THE
BOOK
OF
DRAGONS

ALSO EDITED BY JONATHAN STRAHAN

THE
BOOK
OF
DRAGONS

AN ANTHOLOGY

EDITED BY

JONATHAN STRAHAN

ILLUSTRATED BY

ROVINA CAI

HARPER Voyager

An Imprint of HarperCollins Publisher.

FIRST EDITION

Designed by Paula Russell Szafranski

Illustrations © Rovina Cai

Library of Congress Cataloging-in-Publication Data has been applied for.

ISBN 978-0-06-287716-1

20 21 22 23 24 LSC 10 9 8 7 6 5 4 3 2 1

For Jessica and Sophie,

in memory of Princess Jasmine

and her best friend, Marmaduke,

and for all of the dragons that have helped

keep our dreams safe.

My armor is like tenfold shields, my teeth are swords, my claws spears, the shock of my tail a thunderbolt, my wings a hurricane, and my breath death!

—J. R. R. TOLKIEN, *The Hobbit, or There and Back Again*

CONTENTS

ACKNOWLEDGMENTS

The idea for this book dates back to the very first books I read in the early 1970s, so I should probably thank everyone from Le Guin to Tolkien, but the real thanks are owed to my editor, David Pomerico, who has been kind, understanding, and wonderful to work with throughout; to the whole team at HarperCollins; to the authors, poets, and artists who gave us such wonderful work for this book; to my dear friend Keira McKenzie; to Neil Gaiman, who did everything he could to be a part of this one, but was overrun by time, and to his agent, Merrilee, who tried to make that possible; to my agent, the fabulous Howard Morhaim, who is always in my corner and fights the good fight; and finally, to Marianne, Jessica, and Sophie, who support me through the madness. This book would not exist without you all. Thank you!

INTRODUCTION

When my two daughters were very young, I used to tell them bedtime stories. I'd make the stories up each night but never managed to write them down (much to my youngest daughter's frustration). They were stories about a girl named Jasmine—who lived not far from their grandmother's house and who kept her dreams in a snow globe on her bedroom dresser, safe from a witch who sought to steal them—and of her best friend, a small orange dragon named Marmaduke, who was wise and brave and helped Jasmine to understand how she could save herself. Marmaduke even engaged in some glassblowing, not too long after a family vacation during which we watched a glassblower at work. The memories are hazy, but I think the glassblowing had something to do with the unmaking of the world, which seemed a lot for such a tiny dragon, but magic can make heroes of us all.

My own first memory of dragons, if it's possible to isolate such memories, given how pervasive dragons are in our culture, is probably Pete in the not-particularly-excellent Disney film *Pete's Dragon*, in which a young boy finds an invisible friend, Elliot, who helps him when he needs it most and brings adventure into his life. If I can't quite be sure about the first dragon I encountered, it's hard to forget the many that followed: the greatest wyrm of them all, Tolkien's Smaug, raining fire down on Lake-town in *The Hobbit*; followed by Yevaud and the archipelagos of Ursula K. Le Guin's *A Wizard of Earthsea*; the white dragon, Ruth, from Anne McCaffrey's Pern; Naomi Novik's Temeraire; and George R. R. Martin's dragons of Westeros: Rhaegal, Viserion, and Drogon.

What do all of these great and mighty dragons have in common? Perhaps that they reflect some aspect of ourselves back to us through story. They can be wise friends and counselors, devious enemies and fiery opponents, and pretty much everything in between. Mayland Long in R. A. MacAvoy's *Tea with the Black Dragon* is a wealthy older man who simply wants to help a mother find her daughter, but it seems he is also a two-thousand-year-old dragon. Lucius Shepard's great and maligned Griaule from *The Dragon Griaule*, possibly the greatest dragon to enter fantasy literature in the past thirty years, is a slumbering beast the size of a mountain range on which towns and villages are built, and whose human population both depends upon and hates him in equal measure. Dragons, it seems, have always been with us in story, and although I am not a researcher of folktales or an ethnologist, I could be convinced that dragons can be traced back to the first fires around which our distant ancestors gathered, inspired by dark places beyond the light of the fire and the reptiles that lived there—I'm much more skeptical that they are some sort of species memory of dinosaurs, but let's not rule that out.

Regardless, the way we see dragons depends on where we are in the world. In the West, the image of the fire-breathing, four-legged, winged beast arose in the High Middle Ages. Perhaps a variation on Satan, the Western dragon is often evil, greedy, and clever, and usually hoarding some terrible treasure. There are the dragons of the East, long, snakelike creatures seen as symbols of good fortune and associated with water. Serpentine dragons, like the naga, are found in India and in many Hindu cultures, and are similar to the Indonesian naga or nogo dragons. Japanese dragons, like Ryūjin, the dragon god of the sea, are also water creatures. And so on and so on around the world.

Lizard- or serpent-like features are a constant, but the dragon itself may or may not take human form; can be a creature of any of the four elements (air, earth, fire, or water); may crave wealth or not; and may or may not be able to take flight. But it will live at the heart of its story, as the dragons do in the stories in the book you now hold. *The Book of Dragons* grew out of my desire to spend some time with a new group of dragons and the people who encounter them, and so I turned to some of the best writers of science fiction and fantasy of our time and asked them to tell you the story of their dragon, the one that filled their dreams, and they responded with a bestiary of dragons as rich and varied as you could wish for. In these pages, you will encounter dragons on distant worlds as they follow us out to the stars, in the rain-drenched mountains of the Malay Peninsula, in the barn, and living just next door. They are alternately funny and fearsome, fiery and water-drenched, but they are all remarkable.

The stories and poems in the pages here, from Daniel Abraham, Kelly Barnhill, Peter S. Beagle, Brooke Bolander, Beth Cato, Zen Cho, C. S. E. Cooney, Aliette de Bodard, Kate Elliott, Amal El-Mohtar, Sarah Gailey, Theodora Goss, Ellen Klages, R. F. Kuang, Ann Leckie and Rachel Swirsky, Ken Liu, Scott Lynch, Todd McCaffrey, Seanan McGuire, Patricia A. McKillip, Garth Nix, K. J. Parker, Kelly Robson, Michael Swanwick, Jo Walton, Elle Katharine White, JY Yang, and Jane Yolen, are all I could have wished for, and I hope you will love them just as much as I do!

JONATHAN STRAHAN
PERTH, AUSTRALIA, 2019

WHAT HEROISM TELLS US

Jane Yolen

There is the smell of the heroic in the air:
a pair of hawks circling their nest at feeding time.

Rabbits escaping the talons and claws of destiny.
The flesh of impala laughing in the hyena's mouth.

Flash of sword repeating in the dragon's eye.
The princess repelling down the tower on a rope of her own hair.

Even more, I think it's the sight of you, my friend,
pulling love out of despair,
snatching happiness from the ash of winter,
pushing open the closed door, letting in spring.

MATRICULATION

Elle Katharine White

Elle Katharine White (ellekatharinewhite.com) was born and raised in Buffalo, New York, where she learned valuable life skills like how to clear a snowy driveway in under twenty minutes (a lot easier than you think) and how to cheer for the perennial underdog (a lot harder than you think). She is the author of the Heartstone series: *Heartstone, Dragonshadow,* and *Flamebringer.* When she's not writing, she spends her time reading, drinking tea, and having strong feelings about fictional characters.

She should have been ticketed.

The cop stationed on the roof stared at her as she flew past, heedless of the portable speed-scryer screaming in her hand, her mouth open in a perfect *O*. Melee caught the briefest glimpse, only heard the radar's beep as a smudge of sound whipped past by the wind, but she blessed whoever had assigned a rookie to this route. Clearly the cop had never seen a dragon before. By the time she had recovered, Melee was already out of sight.

Landing in Pawn Row was always tricky, and Melee sensed rather than saw the undead eyes peering at her from under stoops and out of upstairs windows, curious to see whether they would be contacting their insurance companies before day's end. She shifted her weight, and the dragon banked. The steel and alchromium bones supporting its wings caught the red rays of the evening sun, and the light licked along the dragon's chassis with the faintest crackle of magic. She felt it like static, raising the hairs on the back of her neck.

"Down, buddy," she whispered, and signed the symbol for *descend* on the thaumium plate by her right hand. The dragon folded its wings and dived. The stone spires of the university and surrounding shops melted into a salty, grayish blur as the wind tugged tears from her eyes and gravity lost meaning and for one perfect instant she was free and all was right with the world.

Then the world remembered itself and gravity caught up and it was all she could do to sign the landing sequence before the dragon joyously sent them both crashing onto the roof tiles below. Its wings snapped out, billowing like swollen kites, and Melee heard the scrape of metal on stone. Her finger left glowing lines on the thaumium as she traced out the symbol for *perch*, and with the hiss of steam and cooling steel, the dragon settled on the edge of a roof overlooking Pawn Row. She unhooked her harness and swung out of the driver's cockpit.

"You know, there are fines for scratching the façade," a voice from the cornice said.

Melee yelped. She managed one stuttering step toward the roof's edge before catching herself on the dragon's outstretched wingtip, as an image of tomorrow's headline flashed through her mind's eye in all its ironic glory: YOUNG MAGITECHNICIAN'S SCHOLARSHIP WINNER PERISHES IN TRAGIC ACCIDENT TWO DAYS BEFORE TERM STARTS.

"Careful now," the gargoyle said dryly. "Forget the fine—you don't want to take a tumble."

Yeah. I'm not that lucky, she mused, glancing over the tiled parapet. It was only two stories to the cobbles of Pawn Row below. A fall from that height might merely result in a mess of broken bones and bloody gashes, especially if she hit the roof of the stoop first. Not that that would improve her situation. Spilling blood on Pawn Row was as good as a death sentence anyway.

"You could try a sign," she muttered.

The gargoyle crouched on the corner of the building, tilted its head, and peered at her with one obsidian eye. "You could try not parking on the roof, love."

"And miss the view? Nah. He likes it." She pulled off her flying goggles and patted the dragon's chassis. "Dontcha?"

The gargoyle gave a pointed look at the guano-streaked crenellations of the row of shops opposite them. Beyond, just visible through the smog of wood smoke and industrial alchemicals, the spires of the University of Uncommon Arts and Sciences rose to dizzying heights above the city to which it had given birth. He sniffed. "Ah, well, can't fault him for that."

She smiled slightly. She didn't make a habit of smiling, but then, who was the gargoyle going to tell? If she had to guess, he was up here for the same reason she was. It would take a dedicated vandal to paint obscenities on anything parked on the roof, dragon or gargoyle.

"You're not going for, er, dinner, are you?" the gargoyle asked as she stuffed her goggles into the satchel at her side.

"No," she said firmly. "Just a bit of shopping."

There was a grinding sound as the gargoyle turned to face her. Expressions on gargoyle-kind rarely branched out into anything that couldn't be described as "stony," but even so, she could see he was surprised. "Starting at the university on Monday?" he asked.

It would have been so easy to lie. Just a nod and the conversation could be over, but then again, why should she lie? It wasn't as if she *wouldn't* be attending the university. The two were on the same grounds. "Institute," she said. "Technical branch. Keep an eye on him for me, will you?"

The gargoyle's eyes twinkled. "Good on you, love. The world could always use more magitechs. Sure I'll watch your ride. Just don't be long, and, please, if at all possible, be human when you get back. It's awful disorienting when they're not."

"Don't worry, I will be."

"I assume you know who you're dealing with down there?"

"Carl's an old friend," she said.

The gargoyle gave a gravelly chuckle. "Well, well, if you say so. You take care of yourself, all right? We'll both be here when you get back."

She thanked him again and turned to the dragon. It sat motionless on its haunches, surveying the street below with what she liked to imagine was a protective gaze. "I'll be right back, buddy," she whispered, and whistled the locking sequence her father had taught her: a few notes, carefully arranged, changed every month or so, and nonsensical to the casual listener. To a keener ear, or to anyone who'd been close to Melee for longer than six months, the random sequences might begin to form a pattern, just discernible as the beginning of a song. A more patient listener would find the entire tune laid out within a year, and they might wonder why such a pretty lullaby had earned this practical vivisection. Fortunately, no one ever managed to stick around for more than a few months. Melee made sure of it.

The golden light faded from the dragon's eyes as it settled into standby.

"Back in a bit," she told the gargoyle, and headed for the rusty fire escape on the side of the building.

The bell chimed softly as she opened the door. It was dim inside and crowded in a way that made Melee feel right at home. The dark wood of the floor and ceiling glowed in the light of the false electric candles on the walls, the sight of which very nearly made her smile again. Carl had renovated since her last visit. Shelves filled the shop from floor to ceiling, stuffed with the leftovers and hand-me-downs of centuries of university students. She passed piles of mended rucksacks, a bin of shoes made for non-human feet, old microwaves, taxidermy homunculi, heaps of mismatched dishes, and brass alchemical sets on her way to the back where the true treasures lived.

Melee slowed as she approached the last row of shelves. Just beyond shone the long glass counter, sparkling clean. There was the magnificent mahogany cabinet behind it, locking away the tools of Carl's true trade. And there, laying around it in piles as tall as she was, were the textbooks.

Carl, however, was nowhere in sight. She picked her way over a liger-skin rug and began searching the nearest stack, eyes keyed for the distinctive orange cover of *Dragons, Dynamos, and Dirty Jobs: A Primer in Magitech*. It was only after combing through three stacks and nine copies of *Necromancy for the Absolute Beginner* that she thought to glance at the counter itself.

There, spread out on the glittering glass surface, was the primer.

Please, please, be readable, she thought, and eased a finger beneath the battered cover. Gingerly, she lifted it a few inches, waiting for the telltale movement. When no words scurried across the page and out of sight, she breathed a sigh of relief. The magical silverfish she'd found graffitied in the last pawnshop's primer had herded the words into the spine each time it was opened. Probably the parting gift of a senior lexomancer to all those undergraduates who had to stoop to buying their books on Pawn Row. Imagining all sorts of miserable postgraduate fates on the fictional lexomancer, Melee hadn't been able to resist adding a few lines of her own in the margins of that one before shoving it back on the shelf.

The text on the pages of this primer, however, stayed firmly in place, obscured here and there by patterns of oily thumbprints in various degrees of translucence. They testified to at least one previous owner with a love of pizza, and no hope of resale profit. She thumbed through the first chapter, wrinkling her nose at the faint smell of mildew and ensorcelled embalming fluid that wafted out. The pizza-loving owner must've been a necromancy major exploring their backup career options. *Wonderful.* She'd heard of senior students binding unpleasant little creatures within the textbooks they didn't like as practice for their finals, and the last thing she wanted was a pseudo-djinn bursting from the pages and interrupting her studies.

The trouble was, she *needed* this textbook. Term started on Monday, and she was running out of pawnshops where she was still welcome.

"Interested, darling?"

Melee slammed the book shut and let out a stream of expletives her father would be shocked to hear she knew. The man standing behind the counter merely smiled and raised one perfectly manicured eyebrow.

"Good to see you again too, Melee," he said when she stopped for breath.

"*Carl*," she growled, "you can't sneak up on people like that."

"Says who?"

"Says me!"

He sighed. "Next time I'll wear a cowbell. Now: Are you interested?"

She looked down at the fraying cover, the pizza stains, the torn pages. "Yes," she said carefully, "but I think I should get a discount."

"*What?*" At least, that's what she assumed he meant. It came out more like, "*Hwhaaaaaaa?*"

"Look at it," she said. "The professor'll quarantine it as a biohazard."

Carl sucked in his cheeks until she could see the outlines of his elongated eyeteeth, making him look more like a corpse. An impressive feat, given that Carl de Rosia had been legally dead for at least a hundred years.

"Melee. *Darling*," the vampire tried. "Be reasonable. You're going for magitech, aren't you?" He waved a hand before she could answer. "What am I saying? Of course you are. I've known Instructor Groźny for . . . well, for a long time. She's been teaching those technical courses since before I got my fangs. As long as you have it, she couldn't care less about the state of your textbook. Besides, a little battering gives it character, don't you think?"

"A *little* battering?"

He looked again at the weary cover. "I believe the proprietary term is 'well loved.'"

Melee bit her tongue. He was probably right: about the book, about Groźny, about everything. No matter where one fell on the vital spectrum, no one earned a position at the University of Uncommon Arts and Sciences without enough life experience to fill a textbook of their own. *Or a position at the institute technical branch*, she reminded herself. Those who made it that far had learned to pick their battles.

"I'll give you one hundred and twenty," she said.

"One hundred and twenty? *One hundred and twenty?*" The words escaped with more than a hint of a whine, and Melee saw his lips twitch back from his fangs. She guessed he'd added a few more words out of the range of human hearing. "Do you want me to starve, heartless girl?"

"You're being dramatic again, Carl. You're not going to starve."

"I might!" he cried. "I haven't had customers in *days*."

"Liar."

"All right, *hours*. But I have a high metabolism and . . . and you don't understand . . ."

Melee wondered if the University Theater knew what talent they had missed when Carl de Rosia decided to pursue the unlife of a pawnbroker. Really, all that was missing were tears and a lacy handkerchief.

"Oh, come *on*," she said. "You could get four hundred and fifty for that orrery set behind you, no problem." Carl gave the delicate brass instrument a doubtful glance. She pressed on. "I know for a fact there's a first year arithmancy student down the road who needs one before term starts."

Carl's theatrical despair evaporated. "Oh? And is this first year . . . hmm . . . healthy?"

She gave him a look. "Nope. Not playing that game—I'm not your dealer. If you want to know, you're gonna have to ask her yourself. In the meantime, what would you say to a hundred and fifty?"

"I'd say you're laughing at me."

"Never. Two hundred?"

Carl tugged the primer toward him. It was all she could do not to follow it with a look as hungry as his. "Three hundred and fifty, and that's generous. Call it a friends-and-family discount." His expression softened. "For your dad."

Melee swallowed hard. "How about two hundred and fifty?" she asked.

"How about you get out of my shop?"

He said it with a smile, but it was the smile of a cat who knew the score. Melee ran a silent tally of everything she'd spent in the last forty-eight hours, checking off the items on the crumpled list in her pocket. She'd had it memorized for weeks, ever since that final miraculous scholarship had gone through. *Metallurgy for the Magitechnician, Twelfth Edition.* One hundred and fifty. *Nine Parts Iron: A Brief History of Thaumaturgical Transportation.* One hundred and twenty-five. *The Combustible Compendium.* Fifty, but that was only because the pawnbroker had just sold a gilt alchemical set to a senior with three fawning hangers-on who agreed to split the exorbitant fifteen-hundred price tag between them, and he was more than satiated. Melee had been an afterthought.

Three hundred and twenty-five spent in the past two days, and all but one textbook purchased. She touched the cover again and watched the cheap cardboard dimple beneath her fingertips. It was ridiculous, really, considering the shape it was in. Carl was asking too much—he *knew* he was asking too much—but he'd stated his price and showed his fangs, and she knew better than to push now. *Three hundred and fifty for family and friends?* Yeah, that was certainly for her father.

"You won't find it, you know," Carl said, before she could step away from the counter. "This book. Anywhere else in the city. I know that for a fact."

"How did you . . . ?"

"Don't worry, I can't read your thoughts, though in this case I don't need to. You were thinking of trying another shop."

"You'd be surprised what's out there," she said, but her words sounded hollow, even to her.

Carl spread his long, spidery fingers over the glass countertop. They shone like old ivory in the dim light of the shop. His nails, Melee noticed, were very sharp. "I get the lists of all required texts from the professors at the university. And the institute," he added, glancing again at the primer. "All of us on Pawn Row do, and, child, we fight fang and nail to make certain we have those books available for the dear, *desperate* students like you. When I tell you that I was the only broker to get a copy of this one, I can assure you it's the truth. I have the receipt."

Melee looked at his hands, looked at the primer, and drew in a long breath. Sometimes she really hated vampires.

"Three hundred. And," she added over his faint growl, "*and* I'll tell that arithmancy student to come to you for her orrery. That's a guaranteed four hundred within the next twenty-four hours." Then, because she figured she could hardly lose any more ground by it, threw in, "Take it or leave it."

The growl deepened, wavered, and gave way to a throaty chuckle. "You are your father's daughter, aren't you? Well, then, darling, I'll take it."

She stuffed the book into her patched satchel as Carl turned to the cabinet behind the counter, unlocked it, and removed a long black box, its surface gleaming from repeated use. He set it between them and flipped open the catch. The faintest scent of antiseptic wafted up from the crystal vials, plastic tubing, and graduated cylinders tucked inside, the purpose of each Melee had learned intimately, repeatedly, and painfully over the last few days. She rolled up her sleeve—her right one, as she didn't want him seeing how much she'd already paid with her left—and rested it against the glass.

The one thing you could say for Carl, or any vampire in business on Pawn Row: they worked quickly. Leather cuff and tourniquet, iodine swab and tubing laid out, needle drawn ("Brand-new and sterile, I promise," he said at her look) and a stool dutifully pulled up. Then the needle prick, the slow bleed, and the world narrowed to the warm red line traveling from the crook of her arm to the cylinder carefully spread with anticoagulant, the reflection spilling across the glass in strange patterns she felt certain any signometry major would tell her spoke of life and death in no uncertain terms.

"Make a fist, darling," Carl said absently, his eyes fixed on the rising red line. "Helps it move faster."

Melee obeyed. Three hundred milliliters was more blood than she'd thought. It was always more than she thought. She closed her eyes. *The last purchase.* This was the last thing she needed today, the last thing she needed at all. Tonight, she would recover, stuff herself silly with ice cream and sticky rolls and wine, watch her dad's favorite movie, maybe take the dragon out for a quick flight beyond the edge of the city. Tonight would be a good night.

Tomorrow, she would worry about the upcoming term.

"There you are, my dear. All done."

She opened her eyes at the sharp pinch of the withdrawing needle. Carl pressed a square of gauze to the inside of her arm and directed her to bend her elbow as he busied himself with cleaning up the residual payment on his equipment. His touch was cool and firm and clinical, but she knew better than to expect gratitude, or even gentleness. She didn't know a single vampire with good counter-side manners. A thick feeling crawled up the back of her throat at the sight of three hundred milliliters of *her* swirling in that glass cylinder. Only it wasn't her, not anymore, and certainly not by the way Carl was eyeing it. She hoped he'd at least have the decency to wait until she'd left to start drinking.

Melee reached across the counter and tore a piece of tape from its dispenser near the gauze. "Thanks, I've got it." She slapped the tape over the gauze and hopped down from the stool. Now—

That's strange. For such a fastidious vampire, Carl's liger-skin carpet was in terrible need of dusting. Her nose itched, and ten thousand pins prickled along her spine, and she wondered how many dead skin cells she had just inhaled. There was a rushing sound in her ears. Her arm hurt. *Is that a dust bunny, or something* alive? He *really* needed to vacuum, *and—*

Why am I on the floor?

"Easy!" Carl scurried around the counter and hauled her upright. "Not too fast. You know how this works, darling."

Her stomach roiled, half queasiness, half shame, as she sat on the stool again. She could almost hear the gossip circulating around Pawn Row. *Did you hear about Old James's girl? Poor thing can't count, apparently. Let herself get drained dry. Passed out, quick and clean as you like on the floor of de Rosia's . . .*

"I'm fine," she panted. "Carl, really, I'm okay."

"Yes, and I'm an inebriated gargoyle. Here." She flinched at the touch of cold metal and even colder skin as he slipped an iron thaler into her palm. "Dinner is on me. Go get yourself something with sugar in it."

"You don't have to—"

"Nonsense. For three hundred and a reference, it's the least I can do."

Melee blinked and looked at the coin in her hand. Stamped on one side of the thaler was the mark of the Pawnbroker's Order: three circles hanging, staggered, from a Cupid's bow. They should have been spheres, but the engraver hadn't made much effort at shading. What was the old student joke? "What does it take to be a genuine pawnbroker? Brass balls, of course." She flipped it over. On the reverse was the asymmetrical lily of Family de Rosia. She'd asked Carl once why they didn't use a rose, but he'd only smiled and said he'd tell her when she was older.

One iron thaler, properly stamped and sealed. Freely given and freely received, no restaurateur in the city could refuse it. She held a token of credit centuries old and stronger than any human, even a man like her dad, could ever hope to build up. She clutched the thaler tightly. Not one of the half-dozen pawnbrokers she'd visited in the last week had offered her a token. "You know, Carl, for a vampire, you're pretty decent."

He gave her that perfect cat smile and bowed. "You make my great-grandmother weep."

"I didn't mean it like—"

"No, no, it's an old family saying. Granddam is a sadistic hag and all of us civilized de Rosias like disappointing her. Now go on, darling. You're going to need some rest if you want to start term on Monday." Gently but firmly, he ushered her to the front of the shop, avoiding the bars of sunlight that snuck through the slats around the door. "The café on the corner is owned by a friend of mine. He'll give you two meals for that token if you ask nicely."

Melee made sure he was clear of the sunlight before opening the door. "Thank you, Carl. For everything."

"Thank *you*, my dear. Now, ah, this first year. I can expect her . . . when?"

"I'll ask her to come around tomorrow."

The street outside was nearly empty, though it wouldn't stay that way for long. The dinner crowds would be out soon, hawking their blood and other valuable living assets to the vitally challenged for tokens and textbooks and practical tips on how to pass Professor Boynya's first alchemy exam. Both diners and dinees were waiting for the sun to slip behind the spindling brick façades of Pawn Row, but for now, Melee had the street to herself. Nearly. The gargoyle winked at her from the corner of the roof. Next to him, the dragon sat rigid and watchful, its eyes still burning standby red.

She whistled the unlocking sequence, and at the final note, the dragon came to life. Golden fire flared in its eyes and flowed beneath its alchromium scales, tracing the sleek lines of its silver chassis. It blinked once, shook itself, and dropped from its perch without leaving a scratch on the stone façade. The street was narrow, so it folded its wings and dived, falconlike, toward the cobbles. Melee could almost hear her insurance man gasp all the way from his office across town. Its wings snapped out just above her head, casting an early twilight over a few square meters of street and setting the three brass balls over Carl's shop door swinging in the sudden gust. Gracefully, with what she could only assume was the mechanical version of pride, it glided down the last few meters until its steel claws touched the curb. Steam and the sharp, bracing scent of drakeoil hissed out from settling joints as it folded its wings against its chassis. It tilted its head and looked at her with a gleam in its eye.

Good job, buddy, Melee thought, and smiled.

It wasn't alive. It could never be alive. She knew as well as anyone the limits of magitech, and yet there was always that *something*, that little sliver of hopeful doubt, that made her wonder. Her dad always said their dragon was more than the sum of its parts. Her smile dimmed as she patted the upward sweep of its wing. It was only a pity those parts were so expensive.

"You've done a fine job with it."

Melee jumped. Instead of returning to the dim comfort of his shop, Carl had stayed in the doorway, a blackout umbrella carefully angled between him and the last rays of sunlight. He was eyeing her dragon with a hunger that had nothing to do with blood.

"He's not for sale, Carl."

"I didn't ask."

"You were thinking it."

"Who's the mind reader now?"

"The answer is no," she said, and swung into the cockpit behind the dragon's head. The metal warmed at her touch as she signed the starting sequence on the control panel.

"But, my dear, if only you *knew* what collectors would offer for a classic like that . . ."

"It could never be enough."

He raised an eyebrow and muttered something just outside her range of hearing.

"What was that?"

"You clearly haven't received your first tuition bill," he said.

It wasn't the sudden drop in blood pressure that sent the cold creeping into her cheeks and started her hands shaking. "I don't care what you or anyone else offers. He stays with me."

Carl inclined his head, baring his neck in the formal gesture of resignation. "Oh, very well. As you say. I wish you the best of luck this term."

She touched the panel. The purr from the dragon's engine intensified. Though she lacked the layered sight of creatures like Carl and so could only imagine the magic flowing through the creature below her, that didn't stop her from trying. The internal magic channels would pulse golden-red with white sparks, just like her dragon's eyes. From the heart of the engine, the magic branched out in spindling threads of fire, knitting steel sinew to bone gears and bone gears to alchrome pistons, filling the dragon like the soul filled a body.

At her touch, the dragon turned its head again. Impatient to be home, just like she was. Melee drew the sign for the students' quarter with her finger on the square of thaumium. The symbol flared white once and faded. The dragon raised its wings.

"Thanks, Carl," she said over the hum of the engine. "I'll see you around."

The first year was out, so Melee left a note in an envelope. The iron thaler gave the cheap paper enough weight to slip it beneath the door of the girl's flat. It stung, for a moment, letting go of a souvenir of such magnanimity like that, but a first-time customer of Carl's would need it more than she did. Even if she was a keen negotiator, that orrery would take a lot out of the first year. Besides, Melee had other plans.

The dinner crowds were just starting to seep out into the purple light of evening as she signed the dragon home. Chill air with just a nibble of winter whipped her hair into a tangle the goggles could do nothing to prevent. The wind scoured clean the sounds of the new city waking below her: laughter, shouts, growls, the clank of machinery, and the occasional scream from someone who'd failed to specify the terms of their dinner engagement. The close-fitting leather helmet her mother had sent a few birthdays back would've also solved the problem, but that would mean finding it, and Melee had spent a great deal of time making certain she'd never set eyes on it again.

She shifted her weight, and the dragon banked toward the World's End district. The tightly knit cluster of houses and shops sat on the edge of town, clinging to the diamond banks of the river Râu with all the tenacity of people who had refused to accept that their beloved neighborhood was no longer a paragon of respectability, and likely never had been. Still, it had its own kind of beauty. She caught her breath as the dragon swooped low over the water. They'd timed it just right. The sun's reflected glow ignited the banks of the Râu in a bonfire of blazing splendor for a few minutes before fading.

Melee brought the dragon down gently on the well-worn pad above the garage. The sign declaring the ancient shop to be that of JAMES & DAUGHTER, MAGITECHNICIANS gave a tired creak in the downdraft from the dragon's wings, and she made a mental note to oil it. It was a game she played sometimes: chronicle all the little things that needed fixing, order them neatly in her mind, and then carefully, meticulously ignore them. There was always something more important to worry about, but she liked to keep up the fiction that she would get to them all someday.

Between her and the dragon, their maintenance routine was up to half an hour now. How her father managed it in ten minutes was beyond her, and she liked to take her time. The dragon stood patiently on the pad, one wing outstretched, then the other, as she inspected every inch of alchromium. Scouring steel in hand, she brushed and burnished anything with the audacity to look like a blemish. Rust was met with all the fury of her sander, grease rag, and several coats of wax. The two dents on the dragon's front foreleg, however, she scrupulously avoided. She touched them lovingly as she passed. It had been a good day, the day her dad had let her drive for the first time. She'd bumbled into everything, of course, but he'd only laughed, squeezed her shoulder, and gently corrected her. No, the dents stayed.

Its exterior scoured clean, she checked the dragon's fuel levels and fed its chemical tank all the remains of yesterday's organics. It rumbled, gurgled, and belched a short blast of fiery exhaust before settling into the steady churn of digestion. Melee's eyes smarted and the smell stung her nose as she risked a peek into the tank, but everything seemed to be in order. Satisfied, she sealed the tank and patted the dragon on its side. It didn't have a name—that would be silly, her dad had always said—but that didn't preclude endearments.

"Rest up, buddy. You did good today." She slung the satchel with her textbooks over her shoulder, signed the symbol for *power down* on the thaumium panel, and shut the chassis door up tight. "Sleep well."

It was an awkward scramble down from the garage roof, what with the bag knocking into her ribs at every ladder rung and her vision swimming when she was halfway down, but she made it in one piece. Melee avoided the shop's main entrance, unlocking instead the side door that led to the flat upstairs. She had to stop twice on the stairs to quell the sudden rush of dizziness, regretting her altruism with Carl's token. Forget the first year; she needed *food*.

The lights were on in their flat, burning a cheerful yellow between stacks of novels, old journals, maps, schematics, empty drakeoil canisters, gears, and miscellaneous parts even she didn't recognize.

"Hey, Dad, I'm home," she called.

She deposited her satchel on the nearest stack and pulled the primer out. Not for the first time, she reflected on how unlucky it was, given the state of their flat, that her dad didn't already own at least one of her textbooks. He had never been one to learn his trade from books.

A stack of papers swayed dangerously in her peripheral vision. She steadied it without looking, as a hideous cat, or something that had probably once been a cat, tumbled out from the piles of domestic detritus. It landed, paws splayed, on the mail heap in front of the door, and after it had assured itself that Melee was watching, arched its back and began the dreadful endeavor of coughing up . . . something.

"Oh no you don't," Melee said, and snatched the cat up before it could deposit a hairball or the remains of a house goblin onto the day's mail. The cat gave her a look of profound distaste and wriggled free, only to disappear again between the pillars of books. A moment later the coughing began again. Melee sighed. *Add that to the list.*

She picked up the pile of letters and flipped through them on her way to the kitchen. Bills. Bills. An advert for organic wolfsbane. A notice from the World's End Homeowners' Association. Another bill.

"I saw Carl today, Dad," she said. "Sends his love. He said to—"

The envelope at the bottom of the stack stopped her. It was thinner than she expected, warped by a journey in the mail carrier's damp bag and half sticking to a flyer from Count Luigi von Tressor's Deli ("a *meating* place for friends and enemies!"), but the stamp and seal were still readable: *University Institute, Technical Branch.*

With trembling hands, she pulled it free, letting the rest of the mail flutter to the ground unread. The cat leaped out from its hiding place and batted the bills aside before burying its claws in the HOA flyer. Melee reached for the ancient armchair behind her and sank into it without bothering to move the piles of her father's old shirts draped over the armrests. The words were ordinary and there was nothing magical about the paper or ink, but it might as well have been a senior lexomantic hex for all the good it did her. To her bleary eyes, the words burned like black fire against the Finance Department's cheap office paper.

> *Dear Ms. James,*
>
> *Due to recent events connected with the Independent Sphere's rally last week, we regret to inform you that the Institute is unable to accept the contribution from the Young Magitechnician's Guild and Scholarship Fund toward your tuition payment for this next term.*
>
> *Please find your final bill below. Payment must be remitted no later than the first day of classes.*
>
> *Kind regards,*
>
> *M. Nauda Nakvispirms, MtPhD, CPA*
>
> *University Bursar*
>
> *Institute Liaison, Technical Branch*

Melee read it again, then once more, giving particular attention to the number below the bursar's note. It did not change.

There was a snuffling sound and the cold touch of a nose against her ankle. She folded the letter. Her hands had stopped shaking. "You're hungry, aren't you?" she said quietly, and leaned down to scratch the cat's chin. "So am I. You hungry, Dad?"

She didn't wait for an answer. *Breakfast.* Breakfast sounded good. It would be overhard eggs for her, sunny-side up for him, frozen hash browns zapped to a crispy death in their ancient microwave and smothered in cheese, bacon barely browned so she could pull off the extra fat, and as many pancakes as she could make before her appetite drove her to the table.

The cat followed her into the kitchen. Melee left the letter on the armchair.

They didn't have any pancake mix, and the milk was starting to spoil, so she settled for toast with pepper-and-nightshade jam. The rigors of frying bacon and unsticking the eggs from the cast iron skillet proved a worthwhile distraction for a while. She could still feel the letter, hanging like a wraith in the crowded doorway between the kitchen and front hall, the silent presence presiding over their tiny table. Three skillets in she ran out of bacon. She scowled at the empty fridge as she set the table for the two of them and pulled her father's wheelchair up to his customary spot.

"Eat up, I made enough for twenty," she said.

The cat meowed at her feet. Melee picked off a few strips of bacon fat and tossed them to the floor. For a long while the sound of chewing filled the room.

"They're not taking the YMG scholarship," she said at last.

The cat nudged her leg.

"Something to do with that stupid rally last week. I wasn't even there."

She flicked a few more bacon bits to the waiting mouth beneath her.

"The bursar says the tuition's due Monday."

A bit of pepper jelly stuck in her teeth. She worked it free.

"I mean, it's not like I didn't have it, right? It was in their hands. It's their fault if they give it back."

The fork scraped the last of her eggs from the paper plate, cleaned as ruthlessly as by any dishwasher.

"This is ridiculous. *I'm* not the one who should have to figure this out!"

She tipped back a mouthful of coffee so hot it brought tears to her eyes. The tears didn't stop, streaming down her cheeks and dripping onto the greasy smears on the table in front of her.

Her father said nothing.

"I'm sorry, Dad," she said after a minute. "I just—I don't know what to do."

The cat nudged her again, but she'd run out of bacon.

"I know I promised." The words came slowly. "I know what you want for me. I want it too—I really do. If I could get the shop up and running again without that stupid certificate, I would. You know I would. But . . ."

It hung out there, an invitation, pleading for conciliation, forgiveness, anything.

Her father said nothing.

Melee hung her head. "But I *promised*," she whispered.

No more tears came. She wished they would, wished she could curl up somewhere and cry for hours, could let herself wallow in self-pity for the sheer selfish pleasure of it. A sharp, double-edged pleasure that solved nothing, but it would feel better than this.

She stood up and cleared the table in silence: one plate scoured clean, one untouched. Her dad's dinner went into an empty cottage-cheese container in the fridge. It would be her breakfast tomorrow. The cat watched her as she paused for a moment behind her dad's wheelchair. Fresh tears sprang to her eyes as she touched the armrest.

"You know what I wish more than anything?" she said.

Still he said nothing.

"Yeah, actually. I bet you do."

She swept up her satchel and jacket and slipped through the labyrinth of memories occupying their living room. At the door, she paused. She could just make out the kitchen, the table, and the wheelchair that had been empty for nearly a month.

"I miss you, Dad."

She didn't bother parking the dragon somewhere away from the night crowds. Their gawping didn't depreciate it, and most were too drunk to remember in the morning. The lights in Pawn Row were, of course, burning brightly as the proprietors turned to their true business. The dragon settled into an easy crouch by the curb outside Carl's shop as she whistled it locked. The golden fire flowed out of its eyes, and in that moment Melee wondered if she should have considered the institute's alternate tuition payment plan. After all, what more use had she of her soul? There were always those buy-back options after graduation. Risky, but maybe worth it . . .

"Melee?"

Carl appeared on the doorstep, his velvet dressing gown swishing dramatically even though there was no wind. His fangs protruded from beneath his upper lip and he had the tiniest smudge of blood on his chin, but he looked down at her with genuine concern.

"Are you all right, darling? What are you doing out this late? After what you paid today, you should be resting!" His eyes flicked to the dragon, and Melee caught the glimmer of understanding in their red depths. She'd never parked it on the street before.

"You said collectors would be interested in my dragon, right?" she asked.

"Well, yes. Naturally. But you said—"

"I know what I *said*." She straightened. *Don't cry. Don't cry. Never let them see you cry.* "This is what I'm saying now. Do you know any of these collectors personally?"

"One or two, but, Melee . . ." Carl trailed off as he searched her face. After a long moment, his fangs retracted and he put a hand on her shoulder. Despite its inhuman chill and frightening strength, his touch was comforting. "What do you need from me?"

The words weighed on her tongue, weighed on her heart. She felt the dragon's eyes on her and somewhere, somehow, her father's eyes too. *I'm sorry, Dad.*

"How much?"

HIKAYAT SRI BUJANG, OR, THE TALE OF THE NAGA SAGE

Zen Cho

Zen Cho (zencho.org) is the author of a short story collection, *Spirits Abroad*; two historical fantasy novels, *Sorcerer to the Crown* and *The True Queen*; and a novella, *The Order of the Pure Moon Reflected in Water*. She is a winner of the Crawford, British Fantasy, and Hugo awards, and a finalist for the Locus and John W. Campbell awards. She was born and raised in Malaysia, resides in the United Kingdom, and lives in a notional space between the two.

The day that ruined the naga sage Sri Bujang's life dawned like any other, free of untoward omens. The mountains were wreathed by a romantic mist, out of which the peaks rose like islands in a vague gray sea.

A sage must be self-disciplined if they are to acquire sufficient merit to achieve liberation. Sri Bujang followed a strict daily routine. Every morning, he rose when it was still dark and did his stretches. These helped keep his long serpentine body limber and were good for opening his third eye.

As he contorted into spiritually rewarding shapes, sunlight spilled over the horizon, burning off the mist. Sri Bujang had all three eyes fixed on the ground, his mind a perfect blank, when suddenly the gold light turned gray. Lightning blazed across the sky, followed by the rumble of thunder.

The rain would have been obliterating for anyone who was not a naga. For Sri Bujang, of course, water was no different from air. With perfect clarity he saw the naga emerge from the forest—and recognized her.

"Kakanda," said his sister.

Sri Bujang froze. His third eye snapped shut. It had always been considered rude in his family to have it open in mixed company.

"Adinda," he said. If he'd had time to prepare, he might have come up with a greeting befitting a naga sage, suitably combining the gnomic and the nonchalant.

But he was not prepared. He had not seen any member of his family in centuries.

"How did you know I'm here?" he blurted out.

Sri Kemboja looked puzzled. "This mountain is named after you. Gunung Sri Bujang."

"Oh, right," said Sri Bujang. *What would a sage do?* he found himself wondering for an absurd moment.

He pulled himself together. Whatever he did was what a sage would do. Also, a sage would be gracious but detached. He would not greet his sister with the usual platitudes: comments on whether she had lost or gained weight, or questions about their relatives' health. A sage would not care to know if anyone was missing him, or if they regretted how they had treated him back then.

"How can I help you?" he said.

He was pleased with the dignified sound of this, but Sri Kemboja's expression was stony. She looked exactly like their father had the last time Sri Bujang had seen him, when they had quarreled and Sri Bujang had left home for good.

"It's not me who needs help," she said. "You have to come home, Kakanda."

For years Sri Bujang had dreamed of receiving this appeal. It was not sagelike to feel vindicated, but nevertheless, Sri Bujang felt a little flutter of satisfaction below his rib cage.

"I told Ayahanda and Bonda already," he said. "This is my life now. The sage of Gunung Sri Bujang cannot simply go off like that. I have responsibilities. This mountain is a keramat; people come on pilgrimage to see me. I'm the number two attraction in this area on TripAdvisor, you know, second only to a very famous nasi lemak stall!"

"Ayahanda is dying," said Sri Kemboja. "Are you coming or not?"

Sri Bujang trailed after his sister as they descended toward the sea, hunching under the storm raised by their passage.

He was being magnanimous, he told himself. One couldn't pick fights with one's dying father. He would go and see his family, and then he would return to his work. He was *not* being feeble.

The plains had altered since he had last come down from the mountain. Humans had left their mark everywhere, with typical lack of consideration.

"They think this is their grandfather's land, is it?" Sri Bujang grumbled. It wasn't so bad for the gods and hantu, who had other dimensions to occupy; besides, small human-made altars dotted the earth, stocked with incense and offerings for tutelary spirits. But the humans had left little room for other corporeal species. "They should think of the other animals, not just themselves."

"Ah, humans are like that," said Sri Kemboja.

As they threaded their way around the various buildings, roads, and other human rubbish that littered the landscape, Sri Bujang began to develop an ache behind his sealed third eye. He paused at the shore, looking back. He could see the peak of his mountain in the distance, covered with virgin forest—a sanctuary from human thoughtlessness and familial encroachments alike.

"Come on," said his sister impatiently. "At the rate you're loitering, this whole seaside development will wash away in the rain."

Sri Bujang found himself opening his mouth to snap, "So what?" He shut it before the words could escape, shocked at himself. The retort belonged to Sri Bujang before the mountain—the unenlightened young naga who had retreated precisely so he could transcend such pettiness.

"I was allowing a moment for reflection," he said, with dignity.

Sri Kemboja's answering snort did not improve his mood. He followed her into the sea, resentment brewing in his chest.

He cheered up as they approached his father's kingdom. By the gates stood the proud figures of the white crocodiles who had guarded the kingdom since it was founded. Sri Bujang had always been a favorite of the captain of the King's Guard. Pak Laminah had trained him in the military arts. Sri Bujang would have recognized his profile anywhere.

"Pak Laminah!" he cried gladly. The crocodile looked around.

It was not Pak Laminah. She had the same snout and the same green eyes, but she was a stranger.

"Ah, Your Highness is back!" she said to Sri Kemboja. She gave Sri Bujang a wary glance.

"Captain, can you spare a messenger to the istana?" said Sri Kemboja. "Tell them the princess has returned with the raja muda."

When they had passed through the gates, Sri Kemboja said, "Pak Laminah is dead. Captain Hartini is his great-great-great-grandniece." She seemed bemused that Sri Bujang hadn't already known this.

Of course, he should have known Pak Laminah would no longer be living. It had been a long time since he had left home.

But the incident lent a nightmare quality to Sri Bujang's procession through the kingdom. He felt like a mother who, having left her eggs safely buried, returns to find the sand scattered, her children devoured in the shell. This was no homecoming, but an arrival at a strange place—a place he did not know, that held uncertain welcome for him.

At the istana they were led into the audience chamber. It was empty, save for two dugong handmaidens and a faded heap on an ornate golden couch. For a split second Sri Bujang took this for an old bolster, limp and bulgy from too much use. It was only when Sri Kemboja went up to greet it that he realized what he saw.

The Naga King of the South China Sea, He Who Is as the Dust of the Almighty, Sri Daik lay coiled on the golden couch. His sides rose and fell irregularly. His scales were dull, as though he were molting. When he opened his eyes, there was no spark of recognition in them.

All resentment fled. Sri Bujang said, appalled, "Ayahanda!"

He was immediately conscious of a wave of cold disapproval from Sri Kemboja at his failure of tact.

"You look better today, Ayahanda," she said. "Look, here's Kakanda."

Sri Bujang touched his snout to his father's foreleg in a salam. Sri Daik said nothing at first, and Sri Bujang remembered that they had parted in extreme acrimony. In this very room Sri Daik had called him anak derhaka: ill-taught, unmannerly, and irresponsible; a traitor to God, his father, and his king. Sri Bujang for his part had said nothing, repeating a mantra in his head: *I am going to seek liberation. I am going to seek liberation.*

In a way, it was the same thing as asking himself: *What would a sage do?*

It was not what a good son would have done. Sri Bujang had departed in peace, making no apology, taking with him as little as he had ever given his parents.

He had not spoken to his father since. He winced now, bracing himself for rejection, dismissal, storms.

"The raja muda has come?" said Sri Daik finally. "Good, good. Have you seen Bonda?"

It was the voice that pierced Sri Bujang like a spear in his flank. Sri Daik was venerable—he had inhabited the South China Sea ever since there had been a South China Sea—but he had never before sounded *old*. Sri Bujang shook his head, speechless.

"You must go and greet her," said Sri Daik. "She is somewhere around. These girls can tell you. She will be very happy."

Even saying so little exhausted him. He shut his eyes. There was a silence, long enough that Sri Bujang wondered if his father had fallen asleep. But Sri Kemboja and the handmaidens waited, watching Sri Daik with calm expectancy.

After a while, he opened his eyes and lifted his head. A dugong rushed to his side.

"Which one are you? Balkis?" said Sri Daik. "I almost forgot. We must have the raja muda crowned as king. You will arrange the proclamation? Thank you."

His eyes fluttered. Sri Bujang opened his mouth, but before he could object, his father roused again.

"Balkis! Are you still there? The regalia, remember to bring out the regalia. You must see if the royal dress fits the raja muda. Don't forget, yes? You're a good girl, Balkis."

They waited for another half an hour, but this time it seemed Sri Daik had said all he had to say. The handmaidens ushered Sri Bujang and his sister out of the chamber.

"We'll call you if His Majesty wants you," said the one called Balkis. "The raja muda's room will be made ready."

Sri Bujang was staring straight ahead. Sri Kemboja had to repeat herself to get his attention.

"What?" he said.

"I said," said Sri Kemboja, raising her voice, "are you sure my royal brother wants his room?"

The dugong Balkis's forehead wrinkled. "But where else will His Royal Highness sleep until the coronation? We will prepare the royal bedchamber, but it cannot properly be used by His Royal Highness until after the ceremony."

"Where, indeed?" said Sri Kemboja meaningfully. When Sri Bujang did not react, she lowered her voice and hissed, "You said you'd come back for a visit only! Then you were going to go back, no?"

The handmaidens looked away in embarrassment, pretending not to hear. Sri Bujang said absently:

"Did I say that?"

He had been too distracted by his distress over Pak Laminah to pay attention to his surroundings when he had entered the istana, and interior decoration had been the last thing on his mind during the audience with his father. But now that Sri Bujang looked properly, the signs of decay were everywhere in his father's palace: buckling floorboards and rotting timbers, black mold creeping out from the corners.

The istana took its measure from the king. As Sri Daik faded, and his magic with him, the istana would follow. And the sphere of influence radiating out from the istana, which Sri Daik had built over so many hundreds of years—the nobles he had cultivated, the followers who depended upon him and gave him importance—all of that too would fall away.

"Well, that won't work," said Sri Bujang.

Someone would have to take it on. There was no one else. He was the raja muda. His parents had selected him to be the chief bearer of their hopes and disappointments.

It had been mostly disappointments so far . . . but that would change.

Sri Kemboja gaped. "You're going to let them crown you? I thought you wanted to attain liberation?"

You couldn't be a prince and a bodhisattva, which was why Sri Bujang had left home. Being a king would be even more of an obstacle to liberation.

Sri Bujang thought of Pak Laminah. He had been Sri Daik's nest brother, closer to Sri Bujang than any of his blood uncles. When he had left home, it was Pak Laminah who had met him at the gates and pressed gold into his paws, refusing to take it back: "Up there, even to breathe you must pay. You will need it."

Now Pak Laminah was dead, all that was left of him the eyes and snout of a stranger. What would be left of Sri Daik after his death, if Sri Bujang did not step up now?

"It doesn't have to happen in this life," he said, trying to ignore the wrenching at his heart. "Since Ayahanda intends to abdicate, I must discharge my duty as king. The next life will be soon enough to become awakened."

"Really? You don't mind waiting?" Sri Kemboja evidently could not believe her ears. "So you're going to give up your mountain and all that nonsense?"

"No," said Sri Bujang. If it mattered what became of his father after his death, so did it matter what became of Sri Bujang. To cease his efforts now would be to lose the prospect of liberation even in the next life.

Sri Kemboja was frowning, back on familiar ground—Sri Bujang the unreliable, from whom nothing could be hoped for. "Don't play around, Kakanda. This is a serious matter. Ayahanda and Bonda have suffered enough. Either take it up, or let them know what to expect."

Sri Bujang told Balkis, "I will sleep in my old room." The hand-maidens made an obeisance and left.

"You have to commit," said Sri Kemboja. "How are you going to be king if you're not willing to sacrifice?"

Sri Bujang assumed his most enigmatic smile, honed by centuries of practice. "I guess you'll have to wait and see."

Tapping the steering wheel, May Lynn noticed that her fingernails were too long.

It was not a new observation. They had been too long for weeks. The thought had gained the familiarity of a landmark one saw every day, like the mountain rising out of the bottom right-hand corner of the windshield.

May Lynn dug in her handbag for her phone and texted her mother: *At Gunung Sri Bujang.* The predictive text brought up the name of the mountain even as she typed *At*. She sent the same text message at the same time every day, to let Ma know she was almost home.

Ma wouldn't let May Lynn cut her fingernails when she got back from work. Cutting your nails at night was bad luck, she said. She was not a woman who was easily parted from her convictions and it was not possible to persuade her that that was a superstition belonging to a time predating electric lights.

". . . said the recent unseasonal rainy weather has increased the risk of accidents and asked motorists to avoid driving during storms. The government has formed a taskforce to investigate measures to prevent further landslides . . ."

Avoid driving, your head, thought May Lynn. How to avoid driving unless you want to sit at home all day? Maybe if there's good public transport, that's another story . . . What she needed to do was bring a fingernail clipper to the office and sort it out there during the day, away from Ma's censorious eye.

But as she imagined it, she could see her coworker gazing incuriously over the divider between their desks. Her resolution wilted. Yasmin possessed the preternatural elegance generally found only in the very wealthy; she looked like she had never sweated in her life. It was impossible to clip one's fingernails in front of Yasmin.

At this point, May Lynn's train of thought was run off its tracks by an enormous crash of thunder. The world was plunged into darkness. As May Lynn peered up at the sky in confusion, it was split by a forked bolt of lightning.

Blinking away the dazzle, she almost missed the sight that would fill social media feeds and preoccupy the press for the next several weeks. By the time she rubbed her eyes and opened them again, the dragon had already leaped across the highway. It retreated into the distance, heading toward the mountains. The traffic light turned green, but for several long breaths, May Lynn and all the other motorists stayed where they were, watching after the dragon until it was lost behind a veil of rain.

"Ah, Adinda," said Sri Daik. "You're here?"

Sri Bujang was engrossed in studying a stele, so he didn't look up until Sri Kemboja said:

"How could you?"

There was no mistaking who she was addressing; she would never have spoken to their parents that way. Sri Bujang said, "What?"

"I know what you've been doing," said Sri Kemboja, in throbbing tones. "You don't think I don't know!"

Looking at his sister's accusing face, Sri Bujang felt suddenly that he had hit his limit.

He had already been feeling hard done by. It was not that any drudgery was expected of him. Princes do not rub unguents on invalids' scales, or feed them healing soups. Sri Daik was attended by physicians, magicians, great-aunts, lesser cousins, handmaidens and manservants, not to mention Sri Bujang's mother, Sri Gumum. He had only to crook a talon for his every need to be supplied.

So it was not clear why Sri Daik and Sri Gumum felt it necessary to take up all of Sri Bujang's time. Sri Gumum had difficulties with the servants. Sri Daik had a mind-boggling array of ailments. They both had strong views on tax policy and zoning, public transport and foreign affairs—the various matters of government with which a king should be well acquainted. They were determined to tell Sri Bujang about all these things, at length.

For one who had spent hundreds of years alone in a cave, this was acutely aggravating. Sri Bujang was accustomed to considering his spirit a precious commodity, to guarding his energies jealously from incursion. It was an unpleasant novelty to be treated as though his spirit was of no account.

"You!" he began, but before he could tell Sri Kemboja what he thought of her tone, their mother said:

"What do you mean, what Kakanda has been doing? He's helping us with Ayahanda's prescriptions."

Sri Kemboja seemed to notice for the first time the stele propped up before Sri Bujang. The pawang's inscription was as illegible as doctors' handwriting is said to be, but still the occasional name of a healing spell or electuary could be discerned.

"What's this?" she said.

"The girls are doing their best," said Sri Daik. "But this old carcass needs so many spells and medicines, it's hard for them to keep track."

"Those naughty dugong forgot to give Ayahanda his dose," said Sri Gumum. "Now the pain in his last pair of hind legs has come back! Whatever you say, it is not like having your own child tend to you."

Before his parents could rejoin battle over what the handmaidens had done and what should be done to them in consequence, Sri Bujang said:

"I'm going to supervise the dosings from now on, make sure Ayahanda gets what he needs. Don't worry, Bonda."

Sri Daik nodded. Sri Gumum smiled. Their approval was a balm to Sri Bujang's irritated soul, but the relief proved fleeting.

"Yes. Fine. Okay," said Sri Kemboja. "That's all very good. But have you told Ayahanda and Bonda about the destruction you've been causing?"

Sri Bujang glared at her. "What are you talking about?"

"Come, Adinda, this is not becoming," said Sri Daik. "Even if you feel your royal brother is wrong, you should tell him gently. What is the matter?"

"Kakanda has been *commuting*," announced Sri Kemboja. She turned to Sri Bujang. "You've been going back to your mountain, haven't you? Did you think nobody would notice?"

Sri Bujang had indeed thought no one would notice. It wasn't like his parents had shown any interest in what he'd been doing for the past several centuries.

He drew himself up. "Is that all? I've been going back, yes. I need quiet time for contemplation. It's not like it's interfered with my duties here." He turned to his parents. "I haven't neglected you, have I?"

He had thought this was a safe appeal, given how devoted he had been. But he saw at once that he was wrong. Sri Daik and Sri Gumum wore identical expressions of horror.

"Oh, Kakanda, how could you?" said Sri Gumum. "You said you were going to postpone all that nonsense to the next life."

Sri Bujang had never mentioned this plan to his parents. He gave Sri Kemboja a burning look of reproach, which she pretended not to notice.

"I have postponed it," he said. "But I'm not going to become awakened in *any* life if I stop self-cultivating altogether."

"This is my fault," said Sri Daik, with the quiet dignity of a martyr. "I am the one who called Kakanda back when he preferred to live on his mountain. In my youth, that was how things were done; children looked after their parents. But times are different now."

Sri Bujang felt as though the floor had opened beneath his feet. "I—what—but what's wrong with me going back? It's just so I can keep up my practice."

"Every time you come down your mountain, you cause a land-slide," said Sri Kemboja. "Did you not *notice*?"

Sri Bujang was about to protest that this was ridiculous, baseless, uncalled for. But as the memory of his last trip to the mountain came back to him, the denial died in his throat.

Could he really swear to the fact that there hadn't been a landslide? As always, his arrival and departure had been attended by incalculable fuss. The mountain's resident jungle spirits and animals were obsessed with protocol, and they loved a party. What with the clamor of their rites, he hadn't had time to pay attention to the state of the soil. It was possible there had been a small landslide or two while he hadn't been looking . . .

"And the flooding, whenever you go up from the sea," said Sri Kemboja. "You didn't notice that either?"

"Of course there was flooding," said Sri Bujang crossly. "There's always flooding whenever any of us goes anywhere. It's just because of the rain."

"And you don't think that's a problem?"

"Don't fight, children," said Sri Gumum, forgetting in her anxiety to prevent a quarrel that she was angry with Sri Bujang. "It's natural of Kakanda to think the humans will be grateful. After all, they used to worship us for bringing rain. He doesn't realize they have changed."

"Kakanda can try to claim he's doing it for the humans' sake," said Sri Kemboja. "But I don't believe it! When did the humans ever like us bringing floods or landslides?"

"Adinda has a point, you know," said Sri Daik to Sri Bujang. "Rain is good, but it must be the right amount. Too much causes difficulties for the humans. Maybe you forgot?"

Sri Bujang was not accustomed to considering humans outside their role as pilgrims to the mountain who left one offerings and made importunate requests.

"That's what all this hoo-ha is about?" he said, baffled. "The *humans*?"

"Tok Batara Guru!" said Sri Kemboja. She flung up her forelegs and turned away.

Sri Bujang had so scandalized his parents that they did not even reprove her for the blasphemy.

"The humans have changed, Kakanda," said Sri Daik. "They are not scared of anything nowadays. If you cause trouble for them, they will cause trouble for you."

"We cannot take trouble right now," said Sri Gumum. "Ayahanda is sick."

The way they looked at Sri Bujang was familiar. This feeling, of being the cause of worry, the troublemaker, the disappointment, was one he knew.

"I know Ayahanda is sick," said Sri Bujang. There was a bitter taste on his tongue. "Do you think I'm doing all this for fun?" He gestured at the stele.

"No. You are doing it because I asked," said Sri Daik. "I should not have asked. It is better not to demand things of your children."

"Kakanda, you spent so many years already on your mountain," said Sri Gumum. "Isn't it time to stop being selfish?"

"Selfish?" Sri Bujang echoed.

But it was true, wasn't it? For he had escaped. All those years ago, he had hardened himself against the demands of love and duty, knowing that he would be used without mercy if he showed the least sign of yielding.

By his own creed, Sri Bujang's life on his mountain required no justification. To gain enlightenment, to free oneself from the shackles of illusion, all expedients were permissible—even necessary. To his family, however, Sri Bujang had been born a debtor. His debts would not be paid off with anything less than his life.

He was distantly aware that Sri Kemboja had come back. She looked from him to their parents.

"Enough," she said abruptly. "There's no need to talk so much. Kakanda's got the point already."

Sri Bujang stared, too miserable to be comforted even by this un-expected show of solidarity. Sri Gumum, who could never resist having the last word, said:

"You cannot have both, Kakanda. You've had your fun, but you're not young anymore. Now it's time to focus on the family. Put aside other things. You understand that, right?"

"Yes," said Sri Bujang, "I know." But everything in him rose in revolt. They could try to take all that mattered to him, he thought, but they couldn't make him believe his soul did not matter. That was the one thing they could not do.

The dragon had become such an everyday sight that May Lynn barely spared it a glance before turning back to her phone. Unbelievably, the message on the screen had not changed.

Besok? Where you want to eat?

The good thing about having overly long fingernails was at least you always had something to chew.

Besok boleh, she typed. It wasn't too much to respond straight away, right? It was normal. They were arranging a normal evening meetup between colleagues, outside working hours, for general socializing purposes. *Anywhere also can.*

The blue double-tick appeared next to her messages, but Yasmin didn't answer immediately. To distract herself, May Lynn looked up at the long line of traffic snaking ahead of her. The cause of the jam was still to be seen, framed between the trees by the side of the road.

The dragon was motionless, its head turned toward Gunung Sri Bujang. It was strange that it was lingering for so long. Usually it was only possible to catch a glimpse of the dragon as it made its way between mountain and sea.

Yasmin's reply said, *I'll surprise you then. Can't wait. ;)*

The traffic inched forward. May Lynn disengaged the brake and let her car slide along, smiling helplessly. Outside, the dragon appeared and disappeared between the trees.

She was in a mood that conferred meaning on everything; the world seemed light and clear, bursting with possibility. The dragon's silhouette was suddenly unbearably poignant, the swoop of its neck full of yearning.

The thunder made her jump and drop her phone. There was a cracking sound, but May Lynn barely heard it through the howling of the wind. Her phone had better not be broken. It would be the worst possible moment for it to happen. What would Yasmin think?

She saw the edge of her phone case and dived to scoop it up. Perhaps that was for the best. It meant she didn't see the tree give way under the force of the storm, or the branch tumbling toward her, crashing through the windscreen.

Sri Bujang woke up under a ceiling of wood, not stone. This would be the case now, till the end of this life. Today and all the days after, he would be king and this would be his kingdom. The thought had the peaceful finality of death.

He slithered out of his bedchamber, raising his head to meet the day.

Sri Gumum was charging down the passage, followed by a thunderous-looking Sri Kemboja. With great weariness, Sri Bujang recognized on them the marks of a tempest in which he would unavoidably be involved.

"Kakanda, where have you been?" said his mother. "We couldn't find you anywhere yesterday! I wouldn't even have known you were back if Balkis hadn't told me."

"Do you need to ask where he was?" said his sister. "He was at his mountain, obviously."

"Oh, no," said Sri Gumum. "Kakanda wouldn't do that, not at a time like this."

"Wouldn't he?" said Sri Kemboja. "You ask him!"

"What do you mean, 'a time like this'?" said Sri Bujang. A chill presentiment touched him. "Is Ayahanda okay?"

His mother shook her head.

"Where is he?" said Sri Bujang. It was too soon. He had made his big sacrifice, the grand gesture that was to put him right with the family. Surely Sri Daik could not have left before Sri Bujang was able to tell him. "Can I see him?"

"Better not," said Sri Gumum. "He's very disappointed. You children don't know, you think your father is invulnerable. All his life he has worked to build his reputation. Now he is having his name dragged through the human courts, and for what?"

"What?" said Sri Bujang.

The letter was written in the new Roman alphabet the humans had adopted in the past century. Emblazoned at the top were the words:

HANTU v Raja Naga Laut China Selatan, Sri Daik

"Ayahanda said the humans would cause trouble," said Sri Gumum.

Sri Bujang scanned the letter slowly. He wasn't used to the humans' new script, and the legal jargon didn't help. "But it says the case is brought by hantu."

"H-A-N-T-U, not hantu," said Sri Kemboja. "It's an acronym." She tapped the sheet with a talon. "See, it explains it here. Humans' Association for the preservation of NaTure from the Unnatural. It's an organization to tackle the ecological impact of spiritual and supernatural activity."

"Humans are scolding *us* for affecting the environment?" said Sri Bujang.

"Not just scolding," said Sri Kemboja. "Suing." She flipped the page and pointed to a row of figures.

The numbers were more familiar than the words. Sri Bujang digested them in a horrified glance. "They're asking for *how* much?"

"For the damage caused by your landslides and floods," said Sri Kemboja. "If it wasn't for the fact that Ayahanda and Bonda have to suffer, I'd say they should be claiming more. You're lucky they're not trying to send you to jail. If there was any justice in the world, you'd be facing criminal charges."

As always, by going too far, her anger ameliorated their mother's.

"Adinda, that's too much," said Sri Gumum.

"No, Bonda, it's time we stopped coddling Kakanda," said Sri Kemboja. "Maybe if we had spoken up before, we could have prevented all this."

To Sri Bujang, turning the pages of the letter with increasing dismay, this attitude seemed less than helpful. It was like his sister to fly off the handle when what they needed was a level-headed discussion of next steps.

"I don't think anyone could blame you for not speaking up enough," he said tartly. "There's no need to be so emotional. It's not like anyone's died."

Sri Kemboja stared at him. "A woman was critically injured in the storm yesterday—the storm *you* raised. The newspapers are all talking about it."

"Newspapers?" said Sri Gumum. "You've been reading human newspapers?"

Sri Kemboja hadn't taken her eyes off Sri Bujang.

"What are you looking so shocked for?" she said. "You must have known your floods and your landslides were destroying roads and buildings, turning people out of their homes. It was only a matter of time before you hurt somebody."

"Adinda, have you been playing human again?" said Sri Gumum, raising her voice. "Going around calling yourself Yasmin and wearing shoes and all that kind of thing?"

"So what if I am?" snapped Sri Kemboja. "Why can't I have an outlet, if the raja muda gets to play sage whenever he feels like it? At least I'm not laying waste to cities and killing innocent humans!"

"Aduhai!" Sri Gumum wrung her paws. "What will Ayahanda say? What is his sin that he has been punished with two such wayward children?"

Sri Bujang had learned several new things about his sister in the past couple of minutes, which at any other time would have been of enormous interest. But there were more important things to worry about now.

"Who got hurt?" he said. His voice cut through the din.

Sri Kemboja said, "Her name is Yap May Lynn." Her eyes filled with tears—the jeweled naga's tears that were once so highly prized among humans that they were traded between rajas as gifts. "She was driving home to her mother. One of the trees by the side of the road, the branch broke because of the storm, and it fell on her car. She's in the hospital now. She may never wake up. I may never see her again. And it's because of you."

"Didn't Bonda already tell you? Don't make friends with humans," said Sri Gumum. "They die after a short time and then you feel bad. That's what humans are like. Anyway, how do you know Kakanda caused the rain?"

"He did," said Sri Kemboja. "He went back to his mountain again, even after everything we told him. Didn't you? It was your storm, wasn't it?"

"Yes," said Sri Bujang, heartsick. "It was my storm."

A man trailing a thunderstorm paused in the hospital car park, watching a car from under his umbrella. A woman got out, struggling with a large plastic container.

Sri Bujang knew Sri Kemboja at once, and she recognized him, though neither was wearing their usual face. They gazed at each other in mutual embarrassment.

"What are you doing here?" said Sri Kemboja.

"Do you want to keep that dry?" said Sri Bujang, at the same time. "I can cover it with my umbrella." He pointed at the plastic container, noticing its contents for the first time. "Is that human food?" he asked, intrigued.

"It's for a friend," said Sri Kemboja. Then she flung back her head. "Actually, it's for Mrs. Yap, May Lynn's mother. You can tell Ayahanda and Bonda if you like. I assume that's why you're here."

Sri Bujang gave her an odd look. "I think Ayahanda and Bonda could probably tell me more about your human career than I could tell them. Anyway, you can't see Mrs. Yap."

Sri Kemboja bridled. "What makes you think you can come here and tell me what to do? Just because you're older and the raja muda—"

"Mrs. Yap is with May Lynn," Sri Bujang continued. "They should be discharging May Lynn in a few days' time, but they want to keep her under observation for a while."

"What?" said Sri Kemboja.

"May Lynn's made a miraculous recovery," said Sri Bujang. Something had been niggling at him, an unanswered question Sri Kemboja's appearance had brought to mind. "Eh, how do you go around without bringing rain with you?"

"What do you mean, a miraculous recovery?"

"I mean me," said Sri Bujang. "I wrought a miracle. Now she's recovered."

Sri Bujang had almost forgotten what his sister looked like when she was not angry. Without the usual expression of impatience, her face was rather nice. She said, "How?"

A flash of lightning briefly blinded them. The sky crackled in its wake, and the rain intensified.

"I'll tell you," said Sri Bujang, "but do you want to go wait somewhere till she's done with her mother? I should move before I cause a flood."

Sri Kemboja ordered at the coffeeshop with the confidence of an old hand:
"Limau ais kurang manis," she told the waiter.

"You've been human for a while, haven't you?" said Sri Bujang.

Sri Kemboja gave him a suspicious look, though he'd only meant to express admiration. "You were going to tell me about May Lynn."

"There's not much to tell," said Sri Bujang. "I gave her my next life. She should be okay now." There was a point that had been making Sri Bujang a little uncomfortable. Sri Kemboja's unblinking gaze made him bring it up.

"She might live for longer than usual," he added. "That's okay, right? Humans are—were—always asking me how to live longer."

Sri Kemboja came back to life.

"What do you mean?" she said. "How long?"

"Not too long," said Sri Bujang, anxious to reassure. "She's still human. Her body couldn't take too much longevity. She's not likely to live more than three hundred years or so, unless she's very careful with her lifestyle."

"Kakanda!"

"I know," said Sri Bujang. "It's not natural for humans to live so long. But it was either that or let her die. I know you all think I'm selfish, but the whole point of going to the mountain was *not* to do harm."

"I thought the point of going to the mountain was to seek liberation," said Sri Kemboja. "How are you going to become an awakened one in your next life if you've given it away?"

Sri Bujang was proud of himself for not wincing. "I'll have to start over from scratch in the next life, that's all. I've lost all the merit I built up before."

He tried not to think about the work his next incarnation would have to do to recover his progress toward liberation—supposing the next incarnation even knew enough to desire enlightenment.

"Hopefully, I'll at least be reborn as a human and not one of the other animals," he said. Even if he'd avoided ending any human lives, he'd probably racked up too much moral debt with all the natural disasters to be reborn as a naga. "Humans are supposed to be able to attain liberation also."

Sri Kemboja folded her hands with the ease of much use—Sri Bujang would have had to practice to reproduce the maneuver.

"I trained myself to suppress the rain-bringing instinct," she said. "It wasn't easy. It took a lot of work, and I don't know if the technique can be reproduced. But I can teach you. If you learn how to do it, you can keep your mountain."

Sri Bujang was touched. "That's really kind, Adinda, but—"

"I'm not offering to be kind," said Sri Kemboja brusquely. "You saved her. That's what I can do for you. So I'll do it."

Sri Bujang paused. Sages did not have hurt feelings. Just because he was not going to be a sage anymore didn't mean he couldn't act like one.

"I was going to say, I'm not keeping my mountain," he said.

He'd already made up his mind, but saying it out loud gave him an acute pang. They'd laid flowers outside his cave, not just the humans but the spirits too; they knew it was good luck to have a naga on the mountain. He had gone for months at a time deep in meditation, joyfully forgetful of self.

He pushed the memories to the back of his mind. They would have to stay there, sunken treasure in a dark sea.

"I'm selling it," he said.

His sister's head whipped around. "What?"

"To pay for the lawsuit," Sri Bujang explained. "It's quite a valuable mountain—central location, good soil. The proceeds should be enough to cover legal expenses and compensation."

"But you can't do that," said Sri Kemboja.

"I can, actually," said Sri Bujang. "I own the mountain under the humans' laws. There are some humans who've lived nearby for millennia—very decent people—but because they did not have the right papers, the other humans have been stealing their land to grow pineapples and build housing developments on. They advised me to make sure my papers were in order, so I did. My lawyer says there should be no problem with passing title."

"You have a *lawyer*?"

"The neighboring humans suggested it." Sri Bujang sighed. "I only went back that last time to say good-bye. I lived there for centuries. I was friendly with the humans, the hantu, the animals . . . I couldn't leave them all hanging. If I knew how to turn off the rain, I would've done it. But I didn't. I never planned on going back and forth."

Sri Kemboja was silent for a moment, staring down at her limau ais. "You never planned on coming home at all."

This was too close to the truth, and a mortal wound.

"Never mind," said Sri Bujang. It would hurt less presently, but he did not want to talk about the life he'd carved out for himself, or the dream that had sustained it. "I thought I could balance the two—the mountain and the sea—but this was a lesson. Like you said, I have to commit. So I'm committing. Ayahanda and Bonda won't have to worry about the lawsuit anymore. Or me."

"They don't have to worry about the lawsuit anyway," said Sri Kemboja. She was looking angry again. Sri Bujang's heart fell. What had he said wrong now?

Sri Kemboja went on, "I told them I'd handle it. There's plenty to challenge. They named the wrong defendant to start with, and then there are the jurisdictional issues. That's not even getting into the substantive case."

"Is this a human thing?" said Sri Bujang cautiously. "Is that why I don't understand anything you're saying?"

"Oh," said Sri Kemboja, "I'm a lawyer. That's why I started living secretly as a human, because Ayahanda and Bonda said princesses can't practice law. You know I always loved the law."

This was even more surprising than it had been to find out that Sri Kemboja moonlighted as a human. "You did?"

"Okay, I assumed too much," said Sri Kemboja. "I forgot who I was talking to. I fought with Ayahanda and Bonda about it all the time, but you wouldn't have noticed. The point is, there's no need to sell your mountain. You'll have money once you're crowned—you can use that to help the people who suffered from your natural disasters."

Sri Bujang felt adrift, his sacrifices taken from him.

"If you could help all along," he said, "with the rain and the court case, why didn't you say so?"

Sri Kemboja looked a little ashamed. "You can only learn to stop the rain if you can see beyond self. How was I to know?"

"I spent centuries training to pierce the veil of self!"

"You didn't know I wanted to be a lawyer," Sri Kemboja pointed out. "Ayahanda had me detained in my room for a month for doing work experience! Do you even remember that?"

Sri Bujang did, now that she mentioned it. "Oh, is that why you spent that month in your room studying the classics?" At Sri Kemboja's look, he said, "Okay, I take your point. But that doesn't apply to the court case."

"I was *mad* at you, Kakanda," said Sri Kemboja. "You got away with everything. You wanted to be a sage, so you went off to this mountain and sat in your cave refusing visitors. I've been the one living with Ayahanda and Bonda, listening to them tell me what they wanted to tell you. But they never sent a messenger to your mountain or asked you to visit them. They always gave you face, because you were the raja muda."

Sri Bujang couldn't think of anything to say except, "I came back."

"Yes," said Sri Kemboja. "Anyway, even if we have a good case, that doesn't mean it's fun to deal with a lawsuit against my sick father. I'm busy at work, I have my own life. I've got enough things to handle as it is."

"Is one of those things May Lynn?" said Sri Bujang. He had been wondering.

Sri Kemboja choked on her drink. The human face she was wearing went bright red.

47

"No! Shut up! Who gave you that idea? We just work together!" she sputtered. "Wait, did May Lynn tell you that? What did she say about me?"

"Oh, nothing," said Sri Bujang. He gazed dreamily at the menu on the opposite wall. "I couldn't betray any confidences, of course. We sages get told things because we are trusted."

"*Kakanda!*" said Sri Kemboja.

But Sri Bujang could tell she wasn't mad at him anymore.

YULI

Daniel Abraham

Daniel Abraham (danielabraham.com) is the author of the Long Price Quartet, the Dragon and the Coin series, and, as M. L. N. Hanover, the Black Sun's Daughter series. As James S. A. Corey, he is co-author of the Expanse series with Ty Franck. His short fiction has been collected in *Leviathan Wept and Other Stories*. He has been nominated for the Hugo, Nebula, and World Fantasy awards, and won the International Horror Guild Award. He lives in New Mexico.

Forty-nine is too young to be raising a teenage grandson, but here he is. The boy spends most of his time downstairs—Yuli won't call it the basement, because the shitty little house they're in was built on a hill, so there's a window down there. Basements don't have windows. But the boy stays downstairs most of the time, either with his little friends or alone. Yuli sits in the kitchen, smoking his cigarettes and watching TV with the sound off, and he can hear them down there, like mice.

They've started playing pretend games, rolling strange-shaped dice and making up stories. Yuli preferred it when they were playing video games. Especially the battle ones where everyone fights against everyone, and the only point is you're the one alive at the end. He's never played those games, but at least he understands them. Every man for himself and God against all is a world he recognizes. There aren't so many things Yuli recognizes these days.

He is living in the United States, which he never thought he would do. He was born in Stavropol, in the North Caucasus, but he doesn't remember it. He was younger than the boys downstairs when he left his family to go fight. He spent more of his childhood in Afghanistan than at home, and that was before he started working private contracts. Since then he's seen the world, if mostly the shit parts of it. But still, the world.

The house he lives in is narrow. The walls were the pale color that Wrona called "Realtor white" when he took the place seven years ago. The smoke from his cigarettes and the grease from his grilled meat have stained them. The kitchen floor is linoleum tile that's curling up a little by the sink where it gets wet. The front room has a sofa that Yuli keeps covered in plastic so that it won't get cigarette stink in the cloth. The backyard he paved over with concrete so he wouldn't have to mow it all the goddamn time, and long fingers of grass still push up wherever there is a crack. His bed is good, though. King-sized, it is so broad that it hardly leaves space enough to walk around his bedroom. He'd had dreams about filling that bed with American girls and fucking his way to contentment, back when he'd first come here, and he'd had a couple girlfriends in the beginning.

Then, two years ago, he'd discovered that he had a son, and that his son had a son. The two had come to visit, and only one had left.

On the silent television news, a black woman and a white man shout over each other, square-mouthed with rage, until the image cuts to a bombed-out city. North Africa, to judge from the architecture. Not Egypt, though. Sudan, maybe. Yuli fought for a time in Sudan.

The boy's friends laugh at something, and Yuli shifts his attention to them. To the boy and what he's saying. It's like listening to a radio with the volume turned down almost past the point of audibility. Almost, but not quite.

"The king presents you with his wise man, and this guy has to be older than dirt. Seriously, he looks like he was born before rocks were invented. He tells you that the first dragons weren't just big, fire-breathing lizards. The first ones were the souls of great warriors who never died. They just became less and less human as they grew in power, until they became dragons. And the gold they guard is the treasure they amassed through their campaigns of violence and terror."

"Fuck," one of his little friends says. "You're telling us Aufganir is one of the first dragons?"

There's pride in the boy's voice when he speaks. "Aufganir is *the* first dragon."

Yuli chuckles and lights a fresh cigarette from the butt of the old one. Dragons and magic swords and the crystals with elf girls' souls in them or some shit. Baby stuff. Yuli was just a year or two older than his grandson is now when he killed his first mujahideen. Shot the man in his mouth. He can still picture it. Can count the moles on the dead man's cheek, that's how clear the memory is.

It was another life. Now he is just a man living a quiet life in a quiet place, letting his days smear together until it's hard to remember what part of the week it is unless the boy has to go to school. But still, it's funny hearing the children down there, talking breathlessly about going out to find imaginary treasures. A hoard of gold.

If they knew what was buried down there, right below their cheap little card table, they'd shit themselves white.

Okay, we set up camp at the edge of the trees. Not all the way out in the meadow where anyone could see us, and not in the forest, but like right at the edge.

All right.

And I'm going to set up a perimeter. Like trip wires all the way around.

Roll your traps skill.

Made it by two.

Okay, what else do you do? Start a fire? Cook dinner?

I'll start a little fire, but I'm digging a hole for it so that the light doesn't show. I don't want anything in the woods getting attracted to us.

Nothing assaults you while you eat. There's the usual forest noises, but nothing to raise an alarm. The moon comes up, with just a few thin clouds. The meadow is quiet and empty. Everything seems peaceful.

This is too easy. It's making me nervous. We set up a watch.

Who goes first?

I do.

Okay, roll perception.

I knew it. I knew it was too fucking easy. All right. Perception? I made it by three.

As you sit there in the darkness, you notice a crow on one of the tree branches. I mean, it's just a crow. There's nothing particularly weird about it, except that it doesn't change places. It's always right in the same spot.

Can it see me?

Well, you can see it, so yeah.

My amulet has passive detect magic. I'm just going to reach in my shirt like I'm scratching an itch. Really casually. And I'm touching the amulet.

Yeah, that crow is not a crow. It's some kind of shapeshifter. One of the dragon's spies. And you don't know how long it's been watching you.

Can I reach my bow?

Roll for it.

Okay . . . ah . . . well, that sucked.

It's not that bad. I'll give you a bonus because you were on watch. I'm going to say that your bow is just out of reach, and your quiver is past it. You can get to them, but you'll have to move.

I want to jump over, grab my bow and an arrow, and shoot at the shapeshifter. I still have one heroic action point left.

Spend it and roll dexterity.

Made it by two.

You would have hit, but the shapeshifter made its dodge. Before you can get another arrow, it's gone. You see the dark wings disappearing into the forest.

Well, shit. Aufganir's going to know we're coming.

Yuli has been losing weight. He hasn't changed his diet or started exercising, but in the last six months twenty pounds have melted away. When someone asks, he makes it a joke and says it's because God loves him, but he thinks it's probably cancer. Or maybe his thyroid. He knew a woman once with thyroid problems, and she lost a lot of weight. He knows he should go see a doctor, and he will. He just wants to drop a few more pounds first.

There are problems that come with his fat going away. There was a winter he was working private in Chechnya when there was snow on the ground for three months. When it thawed, the courtyard was full of bottles and cans and dogshit. All the things that didn't get cleaned up when it was cold that had waited and been revealed. It turned out bodies were like that too. The acid he'd dropped and the weed he'd smoked, maybe some of the heroin he'd used for the pain when he hurt his back outside Kabul, it wound up stored with his fat. Now, with that going, the drugs are getting dumped back into his bloodstream. Dogshit blood.

Most of the time, it's nothing. A little unexpected mellowness, a shift of mood that doesn't relate to anything. Sometimes, though, there's a little synesthesia. His fingertips tingle first, and then noise starts having colors to it. One time, when his hands were like that, he brushed against a wall, and the texture was a deep note, played on a viol. He didn't like it. Another time, he scratched an itch on his elbow just where it got dry and scaly, and for a moment, he was certain that there was a new, different skin underneath. He'd scratched himself bloody trying to peel himself like a snake. At times like that, he tries not to drive, or if he does, he's careful.

When he first came to the United States, he had a sports car. A Porsche. It was a sexy little car, but it leaked oil and there wasn't any room for groceries. He sold it and got a hatchback. It isn't as sexy, but it does what he wants better.

Maybe it's a sign he's getting old. It isn't the money. He has all the money he wants, if he decides to dig it up and spend it, but he doesn't. He keeps his where it stays safe. He's been poor. Living in a shitty house and driving a housewife's car isn't so bad when you know you don't have to do it. And there are reasons not to be so showy.

In the morning, he drives the boy to school. They talk a little, but not about anything. Then Yuli does whatever. Groceries sometimes. Laundry sometimes. He takes himself to a movie if something good is on. He likes action films because they're easier to follow, or at least if he doesn't catch everything, it doesn't matter as much. Lunch is back home if he doesn't want to see people, or Café Gurman if he does.

Today, he does.

Café Gurman is in a strip mall between a musical instrument shop that sells violins to pretentious white parents on one side and a payday loan on the other. The windows have a thin film on them that no amount of cleaning will ever make clear. The booths are red leather, cracked some places and mended with red tape. The walls have pictures of famous people, as if they have eaten there. Maybe they have. It is the home of the expatriate community. Or one particular expatriate community, anyway.

His.

Doria is at the register, doing something on her cell phone. She is the owner's daughter. She doesn't make eye contact with anyone, even as she takes their money and talks to them in Russian. She's a good kid. She'll go away soon, hopefully to college, and then he won't see her again. He orders his usual shawarma, nods to the familiar faces in the other booths. As soon as Wrona comes in, he knows something is wrong.

Yuli has known Wrona longer than anyone else in the United States. They were on the same detail the first time Yuli worked private. He's a tall man with long hands and a face as craggy as tree bark. When he sees Yuli, he lifts his chin in greeting, steps over, and sits in the booth across from him. Yuli frowns. This isn't how they are to each other. Not normally.

"You're looking good," Wrona says, and it is as close to an apology as Yuli will get. A little acknowledgment that Wrona has crossed a boundary, and that he's about to cross others. "You've been going to the gym?"

"No. I don't like those places."

"Me neither," Wrona says, scratching his neck with his long fingers. When he speaks next, it is in Polish. "There was something I needed to ask you. That thing. You know the one?"

Yuli's frown deepens to a scowl. If there was any doubt what Wrona meant, his discomfort clears it away. There is only one subject that would make him this nervous, and it's one that he shouldn't bring up. Not even vaguely and in Polish.

"I know," Yuli says.

"Do you still have it?"

"I know where it is."

Wrona nods but won't meet Yuli's eyes. "Yes, I thought. I mean, I assumed. But I heard something about people coming into town who shouldn't be here. People from Zehak." Now he turns his eyes to Yuli. "You know what I'm saying."

Yuli's mouth is dry, but he doesn't let anything show in his face. He takes a last bite of his shawarma, lifts a hand to get Doria's attention, and signals her for coffee. They're quiet until she brings it. He likes it black, roasted dark enough to hide evidence. That's the joke.

"All right," he says.

"If you have that much money," Wrona says quietly, "someone's going to be looking for it."

"I know."

"If you need a gun . . ." Wrona spreads his hands.

"No, it's all right," Yuli says. "I have guns."

After a long journey, you reach the township of Tannis Low. It's not a big place, but it's seriously defended. A stone wall that goes up thirty feet and then bends backward into the town so that people can hide in the overhang. The gates are bronze, but they've been charred badly over the years so that they look almost totally black. The valley around it is all stone and dirt. There are no trees. Almost no plants.

You know what's weird?

What?

Why does a dragon even have gold? I mean, I know why we want it. Pay off the assassin's guild. But what does Aufganir want with it? It's not like he's heading off to market every weekend to buy lunch meat.

It'd be like a whole cow. Cheaper to just fly out and roast one yourself.

That's my point, right? I mean why have a shit-ton of gold just to sit on?

Hemorrhoids. Definitely hemorrhoids.

Don't be gross.

You laughed.

For serious, though. Is there some kind of magic about gold? Or does he eat it or something? Whatever he wants it for, it's not the same as what we want it for, right?

People, *people*! Can we focus up here?

Sorry. It's just something I was thinking about.

Okay. So like I said, after a long journey, you reach the township . . .

It had been back when Yuli was working private in western Afghanistan, his fifteen years for Mother Russia behind him. Mercenary work suited him, and the pay was good. He'd had more hair back then. And cheekbones. The contract had been all about suppressing the poppy trade. Opium, heroin. Burning out the farms, breaking the trucks, disrupting the flow of drugs and money whatever way they could. Probably the client had been a rival producer. That was fine. Yuli didn't judge. One rule was very clear. The operation stopped at the border. They weren't to cross over into Iran.

They had crossed over into Iran.

There were four of them. Yuli, Wrona, another Pole called Nowak, and a man of no particular nation who everyone called Pintador though it wasn't his name. Yuli was driving. It was a Humvee with customized light armor. He liked it. It felt strong. It was dark, and he had night-vision goggles on that made the hills green and black. The target was a little compound in Sistan and Baluchestan Province that an upcoming warlord named Hakim Ali was using as a base. The target was soft, because the enemy knew that Yuli wasn't permitted to cross the border. Being in Iran kept it safe.

Yuli parked just before the top of a rise, and they all got out, moving quickly and quietly. Pintador whistled under his breath as he took position with a sniper rifle. Yuli surveyed the site through binoculars. Everything matched the briefing except that there was an extra car. A black sedan. Someone had chosen the wrong night to visit.

They moved forward carefully, Yuli and Wrona and Nowak. They each carried a 9A-91 assault rifle with a suppressor. Pintador's soft whistling in his earpiece meant the sniper hadn't seen anything to raise an alarm. The compound was two small houses and a shed, chain-link fence. An American pickup truck that had been white once, an ancient Jeep with a Barrett 82A1 mounted on its frame, and now the sedan. Yuli didn't see a guard, but two dogs were sleeping beside the shed. Yuli shot them first, then Nowak cut the chain on the fence, and they were in.

Three men were eating dinner, served by a woman in a burqa. One of the men wore a Western-style business suit, but except for that, they could have been brothers. Yuli didn't know what alerted them. Maybe they'd made a sound. Maybe the light from their window had reflected off some piece of equipment. Whatever it was, the enemy caught sight of them as they were crossing the yard, and before they could find cover, the enemy was firing at them. Nowak died, but Yuli and Wrona made it to the side of the shed where the dogs lay motionless.

"This is not good," Wrona had said as bullets cracked past them, but Yuli took the barrage of fire as a good sign. The enemy was undisciplined, and the undisciplined were weak. Even now, he can remember the calm of those moments. The focus that left no room for fear. They stayed low and held their fire as he murmured orders to Pintador. Yuli's patience had always been a weapon.

The first came out, circling around to flank them. The urge to shoot back as soon as there was opportunity was hard to resist, but Yuli signaled Wrona to wait. The little pop of the sniper rifle was unmistakable. The woman screamed, and Yuli and Wrona both opened up on the flanking enemy who had been briefly surprised to realize how far out of safety he had drifted. Just like that, two of the men were dead. Killing the last one and the woman took longer.

Afterward, Pintador brought down the Humvee while Yuli and Wrona went through the houses, the shed, the truck, and the cars. The heroin was in the shed, where Yuli had expected it to be. Fifteen bricks wrapped first in plastic and then cloth. It was what they expected to find. The binders in the sedan were a surprise.

Yuli still remembers seeing them: five three-ring binders with blue plastic covers and spines as wide as his hand. They had reminded him of medical records. When he picked one up, it felt too heavy. He remembers his first thought: the paper had gotten waterlogged. When he opened it, each page was a cardboard backing with a grid of clear plastic pockets four across and four high. A gold coin rested in each pocket; some were krugerrands, some American gold eagles. Each was an ounce of gold. Each sheet, a pound. Each binder, between fifteen and twenty pages deep. At the time, it was a little more than half a million dollars. Gold has gone up since then. Now the coins are worth nearly two million.

Yuli had never heard of the target trading in coins. Everything was supposed to be American dollars, if it was anything. This was something new. Yuli had wondered who the man in the suit was and who he had worked for, but there was no identification in his pockets or in his car.

Pintador had loaded Nowak into the Humvee, wrapped in plastic film they'd brought for the purpose. No evidence left behind was the rule, and a dead mercenary was evidence. Wrona went back to the shed and returned with three bricks of heroin. He had tossed one to Yuli.

"Spoils of war," Wrona said.

Yuli tossed it back. "You take it. I'm keeping these."

"You sure?" Wrona said. "The shit will vanish. Show up with those, someone will notice."

Yuli had taken one of the coins out, enjoying its luster in the faint light of the coming dawn. The weight of it on his fingertips. Some part of him had known even then that he wouldn't sell them.

"I'm keeping these," he'd said again, and Wrona had shrugged. Then it had been time to finish up.

Wrona and Pintador took cans of gasoline from the Humvee and soaked the compound. Yuli got the flamethrower and, standing outside the fence line, he turned it on everything. The dead men, the woman, houses, truck, Jeep, sedan. The dogs. The earth.

The flames roared, and he had roared back until his breath and the fire were one thing.

The tunnel narrows down. The roots and soil you were going through at the mouth are thinning out, and you can see the carved stone. This is a worked passage. Not just something natural.

Goblin warren. I'm telling you this is a goblin warren. This is bad.

Better than going in the front door.

The tunnel turns to the right. About twenty feet farther down, you can see an opening. Like it comes to a bigger chamber and ends there. No door, it just opens out. There's light.

Okay, I'm dousing the torch.

Don't kill the fucking torch! We need to see!

We don't need to announce ourselves. Anyway, I'm carrying it, so I douse it.

It gets dark.

We wait until our eyes adjust.

Everyone roll perception, and let me know if you miss.

Ah. I'm down by one.

Anyone else miss? No? Okay, you were looking at the torch before it went out, and so you're taking longer to get your dark vision. Everyone else, you see that the light at the end of the passage is reddish and flickering. Like there's a fire nearby. And because of the way the light hits the stone, you can catch the shadows where something's carved into the walls.

Like runes? Something's written there?

More like there were places for something to be set into the rock. Braces maybe. But they're gone now.

I use my amulet for detect magic.

You don't find anything particular to the marks.

I don't like that. I roll for traps, and . . . make it by two.

Yeah, that's the kind of thing you'd see if someone had put in a winch or something. If you had to bet, you'd say one of those stones is a pressure plate, but you can't tell what the mechanism is that it triggers.

Well, folks, you don't make something like that unless you've got something worth guarding. I'd have to say we're getting close.

Yuli stands naked in front of his full-length mirror and wonders how he let it get this far. His arms are thin, pale, and grayish. His belly doesn't pouch out much, but the skin is slack. He has tits like a twelve-year-old girl. He keeps slouching. He's getting a little bald, a little gray, but that's just time. His teeth are yellow from cigarettes and coffee, because that's how it goes. But he's weak and slow, and that is his fault. Complaisant is another word for stupid, and he is finished with being stupid.

The cigarettes go first. He breaks each one over the toilet, dusting the piss water with tobacco so that he can't go back and fish one last cigarette out of the trash. Next is the alcohol. Then the sugar. He can't believe how much shit he's been eating: frozen pizzas and chocolate candies and bread so white it looks like slices of snow. Now that he sees it all clearly, it's amazing that he isn't in worse condition.

Next is the guns. Those, anyway, are still in good condition. Three pistols—two matching Glock 17s and a Sig Sauer P220 that had been given to him as a present by an old girlfriend. He also has a Bushmaster M4 semi-automatic carbine that he has carried for almost a decade.

There are people who think more guns are better. Yuli thinks that's wrong. Someone who has used ten thousand guns once is an amateur. Someone who has used one gun ten thousand times is an expert.

He puts a clean towel over the kitchen table to keep the oil off it, then cleans them, assembling and disassembling them until all the parts find their familiar places in his fingers. He spends hours dry firing them, aiming at the microwave, the kitchen faucet, the people passing by on the street. *Click click click,* training his hand not to anticipate the kick, practicing like a pianist playing scales. When the boy sees the guns, his eyes get wide. Yuli doesn't talk about them, and the boy doesn't either.

When the boy is at school, Yuli runs up and down the stairs, pushing himself. The first time, he only manages four trips down and up and down again before his heart is tapping on his eardrums and he's shaking. He has to sit on the bottom step and put his head against the wall, a long, slow trickle of Russian profanity dribbling out from his lips. Weak old man. When he gets his breath back, he runs up and down two more times, pushing until he is literally incapable of doing it again. The next day he hurts like someone has beaten him, and he does it again. The third day is worse. The fourth, he does ten rounds before he has to stop. He wants a cigarette. He wants a drink. He feels sick from the pain and the craving, and he revels in his suffering. It is his strength coming back.

He would like to find a boxing club. Someplace he can hit someone and be hit. A way to remind his body what violence is. He should have been doing this all along, and the impulse to do it now is as bad as the nicotine withdrawal. Tactically, going out to a gym is a mistake. He doesn't know where the enemy is, and every trip out of the house is an exposure. Instead, he strips his bedroom bare and works there. Push-ups, sit-ups, lunges. He finds a couple of old cinder blocks half buried in the alley, and brings them in for weights. He starts getting biceps again. He starts seeing gains, and the gains come faster.

He was a predator for many years, and his body remembers what it was like. Wants to return to that way of being. Is hungry for it. He keeps his suffering constant, and his body rewards him. He loses more weight.

His dogshit blood gets worse. The synesthesia and the flashbacks come every few days now, though they are brief. There are a few times he gets dizzy and faints in the morning. He decides to get down to zero percent body fat if he can. Clean away all the drugs. Purge himself of all his old sins.

He leaves the house rarely. When he does, he shifts away from his old habits. He goes to groceries he doesn't like and has never gone to before. He gets gasoline in his car on corners he has to travel to find. Even taking the boy to school, he varies the routes. Drops the boy off behind the gym one day, a half block away the next. Always, part of his attention is on the street around him. Who is where, what they are looking at, who they are talking to. Where the lines of sight are. Where there is cover, and where there is only concealment. He thinks how to flank the fat customer-service man at the bank, if he should need to. He knows what sidewalks he could drive over, what parks he could cross if he were escaping pursuit. Or if he were pursuing. He is aware of the space around him as if it were part of his body. His hypervigilance is almost paranoia.

At night, when the boy is asleep, he stands naked before the full-length mirror, and he sees the alteration in his flesh. He has bulk in his shoulders. He doesn't slouch. His skin has color again. His face is sharp.

Part of him knows that the wise move is to vanish. Pack up his things in the back of the car, take the boy, and drive away to a new city, a new name, and a new life. It wouldn't be his first time, or his second either. He doesn't do it.

He tells himself that it is better to hold to familiar territory and keep his home-court advantage. They will follow him anyway. The truth is that he wants them to come. He is waiting for them.

He feels better now than he has in years.

Everyone roll your stealth.
    I wish I'd kept that heroic action point.
    Did you blow it?

No, I'm okay. Made it exactly.

Everyone else good? Okay, you manage to slip past the stone barrier. The hall you've stepped into is huge. The cave is bigger than a cathedral. A river of lava is running through it, and the air is really hot. Hurts to breathe kind of hot. And the whole floor, where it's not lava, is covered in gold. Coins and goblin bars and jewelry. It's everywhere. And sitting in the middle of all of it is Aufganir. He's huge. His body's forty feet long, easy. Green scales and black wings.

Is he awake?

He is. He hasn't seen you yet, but he's sniffing at the air like he can tell something's wrong.

This is it, then. We attack.

Roll initiative.

Yuli is at the Walmart when it happens. The day is warm and pleasant. He drives over after dropping the boy at school and circles the parking lot twice looking for anything suspicious before he parks. He prefers shopping at Target, but at Walmart, he can carry his guns. He has one of the Glocks in an ankle holster, and the other at the small of his back. He doesn't like the ankle holster. It means he has to wear pants wide enough that they feel like bell-bottoms. It doesn't look stupid, but it feels like it does.

He walks in, stopping at the store's mouth to look back. Two young black men walking together. A blond woman with a pink scarf and yellow skirt. An old woman struggling with an ugly oversized purse. He thinks how he would kill each of them, but only as practice. None of them takes notice of him. He turns back. The fingers of his left hand tingle, and he shakes and makes fists until the feeling comes back.

Inside, the air is cool and scentless. Generic air, the same now as it will be at the height of summer or on Christmas Day. Nothing is different in here. Yuli takes a cart and heads in among the other shoppers. He has a list in his head. Chicken breasts and frozen vegetables to make dinner with. Some Muscle Milk to drink after he works out. And he needs socks.

He's thinking about throwing out all the ones he has and buying a dozen identical pairs at the same time he's noticing all the exits.

Someone coughs, and the sound is wrong. Someone coughs the way you cough when you're used to speaking Farsi. Yuli turns, and it's the blond girl with the scarf. Their eyes meet for a fraction of a second. Her eyes widen a millimeter, and he knows.

He takes his hands off the cart, turns, and walks back toward the entrance. He doesn't run. He doesn't draw down, not yet. She won't be alone. There are others. He needs to find them first, and then react. His heart is racing. Yuli thinks the strange feeling in his head is just adrenaline until a cashier closes her drawer as he passes. The sound is vibrant green.

This is not the time for the dogshit in his blood to be kicking in.

This is the only time he has.

The sun is warm against his face as he steps out into the parking lot. He feels the breeze against his cheek, cool and caressing. For a moment, he is aware of everything. The high, thin clouds almost obscured by the city haze. The faint smell of gasoline. The traffic sound of tires against asphalt on the street. If he can just get to his car and out to the street—

He swings around slowly, and he sees them. Two in a pickup truck by the main entrance. Another pair on the far side beside a white Honda with the engine already running, prepared to intercept him if he goes for one of the cutouts on that side. The blond girl behind him. There should be two more, probably at the back in case he went out the loading dock. They will be coming forward now. Yuli considers the civilians. A father and teenage daughter coming out of the store, bickering. A harried old woman pulling into a parking space. They don't see any of what is unfolding around them.

Yuli walks to his car, watching the hunters as he goes. The back of his neck itches, and he glances back to see the blonde at the entrance of the store. She hasn't drawn a weapon. She isn't walking toward him. They're waiting to see what he does.

If Wrona were here, one could drive while the other put down cover fire. Yuli can't manage both at the same time. A team of seven against just one man, and one altered by ancient drugs at that. He would give himself one chance in six of reaching the street alive. Or less. Probably less.

He wishes now that he'd told the boy about all of it. He doesn't want his grandson coming back home and finding the blond woman and her friends there. The boy won't be able to tell them what they want to know, but they won't believe that. Not at first. Hopefully, they'll find what they want and go while the boy is still in his classes.

Yuli reaches his car. The two in the truck have come to their senses. They drive toward him. He opens the hatchback. If he can get his car started, he won't try to reach the cutout. Straight out over the curb is his best choice. Then, if he doesn't get into a collision, maybe he makes it home. Or away. Or back around behind them to put bullets in their skulls.

One of the pair from the Honda is running toward him hunched over. Making a break for cover. The blond woman sprints toward him, pulling a pistol from a holster under her skirt. The harried civilian gets out of her car, still oblivious to the kill zone she is in.

Yuli hoists his carbine. His hands are both tingling. The blond woman shoots twice. The second shot shatters the hatch window, and Yuli feels a stab of outrage. That's his fucking car. And then there is only pleasure. A sense of overwhelming power flows through him, lifting him up like vast wings. The civilian woman screams and dives under her car. The father is pulling his daughter down as she tries to get out her cell phone to film this.

Yuli turns back toward the blond woman. When she sees the Bushmaster in his hands, she tries to change direction. To find some cover.

His gun roars. The sound is like fire: a brightness of yellow and red.

A WHISPER OF BLUE

———

Ken Liu

Ken Liu (kenliu.name) is an author of speculative fiction, as well as a translator, lawyer, and programmer. A winner of the Nebula, Hugo, and World Fantasy awards, he has been published in *The Magazine of Fantasy & Science Fiction*, *Asimov's*, *Analog*, *Clarkesworld*, *Lightspeed*, and *Strange Horizons*, among other places. His debut novel, *The Grace of Kings*, is the first volume in a silkpunk epic fantasy series, the Dandelion Dynasty. It won the Locus Award for Best First Novel and was a Nebula Award finalist. He subsequently published the second volume in the series, *The Wall of Storms*; two collections of short stories, *The Paper Menagerie and Other Stories* and *The Hidden Girl and Other Stories*; and a Star Wars novel, *The Legends of Luke Skywalker*. Forthcoming is the conclusion to the Dandelion Dynasty. He lives with his family near Boston, Massachusetts.

APRIL

Text on screen: **Town of Mannaport, Commonwealth of Maine and Massachusetts, population 28,528 (human)**

[*Montage of a bedroom community on the shore of Massachusetts Bay. Thick cables pulling a train into a commuter-rail station; families in an ice-cream parlor next to an ammo shop; a block of public housing surrounded by single-family homes; a high school football game; a Fourth of July parade; neighbors browsing a yard sale. The scenes are shot on phones, showing the artless application of filters and framing, as well as the unsteady camerawork of amateurs.*

Scenes of frozen seas and muddy snowfields. And then, the spring. The sunlight, after the long winter, is timid and soft, but there's no mistaking the raucous joy of the children as they test out the playground equipment; the blooming forsythias and azaleas—vibrant, living fireworks splashed onto the canvas after a winter in shades of gray; the chitter-chatter of birds, squirrels, baby skunks luxuriating on green lawns in the warm breeze.]

INGRID (*71, hair so white it shines*)

It started a few weeks ago . . . Look at me, can't remember anything anymore—no, it's not my age. (*Laughs.*) I'm going to blame my poor memory on the excitement of so many new residents in town. (*She turns to her granddaughter, sitting next to her.*) Do you remember the date?

ZOE (*16, expression tense, hunched as though trying to disappear, quiet*)

I . . . I'm not sure.

INGRID

Just check the date on your video—you know, that first one? (*Pridefully to the camera*) She was the first to get a sighting! They used her video for the nightly news.

ZOE

Okay. (*Fumbles with her phone until she finds it.*) Exactly three weeks ago, on the vernal equinox.

LEE *(41, town manager)*

I tell people: manage this right, and you'll secure the future of your children and the future of *their* children.

You've read the headlines in the *Globe* and seen the reports on TV. My days are *packed* with meetings: the President, Boeing, the Commonwealth Energy Commission, Westinghouse, DRACOGRID, Caterpillar, BaySTAR . . . everyone wants a piece of Mannaport! This is easily the largest rush in decades.

You've seen nothing yet. Just wait till the gigawatt-class ones show up—

INGRID

Right. On the vernal equinox.

It's not as bad as some people make it sound. I had Ron— that's my son-in-law—and Zoe put in some heavy curtains on the bedroom window to muffle the noise. I hardly know they are there now.

ZOE

(*Takes a deep breath to calm herself.*) I . . . like having them around.

I keep the windows open a crack at night to hear them.

INGRID

All the ones we've seen so far are pretty small. (*Turns to Zoe.*) Not like the ones you used to draw.

ZOE

(*Looks away from the camera.*)

ALEXANDER *(35, eyes so intense they seem to glow on their own)*

I want them gone! They'll have to put me in jail if they expect me to put up with—

HARIVEEN *(53, self-described "inventrepreneur," has an LED clip in her hair that flashes "Free energy isn't free")*

Nobody knows where they're from. Or how they came to be here. Or why.

But that's not the problem. The problem is that no one is even thinking about the right questions.

[Montage of shaky phone footage: silver scales scintillating between docked boats; a serpentine tail disappearing under a thick lilac bush; the crimson clouds of a seaside sunrise interrupted by a loud roar—reptilian, avian, saurian?—the camera swerves to reveal half-glimpsed leathery wings—like kites plunging out of the sky—vanishing behind sandy dunes; a screaming crowd scattering from a baseball field, pursued by dozens of flying creatures swooping low, emitting high-pitched screeches— bats? birds? flying lizards?]

Town of Mannaport, Commonwealth of Maine and Massachusetts, population 7,000 (dragon, estimated)

HARIVEEN

[We are in a garage, something like a modern Da Vinci's workshop, except messier, dirtier, noisier, and devoid of the patina of romanticized

history. Wheels and gears spin; belts rumble; chains rattle; cranks and pistons goose-step in formation.]

These are prototypes, so a bit crude-looking. But I assure you they're all based on proven, centuries-old designs—like this one, first built by Étienne Lenoir—with lots of patented improvements from me, of course. I've got some that run on coal, some on petroleum or gas—the idea that internal-combustion engines require pure alcohol is a shameless lie spread by the energy conglomerates. If I could just get the funding . . .

Are you still filming?

Never mind. I know how I sound. Even if you shoot everything I show you, they'll figure out a way to discredit me. Can't let the public know about real alternatives to the draconic energy monopoly, can we?

More than a century ago, Thomas Edison and Henry Ford teamed up to lock us into electricity as our dominant power source, and we've been racing nonstop to generate more electricity from dragon breath. Bit by bit, we have grown to depend on these creatures, and now all our politicians are in the pockets of the draconic energy-industrial complex, with no way out.

No, no, don't worry; I won't challenge the orthodoxy that dragons are completely safe—I'll keep the interview uncontroversial.

So . . . how do I explain my opposition to our energy policy without . . . ?

It's like this. Everyone sees that air routes and shipping lanes are planned along dragon migratory routes; metropolises survive and thrive based on their dragon population; countries compete mercilessly to attract the giant beasts that drive GDP.

We speak of university dragon endowments and the national strategic reserve—but the language is designed to make us feel better; it's misleading. Dragons are free to come and go as they like, and empires rise and fall at the whim of creatures we have no hope to understand or tame. Did you ever read *Guns, Germs, and Dragons?* The hypothesis is that the rise of the West was largely due to the good fortune of the presence of fire-breathing dragons in Europe. East Asia fell behind in the Industrial Revolution because their dragons breathed cold mist and water, not fire. It wasn't until Long Ruyuan of Tianjin, inspired by the work of Robert Stirling, invented the yin-yang engine, powered by both fire- and mist-breathing dragons, that the shift of the power to Europe stopped. And even today, the prevalence of city-states and small countries has to do more with our dependence on dragons than culture or politics.

(*A deep sigh.*)

I want to free us from this addiction to cheap energy from dragons. We celebrated when the Warsaw Pact fell as their dragons decided to depart en masse, but how do we know that dragons won't do the same to us here in the Commonwealth of Massachusetts and Maine one day? We forget history at our peril.

For my troubles, people call me a crank, a fool.

ZOE

[*There's a fresh lightness of spirit in her—not quite joy, but perhaps a tentative step toward it. She's still shy and speaks haltingly, but she's talking a lot more than before.*]

The pictures? (*Laughs nervously.*) No, I don't think so. Just childish scribbles. I've no idea if they're even around; I didn't save them.

I want to talk about real dragons.

Some complain about the noise and smell, the droppings everywhere. Some rant about the danger of dragons rampaging through the streets. The first week, there were like twenty accidents over on Route 17, next to the state park, and they had to block off the whole road. Then they had to evacuate and close

Astrov Elementary School because all the dragons roosting on the grounds made parents nervous. Just now, on the way here, I saw a dozen lawyer types around the parking lot of the town center, like a cloud of flies around a heap of dragon dung. I don't know who they're planning on suing. Dragons aren't afraid of lawyers.

I hear the gripes. "Mannaport isn't Boston. We don't have the infrastructure to handle them!" I guess they mean things like walls and fencing. They want the General Court to declare a state of emergency and maybe send in the minutemen to chase the dragons out.

I've been reading up on the history of dragon-rushes . . . Here's a summary from Memexpedia: "Most modern dragon-cities are at least semi-planned: Boston focused on libraries and universities, attracting dragons with scholarship; the California Republic went with a dual strategy of invention and art, and Silicon Valley and Hollywood are now the two biggest dragon centers in all of North America. Down in New York, they stuck with a most old-fashioned technique: hoarding gold and treasure on Wall Street until the Old World dragons of Europe left their havens in the Bahamas and the British Virgin Islands to settle in Manhattan, curling their bodies around the vaults for weeks at a time before stints in the giant power plants on Long Island." Oh, that last bit has a "citation needed" question mark.

But the example that spoke to me the most is Titusville, Appalachia. Back in 1859, a spontaneous gathering of dragons descended on the small settlement out of nowhere. Everyone rushed in, trying to make a profit, and the very fortunately named Edwin Drake managed to build the first dragon derrick, harnessing a fifty-foot obsidian scale that powered the cable railway between Lake Erie and Baltimore. For a while, the dragon-boom made Titusville the wealthiest town in the world. The people became addicted to the dragon money and built more cooling ponds, more dragon derricks, more power plants—until the day the dragons suddenly got up and left.

Edwin Drake is my great-great-great-grandfather, on my mother's side. And my mother—

I'm not ready to talk about that.

Ever since I was little, people would tell me that I have an old soul. I like to read and be by myself. Crowds making speeches make me nervous, but I make it a point to go to the town meetings. To find out what the adults are planning.

They argue about eminent domain and Commonwealth aid, property values and tax credits, isolation walls and safety zones. They want the town manager to make the best deals with the big corporations to guarantee jobs and get every resident a share of the dragon revenues.

But no one seems to be thinking about the *meaning* of dragons coming here, or how to stop Mannaport from becoming another Titusville.

Mannaport has no natural wonders, no great universities, no money, no art. We're like a lot of other small towns in the Commonwealth: clean and peaceful on the outside, but full of pain and desolation behind the walls. My high school feels big and empty because people leave, if they can, and don't come back. Good jobs are hard to find if you want to stick around— all you can look forward to are "gigs." Drugs are a problem, and late at night, sometimes you hear *pop-pop* in the distance. I used to think it was drunk teenagers setting off fireworks, until the day I saw the flashing lights of the police cars hurtling down Route 17 and read about the dead body they found.

[We're on a hill, overlooking a park below. Dragons are slithering, crawling, shambling, gliding, as colorful as the wildflowers dotting the grass. From a distance, they resemble butterflies, birds, bits of living paint swirling to find a shape.]

Worth the climb, isn't it? I come up here almost every day

just for the view. The police tell us to stay away, but I can't imagine them hurting anyone. They sure look better tempered than the turkeys that clog the streets every fall. When I'm up here, I don't worry about the SRATs, school gossip, Dad's nagging, Grandma's lawn that needs mowing—it's just nice knowing that there are these beautiful creatures in the world whose concerns we'll never understand and who'll never care about our troubles. The universe feels just a little bit bigger, you know?

I ask myself: Why have the dragons come here? Why?

But seeing that view, it almost doesn't matter.

JUNE

INGRID

[*Children are playing in a field.*

The focus of the lens changes to be on a towering tupelo in the background. There's something odd about the branches: they seem too bent, too laden with foliage.]

The mood in town has definitely shifted. Not nearly so many are talking about all the money we'll make from selling land to the developers, and also not nearly so many are scared about all the changes. I'd say we are getting used to the dragons.

[*A baseball crashes into the tupelo tree, and the scene explodes. What but a moment earlier had seemed to be mere clumps of leaves transforms into shimmering scales, unwinding limbs, unfolding wings, unfurling whiskers, snapping nictitating membranes. The camouflaging green gives way to reds, golds, brilliant swatches of blue and indigo as a cloud of dragons, disturbed from their chameleon-like rest, take to the air. The flock is a mix of North American elk-horns, Siberian zmeys, Mesoamerican feathered serpents, wingless East Asian loongs, flare-tailed South Asian nagas, European gossamer-wings, and other species. None of them are bigger than a peacock, and most are much smaller.*

For a moment, the children admire the aerial display, but soon lose interest. A girl runs up to the foot of the tree and gingerly steps among the droppings until she recovers the ball. The children resume their game. One by one, the disturbed dragons land back on the tree, settle in, and take on their camouflage.]

They are cute, aren't they? Some people are disappointed; most are relieved. These dragons are nothing like the giants in Widener Library that power Boston or even the smaller ones that drive the jumbo jets crossing the Atlantic and the continent.

Oh, I don't mean to sound like a dragon expert. I didn't see a dragon in person until I was eighteen, the day I showed up at Wellesley, a wide-eyed first-year.

[Archival photos of Wellesley College, presented Ken Burns style.]

Back then, the Wellesley endowment numbered only five: three American bison-horns, a Welsh wyvern, and an English wyrm. It couldn't possibly compete with the five-hundred-strong endowment of Harvard-Radcliffe, but to me, it was wealth and power beyond imagination.

While the other girls were still settling in, I took a walk around Lake Waban, where the smallest bison-horn, Delirious-borne, made her home. It was evening, and I wasn't expecting to see anything. The dragons, I knew, were very busy and rarely home. Although they, like most university dragons, came to Wellesley because they were attracted to the hoard of learning in its libraries and lecture halls, Wellesley's compact with the Commonwealth meant that the university had to persuade the dragons to power the factories and mills in the surrounding towns with their fire breath.

But the professors also knew that the dragons needed time at home to recuperate. Dragons didn't live on grain and meat alone: their spiritual well-being required them to be steeped in the academic atmosphere of the college, to have time to be alone and to think—I know modern experts say this is all nonsense, but I believed it back then, and I believe it still.

Not a bad metaphor for the life of a college student, I think.

The shoreline trail was shrouded in mist and fog, as was the lake itself. As I continued my stroll, energized by the excitement of being on my own, away from the eyes of parents and chaperones, I imagined myself a hero in the ballads of old, hiking through vale and dale, traversing swamp and bog, hot on the trail of a dragon guarding treasure. The heavy mist made it impossible to see the other shore of the lake, and it seemed to expand in size until it was as large as an ocean—I didn't know then that loss of spatial sense and judgment was said to be a common psychological effect of proximity to a dragon.

Abruptly, the air was rent by a loud trumpeting, the way I imagine a jet engine sounds. I turned and was greeted by the sight of the water in the lake erupting like a volcano. The mist parted for a moment to reveal a long, sinuous neck, like in the drawings of the brontosaurus in books, topped by a massive horned and furry head. Sunlight, refracted by the mist, haloed that head with a thousand colors I could not name and had never seen. The head turned toward me, and those eyes, blue orbs that seemed to glow with an inner light, locked with mine.

Then, almost casually, Deliriousborne opened her mouth a crack and let out a gentle hiss, like a whisper; the mist swirling around her maw glowed a faint blue, like an iceberg. My heart was in my throat.

She looked away and up, turning heavenward. The jaws opened wide, and out shot a widening tongue of flame, a fiery flower blossoming in the middle of the lake.

I don't think I ever understood the literal meaning of *breath-taking* until that moment. I had seen plenty of scientific illustrations and photographs of dragons curled inside power plants, using their fire to generate the steam that spun the turbines that produced the electricity that was the lifeblood of the mechanized world. But those illustrations made dragons seem tame and controlled, organic components of the machinery of the modern metropolis.

Coming face-to-face with a dragon was indescribably different: *sublime*, as the Romantic poets would have said. Instantaneously, I understood why so many explorers and engineers of old would brave lightning-filled storms, ice-bound Arctic waters, pathless deserts strewn with skeletons, and swamps covered in poisonous vapors—just for a chance to glimpse one of these magnificent creatures.

Years later, after I had Julie, that was one of her favorite stories, and she demanded I tell it again and again. As a little girl, she was obsessed with dragons, and she used to draw all these pictures—just like Zoe. She always left the eyes till last, and when she painted in the brilliant bits of blue, with shiny streaks bleeding into the misty air, the dragons seemed to come alive.

HARIVEEN

For all our modern dependence on dragons, most people never see one. The trend to deprive people of the knowledge of the reality of our energy policy has only accelerated in recent decades. In the same way we keep death out of sight in hospitals, we keep the dragons out of people's view behind concrete walls and steel doors, behind secretive employment contracts and ironclad NDAs, maintaining the illusion that modernity is cost-free.

If dragons are so safe, as the government and the energy companies keep on insisting, why the thick prisonlike fence around Harvard Yard and the high-security isolation barriers that gave Wall Street its name? Makes you wonder what they *aren't* telling us, doesn't it?

Anyway, the problem isn't limited to the Commonwealth of Maine and Massachusetts, or even to the other countries in North America. Everywhere in the world, from the Hibernia Republic to the city-states of the Sinitic League, people are content to let mysteries be mysteries.

You can find a hint of this modern state of affairs even in antiquity.

[Animation of an aeolipile revolving, with jets of steam shooting out.]

The first person in recorded history to harness draconic energy was Hero of Alexandria. He constructed a brass sphere with two bent pipes coming out, pointing in opposite directions. The sphere was free to rotate about an axis perpendicular to the pipes.

Hero then lined the inside of the sphere with pieces of amber, carved into intricate mythological scenes. A handful of fireflies were trapped inside the sphere to provide illumination, like shooting stars revolving in this inner empyrean. The intent, evidently, was to create a piece of temple art, whose hidden beauty could be appreciated only by the gods and imagined by the worshippers.

However, to the surprise of everyone, Hero's creation aroused the curiosity of local Egyptian dragons, and two juvenile specimens slithered into the device through the pipes, asplike. Pleased by the art they found inside, the dragons filled the interior with heated steam. The scalding steam, jetting out of the bent pipes, spun the sphere as though it were a living thing, bringing joy and wonder to all viewers.

Hero went on to create more and more elaborate versions of the aeolipile, and died relatively young, raving mad. Few writers in antiquity drew any connection between his work and his death.

LEE

Of course I'm disappointed. I thought the little dragons were going to be the appetizers for the main course, not the whole meal!

The one good thing is that the "Knights of Mannaport" are no longer bugging me all the time to "do something" about the safety of the town. I guess even the anti-dragon conspiracy videos they watch online don't consider little dragons much of a threat.

One by one, the corporations stopped calling.

So I called them.

"Our engineers have done the feasibility studies. It's just not economical to exploit the little dragons you have," they'd tell me. Then they'd drone on and on about megawatts and gigawatts and ROI and capitalization and utility rates and depreciation.

Turns out that the dragons in Mannaport are barely in the kilowatt range. Back in the days when James Watt used to strap a pair of kaleidoscopic goggles on a donkey-sized nessie and call that a steam engine, such low output might have been commercially acceptable. But now? Not so much.

"Little dragons will grow into big ones, right?"

"Not always," they'd say. Full-grown dragons come in all sizes, even within the same species. And our miniature dragons, according to the biologists they sent, are already done with growing.

"But we have so many of them!" I'd say. "Can't you corral a bunch of them to do something useful together?"

They'd lecture me on the biology and habits of dragons, the lack of qualified dragon-whisperers, and the dangers of "over-engineering."

Turns out that dragons rarely, if ever, work well in teams. And they can only be enticed, not coerced, to work. The last time anyone tried to force a bunch of small dragons to work together was at Chernobyl, and that was a disaster no one wants to repeat.

"I've heard of places that make single-person vehicles and

household power plants that run on small dragons," I'd plead. "Surely there's *some* way to make that work?"

"The only places where that's economical are kibbutzim and big, dense metropolises where the rich might want to show off," they'd say. "Remember, dragons like to stay where they are, or migrate between fixed points they pick themselves."

"But the dragons may start migrating."

"Who wants to go to Mannaport unless you already live there?"

Then they stopped taking my calls altogether.

I'm not giving up, though. Someone told me that over in Japan, they've made big strides in miniaturization that we can only dream of. There has to be a way to make a profit from our tiny dragons. Has to be.

ALEXANDER

I tell people to stay as far away as possible. The dragons look cute and harmless, but I know the truth.

Joey was the smart one in the family. Went to an exam school. He had the grades and test scores to get out of Manna-port, to be anything he wanted.

But the only thing my brother wanted was to be a dragon-whisperer, to work with the dragons up close, not just to "bask in the glory of the fruits of their labor from afar"—yep, that was how he talked, like an old novel they made you read in school. Used to make me want to punch him. Talk properly, you doofus!

"Lawyers, bankers, coders—they're all parasites, mere leeches," he used to say. "What do they do except manipulate symbols to generate more symbols? But a whisperer is someone who coaxes the breath of life out of the dragon, who makes civilization possible."

He left home for the DRACOGRID plant in Boston Harbor the day he turned eighteen. They pay dragon-whisperers well, but that's because the job is so dangerous, and so few have the talent for it.

Joey told me that you cannot force a dragon to work; you have to *beguile* it. He told me how a czarina in Saint Petersburg once built a whole room in her palace out of amber in order to tempt the dragons into breathing fire—I think she was imitating some hero in Alexandria?—and she got badly burned. That gave me nightmares as a kid.

Let's see, my mother kept Joey's scholarship essay around here somewhere . . . There it is. "Howard Hughes ended up in Las Vegas because he thought the bright lights and endless glamour would keep the flight of dragons that kept his aviation empire aloft entertained. During the Cold Race, NATO and GEAIA both secretly funded artists to try to entice the Warsaw Pact dragons to defect. But hundreds of years after Newcomen and Watt, dragon-whispering is still more art than science.

"I intend to become a great artist."

Dragons are fickle, lazy, and easily bored. Even if you manage to lure them to settle in a city with treasure, books, or novelty, they'd rather nap near the hoard than work. That last bit, getting a dragon to breathe fire while remaining docile, is where they need the dragon-whisperer.

No one knows how dragon-whispering works. There's a code of silence among the whisperers, a secretive guild passing their wisdom down the generations by word of mouth. When we were boys, Joey and I used to play games where I'd be the dragon, and he'd try to get me to do chores—usually by promising me time on the game console he built himself.

Maybe that really is how they do it. Didn't old-time rail-road engineers out west strap kaleidoscopes over their locomotive dragons? Wouldn't surprise me if they now make dragons live in virtual reality headsets. On talk radio, Teddy Patriot said they make the whisperers in power plants stroke the dragons in a weird way, almost like sex, turning them on. I don't know if I believe that. In school, they're still teaching children that dragons enjoy music, literature, and art. Joey used to mock that one as the "Scheherazade theory of dragons."

I'll never know the real answer. Dragon-whisperers, if they aren't torched to charcoal in the line of duty, retire only when their minds have been burned away, which is almost worse.

Joey came home at thirty, but he looked like a man twenty years older. He didn't recognize me or Mom; he didn't laugh or cry; he ate when food was held to his mouth, and wasted away when it wasn't. His mind was like a sieve dipped in water. No matter how many times I showed him old family photos or Mom made his favorite dishes, his eyes remained blank and his speech a nonsensical babble. His heart stopped beating eight months after he got home, but he was really dead long before that.

I have no idea what horrors he had suffered; what he had seen and could not unsee.

There was a generous pension, of course, but no way to make the dragons or the company that sucked the life out of him pay what they really ought. The contract and the laws were impenetrable. Assumption of risk. Willing suspension of rights.

Attacking a dragon is a crime. And I won't ever do anything illegal. But short of that?

JULY

ZOE

[*The camera is on her as she walks, keeping pace. From time to time we see tourists gathered around some empty lot, necks craning, phones ready. Uniformed officers stand behind police tape to keep the crowd at a distance.*]

The tourists want to see it happen again, up close. Now that

we have a bona fide attraction in town, the selectmen are terrified. They want the President to send in the minutemen. (*Shakes
head.*)

No, I still don't know why the dragons have come to Mannaport.
But, I think I've made a new friend, or maybe two.

It started before Independence Day. The town manager and
the selectmen, still trying to figure out a way to make some
profit from our "useless" dragon infestation, had settled on tour-
ism. They sent a photographer around to take pictures and hired
a consulting company to brand the town as the "Dragon Garden
on the Bay." Tour buses came to town twice a day from Boston
and Portland, and there was talk of partnering with the cruise
ship companies too.

I didn't like the idea. I was afraid that the tourists would scare
the dragons. Most had settled around abandoned lots and fore-
closed houses, living off insects and vegetation. Some of them
had even learned to leave their dung in one place, where the
sanitation company could cart it off in weekly rounds. I thought
the dragons and the people of the town were figuring out how
to live together in peace. I didn't want that process interrupted.

But there was an even bigger threat than tourists.

An anti-dragon group had been organizing: parents worried
about dragons rotting their children's minds, bored people looking for something to do, property owners fed up with the mess.
They called themselves the Knights of Mannaport and shared
ideas online about how to drive the dragons out.

I lurked in their forum under a made-up name. When they
decided to use the Fourth of July celebration for "Operation St.
George," I made plans of my own.

Near sunset, while many families were heading to Skerry
Field for the fireworks display, the Knights got into pickup
trucks and minivans. From all around town, they drove toward

the abandoned lot on Hancock, home to one of the largest flocks of little dragons.

I got there just before sundown. The yard was covered in thick, lush grass as tall as my chest, while the house, half of its roof gone and gaping holes in three walls, sat quietly in solitary decay. Dozens of little dragons were already roosting in the ruin or the yard. While a few flapped their wings and opened their eyes, cooing at my approach, most remained asleep.

I ducked down among the grass, out of sight. The soil gave off an acrid odor, not unlike feral cat colonies. As the dusk faded, more bird-sized dragons returned from foraging. They found places to perch, tucked their heads under a wing or a clump of grass, and went to sleep.

I could hear the snores of those nearest me, a faint, even wheezing. A cool breeze whisked away the sweat on my forehead and brought some relief from the stifling summer air. I shivered involuntarily, suddenly remembering this was the house where a man had been shot a couple years ago over an opioid deal gone wrong. The sirens and the flashing blue lights rushing down the street had woken me up.

Pain gripped my heart like a fist. I couldn't breathe. I fought hard to keep the darkness that threatened to awaken in my mind, to burst through the locks on the mental vault I had sealed it in, the piles of psychic rubble I had piled on.

I couldn't think about her couldn't just couldn't couldn't.

Bright beams pierced the darkening evening, sweeping through the air above me like luminous lances. The humming of electric engines subsided; the lights went out. Slamming doors and footsteps. Urgent whispers. The Knights had arrived.

I heard the sounds of heavy objects being unloaded. The vehicles were filled with extra power cells, spools of wire, and home-defense electric prods. Their plan was to cover the lot with a net of charged wires and then wake the sleeping dragons with a few well-placed firecrackers.

The more of those nasty creatures electrocuted, the better, someone had posted in their forum.

Poetic justice to use dragon-generated electricity to kill dragons!

My cousin is a lawyer. He thinks that if we do it this way, we can argue to the judge that the dragons flew into the wires on their own, so it wouldn't count as assault.

I got up from among the thick grass.

"You can't do this," I said. I was so scared and riled up that my body shook as much as my voice.

The startled Knights, lit only by the glow of a distant streetlight, stopped. After some confusion, a man stepped out from the crowd. I recognized him from his picture on the forum: Alexander.

"What are you doing?" he asked.

"Stopping a mistake," I said.

"The dragons don't belong here," he said. He stepped closer so that I could see the grief and rage on his face. "They hurt people. You don't know."

"Not these," I said, struggling to keep my voice calm.

"Yes, these." I heard the pain in his voice, the helplessness of loss and the inability to explain.

I felt equally helpless. I didn't know how to describe seeing the dragons forage over a park in late afternoon. I didn't know how to explain why I felt like smiling *and* crying when I heard the dragons chirp and cheep at night.

So I picked up the whistle hanging around my neck and blew into it, as hard as I could. It was so loud I thought I was never going to stop hearing it, like the sirens in my nightmares.

Around me, the yard and ruined house disintegrated into a maelstrom. The little dragons, awakened by my shrill whistling, bolted into the air. Wings darkened the stars; claws trampled the grass. A cacophonous chorus joined my whistle, and the pungent smell of wild urine saturated the air.

Moments later, the agitation subsided, almost as quickly as it had begun. The dragons were gone. I took the whistle out of my mouth, sucking in a deep breath. Alexander stood rooted to the spot, looking stunned.

A rustling at my feet. We both looked down.

A creature was struggling among the grass. I knelt down: it was about the size of a puppy, though slenderer and a little longer. A calf-shaped head; a pair of tiny, curved horns; whiskers like those on a Maine lobster; a collar of bright, colorful feathers; silver scales over the back; leathery belly; four clawed, birdlike feet; a long, serpentine tail—it was a mutt, descended from the many dragon species that had followed the people here and adapted to life on this continent.

The batlike wings, however, were torn. It couldn't take off. Gently, I picked it up and cradled it in my arms like a kitten. It trembled against my skin, a little whirling dynamo.

It opened its eyes hesitantly. They were a bright, shining blue. I shuddered, almost dropping the dragon. That was the last color I wanted to see.

"Drop it!" Alexander shouted. I looked up and saw that he was holding an electric prod, the kind that would kill a home invader in one wallop.

I turned to shield the dragon from him with my back. "Shhhh. It's okay. I won't abandon you."

The little dragon keened like an injured rabbit, a sharp, almost unbearably painful scream. It trembled even harder against my arms. I tried to stroke its back the way I'd pet a cat, the way my mother used to stroke my hair when I was little to get me to sleep. The scales felt warm and soft to the touch, not at all what I expected.

"Listen to that!" said Alexander. He sounded horrified as he raised the prod. "It's going to breathe fire! You've got to drop it now or you'll die!"

"No! It's screaming only because you are frightening it." No one had ever seen the little dragons in our town breathe fire—I was sure they couldn't. I tried to cover the dragon's eyes with one hand, hoping to keep it from seeing the approaching Alexander, hoping I wouldn't lose my courage from that piercing, bright blue.

He stumbled another few steps, looming over me. "You killed Joey! You killed Joey!"

I looked up into his eyes. They were wild, unreasoning, unseeing. Was that how I looked when I woke up from my nightmares and Grandmother had to hold me down?

"No! It didn't do anything!" I shouted with all my strength. "You got the wrong dragon! The wrong—"

Alexander raised his prod. I had no doubt he was ready to plunge it into me if that was what it took to slay the dragon in his mind.

The dragon lurched in my arms. I strained to hold it down. But the diminutive dragon was too strong for me. With a quick flick of its head, it threw off my covering hand. I felt a sudden wave of heat as I instinctively leaned back. Time seemed to slow down. My vision grew hazy, indistinct.

I saw the dragon's jaws open. I saw the prod's tip suspended, barely inches away. I saw the dragon lock eyes with Alexander. Could I interpret what I saw in those bright blue, inhuman orbs?

Then it looked away, as though the threat of imminent death was of no more consequence than the trail of a distant shooting star. The little dragon, moving as ponderously as though it were the Three Gorges, the largest dragon ever verified, gazed up at the stars, and a blinding plume of light and fire shot up and out of the wide-open maw.

It was like watching a flowing river of liquid gold and silver, a kaleidoscope of migrating butterflies, a galaxy of dew-dappled gossamer and pearl-studded tulle unfurling across the heavens. At the apex of the superheated plasmic stream, the cooling flames ramified, arced, took on new colors: September indigo, blood-of-martyrs red, marigold yellow, dragon-whisper blue . . .

My mouth was agape, an unconscious imitation of the dragon's jaw. It was the greatest fireworks display I had ever seen.

I was again in the aisles of the art supply store, a girl of six. My mother and I were racing around, laughing, throwing tubes of paint and watercolors into the shopping cart. We didn't like the names the manufacturer gave to the colors, so we came up with our own. We were going to spend all day doing nothing but painting and being together. We were going to paint the dragon that Grandmother had seen.

"You'll always be with me, right, Mama?"

"Of course. You'll never be rid of me, baby drake."

Tears drowned my eyes; everything was a blur. I had not dared to recall this memory in years.

Next to me, Alexander's upturned face was bathed in the shifting liquid light of the magnificent display overhead. The prod lay on the ground. "I never imagined . . ." I heard him mutter. "So this was what you saw . . ."

The dragon keened again and let forth a new eruption of sparkling, fiery wonder.

Heat passed over my face—or rather, *into* my face. I don't know how to describe it, really, except it felt like a hand stroking my mind, soothing away something painful, something obstructing, like a rock just beneath the surface of the water. For a moment, something dark and hard and full of jagged edges, an underwater shoal, threatened to thrust through the placid surface, but then, as the invisible hand caressed my mind again, the shoal dissipated and dissolved, carried away by the stream of light and heat.

[*We are at the abandoned lot. Zoe holds up a hand to indicate that the camera crew shouldn't disturb the roosting dragons camouflaged in the grass. She pulls out her phone to show us a picture.*]

I've been trying to paint what I saw. Not very successfully.

Follow my finger. Just by that broken slat in the fence, do you see it? Yes, that green hump in the grass. That's Yegong. I don't think it's going to come out, though, not with so many people around.

I named it after a man in an old fairy tale my mother told me. It's a bit of a joke, see, because in the story, the man *thought* he liked dragons and painted dragons all the time, but then, when a real dragon showed up one day, he was terrified. Do you see— never mind.

It's recovering well. A dragon doctor from Wellesley—well, that's what I call her; her real title is Endowment Maintenance Specialist or something like that—told me that the tears in Yegong's wings will heal on their own in another week. I bring it raspberries; Yegong really likes them.

The Knights still post in their forum, complaining about the dragons. But I haven't seen Alexander post there.

November

LEE

I've been talking to Zoe.

After the video of the dragon fireworks went viral, there was an influx of tourists like you wouldn't believe. Took a while to sort out the security and cost us a lot of overtime pay to the police so no one got hurt. All the publicity also brought in a few companies interested in hiring Zoe as a dragon-whisperer. She turned them down flat.

I was just about to work out how best to take advantage

of Mannaport's newfound fame when little dragons began to show up at a few other towns in the Commonwealth: Brockton, Plymouth, Lowell, Falmouth . . . No one knows how many more dragon-rushes there will be.

Overnight, we lost our competitive advantage.

But that got me thinking. We still have Zoe.

I'm thinking of hiring her to run a training program to teach people how to behave around dragons, maybe do some demonstrations for the other towns—I'll get Beacon Hill to pay for the program. She's at least open to the idea, but she told me she won't make the dragons do fireworks again. "Too much of a good thing is bad," she says.

She told me that the little dragons, if treated right, can make people happy. I called around and found some specialists who want to talk to her about the feasibility of "dragon-therapy" for depression, both kids and adults. She seems really excited about that.

It's not the goldmine that I was hoping, but we'll get something for Mannaport yet, just you wait.

INGRID

[A Thanksgiving meal is being prepared: siblings and spouses squeezed into a too-small kitchen; dishes clattering against serving spoons; in-laws fussing over grandchildren; cousins arguing and laughing; the TV blaring.

Alexander is also in the house, trying to help and looking awkward. But the others are making an effort to make him feel welcome.

Zoe is showing a group a video on her phone. Everyone is rapt. She's smiling.]

Zoe is a big star now. I hear videos of her and Yegong get millions of views. She never makes it breathe fire, though—says it's too dangerous.

Alexander helps her out as the cameraperson. He was telling

me earlier that Zoe, him, and Hariveen are planning to partner up to raise awareness about the plight of dragon-whisperers and raise money for their care.

I'm just glad to see her happy. Haven't seen her smiling like that since the night she found Julie.

HARIVEEN

Here's a question for you: How do you think dragons breathe fire?

Think back to your high school physics and biology classes. You probably learned that dragon power plants are essentially heat engines, which convert the thermal energy from dragon breath into mechanical energy to perform useful work. You probably also learned that dragons, like other living organisms, generate energy by breaking down food via chemical processes. But your teacher probably glossed over the math, which would have shown you that the berries, insects, hunks of beef, and bushels of corn eaten by a dragon could never be enough to generate the heat output of dragon fire.

If your teacher was particularly conscientious, they probably also mentioned Maxwell's demon.

In 1867, James Clerk Maxwell, in the course of formulating the laws of thermodynamics, found the puzzle of dragon breath nigh insoluble. The demon was a thought experiment he used to explain how dragons could seemingly generate energy out of nothing, defying the laws of physics.

Imagine a chamber filled with gas at a certain temperature, divided into two halves thermally insulated from each other. In the middle of this barrier is a tiny, frictionless door, operated by a demon of great cunning. Since temperature is a measure of the *average* kinetic energy of gas molecules bouncing around inside the chamber, it follows that some of the molecules are moving much faster than the average, while others much slower. The demon observes the motion of the molecules and opportunistically opens the door so that fast moving molecules from the right side would be allowed into the left side, while slow moving molecules from the left side would be allowed into the right side.

Over time, this would shift the average kinetic energy inside the two separate halves such that the right side would cool down while the left side would heat up. You could then use this temperature differential to drive a traditional heat engine until the temperatures in the two halves equalized, at which point the demon could start the process again.

Maxwell's demon turns information about the motion of the molecules of gas into "free" energy without increasing entropy, creating a sort of perpetual motion machine out of the two dragons chasing each other in the yin-yang symbol, a perfect heat engine that defies the second law of thermodynamics.

For more than a century, theoreticians and experimenters labored to find a satisfying way to reconcile the demon with the laws of thermodynamics, and they finally reached the conclusion that the key is the information possessed by the demon. The system of demon plus container must increase in entropy because the demon must erase old information in order to record new information.

If dragons are indeed Maxwell's demons, converting information into heat, then it follows that to do what they do, they must erase information.

No one ever said that the information erased must be inside the dragon's own brain.

Have you ever wondered why so many dragon-whisperers retire young with dementia, their brains like Swiss cheese? Or why dragons are always attracted to places with lots of people, books, inventions, novelty? Or why every major advance in our use of dragon energy has been accompanied by a revolution, a massive forgetting of traditions, of folklore, of history?

I think dragon breath is powered by mass amnesia, by the erasure of memories, both painful and joyous. In our grand dragon-powered metropolises, books decay, collective memory rots. Dragon-whisperers, closest to the dragons, also bear the brunt of such damage.

I know, I know. You want to hand me a tinfoil hat now and book me on Teddy Patriot's show. But try, just try for a moment: Isn't there just the slightest chance that I'm right?

Ever since we became addicted to dragon energy, wars have become less frequent, and former enemies quicker to let bygones be bygones. Forgetfulness isn't the same as forgiveness, but it helps.

As our civilization has grown ever more complex, have we created new forms of pain, and the need to forget grown more convoluted? Maybe that is why the little dragons have appeared, a kind of adaptive radiation in response to the lush, entropic jungle of our multiplying desires.

If dragons destroy, they do so in the name of creation.

Friends tell me that I've mellowed out and grown more phil-osophical in the past year. I don't know about that . . . but the little dragons sure are cute.

INGRID

My daughter was a good mother, or she tried to be. But she was always kind of dreamy, had trouble making and sticking to plans. She tried to make it in California after high school as an artist, but she didn't have much luck—she told me that the crit-ics who supposedly had the ear of the dragons never seemed to respond to anything she did—and had to come back. After she and Ron had Zoe, things got harder. But anyone could see how much they loved one another.

[The camera moves into the upstairs hallway, around a corner, into a part of the house rarely seen by outsiders. Framed pictures of dragons line the walls: watercolors, oils, pastels, markers, pencils. Some show a

mature style and are signed by Julie. Others, more childish, are signed by Zoe. There's one showing a mother and a little girl as stick figures, riding a powerful winged dragon together. The dragon has bright blue eyes, like the spinning light on top of police vehicles.]

They ran into money problems, and Ron and Julie separated. Every time I went over, the house was a mess. Julie started drinking to make herself feel better. When that stopped working, she turned to something stronger to stop the pain.

Zoe, just seven then, woke up that night, probably from the sirens of police cars responding to the killing of the man down the road—he was Julie's dealer. Zoe went into her mother's room and found Julie not moving, her body rigid.

She called me, and all she could get out through the sobs was "Mama's lips are blue! They're blue!" I called 911. By the time they got to the house, it was too late.

When Zoe lived with me, she'd have nightmares all the time, but she wouldn't talk about them. For a while, she drew pictures of dragons, the way her mother and she used to do, but she would never use the color blue. I tried to get her help, but she wouldn't go to the therapists. "They'll try to make me forget," she used to say. "I don't want to."

There are many forms of addiction, and one of the most insidious is a helpless devotion to the pain of memory, a self-imposed punishment to be chained to a jagged shoal made up of one moment in time. Her memory of Julie on that night—grief, betrayal, rage, guilt—dominated her life. It was a scar that consumed everything, one that she couldn't help but pick at again and again.

Oblivion isn't solace, but sometimes healing does require erasure, as does forgiveness.

ZOE

Alexander thinks that the dragons came to Mannaport first because of our pain.

I don't think that's true. Like I said, there's nothing special about Mannaport. We have an average amount of heartache and grief, of abandonment and betrayal, no more and no less.

But the little dragons *are* special. They can't be harnessed to do useful work, at least not the way the adults want. But just because a scalpel can't be used to chop down a tree doesn't mean that it can't help.

I made this bowl of cranberry sauce for Yegong, and I'll bring it over later. See how I put blueberries in it? Not quite the same shade as its eyes, but it's the best I can do. Blue is such a pretty color.

Author's note: For more on Maxwell's demon and the thermodynamic properties of information erasure, see Charles H. Bennett, "The Thermodynamics of Computation—A Review," *International Journal of Theoretical Physics* **21, no. 12 (1982): 905–40.**

NIDHOG

Jo Walton

First of all and last of all
And gnawing at the root
Beside the wall, beneath the hall,
In darkness absolute.

Far below feasts and fighting
Far from the folk of Earth
Relentless in her biting
At courage, love, and mirth.

The deepest dragon coils and curls
Nose twitches, ears flick
Through all the noise of all the worlds
She hears the mistle trick.

Light and the gods are far away
Bound fire will never bend
So broken promises today
Mean worlds and trees will end.

She learned the lore so long ago,
She silently keeps score,
The dragon in the shadow,
The worm at the world-tree's core.

For when the new world comes to be
She'll spread her wings and rise
And fill the world with dragons free
It is her promised prize.

Then dragon wings will crease the sky
Humans and gods will learn
That dragons speak, and dragons fly,
And dragonfire will burn!

Deep down impatient Nidhog toils
Until the tree shall fall
Around the root she curls and coils,
First of all, last of all.

WHERE THE RIVER TURNS TO CONCRETE

Brooke Bolander

Brooke Bolander's (brookebolander.com) fiction has won the Nebula and Locus awards and been shortlisted for the Hugo, Shirley Jackson, Theodore Sturgeon, World Fantasy, and British Fantasy awards. Her work has been featured on Tor.com and in *Lightspeed*, *Strange Horizons*, *Uncanny*, and the *New York Times*, among other venues. She currently resides in New York City.

As one of Raymond Sturges's hired goons finally forced his muscle car off the road—as the Dodge Super Bee jounced through the weeds, rolled over the high bank, and did a final handstand on its high beams—the rest of Joe's memory came roaring back, and he knew himself.

The smell of sage and sewage. Shopping trolleys, dirty diapers. Styrofoam takeout clamshells bobbing along in the current, jaws flapping. The gleaming eyes of a roadrunner, herky-jerking down to the water's edge for a drink.

Feathers like a gasoline spill. Ripple and rush from snout to tail tip. Oily fur. A girl's kind eyes as she reached out, brave as anything, and—

Joe's big hands clenched the steering wheel so hard there was an audible *snap*. The Super Bee landed nose first. The desert night splintered into shards.

The Super Bee had been a gift from Raymond, as if fishing Joe out of the gutter and giving him a name and a job hadn't been gift enough. Most big important fellas, they came across a confused guy huddled in the farthest corner of a parking garage, naked as the day God made him, they didn't stop until a valet, a bodyguard, and the shining black shell of a limo door were between them and the Public Disturbance. Raymond was not most big important fellas. The way he told the story, he'd done a mid-stride double take, said something along the lines of "Holy Jesus God, you're a big son of a bitch," and hustled a couple of his boys over to get the big son of a bitch in question covered up before anybody else more inclined to call a security guard happened along. Raymond Sturges knew an opportunity when he saw one. Any man planning on building a condo across a damn riverbed, mostly dry or otherwise, had to have some kinda damn vision. Either that or a screw loose.

Joe couldn't remember any of it. Everything before the moment he woke up in Raymond's clubhouse squeezed into a too-small dressing gown was the darkness beyond headlights on a two-lane mountain road. No clothes, no ID, no memory. No name. The rest of it hadn't bothered him too much, but the lack of a name had felt important in a way he couldn't quite pinpoint. He needed that. Not so much for other people, but as a way of grounding himself.

"Too scary-looking to be a Chaz or a Don," Raymond had pronounced loftily. "Not blond enough to be a Brad, too pretty for a Vince. You got honest eyes, though. Weird color, but honest. Good square jaw. We'll just call you . . . Joe. Had a dog named that when I was a kid. Very all-American. You got any problem with that?"

No, he didn't have a problem with that. Something way back in his skull had rattled the blinds and hissed, but he ignored it and he was Joe. Easy as that. Big Joe Gabriel, one of Raymond Sturges's boys. The one quietly summoning you to court above the nightclub downtown. The one stepping out of the darkness to Raymond's left with a ball-peen hammer clutched in one long-fingered hand, mitts so big they made the tool look like a toy, a joke. Until it wasn't a joke.

Nothing personal, his eyes always said. They were the color of a starling's feathers, iridescent. One of Raymond's ex-wives had sported a ring with a black opal inset as big as a quarter. That's what Joe's eyes looked like, he said, that gaudy piece-of-shit ring of Tina's. *Girls must go gaga when you flash those at 'em.*

Joe didn't get a lot of opportunity to flash his eyes at anybody. Mostly he just did as Raymond told him to do. He loomed. He punched. He broke what needed breaking, picked up whatever needed picking up, and dumped whatever required sawing apart and dumping in the farthest dusty canyons of Out East. Raymond got him set up in a little fleabag apartment property he owned called the Riverview and only took 10 percent out of Joe's wages each month to make up the rent. The cheap doorknobs and drawer handles came off in Joe's hands so regularly he learned other uses for a toolbox besides the ones his boss occasionally set him.

He wanted for nothing. Joe owned six tailored suits, a couple of the kind of white T-shirts that came in packs, two stained pairs of blue jeans, and a pair of swim trunks he had been told were "alarmingly tight" by a lifeguard at the city pool where he swam laps. As the days melted into weeks and months, and the years bred like jackrabbits, and his stature in Raymond's organization grew, he was offered a lot of other things—money, houses, new cars—but he couldn't see or feel the appeal in any of it. He politely declined and kept right on flowing down the same path he had worn for himself in the world.

Until the day Raymond took him by the wrist and walked him outside to meet the Super Bee. He was told he couldn't keep driving that piece-of-shit Buick to and from work. *Stay at the Riverview if you gotta, wear the same six suits until the crotches wear outta all of them, but you are taking this car. Don't insult me by arguing. Don't even start.*

Turned out the warning wasn't needed. It was love at first sight.

She was the deep blue of the sky right after sunset and just before moonrise, a sapphire cut like a predatory animal. Like a river with jagged rocks just below the surface. You'd most likely die if you were stupid enough to jump in, but it might be worth it to get your skin wet. It reminded Joe of something. Something like—

a homesick ache, gone, gone and never the same

—an emotion he had forgotten. *Want.* Maybe it was the shape of the old muscle car. Maybe it was how no modern build held itself like that, ready to tear the road to pieces. He had opened the door with something approaching reverence and crammed himself inside while Raymond chuckled, just like he always did when Joe had to angle his limbs into a driver's seat. He turned the key and the engine roared snowmelt and flash flood. It was like someone saying his name. His *real* name. The thought swirled by and was gone, inexplicable, a dead tree headed for the ocean.

He became a little more himself the moment that ignition rumbled to life. That was the end of it, really. The end of Raymond Sturges, Big Joe Gabriel, and, unfortunately, the end of the cobalt-blue 1970 Dodge Super Bee.

There was a pool in the Riverview's central courtyard, surrounded by a rusting wrought-iron fence and a handful of patio tables with listing umbrellas. As apartment pools went, it was a decent size, long enough that you could get a good workout doing laps from one end to the other. Raymond hadn't seen fit to budget for a pool guy when he acquired the place, though, and so the water was a murky take-your-chances green. In the spring it collected jacaranda blossoms. In the summer it got a nice furring of dead leaves and ash from distant fires. Every other season it was mostly dust, pollen, and the occasional drowned possum. In another kind of complex, it might've been a thing to complain to the landlords about. The Riverview was not that sort of complex. Folks came and went as car engines, low-wage jobs, and arrest warrants allowed. Neighbors did not exchange gossip or meatloaf recipes or anything other than sidelong glances.

Not long after he got the Super Bee, a strange interest in the state of the pool awoke in Joe. Swimming had always been the one thing he allowed himself outside of his job. Something about being in the water felt right in a way he could never recapture on land. He wasn't a big son of a bitch underwater. The water was just part of him, like a bird's feathers or a horse's legs. The other swimmers gaped at how fast he was. Lifeguards looked up from their magazines or mobile phones in wonder. Kids scampered up to ask him how he did it. It seemed like the funniest question in the world to Joe, like being asked to give lessons on how to breathe or grow hair. He always smiled and shrugged apologetically. "Dunno," he'd say softly, if pressed. "I just . . . do it."

Joe didn't talk much. He had very little to say with words that couldn't be said with actions. Other people talked too damn much as it was.

He had noticed the Riverview's pool before but hadn't given it much thought. Then one fine spring morning he was walking to the parking lot and he *smelled* it. Algae and frogs' eggs. Waterlogged purple petals. It smelled familiar in a way that made something in his chest twinge painfully. He stopped dead in his tracks and stared at the dirty pool like he'd never really seen it before. Maybe he hadn't.

All day he thought about that moment, through the usual daily grind of fingers snapped and kneecaps crushed into eggshell fragments through surgical use of a baseball bat. When he got off work, he went to the local library branch, signed up for a card (the biddy behind the front desk looked him up and down dubiously), and checked out every book he could find on pool maintenance. They stayed in a neat stack beside the stained, bare mattress where he slept until he'd pretty well memorized all the ins and outs. Then he returned them, much to the palpable relief of Front Desk Biddy.

Some fellas kept gardens, or goldfish. Raymond had a few of those gnarled little mini trees you could sculpt into weird shapes. Joe had his job, his car, and the pH balance of the Riverview's pool. It was more than he had started out with, naked and blank-eyed in a parking garage.

Under Joe's care, the water grew glossy. He bought nets, chemicals, skimmers, and suckers, all the other filthy-sounding devices one needed. Pretty soon it started looking like something you'd see in a brochure for the kind of apartments where the rent bought you a gym and a doorman. Summer rumbled to a halt at the curb. Joe didn't bother renewing his membership to the city rec pool. Swimming outside felt better, especially early in the morning and late at night. Grackles squabbled over predawn turf disputes in the oaks. Warm yellow light shone down on the pool's surface through smeary rectangles of sliding glass. He could always feel eyes watching him as he rippled through the water, but nobody ever came down to chat.

Nobody adult-sized, anyways. Eventually he gained a single admirer: a black-eyed, black-haired kid, couldn't have been older than six or seven. The way he crept closer every day reminded Joe of the stray cats who hung around the complex. First he watched from the door of his family's apartment. Then, when his babysitter presumably wasn't looking, he sneaked down to the wrought-iron fence, where he played with Matchbox cars and pretended to do anything other than pay attention to the big man in the water. By the end of the week, the toys and the ruse were both abandoned somewhere in the bleached-grass jungle of the courtyard. The boy sat with his face smashed between the fence's bars, watching the oily ripple and flow of Joe. He never said anything or tried to get any closer. Watching was apparently enough. Occasionally whoever was looking after him that day would notice he was gone and call him from the balcony, and he'd run on back upstairs, brown cheeks smeared with lines of rust.

Kids weren't supposed to get in the pool without adult supervision, but the kid had never even come inside the fence, so Joe didn't bother scolding or ratting him out. He also didn't bother latching the gate behind himself as securely as he maybe should've. Those two facts didn't connect at first when he heard the mother screaming. That came a few seconds later, stepping out of his apartment to see her crouched by the poolside, fully clothed and dripping wet, boy laid out unconscious in front of her. Puddles of water from the both of them stained the concrete in slowly widening circles. The pool gate creaked lazily in the breeze.

He covered the distance between his front door and the pool in record time, the faces of other tenants peering cautiously from their windows blurring as he passed. The woman didn't look up at the sound of Joe's footsteps. She just squatted next to her boy, wailing like a coyote. Water trickled from his nostrils. His eyes were closed. Joe pushed the mother out of the way as gently as he could—she barely seemed to notice, eyes locked on her child—and took the boy in his arms. He didn't know what to do. The kid looked tiny and breakable cradled in Joe's big mitts. He also looked dead. His chest was still, black hair slicked to his head like motor oil.

Vaguely Joe remembered a thing called CPR, where you pumped at the drowning victim's chest and breathed into their mouth and hoped like hell they'd wake up. He didn't know how to do it properly, had never taken a lesson in his life far as he could remember, and would've worried immensely about smashing the boy's ribs to matchsticks even if he had known the trick. He decided to start with the mouth-breathing part, crouching down to place his lips against the child's blue ones. He huffed into the eggshell delicacy of the boy. Nothing. Again, as the seconds ticked downhill like pebbles splashing into a stream. No change.

Joe placed his hands on the kid's thin chest. He glanced at the mother, still rocking and crying and praying. A thought traveled down his arms and into his damp fingers as he leaned down to give the breathing method one last shot, garbled and nonsensical: *God dammit, come outta there. You got no business being trapped in some little kid. The hell's wrong with you?*

(*—water is free, he is free, he goes where he pleases flashing beneath the desert sun, minnows and crayfish dart in the bubbling green spaces between his scales and all is rush and slither and it's a hundred years before the first full diaper, the first beer can bobbing, the first net of concrete laid to catch and control—*)

There was a noise beneath his hands and lips like a drain clog letting go. Joe felt something pull, then *pop!,* then his own throat and lungs were full of water, so eager to get out of the kid and into him it spilled from his mouth as he pulled away. It tasted like chlorine. Weirdly, it didn't make him choke, despite the fact that there seemed to be a river's worth of it. All the world's coughing was saved for the boy, suddenly sputtering and gasping to life beneath him like a flooded engine coming back from the dead.

And Joe got a little more human, with that young mother sobbing her thanks at his elbow. He learned their names and evicted a tributary straight from Lucian's lungs to save the kid's life. Even with all the things that happened, he never regretted that part a damn bit.

She found him a few days later. Petite as her son, tiny, really, but blond where he was dark. Joe opened his front door and there she stood, a store-bought chocolate cake in her hands, eyes turned way up to find his a couple feet overhead. "Brought you something," she said. "For saving his life. I know it's not much, it's really kinda silly, but—"

Joe had always done his best to have no truck with the neighbors. For years he had succeeded admirably at this, not that it was hard in a place like the Riverview, working the hours he did. All it took to bring that record crashing to earth, it turned out, was a near-drowning, a pretty face, and free food. He found himself inviting her inside, pulling chipped plates the previous tenants had left from the cabinets and setting them on the tiny dining table he never used. When he tried to sit down at it across from his guest, his knees lifted the entire thing a half inch off the ground. Plastic takeout forks and chocolate cake skated dangerously across cheap maple, saved at the last minute by his neighbor's quick hands.

Joe sat at an angle after that.

Her name was Rita. She worked as a maid at the Eaz-E-Rest out by the interstate. A teenage girl from next door was supposed to watch Luce while she picked up shifts, but sometimes the girl got distracted—by the phone, by the television, by her own reflection in the mirror—and he wandered off. He was a good kid, smart kid, knew better than to talk to strangers or go playing in traffic, but he was drawn to water like some kind of duck or something, couldn't keep away from it. If there hadn't been a high fence between the complex and the concrete bed of the river out back, she knew she would've found him ankle-deep in that nasty run-off ages ago, chasing minnows or frogs or whatever else managed to survive in the stream. Not that she hadn't been the same way at his age. She had ruined a lot of shoes and gotten chewed out a lot for playing in that same river, back when twenty-three seemed like the kind of birthday they handed you black balloons decorated with cartoon vultures for.

Joe listened and ate his cake, happy to let her talk. It meant he didn't have to, and that was his favorite kind of conversation. Too often Raymond wanted him to respond, or laugh, or most horrible of all, to share his own thoughts on a matter. This was fine. Occasionally he smiled, or nodded. She seemed satisfied with that, even when they made eye contact and she lost track of her words for a moment or two.

Rita didn't think the boy would go near the pool even if the gate did somehow get left open again (Joe reassured her that wouldn't happen, feeling plenty guilty), but she worried. She worried about a lot of things: rent, her job, health insurance, making sure Luce ate his veggies, the size of the water bugs in their apartment, you name it. She stared at the crumbs on her plate and tugged at a strand of her short hair as she reeled off this list. If he had known how to swim, none of this would've happened in the first place. She should've taught him, but the pool had been so nasty before and there was no time, there was never any time—

Somebody said, "I can give him lessons if you want." For a second Joe wondered if he had left the police scanner in his bedroom on. By the time he realized it was him talking, his tongue was tripping over "free of charge" and "nah, no trouble," and Rita was staring at him from across the table like he was Jesus, Buddha, and Bob Barker all rolled into one. No backing out after that. Yes, he meant it. He wasn't quite sure *how* you taught someone else to swim, but the look in her eyes meant he'd give it a damn good try twice a week.

They ate the rest of their cake in shy silence, not looking at each other, like a couple of kids.

He thought of her smile as the Super Bee exploded around him like a cactus blossom unfurling. Her smile, and the way she had glanced at him over Lucian's head from the passenger seat on their sunny weekend drives, eyes full of some emotion he didn't dare interrogate. He thought maybe he had looked back at her the same way. God, he hoped he had. For those eyes and that expression he would've submerged entire cities and picked his teeth on their drowned memories.

There was no fireball. The car just came apart and fell back from the liquid length of him like a shed skin as he tore through the vinyl roof. Good-bye, Super Bee. Good-bye, human form. The moon was bright and cold. He flowed through the air in the direction of the city, toward Raymond's clubhouse. His mane was the deep green of water weeds, his teeth jagged as flint. Late-night commuters glancing up at the sky thought he was the contrail from a commercial airliner, silver-white in the moonlight.

Teaching someone to swim, turned out, wasn't as hard as it sounded. It didn't hurt that Lucian was a fast learner. First the doggie paddle, then the scissor kick. On to a simple crawl, the boy's tiny limbs knifing determinedly through the water like starlings diving for takeout wrappers.

Joe made him keep the pool floaties on way past the point where he probably needed them. Just in case.

Rita started inviting Joe over for dinner after lessons. Unless he had business, he usually accepted. He liked how their apartment was a warm mirror of his own, full where his was empty. He liked the toys scattered on the floor and how the TV chattered mindlessly in the background even when nobody was watching it. He liked helping Rita in the kitchen, as big and useless and in the way as he was in that tiny space. She never seemed to mind. Chop this, peel that. They would stand shoulder to shoulder (mostly it was his shoulders), working together in a comfortable silence that smelled of browning meat, frying onions, cumin, and garlic. Occasionally he caught whiffs of Rita herself: Cheap fruity shampoo, powdery deodorant, laundromat detergent. Cleaning solution from her job, soaked permanently into her hands. Lucian was bubblegum toothpaste, die-cast metal, and chlorine.

When dinner was finished and Luce finally put to bed, they would crack a couple of beers and talk. Small stuff at first, nothing heavy. Rita never pushed Joe into saying more than he felt like saying, which he appreciated immensely. Not having someone breathing down his neck to keep the conversation going actually made him want to talk *more*, which was a new and not-unpleasant discovery.

He told her what he could. His job? Private security. Yeah, like a security guard, just like that. It paid the rent. Where had he grown up? Here and there, but mostly here. That wasn't a lie, not as Joe figured it. You grew up every day for most of your life, learning new things. At this stage it was easier than *I'm an amnesiac and don't remember a thing before my boss found my naked ass squatting in a parking garage.* But enough about him, his life was boring, what about Rita?

Rita had also come up in the city. Her dad had died in a construction accident when she wasn't much bigger than Luce, leaving her mother to raise three kids on her own. Luckily, Rita's mother hadn't been just any ordinary lady, and neither had Rita's grandmama. They had known things nobody else knew and saw things nobody else saw and heard things nobody else heard. The neighborhood had relied on them for charms and cures, blessings and curses. It had put food on the table, if barely.

"Here," Rita said after the last longneck of the first six-pack was snuffed. "Gimme your hand."

"My hand?" Joe said rather stupidly.

"Yeah, your hand. I wanna read your palm. My grandmama taught me how." She reached out and grabbed one of his big mitts with both of her own. His entire body stiffened at her touch. "See," she went on, flipping it palm-side up, "I can just look at the lines on them and tell your entire life . . ."

Her voice trailed off like someone had smashed the volume button. Her finger froze in mid-trace. Confusion knitted her brows. Her eyes climbed up and down the creases of his palm once, twice, three times, back and forth, trying to make sense of whatever she was reading. Words with no wind behind them formed rapid fire on her lips and died there.

"Rita?" He was almost afraid to disturb her. "You all right?"

She didn't let go of his hand, but she did look back up at him after several more molasses-slow seconds. Her eyes were reddish-brown with gold flecks, like river mud at sunset.

"*Where* did you grow up again?" she said.

Raymond knew Joe had arrived when all the taps and all the pipes and all the sprinklers in the clubhouse burst their seams the way old men's belts whip loose after a big meal. Joe was the flood and the wrack, the water damage unstoppable, pooling around expensive shoes before coiling up in a shining spiral that blew the roof clean off. A fire, the authorities would say later on, a fire that set off the sprinklers before a leaking gas main did the rest. It didn't make a lick of damn sense to anybody who thought about it for longer than a second, but most people were too happy about the world being rid of Raymond Sturges to question piddling details.

"I thought you were my friend," the elemental that had briefly been Joe Gabriel gurgled. His true form was wolf-muzzled, his neck as long and curved as a cormorant's. You could hear the rumble of the words before he spoke, like water working through a hose kink. "You said you helped me."

"What, you calling me a liar?" Ankle-deep in water, staring up at an enraged river spirit, and still Raymond was unflappable. A man got good enough at as many things as Raymond—murder, racketeering, the occult arts—and it probably took a hell of a lot to flap him. "I *was* helping you, dumbshit! The sooner what's left of you dries up and gets filled in, the better. Here you had a good job and a nice little life and even a pretty little girlfriend, am I right? As a spirit you got about ten years tops before there ain't nothing left of you but a hole in the ground."

"Leave the woman and boy alone," Joe said. The rest—he couldn't say it didn't matter, because the betrayal felt like a fishhook biting into his neck, but right at that moment it was of little concern. "Please, Raymond. Give me your word. Give me that much. Don't send any more people after them."

Raymond looked at him steadily. His face and his eyes were flat, soaked suit bloating around his body. Water dripped off the spiky overhangs of his eyebrows.

"You know I can't do that, Joe," he said. "You know that ain't how this works. She saw too much. I'm sorry, kid."

And he meant it. You could see it in his eyes. Joe was sorry, too, as the mournful eel's length of him snapped forward and down.

"You wanna hear something crazy?" Rita was staring out to where the river dragged itself sluggishly across the concrete.

"Sure," Joe said. He couldn't join her in perching on the hood of the Super Bee—he loved the Super Bee too much to crumple the poor thing's snout like that—but he leaned in as close as he could get, hot metal baking his palms. Luce stood a few yards downriver chucking tiny pebbles into deeper parts of the channel.

"Okay. Okay. Promise you won't think I'm crazy?"

He promised.

"No, really, you promise promise?"

Promise promise.

"All right." Deep breath. "I saw a dragon down here once. Swear to Jesus I did."

This was his favorite time of the week. If he didn't have any work, and Rita didn't have any shifts at the Eaz-E-Rest, on Sunday afternoons they had started taking the Super Bee out for what Lucian called Flying Time. They rode with the top down and no destination in mind, until the traffic lights glowed in spangled firework colors and the first stars winked like silent movie starlets. There weren't any bodies rolled in carpets or bathrooms covered in other people's shit during Flying Time. Bed bugs and bloodstains ceased to exist. It was as good as swimming laps, but better, because Rita and Luce were there, too, and in all his short, violent, empty memory, Joe could not remember ever enjoying the company of anyone as much as he did theirs.

Their wanderings this evening had taken them through many back alleys, access roads, and restricted areas, down to the river's edge, or what was left of it. So long as Luce stayed *out* of the water, Rita said, and so long as he stayed within eyeshot, it was fine for him to play *near* the water while Mama and Joe talked. Joe had already seen him getting the toes of his sneakers wet, but as Raymond could've told the kid, Joe wasn't a snitch. He kept his mouth shut tight and listened as Rita spun her tale.

"So, back when I was Luce's age, I used to come here about as much as I could, after school and on weekends. We lived as close to it as the Riverview is, but there weren't any fences or 'keep out' signs. There seemed to be a lot more water back then, too. You could catch catfish sometimes, and minnows and tadpoles and stuff. In the place near our house, it wasn't even paved over yet, and there were rocks and this deep little pool. Anytime Mama didn't need me to help out in the shop, I was down there messing around. Dunno why it seemed so cool. Kids are weird, y'know? It's just a nasty little creek now, but it was like a magic, secret place or something. Nobody else ever went there but me. I guess I kinda started thinking of it as mine."

She shrugged. Joe got the feeling that if she had been a smoker, she would've taken a big drag.

"Anyway, like I've told you before, sometimes I . . . see stuff. Shapes.

Ghosts, spirits, whatever. All the women in my family do. Most of the time it's like seeing something out of the corner of your eye, but I came down here right before dark when I was a little older, maybe twelve or thirteen, about the time of day it is right now, and there was a huge, real animal all messed up in the water, thrashing around, tangled in garbage. It had a head like a coyote or a wolf, and a long body like a weasel, with . . . like, greeny-white fur all over. And weird purple-black feathers. And scaly front legs with claws like a—like a big bird or something. Jesus, the more I describe it, the crazier it sounds. I've never told this to anybody. You think I'm nuts yet?"

No, Joe didn't think she was nuts. He had seen some weird shit himself in his time, he said. It was a lie, he never had, but something about the story seemed unsettlingly familiar, like a bedtime story someone had told him once. He knew what she was going to say before she even said it, could see the entire thing play out in his head.

"Shit, maybe you're nuts, too, then. It gets better, though. I see this weird animal, and it's hurt, and it's also huge, with giant teeth and claws. I'm pretty sure it's a dragon. Do I run the heck away? Do I go home?"

No, Joe thought, but didn't say. *No, you were always braver than that.*

"No! I feel bad for the thing, because I'm *crazy*! I can see its front legs are wrapped in fishing line, so I creep up and I start snipping away with my pocket knife every time it stops thrashing around. And I swear to Jesus, Mary, and Joseph, hand on the Bible, it sees me and it chills the heck out until I finish, like it knows I'm trying to help. I get all the line untangled and the only thing that's left is this plastic six-pack wrapper holding its snout shut, right?"

Oh yeah, he knew how this one ended. *Gentle hands reaching out to pull the nasty trap away, hands that would barely make a mouthful but they don't even shake, and the girl's eyes are kind and unafraid—*

He was beginning to worry she was right about the both of them being bananas.

"So, what'd you do?"

"I . . . I mean, I pulled the six-pack ring off. I could tell by then it wasn't gonna hurt me. It had the weirdest eyes I've ever seen. They were people-smart, and colored funny. Kind of like yours, actually." She laughed. It was a laugh that had some thoughts about things but wasn't telling. "I pulled it off and freed the thing and the air sorta rippled and it was gone."

Plop, went Luce's stones. The water was too shallow here for a really satisfying splash. These were just enough to pleasantly break the dusk quiet. *Plop plop*.

"Jesus. I've seriously never told anyone that story before. Not even my ex-husband."

Joe didn't know how to respond.

"Well. Thanks for trusting me," he finally said, and meant it. He really, really meant it. He didn't quite know why he meant it so damn much, but he did, with all his heart and kidneys and every other plentiful organ inside his big dumb body. "Thank you."

She smiled. For the second time in a month she reached out and took his hand.

But nothing gold could stay. Dragons knew that. They fought their whole long existences against it, for all the good it did them.

All opposition to Raymond's river-spanning construction project had been bulldozed, bribed, and broken down. That only left the cleanup—the ones that knew a little too much, the associates who had helped and lent a hand at risk of outlasting their shelf lives. Raymond had a list. There was nothing personal about the list. It was all business. Raymond gave the list to Joe, and Joe did what he had always done. He followed orders. He went home and washed the Super Bee and splashed Rita and Luce with the hose and gave work no more thought. Most of the ones getting their *t*'s slashed and their *i*'s dotted were bad men, like him. No great loss, he told himself. None of my business.

The number of names on the list dropped. Autumn loomed. Only a few more loose ends flapped in the desert breeze. One was a drifter named Maria.

Maria was about ten thousand years old. She had come to town to collect on a debt Raymond owed her and he had graciously put her in a motel for the weekend while he got the paperwork drawn up. He didn't explain *why* he needed a toothless old woman crossed off his special list, and as usual Joe didn't ask. He took a look at the photograph, pocketed the address and room number Raymond gave him, and headed off with another one of Raymond's fixers, a no-nonsense guy with a pencil-thin mustache named Dave. Dave never talked a lot of shit. He just did his job, like Joe.

The hotel looked nondescript when they pulled into the parking lot, indistinguishable from a million others slowly rotting beside the exit ramps of every major and minor city across the sad, scarred continent. Peeling paint, grackles picking through the gravel, vacancy sign valiantly flashing against the midafternoon sun. Only one or two other cars parked, none of them in great shape. But as soon as Joe stepped out of the Lincoln they were driving, a cold shiver ran down his back. He looked down at his goose bumps in wonder. The thermometer on the car's side mirror had said 98°F.

He exchanged a look with Dave, who nodded.

"Yeah," he said. "I feel it too. Something's frickin' weird. Watch your back in there, buddy."

Maria was in 15, a downstairs room opening onto the parking lot. Joe had expected they'd have to pick the lock, but the knob turned easily in his hand. They eased into the ruddy gloom with way more caution than one old women necessarily called for. The lights and TV were off, the shades drawn. A hunched figure sat against the far wall opposite the window and bed.

"How kind of Raymond to send me company," the shadow said. Her voice was drier than August. Something in her hand went *click*. In the flare of the lighter Joe saw a withered face, iron-gray hair, a hand like a claw tattooed with a warding eye. Inexplicably, she was also wearing a battered top hat. The smell of fresh cigar smoke cut through the motel room mustiness. "Who needs one of those bracelets in case you fall over in the bathroom when you've got such good friends? Come to carry my groceries for me, boys?"

Joe's eyes were adjusting to the shadows. He could see other things now, too: symbols drawn on the walls, a broad circle scrawled overhead on the ceiling. Tarot cards fanned out on the stained carpet. The air was vibrating on some frequency that made his teeth itch. His thoughts and words felt as if they were bubbling through tar. Beside him Dave winced and rubbed at his temples.

"Nothing personal, lady," Joe managed. "It's just . . . business."

Cackling laughter. The cherry of her cigar bobbed merrily in the semi-darkness like a red eye.

"Is that what you tell yourself, boy?" she rasped. "If it wasn't personal, he wouldn't have sent *you*, of all people. Or should I say, of all un-people. What an incredible bastard that man is. Asks me to do a job and then kills me for doing what he asked without even paying. The cheek! I hope the next witch he double-crosses opens a portal to hell in his asshole."

Dave took a lurching step toward her, fumbling at his holster. He moved like a blind man in a drainage ditch.

"Is that all you got to say for your last words, a bunch of crazy talk?" he said. "You don't wanna pray or something?"

"Oh, I don't need to pray," came the retort. "You're wading through my last wishes right now. I wish for Raymond Sturges to fetch what all his double-dealing has got coming to him. I wish for that ugly *condom-minimum* he's building to tumble into the riverbed like a house of cards. And I wish *most* fervently, with all the hearts I stole as a fine young thing and all of the soul I sold for scrap, that the spirit standing over there that he asked me to summon and bind, trapped in the body of a mortal man, remembers what he is and drowns the *shit* out of his 'boss.' Any of those come to pass, I'll join the unseen world happy." The cigar gave a vicious little jerk.

Nothing she was saying made any kind of sense. Joe tried to shake the mud out of his head.

"Jesus, lady, what the hell do you think I am?" He stepped closer. Tarot cards slipped and cracked beneath his bootheels. The whites of the old woman's eyes flashed up at him.

"I think you know what you are." Her voice was a low hiss. "He needed you out of the way, same as he needs *me* out of the way. But you can't just put a bullet between a river god's eyes. For that, you need *specialists*. You need someone who knows what they're doing to teach you. You nee—"

"My head hurts," Dave said. He dragged his pistol to bear. "Let's just get this done with already."

"No, Dave, wait, hang the hell on, I wanna know what she's—"

"You'll remember soon," Maria said calmly. "He wanted you on a leash, and—"

The silencer on Dave's gun choked the pistol's roar into a muffled cough. Maria slumped. Her top hat and cigar tumbled to the floor at Joe's feet.

"God DAMMIT, I was trying to talk to her! Jesus, what part of 'wait' don't you understand?!"

Dave threw his hands up in the universal *chill the hell out* position. "I'm sorry, did the boss send us here to chat with the old bag or kill her? What the hell are you so upset for all of a sudden?"

It was a great question. Like most questions, Joe didn't have an answer. He felt . . . weird. Now that Maria was dead, Dave seemed fine. Joe was a hundred miles west of fine in a bus headed east. It had just pulled past the city limits of Gut-Churning Anxiety in a cloud of exhaust and the next stop was someplace he desperately did not want to think about. He could see the happy life he had managed to scrape together receding in the rear-view mirror.

"No," he muttered, clutching his head. "No no no no. She was nuts. I don't know what she meant."

But lies didn't hurt like this. He could feel all the little shards of his past coming back together, intrusive and cold as men with guns, men with concrete, men with summoning spells, and there was only so long he could hold them off before—

The slightest, softest of gasps from behind. Joe and Dave both went rigid.

Standing in the doorway, haloed by the late-afternoon sun, was Rita.

Done with Raymond, he swept on to the Riverview. It hurt to pull himself back into human form—hurt like hell, in fact, like wearing a shoe three sizes too small—but he kept it together long enough to limp into his dingy little apartment one last time.

He wrote her a letter.

> *Rita,*
>
> *I have to go. I'm so sorry. Nobody else will come after you, I promise. That's all been taken care of.*
>
> *There's a lot of money stashed under my mattress, and a lot more at the address below. Please take it. Spending time with you and Luce has made me happier than I can say.*
>
> *Thank you for everything.*

He slipped it beneath her door, where she'd find it when she returned. Then he walked into the night, down to where the riverbed was visible through the chain-link fence.

She was holding a stack of towels that rose almost to her chin. Joe couldn't see her eyes with the light of the open hotel room door at her back, but from the way she had frozen, he could imagine the look in them and it broke his heart.

Dave sighed "God dammit" in the way someone would looking at a huge mess that had just gotten a little bigger, and raised his piece. He was good at cleaning up messes, smooth as a well-tended engine.

Joe had never been what you'd call "smooth," but what he lacked in slickness he made up for by being very, very big. The desperate blow he landed on Dave's elbow knocked the shot wide. It also shattered the bone with a *crack* and sent the pistol cartwheeling as Dave shrieked, smoothness temporarily splintered.

That would've been the moment to put him down, to crack his neck or put a bullet through his head, to lie to Raymond and pin the blame on Maria. Instead, Joe spun, pushed by his howling, cursing ex-partner, grabbed Rita as he sprinted through the door, and made for the Lincoln. Sirens were already howling in the distance. Rita didn't make a sound as he threw her into the passenger seat and lurched for the driver's side, still wide-eyed and wordless with shock.

The big old car's tires chirped as it fish-tailed out of the parking lot and into early evening traffic. Joe was doing math in his head. It wouldn't take long for Dave to report back to Raymond, even with no ride and a busted arm. Raymond already knew about Rita. He knew where she lived. Once Dave got him on the phone and he put two and two together—

"Shit. Shit shit shit *shit*." He punched the console into plastic splinters and pulled his fist away bloody. It was all too much. Maria's talk, Rita sitting beside him flinching at his rage—all of it was just too damn much. He wanted to fly apart and sweep the entire city away, Atlantis style. "Rita, I'm so sorry. I didn't—I couldn't—"

"Are you going to kill me?" Her voice was so small he could barely hear the words over the noise of traffic outside. Jesus, how many times could his heart crack in a single day?

"No," he said. "I would never hurt you. Never." He licked his dry lips and swallowed what felt like an ostrich egg–sized lump in his throat. Her posture relaxed a little, but there was still a justifiable guardedness there that it hurt to look at. Private security, he had told her. That was his job. Sure. "Is there somewhere safe you can go for a few days? Somewhere outta town?"

"I—my sister lives in Tucson, I could—"

"Take Luce and go there. Stay for a couple of weeks. Don't come back for a while, all right?"

"My job, I can't—"

"Your job's the last thing to be worrying about. Please, Rita. A very bad man is probably hearing you just saw some shit you shouldn't've. Give me time to fix this." *The spirit standing over there that he asked me to summon and bind, trapped in the body of a mortal man.* What had that meant?

Flashes. A much younger Rita standing before him, looking about as scared as she did right now but still reaching up and out, gently, slowly—concrete trucks on the banks of home—a feeling of being pulled away from where he belonged and tethered to something small and clumsy and slow—and Raymond's voice, clear as if he was sitting beside Joe right now: *Holy hell, it worked. You did it. You crazy old witch, you did it. Nico, Bobby, get him some clothes!*

"Rita," he said, slowly, carefully. "What exactly did you see on my palm that time you read it?"

One of the towels from the hotel was still in her hands. For a long time she didn't respond, twisting it into tortured knots in her lap as she thought about the question.

"You don't belong here," she said at last. "Your home is . . . somewhere else."

Neither of them said another word until they pulled into the Riverview's parking lot. Just as he had feared, there were cars already there that he recognized, had driven and ridden in before. Dark shadows loitered on the staircase leading to the second-floor balcony.

"Where's Luce?" he said. His eyes never left the figures on the catwalk.

"At Sarah's."

Sarah's. Downstairs. Thank storm and spring and dew on the grass. "Okay. Here's how we're gonna play this. I'm getting out of the car. I'm walking upstairs. You get out after me, and you go get Luce. Then you get into *your* car, and you drive away to your sister's. You are *not* to look back, no matter what you hear. Please."

124

"Joe, I—"

"*Please.* Just walk over to Sarah's, get Luce, and walk back to your car. It'll be okay."

"Will I see you again?" She blurted it out so that all the words ran together: *WillIseeyouagain?* Rita was not a blurter. There was nothing left of Joe's heart now but the kind of slivers you had to use a wet paper towel to sponge up.

"Never know," he said. He didn't look back at her as he said it. He opened the car door. "Count to fifteen and then get out."

He cleared the space between the parking lot and the staircase at a sprint. He was a big target for the guys up above to miss, but even a big target was hard to hit at a dead run in bad lighting. The flimsy metal-and-plywood shivered and boomed beneath his feet as he began his ascent. Two steps at a time and then two more and he was plowing into the dark mass of bodies with all the blundering force his lumbering steamroller of a human body contained. He saw faces he knew and smashed them with his fists. A gun went off beside his ear and he barely noticed. The world was reduced to churning, boiling action, things swept up and tossed aside by his rage. It felt *amazing.* It also felt awfully damn familiar.

Far away a car door slammed. From inside the maelstrom Joe registered it and thought, *Good.* All he had to do was keep them distracted until Rita and Luce got clear, and then he could go confront Raymond himself: boss, benefactor, and betrayer. Someone's skull bounced against the metal railings with a *clong.* A guy who had baked the best peanut butter cookies Joe ever tasted for Raymond's birthday pressed the muzzle of a pistol against his shoulder and pulled the trigger, and Joe felt the bullet sear a path through muscle and bone and more muscle. He roared. There was no better way to describe it: he opened his mouth and an animal noise ripped out, and then he tore the gun away and broke the man's jaw with it.

He came up for air, clawing at shoulders and heads and necks. Down below, Rita was making her away across the courtyard back toward the parking lot, Lucian in her arms. The light was getting worse by the second, the world long since melted into shades of blue and gray and black, but he saw her just the same. And she saw him. *Don't look back*, he had told her, begged her, but she was her own person—her own wonderful person—and she looked up and saw him and their eyes met across the divide. She paused. He shook his head, frantically. She gave him one last anguished glance and kept going.

"Good-bye," he whispered. The churn of bodies sucked him back under.

"Hey," Luce said to the river, and Rita's breath snagged, ragged in her throat. "Why did you go? You still hadn't taught me to do the butterfly kick."

Their new place wasn't anywhere near the river. It was high in the hills, in a nice neighborhood Rita had driven through a thousand times before in her bombed-out Chevy, never able to glance at the pretty bungalows with their pretty front lawns for long before a police cruiser edged into frame to hurry her along. Half of her reasoning when she had bought the house had been purely petty: *Screw those people, let's see how they like having me as a neighbor.* It was also a really cute house, in a really good school district, and only a couple of miles from the community college to boot. The pettiness had just been the thing that finally pushed her over the edge, a gentle nudge that said, *Girl, you deserve this.*

But the river wasn't nearby, at least not near enough to walk to. Her neighbors said that was a blessing; the way it had suddenly begun to rise, like a dam had gone bust somewhere upstream; there was no telling what would happen the next time a hard rain fell. A lot of new construction along its banks had been put on indefinite hiatus. Some said it was due to snowfall in the mountains; others said the weather patterns were all outta whack. Rita had her own ideas, but she kept them to herself. She dropped Luce off at kindergarten and bought groceries and went to class three times a week, and on the weekends they drove to the river, glittering and fanning beneath the desert sun like dirty silk.

It was still filthy. Tan scum still gathered on its concrete shores, full of takeout cups and plastic bags and all the other garbage the people of the city felt like tipping in. Something about it had changed, though. Something besides the water levels. There was a watchfulness that had been missing for a long, long time. It rippled its oily coat when they got out of the car, like a cat stretching and yawning and rising to greet them. It gentled when Luce got too close, ready to catch him if he tripped and fell in. Or maybe that was Rita's wishful thinking. She didn't know what she expected, really. Despite the windfall Joe had left them, there was a want so big in her she couldn't sleep some nights. It only really went away when she could hear the water. Her heart was only satisfied when she could keep a weather eye out, for—

For what, exactly? Eyes like weird jewels? Feathers and fur and fangs? A Super Bee rising up out of the nasty water like a damn dolphin?

"Where did you go?" Luce asked again.

HABITAT

K. J. Parker

K. J. Parker was born in London in 1961, and has been, at various times, not very good at coin dealing, lawyering, farm laboring, lumberjackery, and auction-house portering. He is an indifferent metalworker, inept carpenter, two-left-footed fencer, timid horse rider, lackluster archer, so-so armorer and sword-smith, barely adequate stockman and forester, run-of-the-mill mid-list novelist, skilled textile worker and crack shot, who won the World Fantasy Award for novellas twice hand running some years ago and has since produced relatively little of note.

The desert grows: woe to him who harbors deserts!
—NIETZSCHE, *Also sprach Zarathustra*

He looked at me.

I looked back at him, trying to think of something to say. *Go to hell* isn't something you say to a prince, not when you've been obliged by protocol to leave your sword at the porter's lodge, and the royal grooms have control of your horse. I might just get away with *No*, but then again, I might not. *Yes* was out of the question.

"I'm sorry," I said, "I'm a bit deaf in one ear. Could you just say that again?"

He sighed. "I want you," he said slowly, as if to a foreigner, "to catch me a dragon. A live one. You can do that, can't you?"

Well, I'd bought my time. Paid through the nose for it. "Probably not," I said.

Not what he'd been expecting to hear. "Why not?"

I know a lot of people who complain, quite justifiably, that one small failure has ruined their lives. In my case, one success completely screwed up mine. No good saying I was just a kid at the time, that I didn't know what I was getting myself into, that if I'd known, I'd have run a mile; too late for that now. It's on my record; I'm branded with it for life (so probably not for very long, given the nature of that brand). I have HERO burned into the skin of my face, too deep for rouge, too tall for the shadow of a wide-brimmed hat.

I was nineteen, youngest of three sons of an impoverished knight. What that meant in practice was that we had a damp, leaky hall decorated with rusty inherited armor, and we looked after our own sheep. Correction: Juifrez and I looked after the sheep, because Raimbaut was the eldest, therefore the heir designate, therefore too grand to get his hands dirty with anything useful. He spent all his time bashing a wooden pole with a wooden sword and learning heraldry, while we clipped shitty wool off the arses of the pregnant ewes. I can't tell you who got the worst of it; they were both miserable ways of spending a day, but at least ours put food on the table.

We had two hundred and six sheep, and then one day we had two hundred and two. The other four had vanished. Juifrez and I went looking for them and found a few bones and straggles of wool. That made no sense. A wolf leaves a big red mess; rustlers leave nothing at all. We split up. I wandered around for an hour or so and saw nothing at all. Then I went back to where I'd told Juifrez to wait for me. He wasn't there.

I hate that feeling when panic sets in. I felt it rather too often in

Outremer, but never quite so badly as I did then. Juifrez was a year older than me, but somehow he was always my kid brother; I was smarter, more sensible. It had always been understood it was my job to look after him. *Let's split up*, I'd said. I could picture myself telling my father that. It wasn't a comfortable thought.

I tried to find a trail, footprints—I was good at that sort of thing—but I couldn't find any, and that nearly made me burst into tears. I started running, just to cover the ground quicker, and it was only when I stopped that I realized I'd run myself out of breath and could hardly breathe for the cramps. I'd been yelling his name for God knows how long, and my throat was raw. I put my back to a tree, to keep myself from falling over, and slid to the ground. I'd had enough. I was beaten.

I was sitting there with my face in my hands when I felt something splash on the top of my head. It was light enough to be a raindrop, but rain generally comes thicker than a drop at a time. I put my hand on my head, then looked at the fingertip. Red. I looked up and saw Juifrez hanging by his heels from a high branch, with his head twisted around a full half-turn.

And I heard a voice, in my mind. *Go away*, it said.

I was in no state to be bothered with voices. A moment or so frozen stiff, unable to move; then I was scrabbling at the trunk of the tree, trying to climb it, but there was nothing to get a grip on. *Go away*, repeated the voice in my head, but that made no sense, and there was my brother, my elder-kid brother, hanging just out of reach like the biggest, fattest plum always does. *I warned you*, said the voice, and something shifted, right up in the canopy.

At first I took it for a pig, except pigs don't climb trees, and they aren't that big, or that color. A great big blue-gold pig, with tiny eyes with human eyelashes. Then it raised its crest, a collar of flat spikes, like flag iris leaves as long as your arm, and stuck out its ridiculously long neck, thick as your waist. At which point I realized what it was. *You've got to be joking*, I thought, because of course they don't exist.

Which hardly mattered. This thing, whatever it was (didn't matter what it was), had killed my brother, twisted his neck like a chicken's and hung him up in a tree, like you'd do with vermin, stoats and weasels and rats, to scare away their nasty little relatives. *The hell with that*, I thought.

I believe anger is a gift from God. I bent my knees and jumped, but I still couldn't get a handhold, and all I did was rip my fingernails.

Suit yourself, idiot, said the voice in my head, and the thing—let's call it what it was even though it sounds ridiculous just saying the word—the *dragon* slid down the tree straight at me, jaws open, so I could see inside. The roof of its mouth was pink, and its fangs, tusks, I don't know the technical term, were the pale buttermilk color of mature ivory, except one of them was split at the point.

I was unarmed, and according to our old bestiary, dragons' fangs are deadly poison. Which is why I believe anger is a gift from God. It allows you to confront the risks and say to yourself, *Be that as it may.*

I'm neither brave nor clever, but over the years I've noticed that an overpowering desire to kill someone or something brings out the best in me. I let it come on, watching it—anger makes me calm, sometimes—until it was right on top of me, jaws wide open. At which point I stuck my right arm in its mouth, grabbed its tongue as close as I could to its root, and planted my elbow against the floor of its lower jaw.

It tried to close its jaws, but it couldn't. My forearm was propping its mouth open, and the force of its jaws drove my fist and elbow into its soft palates, anchoring them. I kept my arm straight; I knew that if I didn't, my wrist would break and that would be that. I noticed, almost dispassionately, that the lower jaw fangs were half an inch from digging into my upper arm.

It tried to pull away, found that it was ripping its own tongue out, and gave up in a hurry. Then it paused, just for a moment, trying to figure out what to do. Fortuitously, it took me precisely a moment to stick my thumb in its eye, as hard as I possibly could.

I broke my thumb, of course, but that was the least of my concerns. The dragon yanked its head back sharply, so sharply its tongue came away in my hand.

I learned a useful lesson that day, one which served me well in later life, when I managed to get myself into real trouble (as opposed to minor inconvenience, like fighting a dragon bare-handed). I pass it on to you in the hope that you may find it as useful as I did, and always have done. If you're fighting an enemy who's much bigger and stronger than you are, don't try to kill him. Just cause him as much pain as you possibly can. There'll be a split second when it hurts so much that for all his strength he just can't think straight; and in that split second you can (for example) stoop and pick up a big stone and smash his head in.

Later, we found out that I'd been incredibly lucky. A dragon's skull is far too thick to be crushed by anything less than a direct hit from a trebuchet; except for a little spot, no bigger than the palm of your hand, right on the very top, where the two main plates of its skull form a weak seam.

When things go badly wrong, I've always found, there abide these three: terror, dumb luck, and anger. But the greatest of these is anger.

"Why not?" he said.

What a question. "Because it's too difficult," I said. "It's difficult and dangerous, and I don't want to get killed."

He gave me a hurt look, as though I'd just refused to marry him. "You're too scared," he said.

"Yes."

He nodded. "Yesterday I bought up all the mortgages on your land," he said. "If I foreclose, can you find two thousand angels within fourteen days?"

"No," I said.

"Will you do this perfectly straightforward little job for me?"

"Yes," I said.

Two thousand angels is a lot of money. It's about half what our estate is worth: two angels an acre. It's roughly what it costs to fit out two knights and send them to fight in Outremer.

When my brother Raimbaut was twenty-four, my lord the duke decided to follow the call of his conscience and his heart and join the soldiers of God fighting the heathens in Outremer. It was a noble, beautiful thing to do, or so people said. And of course he called up his tenants and his subinfeudees to go with him, since one man on his own can't achieve very much in a war, even if he's a peer of the realm whose ancestors were dukes in the Cascenais when the king's ancestors were still chasing goats up mountains. My father was too old to go, so Raimbaut went instead.

Have you ever stopped to think how much all that stuff costs? Item, one mail shirt. Item, one pair of ankle-length mail chausses. Item, one coat of plates. Item, one helmet, with nasal. Items, one gambeson, one aketon, two gauntlets; one warhorse, one palfrey, two packhorses, three amblers for his squire and his two men at arms. One sword, two lances, one shield, and so on, and so on. Total, eight hundred and thirty-six angels. Add to that traveling expenses and living expenses—

Only he didn't. He died of dysentery three weeks after he got there. The army was in full retreat at the time, so they had to dump his body, and all his expensive kit; presumably the enemy got the kit and sold it to the Tedesci brothers, who buy all their plunder and sell it back to the Defenders of the Faith at the Foregate fair at Aescra. But not to worry, the duke's marshals told him, plenty more where he came from. The obligation was still due, and my father still had a son. So that was all right.

Two thousand angels, which my father raised by pledging his land to the Aechmalota twins, at 3 percent interest, to send Raimbaut and then me to Outremer. You know what they say about a fool and his money.

But if I succeeded, on the other hand, his majesty would give me the mortgage deeds, and a thousand angels cash. A thousand angels is a lot of money.

First, find a dragon. Not as easy as it sounds. The species isn't native to our part of the world; it's too cold, and a good crisp winter will achieve more in the way of pest control than a hundred knights, with or without enchanted swords. The only specimens to be encountered north of the Middle Sea are the handful brought back by noble lords returning from Outremer as souvenirs or gifts for the man who has everything.

It is more blessed, Scripture tells us, to give than to receive; and although I have my doubts about that as a general rule, it surely applies when the gift is a dragon. For a start, you've got to build a special house for it to live in, with very thick stone walls and underfloor heating, and you've got to feed it a ruinous amount of fresh meat every day; and if, God forbid, the wretched thing ever gives you the slip and gets loose on your neighbors' land, you've got to go deal with it, or find some poor fool who'll deal with it for you. Unless, of course, you're lucky enough to live next door but three to a young idiot who'll rip its tongue out and smash its head in free of charge, just to settle a score, but that almost never happens. Who'd be stupid enough to do it?

I said just now that dragons can't survive the northern winter, and that's almost true. Out of the few that escape, a very few of them can. Usually they find a deep cave to insulate themselves against the frost and the bitter wind, and hibernate until spring. Caves that deep are few and far between, and in those places where there are such caves, generally speaking, there aren't enough sheep and cattle for the dragon to feed up on, to build its fat reserves to see it through until spring comes along.

In fact, the only place north of the Saëve where you might reasonably expect to find one is where the moors meet the mountain foothills, near the small market town of Loucy. It's a godforsaken place. The Blood River—so called because it runs red with rust from the iron ore deposits at Weal Jehan; the water's poisonous down as far as Boc Loucy, and nothing grows on its banks for a hundred yards on either side— bisects a deep, windswept valley, half of which (roughly two thousand acres) just about grows oats and barley, while the other half is forested with small, twisted holm oaks, no use for anything except firewood.

There are four tiny villages north of the town, surrounding the small, dilapidated manor house where the de Loucys have lived for about three hundred years, and where I grew up.

We reckoned the dragons escaped from the grange at Emm, the farthest outpost of my lord the duke's estate at Chastelbest, though of course we couldn't prove it. Shortly after my lord's father came back from Outremer, they built an enormous barn in a deep combe between the ridge on which the house stands and the forest (which extends over the Hog's Back and joins up with the Loucy woods at Moyenchamber). They were three years building it, and they had masons and tradesmen in from the city, sixty miles away—odd, don't you think, just to build an ordinary barn? But nobody ever heard of straw or pease or hay being carted there. But flocks of sheep were driven down from the top pastures, and herds of pigs came up from the home cottages; and nobody ever saw them come out again. Proving nothing, of course. But the first dragon showed up in Loucy woods about five years after the barn was built. I was nineteen at the time.

Not so very long after that, the barn burned to the ground in a great fire, which spread to Hog's Back Wood, over the top and down into our woods, though no great harm done, since they're all useless, as I told you; about nine hundred acres lost on our side, which is all tangled briars and withies now. The grange people never rebuilt the barn, and over the years the tenants have helped themselves to the stones for making and mending walls, so there's nothing to see there these days except a long rectangle of foxgloves and gorse.

Anyway, if I wanted to find a dragon, that's where I'd look; just as, if I wanted to look for death, I'd throw a rope over a tree or eat yellow-cap mushrooms.

I was in Outremer for five years.

Doesn't sound all that long. My lord the duke's eldest son has just got back from seven years at the university, where I gather he distinguished himself by reading several books and being seen at a number of lectures, modestly attired in a black silk scholar's gown trimmed with sable. That's two years away from home longer than me, and more or less the same distance, and yet you'd hardly know to look at him that he's been away at all.

Five years in Outremer, however, is a very long time. Half of the new arrivals—my brother Raimbaut, for instance—die within the first three months. Those who don't tend to last anything between six and eighteen months; two years makes you a veteran, someone to be pointed out and stared at. After three years, they send you home.

I was there for five years, and while I was there I met an interesting man. He wasn't one of us. He served the emperor, on whose behalf we were supposed to be fighting, though it was no secret that the emperor reckoned we were worse than the heathens and did ten times as much damage to his long-suffering people. This man told me that before he was conscripted, he'd worked for a master who caught wild animals for the Hippodrome games in the Golden City—lions, bears, elephants, that sort of thing.

(In case you aren't familiar with the high culture of the Cradle of Civilization, once a month, all the citizens of the City crowd into a huge enclosure to watch the fighting; men against wild animals, animals against animals, men against men. Now, I find this odd, since the Empire has been at war against the heathen for six hundred years, doing quite badly most of the time; every family loses at least one man every generation, and the City itself has been besieged twelve times, so you'd think they'd have seen quite enough fighting and killing for free, without paying a silver sixpence for a seat at the back, probably behind a pillar or a woman with a tall hat. Apparently not.)

Oh, and dragons, of course, he told me. We caught half a dozen dragons. Then he stopped and grinned at me. You think I'm shitting you, he said. I bet you don't think dragons even exist.

Oddly enough, I said, I do.

He looked at me. Well, they do, he said, and we had to catch them, alive, undamaged. Bet you can't guess how we did it.

I'm more interested in lions, I told him. Tell me how you used to catch lions.

Same way as we caught dragons, basically, he said. What you do is—

He was a good man, though he took some getting used to, and what he didn't know about dragons—Somehow he never quite grasped that it wasn't a subject I was comfortable talking about, but he was a wonderful horseman and taught me how to shoot a hundred-pound-draw short-bow from the saddle, set a broken arm, and cure mountain fever. I have no idea what happened to him. His squadron was cut off by an out-flanking wing that came out of nowhere. A day or so later, I went back and picked over the bodies, but I didn't find his there. Proving nothing.

A thousand angels. A lot of money.

I met an alchemist once, and he explained the theory to me. All things corrupt, he told me, all things decay and fall apart and go to waste and ruin, except for gold. You can leave it out in the rain or bury it in the damp earth for a hundred years, and it'll come out looking just as shiny and clean as when it went in. There are only two things, he said to me, that survive and pass through the taints and decays and cor-ruptions of this world unscathed and unchanged: God and gold. And one of them is all around us every day, in everything and comprised in and comprising everything, and the other one is very rare, and has to be crushed and sweated out of a rock or sifted, tiny speck by tiny speck, from the stinking silt of a riverbed. Guess which one people value the most. Go on, guess.

And (he went on) neither of them can be reduced to an essential form, since they're both perfect already; but both of them have the vir-tue of rejuvenating, of restoring and perfecting. Both of them, in fact, can work miracles.

I told him I wasn't sure about that. I'll show you, he said, and he led me through the bazaar to an archway in a wall, and through the arch into a courtyard with a door, and he rang a little brass bell. Someone opened the door for us, and beyond it I saw a walled garden, rows of lavender and sage and marjoram, apple trees espaliered on wires, and in the center a fountain. Ten years ago, he told me, this was a tanner's yard, and you could smell the slurry and the rotting brains halfway across town. Then I bought it, and I spent a thousand nomismata making it like this, but it was worth it. Gold transforms, he said, gold purifies. Gold can turn a cesspit into a paradise.

I like a pretty garden as much as the next man, but if I had a thousand angels I knew what I'd do with it. First I'd hire all the casual labor I could get, and I'd clear and plough up all the land in Loucy that's gone to rack and ruin since my grandfather's time, and I'd rebuild all the fallen-down barns and walls, have all the hedges laid so the stock couldn't get out and stray onto my lord's land, never to return. I'd plant out a vineyard on Conegar, clear the weeds and the cow parsley out of the millrace and get the mill working again, get the fish traps and weirs on the river fixed up, order new ploughs and harrows, maybe even go to Chastelbest abbey fair and buy a really good pedigree bull. They'll tell you in the schools that alchemy is abstruse and difficult to understand, but I think it's pretty clear and simple, once you understand the basic principles.

I'll need money, I'd told him, for expenses. He'd looked offended and sad, and told the chancellor to give me a writ for fifteen angels. What I'd actually asked for was fifty, but the prince is slightly deaf in one ear.

Still, fifteen angels is a lot of money. I took the writ down to the chancellery and they counted fifteen coins into my hand and made me sign a receipt.

I've known the blacksmith at Loucy all my life. When I was a boy, I used to hang around the forge watching him, trying not to get under his feet. If I'd been Raimbaut, that wouldn't have been allowed, but a third son has more latitude in precise gradations of status, especially when his father isn't entirely sure when he'll be in a position to pay the blacksmith's bill. It'd be an exaggeration to say that he ever liked me much. I was a small boy who sat in a corner of the room and stared at him and never said anything, even when spoken to. But he got used to me.

Then my lord the duke decided to go to Outremer, and with him went his seventeen horses, and the horses needed a farrier. The blacksmith of Loucy had a son, a promising young man who was already a master of the trade and known to be particularly good with horses. He'd already made his mind up to volunteer, he told me, when my lord's man came with the summons. It was an honor and a privilege, and the money was very good, and he'd always had a fancy to travel.

Two days after he told me that, he was dead. I can't remember offhand whether it was cholera or the flux; one of the two. When we were kids, he used to duck my head in the slack bucket when he was sure nobody was watching, and once, he stole my shoes and I had to pretend to my father that I'd lost them crossing the river. When I told his father, I made out that he'd died bravely fighting the heathen; he dashed forward to rescue a fallen comrade, I said, and a savage stabbed him in the back.

So, Garcio and I know each other tolerably well. Which means he knows me well enough to make me show him actual money before I tell him what I want made.

"What in God's name is that supposed to be?" he said.

I'd drawn a sketch in chalk on a roof slate. "It's to scale," I told him. "I measured it with dividers and calipers." He'd taught me to do that, though he hadn't meant to; I'd watched him, with his back to me. Saved my life once, being able to draw up an accurate sketch. I never told him that, of course.

"What is it?"

"It's a trap," I told him.

He peered at the slate. His eyes aren't what they were, on account of staring at white-hot metal for forty years. "What's that supposed to be?"

"That's the sear," I said. "The tripwire disengages the sear from the notch, which releases the shutter."

He looked at me. "What's it a trap for?"

"Lions," I said.

"What do you want to trap lions for?"

"I don't."

Like I said, he was used to me. "How thick's this strut got to be?"

"An inch. Actually, you might get away with seven-eighths, but what the hell."

"Rivetted?"

I shook my head. "Welded. Better still, rivetted and welded."

He was frowning. "There aren't any lions in these parts," he said.

"Is that right?"

I had reason to believe there'd be a dragon in the caves below Staert, and I was right. They don't exactly conceal their presence.

One of the many things that everybody knows about dragons, and that isn't actually true, is that they breathe fire. Of course they don't, but fires start wherever they've been living for any length of time. My friend the lion-catcher in Outremer explained why, or at least he told me what he'd been told. They're desert creatures, he told me. They're what causes deserts.

Which sounds like drivel, until you read old books and look at old maps. From which you learn that once upon a time, hundreds or thousands of years ago, the endless rolling sand dunes of Outremer were forests and pastures and meadows, quilted with rivers, studded with busy towns and walled cities. Just occasionally you come across them, the corner of a worked stone poking up through the sand, like a bone through the skin. But then, so my friend told me, the dragons came, and something they were or something they did dried up all the water, killed all the trees and the grass. And where you get dead trees and dry grass, you get fires, and before long there's nothing alive at all, which is a pretty good working definition of a desert. Either they poison the water, like the iron ore, or their piss kills the grass, like a sick dog's; anyway, you can tell straight away where a dragon lives, because everything around it is dead.

When I was a boy, there was a big stand of ash trees at Staert. My grandfather had them planted the day my father was born, which I always thought was a nice thing to do, and if ever I had a son, I'd do the same. All gone. At least, the stub ends of the trunks were still there, charred black, sticking up like the grave markers of a hastily buried army. The ground was black and crunched when you walked on it, all the way from the top of the ridge to the point where the earth becomes rock.

I didn't need to go that far, so I didn't. I stood on top of the Calf, the smaller of the two tall knolls on the other side of the valley cut by the little river that races down from the mountains to join the Blood River at Watersmeet. I don't know that that little river ever had a name, not a proper one. We always called it Calf Water. Anyway, its bed was dry and split with deep cracks, and the withies on what had been its banks were starting to droop. The fire hadn't managed to jump the riverbed, but all the heather on the flanks of the Calf was brown and brittle, and you know what dry heather's like. Breathe on it when you've been eating garlic and you'll have a fire you could weld steel in.

No heather in Outremer, naturally. But around the oases they grow marvelous crops of wheat; shorter in the stem than our northern varieties, but with ears as long as your thumb. The enemy used to wait until the corn was just ripening, and then they'd swoop down, drive off the farmers, harvest the corn, and cart it back over what we laughingly called the border. Same every year, and the farmers only stayed there because we wouldn't let them leave.

I'd been there two and a half years. I was still alive because I'd been seconded away from my lord the duke's contingent to serve with one of the emperor's regiments—the locals, in other words, the people who actually lived there and knew what they were doing. They knew about such things as keeping your wounds and water clean, not letting your latrines drain into a river when your allies were camped a mile downstream, that sort of stuff, and they knew about fighting the enemy, which they'd been doing for six hundred years.

The year before, my lord the duke had been given responsibility for that sector, and he'd tried to forestall the annual invasion by fighting a pitched battle on the border. He lost, needless to say, and seventy knights and five hundred and twelve foot soldiers died, and the enemy went about their business in the usual way. The next year, the rotation meant our lot, the emperor's men, got that sector, and of course, they knew what to do.

Which was nothing. We sat on our horses and watched as the enemy column swaggered (no other word for it) across the little brown river that marked the frontier. We'd already evacuated the locals, so the country was empty for as far as an eagle could fly in a day. We sat and watched them ride down the old military road the emperors had built four centuries ago, and we did nothing.

We did nothing while they set about their weary job of *chevauchée*— that's the military word for turning someone else's home into a desert. You trash the houses, cut down the orchards, burn the crops, kill every domesticated animal, and then you move on to the next village. It's hard manual labor, which was why the enemy used prisoners of war— our people—to do the actual work, while they sat in their saddles and made sure they did a proper job. They sat, and we sat, and the chain gangs sweated to death in the blazing sun, destroying the livelihoods of their own flesh and blood. Then, when there wasn't anything left, they moved on to the next village, and the next, until they'd finished their allotted sweep and it was time to go home.

The enemy weren't stupid. They sent the harvested grain on ahead in wagons, but they kept back large areas of uncut grain so the army would have something to eat on its way home. The biggest patch was a flat plain, maybe two thousand acres, all rich, fertile land, with the road running straight down the middle.

One of the men in our company was local born and bred. He knew the terrain, and he knew the prevailing winds. So, one night when the enemy were camped in the middle of this enormous cornfield, we crept out and started our fires at carefully chosen points, knowing that the wind was in the right direction and would blow strongly for the next thirty-six hours. Then we split into two, each party blocking one end of the road.

It worked like a charm, though the fighting at the roadblocks was murderous. But we knew we didn't have to prevail, just hold them up long enough for the fire to reach them—and it did, roaring in like waves breaking on a beach, until the smoke was so thick that fighting was irrelevant, and we broke up and got out of there as fast as we possibly could. Of the twenty thousand heathens who marched in, about nine hundred got out. The technical term for that is victory, though of course they were back next year, and the year after that.

We also burned to death about twelve thousand of those prisoners of war, but that couldn't be helped. As my lord the duke said later, when claiming the whole thing had been his idea; once captured, those men were assets of the enemy and needed to be dealt with; and besides, better dead than in the hands of the infidel. Actually, he may have been right about that last bit. They had a pretty rough time of it, so I gather. I guess it comes down to a choice: Which would you rather die of—fire, torture, or starvation?

Also, said my lord the duke, it's a well-known fact that burning the crop actually increases the fertility of the soil, so once this ridiculous war was over and the heathen had been crushed, future generations would bless us. I won't comment on that, if you don't mind.

Garcio the blacksmith has always done good work. He charged me an angel seventeen for it; extortionate, but it wasn't my money. The change out of the second angel just about paid for the hire of the stonemason's big cart, his big crane, and a dozen of his biggest men. Have you noticed that when you're engaged in something truly difficult and dangerous, everybody rips you off?

So, I had a dragon, and a trap. That just left bait.

When I came home from Outremer, carrying everything I owned in a hemp sack slung over my shoulder, I hardly knew the place. I looked down from the top of the ridge expecting to see cornfields, neatly laid hedges, a properly made-up road leading through coppiced spinneys to our house. Instead, I saw a wilderness of gorse, briars, and nettles. The fields and the hedges and the stumps of the felled trees had vanished, buried like the stones of the ancient cities of Outremer. There was no road, and no house.

Three years after I went away, apparently, there was a fire. The house burned down; it spread to the spinney, and from there to the fields. My father got out in time, but he was never the same afterward. He moved to a cottage for a few months but proved entirely incapable of looking after himself, so the monks took him in and gave him a cell, board, and lodging in return for a second mortgage on the estate. He died six months later, and they buried him in their own graveyard; something of an honor, apparently, for a layman.

It didn't take long for the tenants to find out that I was home. They sent a deputation to the inn to welcome me, and I had to tell them that not everybody comes home from Outremer leading a string of ponies loaded down with plundered gold. They took it reasonably well. Oh, well, they said, and off they went. Later, I went to see them each in turn, with some vague idea in my mind of discussing arrears of rent. But it had been hard times all around, they told me, since the old master died, and what I'd seen inclined me to believe them. Three failed harvests in succession, and the grass so bad, they kept the stock alive by cutting hazel branches from the hedges. That's bad, I told them, thinking of the villages in Outremer we'd been sworn to protect (and where one day the corn will grow so high, because of all that ash), and they weren't to worry about rent until they were back on their feet again.

I was still wearing the shoes I'd walked two hundred miles in, from the coast all the way up the military road to Loucy. They were good shoes. I took them off a dead heathen in a canyon somewhere, and he'd got them from one of our lot, a rich man's son to judge by shape of the last and the quality of the stitching. They still had a good few miles left in them. A man wearing shoes like that wasn't going to worry too much about sleeping in a barn, or living off unfortunate creatures caught in snares, while he sets about clearing fifty acres of tangled briars with an old hook he found in a fallen-down toolshed.

I was good with cutting tools in Outremer. I could slice a man's arm off with a backhand cut. And the worst a bramble can do is scratch you up a bit. I had energy and motivation; best of all, I was angry (and the greatest of these is anger). But I'd been in the sun too long. I got soaked to the skin by a heavy shower, and next thing I knew I had fever. My friend the lion-catcher had taught me how to cure it, but those herbs don't grow here. I was sick as a dog for a week, and when I snapped out of it, I had no strength left. I limped over to the abbey, where they took me in and gave me bowl after bowl of barley broth with dumplings, and showed me the mortgage deed my father had signed. And that was the end of my crusade to take back my inheritance.

I was twenty-eight years old, and I could see no point in anything. But I was still that crazy kid who'd killed a dragon with his bare hands; so I went south and signed on with one of the free companies as a mercenary. I found I fit in well there. I was famous. They called me *ormsbana* and *wurmtoter,* and had a special banner made with a dragon on it, and the enemy ran away as soon as they heard we were coming. We trashed a lot of cottages and burned a lot of corn, and three years later I'd saved up a hundred angels, which is a lot of money, and I bought a farm, down on the coast, a mile or so from the Straits. From my window, I could see the ships setting sail for Outremer, and very occasionally at night I could see the beacons on the other side, lit to show them the way into the harbor.

I had a shrewd idea where would be a good place for my trap, if only I could find it again. I was afraid it would all look different, so much else having changed, but when we got there it was exactly as I remembered it. There was a certain tree, under which I'd sat one day after I'd been looking for my brother. It was taller and thicker, but not by very much.

You can't really hide a machine made of iron girders weighing well over a ton, so I told them to put it down anywhere, gave them their money, and watched them trundle away. Then I walked around it a few times. A trap is a trap. I could tell what it was and how it was supposed to work just by glancing at it. But Garcio the smith hadn't known until I told him, and a dragon is just a dumb brute.

I wound up the shutters using the winch provided, engaged the sear in the notch, disengaged the hook and chain, and hung them back out of the way. There was a pressure plate on the floor. When the dragon stood on it, it would pivot and pull on a cable, which would lift the sear out of the battery, and the front and rear shutters would fall simultaneously. There was also a little wicket gate at the back, between the back shutter and the end of the frame. I made sure it opened and shut easily.

The space between the shutter and the wicket was where the bait had to go. I'd thought to bring a little three-legged milking stool. I ducked under the bottom edge of the shutter and sat down on the stool. Might as well be comfortable while I was waiting.

Not for very long. Dragons have poor eyesight but a marvelous sense of smell. It came, just as I'd anticipated, out of the canopy of that damned tree, unwinding itself like a coil of living rope. Last time I'd been preoccupied; this time I made a point of looking, because a dragon isn't something you see every day. Neck as thick as your waist, head like a pig, tiny black eyes, crest like sword blades, scales like the armor they wear in Outremer, teeth like handspikes. And a voice in my head saying, *Run.*

Nice of it to care. But there comes a point in a man's life when he has nowhere left to run to, and a thousand angels is a very great deal of money. I looked into the dragon's eyes and saw what I'd expected to see.

"Hello, Juifrez," I said.

It lunged at me. I scampered back, fumbling for the wicket catch. As I'd anticipated, it couldn't reach me without sliding into the cage. It arched its spine and slithered forward, and I heard the pressure plate creak. Its head shot forward, just as I threw myself out of the wicket, hit the ground, and rolled. I heard the thud as the shutters fell.

The trap was designed to catch lions. It was far too short for twenty feet of dragon. But the shutters were sheet iron, three inches thick, and one had slammed down on its neck, pinning it to the floor, and the other had trapped its tail. It wasn't too happy about that. It shook and wriggled, trying to jackknife, so hard it lifted the whole contraption a handspan off the ground, but it couldn't get free. The shutters were too heavy.

I heard a voice in my head: *Let me go. Please.* But even if I'd wanted to, I couldn't. I'd have had to get the hook under the shutters and winch them up, and the winch was buried under the dragon's body. And I knew if I tried to get to it, the dragon would kill me. And what had my lord the duke had to say on the subject, or something quite similar? Once captured, he was an asset of the enemy and needed to be dealt with. And a thousand angels is a lot of money.

I looked down at my leg and saw a tear in the cloth, tinged with blood. Maybe I'd scratched myself on a sharp edge of the frame, or a thorn, or maybe the dragon's teeth had just nicked me before I got out of its way. *Damn*, I thought.

"I'm sorry," I said, and walked away.

I waited five days. That's what my friend in Outremer had told me, the one who trapped lions for a living. Oh, and dragons, too, of course. You leave them in the trap for five days, no food or water, till they're so weak, they couldn't hurt a kitten. Then you dose them with a stirrup pump: distilled essence of poppy, about a gallon, which ought to keep them under for a week at the very least. After that, you can load them onto a boatbuilder's cart and ship them out, and get paid.

So I did that. The prince was as good as his word. I got the mortgage deeds to my land (two thousand acres of brambles and self-seeded withies) and a thousand angels in a linen bag, and he got his dragon. What do you want it for, I asked him. Mind your own damned business, he told me.

*An interesting and little-known fact about dragons is that they don't repro-*duce the same way as other animals. Instead of mating, and bearing and rearing their young, they propagate by contamination, like a disease, like the plague that killed two out of three of the inhabitants of Joiauz Saber the year after I came home, brought there by veterans returning from Outremer. All it takes, so my friend told me, is a little scratch, from its teeth or even just the rough edge of one of its scales. If it draws blood, it infects you.

The incubation period is anything from a few days to ten years. Even being dead won't save you. If a dragon bites a corpse, in due course the corpse becomes a dragon. But they prefer to take their victims alive, like my lord the prince, or the heathens in Outremer who rounded up farmers and marched them back home in chains to burn their cousins' corn.

I've given it some thought over the years, but I honestly can't remember if the dragon I killed when I was nineteen managed to scratch me or not. With every year that passed, I persuaded myself to feel a little safer. And I have no idea whether Juifrez, my poor dear brother Juifrez, scratched me, or whether it was a sharp edge on the frame of the trap, or a briar.

It hardly matters. Dragons don't survive here in the north, except in one or two remote places. Their natural habitat is Outremer, where they swarm and proliferate, so that place will never ever be rid of them. It hardly matters, because there are far worse things than dragons in Outremer, and the slightest scratch will turn you into one of them; the sort of man who'll burn his own house down, or kill thousands of his own people so as to kill thousands of the enemy, or who'll come home and start doing for money what he hated himself for doing abroad for honor and fealty.

The prince wanted a live dragon because he was jealous. He didn't like the fact that a poor knight's son had won imperishable glory by slaying a dragon with his bare hands, and he wanted to emulate the feat, but only after having reduced the concomitant risk to a sensible level. So he had the poor knight's son catch him a dragon, and then he had his people draw the dragon's fangs and dope it with poppy juice until it could barely keep its eyes open. Then he staged a tournament and had the dragon carted into the lists, and rode forth on his white charger to slay the monster. Unfortunately, the dragon fell asleep just as he was about to drive his gauntleted fist into the vulnerable place on top of the monster's head, which his people had sensibly marked for him with bright red paint. It fell asleep and rolled over, and in doing so knocked the prince off his horse and crushed him like an egg. He lived for two days in unspeakable pain and then died. Served him right.

POX

Ellen Klages

Ellen Klages (ellenklages.com) is the author of three acclaimed historical novels: *The Green Glass Sea*, which won the Scott O'Dell and the New Mexico Book awards; *White Sands, Red Menace*, which won the California and the New Mexico Book awards; and *Out of Left Field*, which won the 2019 Children's History Book Prize and the Ohioana Award. Her short fiction has been translated into a dozen languages and nominated for or has won multiple Hugo, Nebula, Locus, Mythopoeic, British Fantasy, and World Fantasy awards. Ellen lives in San Francisco, in a small house full of strange and wondrous things.

Author's note: I am often asked what made me want to become a fantasy writer, what my influences were growing up. There are two that stand out: Ursula K. Le Guin and chicken pox. I would not be the writer I am today were it not for one long ago vacation, when nothing went as planned.

April of 1969. I was almost nine, my brother Jack five, and baby Alice had just turned two. It was my elementary school's spring break. Dad had taken off work so our whole family could fly across the country, all the way from Ohio, to visit my mother's only brother and his family. They lived in a small town north of San Francisco, in a modern house on a hillside, overlooking a ravine.

We were supposed to stay for a week, which would have been fine, even though the house was pretty crowded with nine of us: my family, Uncle Russell, Aunt Polly, and my cousins Thom (who was seven) and Nigel (who was already in high school). Mom and Dad slept in the guest room with Alice; Jack got the bottom bunk in Thom's room. Since I was the only girl, my bed was a pullout couch in the basement rec room.

Vacation, in California! I'd imagined beaches, like *Gidget*, but when Dad drove us to the coast on Tuesday while Aunt Polly taught her college class, the ocean was gray and the wind was fierce and cold. Mom held Alice on her lap and wouldn't even get out of the car. We couldn't go swimming, and Jack started to whine, so we just got McDonald's and drove back. The rest of the week we stayed around my cousins' house.

Dinners were loud, and the table was too small for that many forks and elbows. "Well, the more the merrier," Uncle Russell said, more than once. After we ate, he and Dad would go out onto the patio and smoke cigars. The boys all watched TV, and I had to help with the dishes, just like at home.

Jack and Thom had taken over a corner of the yard, under the pine tree, making a big puddle and building houses or forts or something with sticks and clumps of grass, then knocking them down with rocks and building again. They got so muddy Aunt Polly had to use the hose on them before she'd let them back into the kitchen.

Me? I found a comfortable chair in the rec room and hid out with my Christmas present from Aunt Polly. *A Wizard of Earthsea* was the best book I'd ever read, all about a kid who can do magic and has adventures with dragons. The cover was starting to come off because I'd finished the whole book three times and read my favorite parts over and over and over.

Our plane left on Sunday, so that Saturday, the nine of us went to some winery, which was beautiful and scenic and all that, except there wasn't anything to *do*. Mom made me watch Alice while the grown-ups went inside, drinking and talking, and the three boys played tag, falling down and getting dirt and grape stains on their shirts. On the way home, Alice started crying and saying that her tummy itched.

"Oh, no," Mom said when we got back. "That looks like chicken pox." I'd had them when I was a baby, so she knew.

Sure enough. Aunt Polly called Thom's pediatrician, who was a friend of the family and lived one street away. He came over with his black doctor bag, still wearing golf pants.

"I'm afraid you're right," he said after he examined the spots on Alice's arms and stomach. "And she's contagious, won't be allowed on a plane."

"How long until she can fly home?" Dad asked.

"Ten days, maybe two weeks."

Dad said a bad word.

That evening, the grown-ups huddled in the dining room with the door closed. Some of the conversation got pretty loud, and I heard Mom say, "Frank! It's not babysitting when they're *your* kids!" After an hour, they announced that Daddy would fly back by himself, because he had to go to work. The rest of us would stay.

So there I was, in California with a Get Out of School Free card. That sounded swell. Even more on Monday morning when my cousins had to get up and go to their schools, and I got to sleep in.

The first day was okay. Alice was in bed. Mom and Aunt Polly sat in the kitchen drinking coffee and keeping Jack busy with a coloring book. I was more or less on my own. In the morning I watched cartoons and game shows on TV and ate a bologna and cheese sandwich for lunch. In the afternoon, though, TV was only soap operas, which are icky. I'd finished my book again, so I waited for Thom to get home. Even though he was a little kid, and a boy, I figured playing Candy Land with him would be better than watching imaginary people kiss.

But when Thom banged in the door at three thirty, he snatched a handful of cookies from the jar, handed some to Jack, and they both escaped into the backyard to play in their puddle fort. I followed them.

"Hey, this is a secret project!" Thom said, pointing a finger at me. "No girls allowed." He bunched his hands into fists. Jack did the same. I was bigger than both of them, and with our moms just inside the back door, I didn't think Thom would actually *hit* me, but it wasn't worth getting into trouble.

"Fine. It's just stupid mud." I went to the other side of the yard and sat on the cement wall. Lizards sometimes laid on the flat top, basking in the sun. We didn't have those in Ohio, and they were probably descended from dragons, so I wanted to examine one, up close. I waited, sitting for so long that my foot started to go to sleep, and then I saw one! I reached for it, but it was *super* fast and all I caught was the tail, which came off in my hand. The lizard ran away. The fat end of the tail had a drop of blood where it had been attached. Regular red blood, not black, like dragon blood, but still.

I felt sad and went into the kitchen. Mom started to scold me, but Aunt Polly said Nigel used to do that all the time when he was younger. Now he didn't need to catch backyard lizards because he had an iguana and a gecko and a garter snake in cages in his room. Separate cages. She said the tail would grow back, and losing it didn't harm the lizard.

"Would you prefer hunting for snails?" Aunt Polly asked. She'd been born in England and still had one of those Mary Poppins accents.

Snails?

"Not really," I said. My mother shot me one of those "behave, we're company" looks. "I mean, thank you for the idea, Aunt Polly, but—"

She smiled. "I see. Well, snails have been spoiling my garden, and I thought perhaps you might be brave enough to slay a few. Or at least banish them." She rummaged under the sink and came up with a plastic bucket. "Here. Supper's at six. I'll pay you a penny for every one of the beasts you can capture by then."

"Cool!" I went back outside, on a quest now. Turns out snails were all over the place—underneath leaves, on the wall, climbing up the wooden fence. I pulled them off, one by one, dropping them into the bucket with a wet, slimy *plop*. I did slay a couple, by accident, crushing their shells when I grabbed them too hard. I got snail gook on my hand, but I wiped it off on my pants. By the time I went to bed, I had forty-one cents, which was more than my allowance for a whole week.

Tuesday, I went out with my bucket right after breakfast. After an hour, I'd only caught four. Maybe I'd wiped out Snailville the day before, or the snail lords had sent out a warning. Either way, it was slim pickings. I kept hunting for half an hour, then went back inside.

"Good, here you are," Mom said. "Aunt Polly's making a run to the grocery, and I need to do a couple loads of laundry. We didn't pack for such a long trip." She picked up a plastic tub. "Alice is sleeping. Be a big girl and watch Jack while I'm downstairs?" I could tell it wasn't actually a question, so I helped him build a LEGO castle and made us peanut butter and jelly sandwiches. Jack won't eat bologna.

After lunch, Jack was cranky. He said his arms itched.

Sure enough, by dinner, he and Thom were both covered in spots.

"It was just a matter of time, I suppose," Aunt Polly said. "Nigel had the pox when he was seven. I know the routine, so I stocked up on ginger ale and got calamine lotion at the drugstore. We're in for a siege. Another ten days."

Great. Now every kid except me and Nigel were sick, and he wouldn't even play rummy with me. He just stayed in his room, soft thumps of rock and roll music coming out from under the closed door. So I hunted for snails—and made another eighteen cents—until it started to rain, hard. Thursday, Friday, Saturday—three days straight. I couldn't even go outside. The rec room had a shelf of Nigel's old Hardy Boys books, and I read two, but they weren't very good adventures, compared to *Earthsea*. By our second Sunday, I was *so* bored.

That afternoon, I heard Aunt Polly calling me. I was curled up behind the living room couch with my pile of pennies, being Yevaud, the Dragon of Pendor, guarding my hoard. I scooped them all back into my pockets and stuck my head up. "I'm back here."

"Hmm. I see." She sat down. "You look like a girl who could do with an adventure," she said.

I nodded. "Not more snails, though."

"Hardly. A proper outing. Tomorrow. Just us girls."

I liked that idea. I crawled out and sat next to her. "Where?"

"San Francisco. I'll show you some of my old haunts. I was sixteen when I first arrived, a war refugee. Very different times, but it's still a magical city, full of surprises." She smiled. "There are also quite a few dragons."

"Really?" My voice squeaked.

"Absolutely. In the part of the city where we're going, you'll see them everywhere."

I wasn't sure if I believed her, but almost anything would be more fun than hiding behind the couch.

The next morning, Mom insisted that I had to put on my skirt and blouse and good shoes. I didn't like that one bit, but it was the rule that you had to dress up in church clothes when you went into a city.

Aunt Polly saved me. Again.

She wore lipstick and earrings, but had on pants and a jacket. "I'm wearing slacks," she told my mom. "If the fog rolls in, it can get quite chilly. I'm afraid she'll freeze in that lovely frock."

I could see that Mom wanted to argue, but it was Aunt Polly's house, and her city, too, so she gave in with an annoyed huff. I went back down to the rec room and changed into a sweater and my favorite blue cords. The pockets sagged with all my pennies. Aunt Polly chuckled when she saw me, and swapped me dimes and nickels, which was lots better. Then we got into their station wagon and headed south.

Most places, you can't drive into magic. But I swear, we did. The road went up and down hills and curves a couple of times, then through a tunnel, and when we merged on the other side, I gasped out loud. I felt like Dorothy when she first lands in Oz and everything changes from black and white to color.

Ahead of us was the Golden Gate Bridge, which isn't actually gold.

158

It *is* orange, though, not boring gray like every bridge back home. Underneath, there was blue water, with sailboats and huge ships steaming off to faraway lands. To the right was the Pacific Ocean, which goes all the way to Japan; to the left was Alcatraz Prison, on its own island, so no one could escape. Even in the bright sunshine, it appeared both dangerous and mysterious.

At the far end of the bridge was San Francisco, steep hills with streets like straight lines leading from the water right up to the sky. White buildings and towers, more like something from a fairy tale than a place you could go to in an ordinary Chevy.

It felt less magic once we were *in* it—gas stations and stoplights and wood houses that were taller than they were wide. A few streets were flat; others climbed and twisted. Around every turn was a different view: white-capped water; the towns across the bay, where we'd come from; hillsides with Easter-colored houses stacked on top of each other, not side by side, no lawns anywhere.

Aunt Polly took us down Lombard Street, the crookedest street in the world, she said. It was brick and curled around itself like a snake, so tight that she had to drive very slowly. After that, the neighborhood changed to Italian, with signs for wine and pizza everywhere. We stopped for a light, and I stared into a shop window full of round cheeses and more kinds of noodles than I'd thought was possible. She parked the car on the third floor of a cement garage as twisty as the streets, and we rode down in a creaky metal elevator.

We stood at a crosswalk, waiting a long time for the light to change. When the sign finally said WALK, Aunt Polly reached down and held my hand, which seemed a bit babyish, but Broadway was a big, busy street with lots of cars and trucks roaring by, so I let her.

On the other side, she stopped and let go. "Hang on a tick," she said, looking at her watch. "We'll wait here. Shouldn't be more than a few minutes."

"What are we waiting for?"

"A who, not a what. No one should visit San Francisco without seeing Chinatown, but most of it is for ordinary tourists." She shook her head. "That's certainly not you. However, my friend Franny knows her way around, and she's agreed to give us the special, back-alley tour." She winked at me, which made me feel grown up and important.

"Polly!"

We both turned. A very short woman waved from the far side of a bus stop down the block. She wore a long green shirt over a pair of loose black pants. Her dark hair was blunt-cut and chin-length, like it had been styled by someone from *Thoroughly Modern Millie*. When she got closer, I could see that her face was all wrinkles, and her hands had spots like my gramma's.

"Franny!" Aunt Polly said. She sounded so happy. The two women hugged, a good, long hug, not the polite kind my mother did with her friends. Maybe they hadn't seen each other in a very long time?

"This is my niece, Ellen," she said, looping an arm around my shoulders. "She's come all the way from Ohio. Ellen, this is Franny Travers, my oldest, dearest friend."

I held out my hand, the way I'd been taught. "It's nice to meet you, Mrs. Travers."

She snorted. "There is no Mr. Travers, and never will be. Just Franny is fine."

"But—" I bit my lip, caught between two of my mother's rules. It is rude to argue with a grown-up. And it is rude to call a grown-up woman by her first name. "My mom would make me call you Aunt Franny."

"You can if you want." Franny cocked her head. "I don't mind, one way or the other. But let me point out two things before you decide. "One—" She held up an index finger. "Your mother is not here, and no one is going to tattle. And two," she said with a grin, "now that I'm a crone, I don't give a hoot for ordinary rules."

"You never have," said Aunt Polly. To me, "Franny has always been a woman of—exceptional abilities." She glanced around. "Speaking of which, where's Babs?"

"Boston. She's presenting a paper at a mathematics conference," Franny said, and looked back at me. We were almost the same height, eye to eye. "So, do you think you can bring yourself to call me Franny? Everyone else does."

I smiled, then did my best curtsey. "I would be honored."

She burst out laughing. "I like you, kid! Let's see the sights." She gestured around us with one arm. "This is Grant Avenue. The heart of Chinatown's tourist industry. We'll start here, get the lay of the land, ease our way slowly into this fascinating culture."

We started walking up the right side of the street. The sidewalk was crowded with lots and lots of people heading in both directions. It was noisy, too, with so many conversations, most of them in what Franny said were a couple different kinds of Chinese. Only once in that first block of stores did I hear words I understood. The din around me was just—sounds—kind of a mix between talking and singing, the pitch going up and down, loud and soft. It was interesting, though. I could tell when it was a question, and knew that the woman in high heels was angry, but that was about it.

I wondered if that was what it had been like when Ged first learned Old Speech, the language of dragons, because Aunt Polly was right: dragons were *every*where. Most of them were gold and red, long and skinny, like snakes with four clawed feet. No wings. Carved statues with big sharp teeth, dragons painted on the windows of stores, golden ones twined around lanterns at the tops of street signs. Shops called Jade Dragon, Silver Dragon, Lucky Dragon.

Above and below were signs in English, or in Chinese characters that meant nothing to me, and lots that were half-and-half—words I knew, but in letters pretending to be Chinese.

"I've had chop suey," I said, pointing to a tall neon sign with the half-and-half letters running from top to bottom. "The commercials say it's cooked in dragon fire." I shrugged. "That part's probably not true."

"Unlikely," Franny said. "But we *could* have lunch there, if that's a favorite food."

"It's not." I stuck out my tongue. "It's what my friend Mindy's mom made last time I slept over. It comes in two cans, with crunchy fried noodles. Those are okay, but the vegetable half is worse than cafeteria food."

Franny laughed. "It is rather awful, and not even real Chinese cuisine, just an American mish-mosh." She pointed down the street. "Let's walk a few more blocks. I know a little out-of-the-way place where we can have a true feast."

"Ooh, I've never had a feast. Except for Thanksgiving," I said.

"Then let us continue."

The sidewalk wasn't wide enough for all three of us to walk next to each other, so we took turns: two up front, one back, switching every time one of us stopped to look in a shop window, which was about every ten feet.

I had never seen so many things crowded into a single store in my whole life. There were neat shelves, like the supermarket back home, but also jumbles of paper lanterns and purses and SAN FRANCISCO souvenirs hanging from the ceiling, bamboo whistles and wooden puzzles and plastic toys stacked in trays out front, like they were fruit or candy bars. I wanted to buy something to take home with me, but there were so many piles of bright colors, my eyes didn't know where to look. I only had sixty-three cents, and before I made up my mind, I wanted to look at *everything*.

My nose was as busy as my eyes. Strange smells in all directions: incense, flowery and smoky and oddly sweet. Steam that rose up from grates in the sidewalk and basement stairways and smelled like laundry or cookies or chicken soup. An alley reeked of garbage and what I hoped was cat pee.

I stopped in front of one store, open to the street, and stared at rows of barrels full of dried sticks and baskets of twisted roots; a whole wall of glass jars that held beans and seeds and cereal, or odd shapes floating in liquid like alien pickles; dried plants hanging in bunches from pillars. I thought of the healer-witch's hut in Ged's village.

"What *is* this place? Is it magic?"

Franny thought for a moment. "Perhaps, by Western standards. Other cultures often seem mysterious or mystical to outsiders. *I* think that what we call magic is merely the wonders of nature that we don't understand yet."

"Okay—but what's all *this*?"

"A Chinese pharmacy, in essence," Aunt Polly said. "It's an entirely different system of medicine. Thousands of years old. I've found many of the remedies to be more effective than Rexall's nostrums."

I stared. Not a bottle of cough syrup or jar of Vicks anywhere. "Do you think they'd have a cure for chicken pox?"

Franny nodded. "I wouldn't be surprised. Let me ask Mr. Lim."

We stepped inside. It smelled weird, but not exactly *bad*. Like licorice and fall leaves, aspirin and dust, all mixed together with a hint of sour and something at the back of my throat that smelled the way my dad's beer tasted.

Next to me were baskets of—animals. Pale, flattened animals. A cellophane bag full of dead crickets. A dried octopus, complete with tentacles, that I could have slipped into an envelope. A withered lizard splayed on a pair of crossed sticks, like a tiny reptilian Jesus. I tucked my arms in closer to my sides.

Franny went to the counter and talked to a bald man for a few minutes, then came back to us. "Mr. Lim says that what we call chicken pox is an imbalance of wind and damp and heat. He suggested boiling honeysuckle and chrysanthemum flowers and making a strong tea."

"It would be an interesting experiment," Aunt Polly said, "but I'm not sure how my sister-in-law would feel about using her children as guinea pigs." She turned to me. "What do you think? Shall we venture into unknown territory, or continue with toast soldiers and ginger ale?"

"Toast." I took a step away from the basket of lizards. "Jack's kind of a picky eater."

We left the medicine store and continued down Grant Avenue, stopping and walking and stopping, the two women chatting about people I didn't know. We crossed one of the side streets, crammed with even more shops and awnings and sidewalk displays. For the first time, I noticed that beneath all the confusion, the bright colors and intricate ornamental signs, the buildings were old and shabby. Chipped stone and sooty bricks, third-floor windows with torn curtains, rusting metal fire escapes zigzagging across every building, above the tourist shops.

Most of the stores carried the same toys and souvenirs, so the fifth time I stopped and looked at the displays of trick matches, I decided to buy some. They'd be fun to mess around with, and I might even be able to fool my dad when he wanted to light a cigar after dinner.

One kind exploded, one made a thin black snake of ash, and the third burst into miniature fireworks, like a sparkler. All of them had bad drawings of sexy women on the front. They were only a nickel, so I bought one of each.

I caught up with the others and showed them.

Aunt Polly smiled. "Your cousin Nigel used to adore those. He'd buy a pack or two every time we came here for dinner. For his junior high school science fair, I taught him how to make his own." She sighed. "I rather regretted that for a few months."

"You can *make* these?"

"I'm a chemist, and my father was a stage magician, so I was raised on tricks of that sort. This, for example," she said, touching a finger to the exploding one, "is a mixture of sulfur, charcoal, and potassium nitrate. Re-creating it is quite simple, if a bit time-consuming."

"Wow," I said. That was so neat, having a lady scientist in the family.

Another two blocks, and we turned right onto a narrow street. Fewer people, smaller signs, no bright colors. A barbershop, an insurance company—not tourist stores. It was a long block, all uphill, as steep as the sledding meadow at home. I could feel the backs of my legs stretch with each step.

Halfway up, as we passed a playground, a couple of men in shirt-sleeves shooting baskets, Franny said, "This is it." We turned right again. Now we were in an even narrower dead-end alley, a chain-link fence on the playground side and a building the color of liver on the other. Above the door, red and gold lanterns hung on either side of a plastic sign that said HANG AH TEA ROOM.

"We're eating *here*?" It didn't look like any place for a feast. My stomach gave a tumble. "Um—my mom says Chinese restaurants are dangerous, because of opium dens and white slavery." I wasn't sure I believed her, since the only one near our house—Wing's—was in a shopping center, next to the Super Duper. But—

"Poppycock," said Franny.

Aunt Polly hugged me. "Nothing to fear. Franny and I have eaten here for ages. It may not look like much on the outside, but trust me, the food is absolutely scrumptious."

"It's been here for fifty years, the oldest dim sum restaurant in America," Franny said, holding the door open. "*Dim sum* translates to something like 'tasty tidbits.'"

"Oh. Okay." I tried to sound cool about it, because I didn't want them to think I was a wuss, but my voice shook.

"Are you feeling brave enough to try something new? It's all right if you'd rather find a sandwich shop," Aunt Polly said.

"No. I wanted an adventure." I took a deep breath and followed Franny through the door. I did *not* ask what kinds of tidbits, crossing my fingers that they wouldn't be crickets.

The inside was more like a diner than a fancy restaurant. Everyone but us was Chinese. At a table in the corner, I saw three women with hairnets sitting around a huge pile of meat, rolling pieces into little balls. They talked really fast as they wrapped each ball in a circle of pie dough.

"Table for three," Franny said. The waitress took us to a Formica table with paper placemats. She started to give us menus, but Franny raised her hand and said, "Number two tray service, please. And a pot of po-ni." She turned to me. "That's tea. Would you rather have—?"

"Do they have Cokes?"

She nodded. "Make that two teas and a bottle of Coca-Cola."

I felt relieved when the waitress came back with the familiar green glass bottle. The steam from the brown teapot smelled kind of smoky, like burning leaves in a backyard a few blocks away. Two minutes later, she was back with a cafeteria tray that held three round, squat bamboo baskets with lids.

"Ha-gow, sui-mi, bow," she said.

I had no idea what any of that meant, but Franny's whole face lit up with a smile. "Yes, all three," she said. The waitress took off the lids and set the baskets on the table.

Each of them held four—things. I'd never seen anything like them before. Two were sort of round—one big and fluffy, the other like a small squat mushroom with no stem. The third was a translucent crescent.

Aunt Polly pointed. "The big white ones are pork buns. They're one of my favorite treats." She picked one up and put it on my plate. "Go ahead, just tear it open."

I did. It felt like dense, hot Wonder Bread. A wisp of steam escaped when I pulled it apart, revealing a center of shredded meat in a reddish glaze. I took a very small bite. The bread part was *so* soft, just a little chewy, and the meat center tasted like the ribs my dad always makes for Fourth of July. Delicious. I gobbled half of it in two big bites.

Franny clapped her hands. "Score one for bow. Ready to try ha-gow?" She used chopsticks to pick up one of the crescents from the next basket. It was pale and glistening and had one crimped edge. "These are shrimp and pork dumplings. I like mine with a few drops of soy sauce. It's savory and salty." She poured a puddle of brown liquid onto her plate from a red-topped bottle, dipped one end of the crescent into it, then bit the dumpling in half.

I tried one myself. They were tasty, but not as good as the buns. The sui-mi turned out to be little meatballs inside steamed pastry, pinched all around the top. I was halfway through a second pork bun when the waitress came back with another tray of baskets.

"Lo-mein, bow, egg roll," she said.

"Egg roll and bow," Aunt Polly said. She made a face. "I'm not a big fan of lo-mein." More baskets on the table, and shallow dishes of pale yellow mustard and a clear red sauce with bits floating in it.

"That one's very hot," Franny said. "Spicy, I mean. Chili peppers. If you want to try it, start with just a drop."

Even a drop was too much for me. I drank half my Coke trying to put out the fire in my mouth. The egg rolls were crispy fried tubes full of vegetables. Mine crunched when I bit into it, and flakes fell all over the placemat.

The room had paintings on every wall, long and thin, some with trees and clouds, others with dragons. Carved golden dragons over a doorway. Dragons on the menu. "Do you think dragons are real?" I asked, when I'd finished my egg roll.

They looked at each other. Finally, Aunt Polly said, "Well, nearly every culture has a dragon myth or legend. There are too many stories— all over the world—to dismiss the idea entirely."

"On the other hand—" She paused, thinking, and poured another cup of the smoky tea. "—there isn't any archaeological or paleontological evidence to support their existence."

"Huh?"

"Sorry. Professor speak. I mean, no one has ever found dragon bones," she explained.

"But they *have* found dinosaur bones," I said. "Couldn't some of those have actually been from dragons?"

Aunt Polly nodded. "I suppose it's not impossible. As new evidence is discovered, scientists have to adjust their theories. Sometimes that means relabeling fossils. The brontosaurus, for example."

"I must point out that no one has ever proved that dragons did *not* exist," Franny said. "Science and myth may well be describing similar phenomena."

"It's difficult to prove a negative," Aunt Polly said.

I got the feeling they'd had conversations like this before. I was fascinated. Grown-ups *never* take dragons seriously.

"So," I said slowly, "what if dragons were real once, but now they aren't around anymore? Like dinosaurs." I thought for a minute. In the part of Earthsea where Ged lived, there hadn't been dragons for hundreds of years, but everyone still told tales and sang songs about them. "It is one thing to read about dragons, and another to meet them," I said.

"Exactly! Absence of evidence is not evidence of absence." Franny beamed at me. "That was very well put."

"Thanks, but I didn't make it up." I felt my face turning red. "It's from the book Aunt Polly gave me for Christmas. *A Wizard of Earthsea*."

"I'm so glad you liked it!" Aunt Polly patted my hand. "Franny's the one who recommended it."

"I've known Ursula since she was about your age. My partner, Babs, and I were old friends with her parents, the Kroebers, through the university."

"You know a real writer?" I was impressed.

"Many. Writers, artists, scientists. I find that the best companions are people with a spark of curiosity," Franny said.

The waitress came around with another tray. "Sui-mi, chicken feet, pot-sticker."

"Oh. Pot-stickers," Aunt Polly said. I waited, holding my breath, afraid we were going to have to try chicken feet, but the waitress just put one basket on the table. *Whew.*

I would eat pot-stickers again, anytime, anywhere. They were bigger crescents, crispy brown on one side—like a grilled cheese sandwich—and soft-chewy dough on the other, with pork and green onions on the inside. They came with a bottle of white vinegar, which was pretty tasty when you mixed it with soy sauce. Sour and salty at the same time. I got a second Coke.

Franny waved away the next two trays while we nibbled at everything already on the table, stacking baskets on top of each other when they were empty. By the time we stacked the last one, I was full. Almost too full, but everything was *so* good my mouth didn't want to stop. Tasty tidbits, for sure.

When the waitress came by again, Franny said, "Egg tarts, and then I think we're done, yes?"

"And sesame balls," Aunt Polly said. "Sesame brings good luck." She and Franny smiled at each other in a way that made me think it wasn't the first time they'd said *that*, either.

The tarts were a little bigger than a silver dollar, with warm custard and flaky, flaky piecrust. One or two bites and gone. The sesame balls were completely round, like giant seed-studded gumballs, dense and chewy, with a sweet, thick paste on the inside. Franny said it was made out of red beans, which I thought was a weird ingredient for a dessert.

"That really *was* a feast," I said when nothing was left on my plate but colorful smears of sauces and some errant flakes of pastry. I crumpled up my paper napkin and tried not to burp. "And an adventure."

"Brilliant!" Aunt Polly said. "I'm so glad we could salvage a bit of your holiday."

Franny signaled for the bill.

"What's the damage?" Aunt Polly reached for her purse.

Franny shook her head. "Don't be silly. My treat."

I wondered if she was rich. All that food? It *had* to be expensive. But when the waitress gave her the piece of paper, Franny just chuckled. "This whole lunch was seven dollars, with tip. I think I can manage that."

After lunch we walked back out to the barbershop street and climbed the rest of the way up the hill to Stockton Street. It was as wide as Broadway, full of delivery trucks and cars whizzing by in both directions. Franny gestured to the left, at the mouth of a big stone tunnel. "If you walk through there, you'll come out smack in the middle of downtown. Banks, department stores, businessmen in suits and ties. Like traveling from one world into another in the space of a few blocks."

I liked that idea, too. In Ohio, you could drive for miles and miles without anything changing at all.

Stockton Street was different from the tourist part. Markets crowded with people, open to the sidewalk, fruits and vegetables on display. Labels were in Chinese, prices in numbers. Piles of leafy greens that were almost celery or spinach, but not quite. I recognized lemons and oranges, but there was no other Ohio produce. Franny showed me sticks of sugar cane and reddish-yellow mangoes, bright pink dragon fruit and lumpy bitter melon, and a heavy spiked globe called a durian that looked like a land mine.

We passed two bakeries, each with lines out the door, windows steamed up. A quick glimpse inside: pork buns and custard tarts and piles of other dim sum and desserts, baked or steamed or fried. The smell made my mouth water.

The next shop over almost made me hold my nose. White tiled walls and linoleum floors. Dead fish lying on ice-covered steel tabletops. Live fish swimming in a tank. Crabs and lobsters scuttling around in another, waving their claws and antennas. I stood on the sidewalk, looking in the window. The fish seemed to be looking back with flat, cloudy eyes. "What's *that*?" I pointed to the far end of the ice, at a gray animal the size and shape of a football, its skin pebbled and scaly.

Aunt Polly peered over my shoulder. After a minute, she said, "I believe that is an armadillo. It must be imported. Texas or Louisiana. They're not native to California."

"People *eat* them?"

"They're considered a delicacy in many parts of the world," Franny said. "I've been told they taste like high-end pork, but I have no personal experience."

A small grocery store with shelves of foreign cans and boxes and cellophane bags in orderly aisles. A takeout restaurant with trays of noodles and meat and vegetables, roasted ducks hanging from steel hooks in the window, shiny and glazed, their bills drooped to one side. Next to them, great slabs of pork, reddish and dripping. Smells drifted out, tangy barbecue and fried grease.

Then another tiled fish market, men in aprons and white paper hats chopping a huge tuna into smaller parts with cleavers, throwing the guts into a white bucket on the floor. Halfway out on the sidewalk was a laundry tub with six inches of water and maybe fifteen huge green bullfrogs crawling over each other. I'd caught bullfrogs in a pond back home, but I had let them go again. I wanted to rescue all of these, save them from being someone's dinner; the sign above the tub said 34¢/LB. I'd never had that much money in my life.

Another bakery, some offices, a big building with pillars and stone steps. We were almost back to Broadway and the parking garage when I stopped so suddenly that Aunt Polly bumped into me.

"What is it?" she asked.

I pointed to a white shelf, just inside the doorway of a third fish market. On it sat a glass-walled tank with half a dozen lizards, each twice as long as my hand. Three of them seemed to be larger versions of the brown ones in Aunt Polly's backyard. Another was yellow, with big red eyes and flat, fat-toed feet. But tucked in a corner was a silvery gray one covered with rough, spiky scales, like a horned toad, only long and slender. It had a jagged tail that curled all the way around its body.

It looked exactly how I'd imagined the small dragons in Earthsea, the kind Ged's friend's sister had. They don't grow any bigger. "A *harrekki*," I said, touching one finger to the cool surface of the glass.

The sign taped above the tank said 48¢/LB.

I fingered the coins in my pocket. After buying the trick matches, I had forty-eight cents left. If it weighed less than a pound, I *could* rescue this one.

"I want that one," I told Aunt Polly. "I want a dragon for my souvenir."

"Oh. Well. I'm not sure that your mother will—" Aunt Polly started to say.

Franny held up a hand. "I think that's splendid. Every girl should have a dragon."

Silence for a minute. Then Aunt Polly said slowly, "Hmm. Nigel *does* have iguana food. Perhaps he can rummage up another enclosure as well. We could check the basement."

It took a few minutes to explain to the fish-market man what we wanted, and longer to convince him that we did *not* want it skinned and cut up and wrapped in butcher paper.

"I prefer to prepare my own," Franny said. The man shook his head—for the third or fourth time. Then she said something very stern in Chinese and waggled a finger at him. After a moment, he nodded, almost a bow, and went off into a back room.

"I didn't realize you spoke Chinese," Aunt Polly said.

"Forty years of business dealings, you pick up a word or two. And a bit of nuance." Franny said. "I told him, 'You respect grandmother kitchen.'"

The man returned with a small cardboard box. He reached into the glass case with a net, scooped up my silvery purchase, and plunked her inside.

"Let me see," Franny said. She reached a hand into the box, murmuring strange syllables I didn't understand.

"Is that Chinese, too?"

"No, dear."

"Is it Old Speech? The language of dragons?"

She looked surprised. "Something like that." She whispered for another minute, then removed her hand and deftly tucked the flaps around each other to close the top of the box. "There. That ought to do it."

The fish-market man put the box on a hanging scale. Fourteen ounces, including the cardboard. "Forty-two cents," he said.

I handed him four dimes and two pennies.

Only a block back to the car. I carried the box with both hands, as if it were the crown jewels. At the door to the parking garage, we all stopped.

"I'm so glad you called," Franny said to Aunt Polly, giving her a hug. "It's been far too long since we had a proper excursion. But now I believe I'll head home and give my old bones a rest."

"Are you going to—?" Aunt Polly made a folding motion with her fingers that made no sense to me.

Franny seemed to know what she meant.

"No, I'm tired. I'll just hail a cab." She turned to me and rested a hand on my shoulder. "It was a delight meeting you, Ellen. Did you have a good time?"

"This was—it was—the best day of my whole entire life," I said.

"Excellent!" She smiled so big her whole face pleated. "Then you'll come back and visit again?"

"You bet. When I'm a grown-up, I'm going to *live* here."

"I hope you do." She gave my shoulder a squeeze and a pat, stepped back onto the sidewalk, and raised her arm to flag a passing taxi.

Late afternoon. The sun was low over the water, and all the light in the world seemed magic. I sat on the wide front seat of the Chevy, next to my favorite aunt, who was humming to herself. I held the box steady in my lap, my right hand bracing it against my shirt when the car jostled over uneven pavement. On the approach to the Golden Gate Bridge, I untucked one of the flaps with my other hand, just enough to get a finger through, and gently stroked her scaly back.

"Until I learn your true name, what should I call you?" I whispered. "Puff, after the song? Hang Ah? Dim Sum? Silver? Pox?"

As I said the last name aloud, I heard a sound from inside the box, like a tiny, growly burp.

I laughed. "Okay, then. Pox it is. Pox the magic dragon."

Another burp-growl.

The scenery out the window was so beautiful—ocean waves breaking against a sheer rock coast, tendrils of fog sliding down a green hillside as if someone were pouring whipped cream very slowly—that it took my attention away for a minute. Then I noticed a spot on my right palm had started to itch. No, not itching—hot!

I pulled my hand away from the cardboard and leaned over to take a look. Near the bottom of the box was a charred black circle as big around as the tip of one of Dad's cigars, edges curling, rimmed with a thread-thin, neon-bright orange and yellow light. I moved my hand farther away as the edges flickered and the hole grew a little bigger.

"Do you smell something burning?" Aunt Polly asked.

"May—be," I replied, thinking fast. "Have you had the brakes checked? That's the first thing my dad says, when he smells something in the car. And the streets *are* very steep around here." I was talking a lot so she might not notice I was also cranking open the triangular side window.

"I shall ask your uncle at dinner. You're a very resourceful girl."

"I'm learning." I turned the box around, so the hole was facing the window, and tickled my dragon one more time, grinning as a tiny wisp of her yellow smoke drifted out over San Francisco Bay.

THE NINE CURVES RIVER

R. F. Kuang

R. F. Kuang (rfkuang.com) is the Nebula, Locus, and John W. Campbell Award—nominated author of *The Poppy War* and its sequel, *The Dragon Republic*. She is currently pursuing an MSc in Contemporary Chinese Studies at the University of Oxford on a Marshall Scholarship. Her debut novel, *The Poppy War*, was listed by *Times*, Amazon, Goodreads, and the *Guardian* as one of the best books of 2018 and has won the Crawford Award and Compton Crook Award for Best First Novel.

We reach Arlong on the fourth day of the Lunar New Year. In Dragon Province, we celebrate the new year over fifteen days. On the third day, families come home to reunite. On the fourth day, we welcome back the gods.

You've never been to Arlong before. The farthest you've wandered from our home on Ao Island is the local water market over the canal intersection that links together the archipelago where we live. You've never come with me and Baba to Arlong, the provincial capital, on our yearly trips to trade bone carvings and dried salted mayau for silks, knives, and new wire for hooks. Mama and Baba have never let you. They've always wanted to keep you safe from the capital. Ao Island is a tiny and familiar domain, but Arlong is a rich, greedy, dense, and devouring city. If you're not careful, a creature as tiny and pretty as you would vanish into the crowd in seconds.

If Mama and Baba could have had their way, you would never have stepped foot off Ao Island. But even they couldn't stop the coming of this day.

We make the two-hour trip over clear, blue waves in a private, rented sampan. This is a luxury that under any other circumstance would cost three silvers an hour. Father and I usually paddle our own canoe down the coastline to Arlong every autumn. But today is special. Neither of us will lift a finger to labor. Instead, we will sit back, sucking on dried sugarcane sticks while the boatman warbles river songs in a loud, oscillating tone that makes you laugh.

We've been giggling at his songs for the past hour, requesting repeats of our favorites and learning the lyrics to the dirtier ones, but you fall silent when Arlong appears on the horizon. The boatman, reading your expression, stops singing. For a long moment, the three of us merely stare as we approach the Floating City, the sprawling network of canals that link lush, green islands together like emeralds inlaid in sapphire. You've never seen this many boats and shanties wedged together in one place. You've never seen these lily pads thick and wide as frying woks; firm enough for a small child to stand on without sinking.

"Come." I reach for your hand and tug you gently toward the shore. You're still staring in wonder, eyes darting frantically around as if you don't know where to look next. "There's so much more to see."

We must reach Arlong's opposite coast by dark, but the sun is still high in the sky and we have many hours yet. We have time to travel on foot. We step cautiously along the rickety walkways—Arlong's narrow wooden bridges are notoriously unreliable, and on a day like today, when all ten thousand of its residents are outside cramming the streets on foot or bumping their boats against the buoy posts, a single false step could send us tumbling into the chilly water.

Oh, I know. *You* don't need to be careful. You could dance across the canals if you wanted to, jumping nimbly from boat to crate to peg. I've seen you navigate the docks at home like a dragonfly skimming the surface of a pond. But slow down, sister. We are not all so gifted.

Relax. You have time to savor this. Take a look around you; drink in the festivities. Most days, Arlong is a drab, busy market center, all commerce and efficiency, but during Lunar New Year, it explodes with color. Red and gold banners, streamers, and firecracker confetti hang suspended in the air, buoyed up by a gentle wind that has decided, just for today, to arrest gravity just so. Merchants line every inch of the narrow walkways gilding the canals, hawking sizzling red bean cakes, fragrant dough buns, caramelized taro cubes, tea eggs, sticky rice dumplings wrapped in bamboo leaves, and rows and rows of tanghulu skewers.

These immediately catch your eye.

"Is that sugar?" you ask. "Are they—are they *covered* in sugar?"

The tanghulu are dripping with so much sugar my teeth ache to look. I've tried the sweet, sticky mountain hawthorns just once. Baba bought me a skewer when I was ten, and I've never forgotten the taste. "Of course."

"Can I have one?"

Why do you even ask? You know that today you can have anything you want.

I reach into my pocket for my money pouch. "How many?"

"Just one skewer," you say primly, and I don't know whether to laugh or cry. Such a good child. Such precocious restraint, even today.

I purchase two skewers. You protest, but I press the sticks into your palm until you stop trying to pass them back.

"I can't eat that many."

"Then hold on to it for later," I say without thinking. I clamp my jaw shut, but the last word lingers in my throat like the taste of bitter melon. *Later.* But there is no later; that is the entire point.

You pretend not to notice.

It has not rained in Arlong for two months.

The city officials have done their best to conceal this. Lunar New Year must always be properly feted, drought or no drought. The yellowing grass has been cleverly concealed with blankets, tents, and scattered flower petals that must have been shipped in from the mainland at great expense. Fresh, juicy, imported fruits are still on display at every corner, though the prices are triple what I've seen before.

Mainlanders find it strange to think that drought could be a problem in a place surrounded by blue ocean. But salt water can't sate humans or nourish crops. Without rain, the beaches grow hard and splinter like tea eggs steeped for too long. I can tell this drought is serious; the canals are far shallower than they used to be, and in some stretches it's obvious that the boats' bottoms are scraping along the riverbed. But you've never been to Arlong before, and you have no basis for comparison. I glance down at your wide, delighted eyes, and I can tell this city is the loveliest thing you've ever seen.

It's not long before the whispering starts. A pair of old women, walking down the bridge toward us, notice your golden anklets and bracelets and immediately start to chatter. They conceal their whispers behind cupped hands, but they make no effort to avert their stares. I want to slap them as they pass.

In mere minutes, it seems, the entire city has found out you've arrived. Everyone stops and turns their heads, eyes following you as you pass. I'm scared to stop walking, but within an hour we're both starving, and when we pass a cart of fried, flaky lotus seed cakes sizzling in oil, we can't help but stop. The hawker, upon seeing you, stuffs a bag with far more cakes than we could possibly eat but refuses to take our silver. I leave a few coins on his cart, but he runs after us. He won't leave us alone until I let him return the coins to my palm.

"Please," he says. He smells like sugar. His eyes look wet and red around the rims. "It's the least I can do."

A small crowd has gathered around us to watch. I suddenly feel sweaty. I don't know what to do. Father instructed me not to seek special treatment, afraid that the crowds might think we were exploiting our position. Baffled, I glance at you.

"Thank you," you tell the hawker, and keep walking.

I stuff my money pouch back in my pocket and follow.

The crowd stays with us and grows as we make our way through the canals. You don't seem to mind. You're good at deflecting attention; you, who are so used to receiving it. You stare straight ahead as we walk, never baiting your audience, never giving your onlookers reason to jeer. You hold your back straight, chin forward, your expression pleasant and placid as if you haven't noticed the crowd at all.

When someone shouts to ask if you're scared—where did that voice come from? Who was it? I'll kill them—you only blink, smile, and shake your head.

"Have one, jiejie." You pass me a lotus seed cake. "They're still warm."

You were never an ordinary child.

Everyone on Ao Island knew you were special from the day you were born. You came out perfectly silent with a full head of thick black hair, breathing evenly, your lovely dark eyes roving disdainfully around the room as if you were disappointed in everyone else for making such a fuss. The midwife wouldn't accept her full payment because you'd given her so little to do.

You were a slender and graceful toddler, and you only became more achingly elegant as you grew, limbs light and delicate as a bird's.

The rest of us have sun-browned skin the shade of coconuts, but yours gleams pale like porcelain, like moonlight. By the time you were three, your hair had grown down to your waist, and it stayed that way because Mama couldn't bear to snip those thick, silky locks that braided so easily and never frizzed after it rained, like mine.

By the time you were ten, you were praised as the beauty of the village. Yet you never grew spoiled or proud. We never had to remind you to be humble. You possessed myriad virtues, and humility was one of them. You accepted our praise with grave gratitude, reacting no more than a mountain might to being called grand.

"She's going to break hearts someday," said all our neighbors, and our parents agreed.

Not only were you beautiful; you were astonishingly clever. You could recite Tang classics after hearing them only once. You could calculate sums faster than any of us before you turned nine. Mama and Baba hired a tutor to teach you classics and advanced arithmetic, subjects meant for young men attempting to become government officials, an expense that was never spared for me. When you excelled even at that, our parents began suggesting you might try to test into a university on the mainland, even though half of them still don't accept women.

She'll marry a prince. She'll become the first woman court scholar. She'll make our island famous. Everyone loved to fantasize about what you might do and become because the possibilities seemed so endless.

But you never spoke about your future at all.

"Jiejie?"

"Yes."

"What do you think the Dragon is like?"

I can't suppress a flinch.

You know the story of the dragon and the fisherman. You've heard infinite variations of it throughout your short life, from our parents, aunts, uncles, friends, and teachers. Everyone tells it differently, because everyone wants to believe something different.

There are only three constants. A dragon. A grotto. A fisherman.

You heard Baba's version this morning before we left in our sampan. Once upon a time, there was a village dying of drought. The ground shriveled and cracked. The birds flew away and left the forests silent. The grain stores dwindled and disappeared. Facing imminent starvation, the villagers sent their priests to the Dragon Lord who ruled the waters from the grotto in the Nine Curves River and begged him for rain. They offered the Dragon many things—jade statuettes, piles of silver, intricately painted wall scrolls, flocks of chickens and herds of goats. All the valuables the village possessed. The Dragon was not satisfied. Desperate, the priests asked the Dragon to name his price.

"I am hungry," said the Dragon.

"We will prepare you a great feast," said the priests. "All our finest delicacies—"

"I am not hungry for animal flesh," said the Dragon. "I crave a rarer meat. If you want rain, you will provide it."

The priests stared at the Dragon in horror. "We cannot force our own to do this."

"Then don't," said the Dragon. "My meal must come willingly. Fear spoils the taste. I will only accept a volunteer."

The priests, after hours of squabbling, could not decide who should sacrifice their lives for the village. They drew lots, but the loser refused to go, claiming he was too old, that his flesh would be too dry and chewy. At last, an old fisherman, who had ferried the priests to the Dragon's grotto and back, interrupted them and volunteered to go in their stead.

"I die, or my daughters die," he said, when the priests expressed their amazement. "It is that simple."

So the village was saved.

The priests told you a different version. Once upon a time, on a dying island, the starving village priests visited the Dragon Lord, who had until now blessed them with heavy rains, and asked him what was wrong.

"I grow weak," said the Dragon. "I am old. My spirit withers, and I cannot rule this grotto any longer. One of you must take my place. You will have power over the rains, rivers, and oceans. But you must stay in this grotto, which is the source of my power. You may never leave."

In this version, too, the fisherman volunteers, even though he has two young daughters whom he will miss dearly. A year after he enters the grotto, his wife brings their daughters to the cave to visit him. But by then the fisherman's hair has receded; his teeth have lengthened and sharpened, and his skin has turned to glittering blue scales. The girls scream and run away at first sight. They never visit their father again.

The priests told you this version, I think, because they think it is kinder. I hate it.

I think for a long while, and then I tell you my version.

"I think the Dragon is lonely. I think he wants a friend. He does so much for us: warding away hurricanes, bringing us rain, calming the oceans. He deserves a companion."

You mull this for a moment. "So he doesn't eat the tributes?"

"Why would he? Down in the ocean, with all those fish and turtles and shrimp to catch? The Dragon can have shark fin soup whenever he wants. Why on earth would you want to eat *humans*?" I pinch your shoulder. "Who in their right mind would want to eat you, skinny?"

That makes you giggle. I exhale, relieved, and feel like I've finally done something right.

I'm talking out of my ass. None of us knows what happens in that grotto. You know that. None of us will never know which version is true, and by the time you find out, it will be too late.

I like to see you laugh. We haven't laughed together like this—like sisters—in a long time. We have not been friends for a long time. I was afraid this would be a day of forced and fake levity, but walking hand in hand through Arlong with you feels so natural. We've fallen comfortably into our old patterns, and it would be so easy to pretend that the past few years had never happened.

But today we must be honest.

I was jealous of you. I have never admitted this to you before. I didn't want to say it out loud because it would affirm all the reasons I was jealous to begin with. But yes—I was jealous, I was cruel, and I was ashamed. I am still ashamed.

I always knew I wasn't pretty. Mother never ran her hands through my hair and sighed at its thickness. She never braided it in twisting, intricate patterns the way she did yours. No one ever commented on the elegant slope of my nose, or the arched shape of my eyes. I never lingered in front of a mirror, admiring the shape of my face, the way everyone else admired yours.

It didn't used to bother me. On our island, where the myriad schools of colorful fish in the shallows were far more attractive and more exciting than the boys, my looks hardly mattered. I was strong and I was quick. I could fish and run and shimmy up palm trees just as well as anyone else, and it didn't matter that fish clustered self-sacrificially around your ankles when you waded into the water with a net, or that trees dropped their ripest fruit as if by command when you touched their trunks.

Then when I was thirteen and you were nine, the city matchmaker stopped by our home on her annual visit, because by then I was at last old enough for her opinion to matter. She examined my face for all of two seconds before she shook her head and sighed.

"Pity how the looks always go to the younger sister," she said.

Our parents had no response to that. I think they were shocked, and likely nervous in her presence. But they didn't deny it. Of course they agreed with the matchmaker—it would be so silly to protest, *no, both our daughters are beautiful, don't be absurd*—when the shining evidence of your beauty was right there in front of us.

That was the first time I saw, truly, how brightly your star shone over mine. This was even before the priests came. Oh, gods, it became ten times worse after the priests came and started telling everyone you were chosen by the gods and blessed from the day you were born. Not truly human but a faerie sent down from the heavens. Special.

All of that came later. But I started to hate you the day the matchmaker came. It didn't matter how kind, how humble, or how loving you were. All your graciousness only made the gap between us harder to bear. You could afford to be kind, because you were so secure in your superiority.

I interpreted your kindness as snobbery. And the day the matchmaker came was the first time I wished you were dead.

You're too young.

My gods. You're far too young. You haven't even begun to live your life. You've only ever seen the sands of our little island. You've never been to the mainland; never visited the great universities we all thought you might enter one day.

How could they make you throw all that away?

The sun sinks lower over the Daba Mountains, and Arlong's canals reflect burnt gold now instead of bright, searing yellow. Our time is drawing to an end. I know I should cherish these final moments with you and kiss you and hug you, but all I can think is that *you're too young, it's not fair,* and that makes me want to scream, to overturn this sampan, to jump into the river with you bound in my arms, because even if we go to the same watery fate, at least *he* will not have *you*—

No, meimei, I'm all right. I'm just tired. It's been such a long day. Please don't worry about me.

Thank you. I would love some tanghulu.

By the time we reach the grottoes of the Nine Curves River, a crowd—the entire city, it appears—has assembled by the shore. They watch you pass with varying expressions: some cold and expectant, as if wondering what has taken you so long; some with hands clamped over their mouths, eyes wide with horror. Some are weeping. Some of them cry out to you how brave you are, and how sorry they are.

I want to hit them. If they're sorry, then why don't they walk into that grotto themselves? Why are they letting this happen? Why won't anyone try to stop this?

I know why.

Year after year, the people of our archipelago have experimented with this ritual, enough times now that we know its effects even if we will never understand its cause. We know that it rains in the years that we send a sacrifice. We know there is drought in the years that we don't.

We still don't know what happens to the Dragon's tributes. We don't know if they live or die—no one has ever returned from the grotto, and their bones have never washed up on shore. Perhaps the Dragon devours them whole. Or, for all we know, perhaps the tributes step into that cave and vanish into another world entirely.

This is no consolation to the families. This uncertainty will do nothing to assuage our parents' pain. But they are two people, and their opinions mean nothing stacked against the weight of Arlong's. Arlong's citizens have chosen to sentence my sister to death.

Who can blame them?

Droughts are horrible things. Droughts mean withered fields, empty granaries, and stomachs bloated from being stuffed with cotton, goose down, and tree bark. Droughts mean shriveled carcasses littered along the canals with no one left alive to tie rocks around their ankles and roll them into the sea. Droughts are a thousand times worse than the quick, brutal death of one little girl.

No matter how sorry the crowd at the shore professes to be, no one will lift a finger to help you today. I know this. Because I know, better than anyone, how selfish a person can be.

I began to torture you first with my indifference.

You see, when I began to hate you, I wanted to hurt you, and it seemed the easiest way to do that was to ignore you.

The day after the matchmaker left, you asked to come with me when I went out to check my bird traps in the forest, and I said no.

"You'll get in the way," I said. I'd never said that to you before, and we both knew it was a lie; you were nimbler with those traps than anyone. But I said it anyway. "You're always following me around. Can't you leave me alone?"

It startled me how quickly tears sprang to your eyes. I hadn't expected this degree of devastation. For a moment, I was stricken. Then I felt this thick, squirming tendril of delight—delight that you cared what I thought of you *this* much. That I, your jiejie, still wielded this much power over you.

So I began to routinely ignore and exclude you. Jiejie, do you want to fly paper kites with me? No. Jiejie, will you go climbing for coconuts with me? No. Finally you learned to stop asking, but I knew that time hadn't dulled the pain. You didn't have other friends on the island—either you scared the other girls your age, or they scared you. I was all you had and I refused to be that anymore.

But it wasn't enough just to hurt you, because everyone else still loved you. Whenever you cried, someone was always there to pick you up and wipe your tears away and tell you how special and wonderful you were. Hush, hush, don't cry, you little pearl of a girl. You are so lovely. What do you have to cry about?

I thought if I could just convince the rest of the island that you weren't as wonderful as everyone thought, then that would finally make us equal.

That's why I told all those boys that you were a white snake.

We'd grown up hearing stories about magical white snakes—beautiful women who were actually powerful serpent demons in disguise, who used their hundreds of years of magical training to assume human forms and trick foolish men into falling desperately in love with them. On the mainland, white snake stories are love stories. Their new husbands inevitably discover their true form, but pledge their everlasting love regardless. Love triumphs over original nature. The white snakes are not predators; they just want to know the touch of human love.

But on our island, white snake stories are about deception. The wily white snake seduces and manipulates. She blinds everyone to her true nature—poisonous, foul, and disgusting. When the priests discover

188

what she is, they drug her drink to make her lose her human glamour, and then they lop off her head.

This, I told the boys, was the source of your beauty. Why your skin shone white instead of coconut brown. Why you always wore such a mysterious, enticing smile. Why you could predict, days beforehand, when rain was going to come; why you could tell us that Auntie Yeo's eldest son had been injured climbing trees hours before anyone discovered him.

"I've seen her return to her true form," I told them. "She can't maintain her human disguise all the time. It's exhausting; she has to rest. When she thinks no one is looking, she takes off all her clothes and shrinks into a slimy little coil." I weaved my fingers through the air for effect. "That's how she sleeps."

Of course I had never seen any such thing. But the words tasted nasty and delicious on my tongue. They let me speak the truth, through metaphor, about how much I envied and detested your gifts that could not possibly be natural, because if they were unnatural like myth implied, then that meant they were not gifts at all but demonic trickery.

I didn't think the boys would actually believe me.

I didn't think they would go so far.

The boys were rowdy creatures we'd known since infancy. We'd grown up together. We'd played and fished and climbed together. We'd gone swimming naked in the ocean together without so much as a blush, because back then our bodies were just sexless, neutral shapes. The boys were loud and energetic; perhaps too easily excitable, too quick to break out into fistfights, but they had never once harmed us. They were good boys.

I thought they might laugh at my story.

I thought they might jeer and tease you the next time they saw you. At the very least, I thought they might stop adoring you.

Please believe me, sister. I never thought they would hurt you.

"Is it time already?" you ask.

The crowds have grown quiet. Expectant.

I look up at the darkening sky. The sun bleeds crimson through pink clouds, but it hasn't yet started to skim the horizon.

"We have a few minutes still," I say.

"Good," you say. You stand with your eyes closed. I don't know what you're thinking about, and I don't ask. I reach tentatively for your shoulder, then draw my hand back, uncertain. I want to comfort you—this is my duty, the entire reason Baba and Mama sent me here with you—but I don't know how. I have no idea what I could possibly say to make this easier. And I can't comfort you through gestures; I can't be the strong big sister pulling you into my chest. I've long relinquished all claim to that position.

"I'm not scared." You answer my question for me. You don't sound scared. You sound so unearthly calm. You smile up at me and squeeze my hand. "I'm just remembering."

On our island, there live deadly snakes, thin as an index finger and long as an adult's forearm. They hide in used firepits and bushes at the edge of the forest. They are rare but deadly. A single bite makes their victims swell grotesquely, each limb puffed up like an overripe red and green mottled mango. We're taught as little children how to recognize their vibrant patterning like alarm bells—rich red and yellow with black stripes. When our parents find their nests, they clear them out using two remedies—smoke, to choke them out into the open where we stand waiting with shovels to chop off their heads, and sharp white vinegar to pour in circles on the ground, which sears their bellies when they try to slither away.

I wasn't there when the boys attacked you. That is the single, thin veneer of deniability that I've hid behind. I didn't know they were coming. I didn't tell them to do it.

And I still don't know precisely what happened. None of us do. You wouldn't tell us anything when you came home smelling acrid and sour with your clothes torn, burned and singed just like your hair. Your pale skin was crisscrossed with a hundred tiny inflamed lacerations. Tear tracks carved through the soot on your face, but you'd long stopped cry-ing. You wouldn't speak at all. Baba begged you a thousand times to tell him who'd done this to you, but you kept your trembling, wide-eyed silence.

Only I knew. Smoke and vinegar. We all knew that was how you killed snakes. The boys' logic was so plainly clear.

But I said nothing. I was afraid if I betrayed the boys, then they might betray me.

That night the priest visited our home for the last time. By then Mama had wiped the soot from your face and wrapped you in a silk robe to conceal your still-bleeding scars. But the priests didn't seem to notice. They'd come regarding a different matter.

They said the oracle bones had spoken. Your year had come.

"What does that mean?" our mother asked.

The head priest looked her very calmly in the eyes and said, "It means the Dragon is lonely."

And then our mother screamed.

At last the sun is about to set. Its dying, burnished glow twinkles in the shallow waves around our ankles like molten gold.

Our parents aren't here with you. Mama would have come in your stead if they had let her. Baba would have torn the priests apart with his bare hands for you, if he'd thought that would make a modicum of difference. But this they cannot watch. After you told the priests you would go willingly as a volunteer, there was nothing more they could do. They couldn't have locked you up; they would never do that to you. They respected your choice. They said their good-byes on the island. But they didn't want you to be alone in these last moments, so they sent me.

Why had they so quickly assumed I would be better able to bear it? Was it because they knew, or suspected, that I didn't love you as much?

I don't know what to say. I have been swallowing my grief all day;

I've wanted to maintain the illusion as long as I could that we were just here for the festival. But now the moment has come, and my words congeal in my throat like dry rice balls.

You don't wait for me to find my voice. The light is fading fast now, and you need to go quickly, while you might still bring a little light to arm you. You take two steps toward the grotto, then glance back over your shoulder. "You've been a good sister. The very best."

Then you smile, and I want to weep.

"I'm sorry." It's not enough. It's not what you deserve. But I'll never be able to give you what you deserve. It's too late for that. "Meimei, I'm . . ."

You don't turn around.

"Remember," I call out as you wade farther into the grotto, the waves rocking gently against your chest. "All the myths are wrong."

I don't know what will happen to you in that grotto.

I know what they say happens. I know what our mother is imagining now in her grief: the rapid shredding of your lifeless body, ripped apart by fangs as long as you are tall. But somehow I find this act of savagery ridiculous; impossible under this quiet, moonlit night. The Dragon gives and protects life; he brings us rain, and he keeps our islands safe. He is ultimately benevolent, not some rabid monster.

An old fisherman I met at the local market told me a lovely story once. He said he heard it from a bird who heard it from a rainbow-scaled fish that swam north from the Nine Curves River.

He said the grotto leads to a beautiful palace. He said the Dragon is kind to his tributes and treats them well; he teaches them magic and trains them to swim underwater without ever needing to come up for air. He dazzles them with treasures that we above water can only dream of, and that is why they never come back. Their new world is so beautiful, they never want to leave.

Whose fault is it that our monsters are lonely? The white snake became a human because she craved the touch of warm, loving flesh.

The Dragon begs for a new companion every year because he grows lonely in the grotto, the site of his power and his prison.

Our monsters are lonely, and they cannot be blamed that their kisses are poison or that they drown with their embrace. I suspect this is because they don't know how to love, and we never taught them—they ventured bravely into our world and we responded with fire, lye, vinegar, and spears. We take your gifts but still we will cast you out, because you terrify us. You cannot help the way you were made. We cannot help the way we were made. We demand and take everything from you and attribute our ingratitude to fear. We don't know another way.

The sun has disappeared now, and I can only barely glimpse your pale neck and ears protruding over the water.

It has not rained in Arlong in over two months. And if there is any justice in the world, it will not rain for a very long time.

LUCKY'S DRAGON

Kelly Barnhill

Kelly Barnhill (kellybarnhill.com) is the author of the New-bery Medal–winning novel *The Girl Who Drank the Moon* and the World Fantasy Award–winning novella *The Unlicensed Magician*, as well as other novels and short stories. She is the recipient of fellowships from the McKnight Foundation, the Jerome Foundation, the Minnesota State Arts Board, and the Loft Literary Center. Her most recent book is a collection of short stories, *Dreadful Young Ladies and Other Stories*.

Just because the dragon was an accident didn't mean that Lucky loved it any less. From the moment she saw that her science project contained, at its heart, a flaw so fundamentally *awesome* as to produce, in a flash, a tiny, blinking, astonished dragon, so small it could fit inside a teaspoon used by a teaspoon (indeed, it was so small that Lucky almost missed it entirely, which would have been a tragedy—not only would she have failed her project, but she would have missed her chance to hold in her hand a dragon that she felt she could love until the end of time), Lucky realized in an instant that her life was about to become ever so much more wonderful than it once had been. She scooped up the dragon and stared at it, awestruck and gaping.

"Don't worry," she whispered, noting the trembling in her heart. "I'll take care of you." *Forever and ever*, she knew in her bones. She didn't even have to think about it. It wasn't a matter of saying yes, but rather of recognizing that the *yes* was a foregone conclusion—a prior assumption of a seemingly random universe, which had apparently conspired to deliver an epically tiny and magnificent dragon into the palm of an undeniably deserving almost-ten-year-old girl.

Her science project, or what was left of it, began to bubble and froth. The odd glow that shimmered across its surface took on a more sinister sheen. The edges of the glass beaker crinkled and smoked. Lucky didn't care. She stared at the tiny creature standing in her palm in wonder. The dragon—no bigger than a lima bean—stared back up at her.

"LUCINDA BEVINGTON-COATES!"

Lucky jumped at the sound of her name and looked in horror at her science teacher tearing across the room like a foul-tempered rhinoceros. "What on earth have you *done?*" Mr. Shaw's voice was filled with hooks and barbs and disappointment. Lucky was fairly certain he hadn't seen the dragon standing in the center of her palm, staring up at its brand-new universe with its relatively large green eyes, currently slicked with tears. But just to be safe, she cupped her free hand over it quickly, and stared up at her science teacher with what she hoped was an innocent expression.

"Yes, Mr. Shaw?" she said, sliding her cupped hands under the table.

Mr. Shaw had large muscles and a larger neck. His neck had two veins on either side that bulged when he was angry—and did so now. He was not interested in Lucky's hands. He *was* interested in the glowing, melting, flammable mass in front of her. "Step aside," he said curtly, as he doused the whole thing with flame retardant. "OPEN THE WINDOWS," he barked at Mari and Anji. "This minute. The last thing we need is a building-wide fire alarm. You two!" He pointed at Wallace and the boy who always sat by Wallace, whose name Lucky could never remember. "Stand on your desks and fan the vents with your notebooks. STEP UP, SOLDIERS!" Mr. Shaw used to be in the army and had been in charge of training soldiers to stand in straight lines and run thirty miles and shoot guns and say "YES, SIR!" before he decided to try something harder, like teaching fourth grade science. Or that was the story he told, anyway. Sometimes, he made everyone feel as though perhaps they, too, were running through a war zone, with dangers flying from every direction, their feet sore from a long day of pounding in heavy combat boots. He often called them soldiers and told them that learning, like life, was a battle. He called himself Commander, and often said that, for the duration of fifth-period science at least, "your souls belong to me." He said that a lot.

Lucky disagreed. But she didn't tell her teacher that.

"Miss Bevington-Coates, I am frankly shocked at you. I expected so much better. You have been distracted all day. UNACCEPTABLE. Distraction causes destruction. Never forget it." He pulled out his grade book and made three deep, short strokes. An unmistakable F.

Lucky had *never* gotten an F on a classroom project in her life. This one she welcomed with grace and determination, her head held high and a look of what she assumed was calm acceptance on her face. Because this F *came with a dragon.* But no one knew about the dragon—which was, at this very moment, crawling around within the space inside her cupped hands, exploring the lines of her palm and poking her skin with tiny, tiny talons. And no one *could* know about the dragon. It was *her dragon*, after all. She felt certain that if anyone at school knew, it would be taken away from her, and the very thought of it made her so impossibly sad, she worried her heart would explode.

"I'm sorry, Mr. Shaw," she said.

"I will be emailing your parents, detailing your lack of care. I am assuming they will mete out an appropriate consequence."

"Of course," Lucky said.

There was no danger of any of that happening. Mr. Shaw was often threatening to send an email, but as far as anyone knew, he never had. Lucky wasn't sure he even knew how to work a computer. Mr. Shaw was *old school.* And even if he did, it was unlikely that her parents would even read it. Her mother wasn't doing much of anything these days. And she hadn't seen her father since the Fourth of July, when he went out to buy fireworks and hadn't come home since.

Mr. Shaw brought a trash receptacle over and slid the once-glowing mass of . . . well, whatever that even *was* at this point . . . into the metal can. It was heavy—heavier than it seemed it should have been—and hit the metal bottom with a colossal crash. Mr. Shaw, as strong as he was, strained prodigiously to haul it to the back room. The lab smelled funny for the rest of the day.

Lucky missed the bus on purpose and went home on foot, skipping the whole way, her dragon safely ensconced in her lunch box (she poked holes in it, obviously), her head brimming with plans to make the most epic and magnificent dragon terrarium with her very best friend in all the world, Mrs. Hollins.

Mrs. Hollins was 101 years old and lived next door. Lucky didn't have many—or, honestly, *any*—friends her own age. She sat by herself at school. She played by herself on the playground. She was never asked to be part of anyone's group project. These things didn't bother her—or she told people that these things didn't bother her—but she didn't understand it very well, if at all. Most people seemed baffled by Lucky, and Lucky was, in turn, baffled by them.

She didn't have any of these problems with Mrs. Hollins.

Lucky *loved* Mrs. Hollins's house. It was her favorite place to be. Especially since her dad left.

As Lucky rounded the corner toward her block, she marveled at what a fine day it was. Warm for mid-October, the air was sweet and pungent with fallen leaves and rotting crabapples. The sun shone bright and the sky was the same blue as a robin's egg. The dragon scurried around in the lunch box. Lucky crooned to it. "Don't worry," she whispered. "I'll let you out as soon as we get to my friend's house." She tried to keep the thrill out of her voice when she said the word *friend*, so as to teach the dragon that it was no big deal to have a friend and that anyone can do it and it isn't hard. Even for a dragon. She wanted to shield her dragon from life's more vexing difficulties.

She paused as she reached her house. Although every other house on her block glistened in the clear autumn light, her own house was, once again, in shadow. Mail piled in a heap next to the door. Her mom was inside somewhere. Lucky felt her forehead crease and her stomach cramp tight. She knew her mother was likely on the couch, and crying again. Her mother was always crying. She also knew that she *should* go inside and sit with her mother for a while. It didn't actually *help,* but like brushing her teeth and clearing off the counters when they got dirty, Lucky knew it was one of the things a person *should do.* But the dragon scurried about inside the lunchbox. And she wanted so much to show it to Mrs. Hollins.

"Mom!" she called from the porch, letting her backpack fall with a thud. Her mother didn't answer. "I'm going out to play!" She didn't tell her mother that she was going to Mrs. Hollins's house. As far as Lucky knew, her mother had never met Mrs. Hollins, and had never really noticed the house next door.

Lucky clutched her lunch box to her chest and skipped down the steps. Surely, her mother had heard her. Surely, that was enough.

Mrs. Hollins's house sparkled in the sunlight. It always sparkled. It was one of the things Lucky loved about it. Also, there was no distressing pile of mail because the mail didn't even *come* to Mrs. Hollins's house. Lucky assumed it was because the house number, unlike everyone else's whole numbers, was 1425$\frac{1}{2}$, and perhaps the mail carrier didn't trust fractions. The front door of Mrs. Hollins's house had an eight-inch wide convex porthole lens, at just about Mrs. Hollins's height. This was convenient, because it was Lucky's height also. This gave her a fish-eye's view into the house, and allowed her to watch the old woman's slow approach to the front door, her glass-distorted figure becoming more and more garish as it approached until all that could be seen was a single, gigantic eye, blinking in the center of the door. Lucky waved.

"Hi, Mrs. Hollins!"

"Why, Lucinda!" Mrs. Hollins exclaimed through the intercom. "What a surprise!" She always said that. Even though Lucky visited every day. Mrs. Hollins had a very thick accent. She said "Lucinda" as though it was "Looceenda." This was because she came from a place called the Old Country. Lucky didn't know exactly where that was. Only that it was old.

"Just one moment," Mrs. Hollins said. "Let me open the door." This was an involved affair. The door to Mrs. Hollins's house was thick and wide and metal and very, very heavy, and had originally been a door on a top secret, experimental submarine. Mrs. Hollins never said if she had been part of the diving team. But Lucky assumed.

"An interesting house requires an interesting entrance," Mrs. Hollins told Lucky once. Lucky filed this piece of information away. Maybe it might help her mother. You never knew.

There was an uncountable number of different levers, latches, gears, springs, and motors that all worked together to open the door. Mrs. Hollins only had to pull a single cord (it was red and velvet and had once been part of a circus act) in order to open it, but the process took well over a minute. Finally, after a whir, a squeak, a whine, and a colossal jolt, the door rattled open. Mrs. Hollins stood in the doorway, her wrinkled mouth spread open in a smile. She had short gray hair that stuck out all over her head like shiny pins. She wore a thin cotton housedress, its patch pockets bulging with tools, a white lab coat, and a pair of thick black Wellington boots. And while her eyes were small and bright as pebbles, her eyeglasses acted as a magnifying lens, making them look like twin planets, dwarfing her face. She blinked. Blinked again. She inclined her face so close to Lucky's that their noses almost touched.

"Something's different." Her magnified eyes crinkled a bit. "Are you different?"

"No," Lucky said.

"There seems to be less of you. *Is* there less of you?" Mrs. Hollins asked. She pulled a measuring tape out of her pocket and measured Lucky's skull. She frowned.

"I don't think so," Lucky said. The dragon scuttled in the lunch box. Lucky almost fainted with anticipation. Just *wait* until Mrs. Hollins saw!

The old woman grunted. Then she shrugged. "Well, I must be imagining things. Come on then." She hobbled toward the kitchen. "Kettle's on."

Mrs. Hollins was a scientist and an inventor, and every room in the house hummed with mechanical activity. She had machines that opened jars and machines that told you when someone was in the bathroom and machines that closed the blinds when you cleared your throat very, very loud (this was problematic that one time when Mrs. Hollins got pneumonia). She had machines that showed her video images of laboratories around the globe (including one that appeared to be in outer space), and machines that minded her various materials labs in the basement, and a machine that crawled around the house with a feather duster and a damp rag, because you really never can do enough dusting.

Mrs. Hollins walked with a cane with four prongs on the bottom, which wasn't itself very unusual until one noticed that each prong operated with its own gears and optics, re-balancing and responding to her every move. It was impossible to knock over. Lucky knew this, because she once tried knocking it over while Mrs. Hollins was taking a nap on the couch. Not only did the cane right itself instantly, but it then reared on Lucky, chasing her out of the room like an overprotective Labrador.

Lucky once told Mrs. Hollins that she should name the cane something tough and imposing, like Fang or Bruiser or Wolf. Mrs. Hollins told her it was silly to name machines, as they had no souls. "You can't have a name without a soul," Mrs. Hollins had said. "Everyone knows that."

Lucky set the lunch box down on the kitchen table. "Mrs. Hollins!" she squealed. She could hardly contain her excitement. "I have amazing news." She laid her hand on the lunch box and began jumping up and down.

Mrs. Hollins reached into the patch pocket of her housedress and pulled out a pair of ornate opera glasses. She frowned. "No. Something's happened to you. You are missing something."

"I am?" Lucky said. "What am I missing?"

"I don't know," Mrs. Hollins said, her wrinkles pressing around the eyepieces of the opera glasses. "You tell me."

Lucky shook her head. "I don't think I'm missing anything. But I *have* something, Mrs. Hollins. A *new* something. That's what I've been trying to tell you."

The kettle boiled, and instead of a whistle, it belched out a woman's voice singing a song from an opera that Mrs. Hollins had once explained was *La Traviata*, as though Lucky had heard of it. Lucky appreciated this aspect of Mrs. Hollins's personality: she always assumed that Lucky knew more than she did, unlike every other adult she knew, who assumed the opposite.

Lucky shook her head. "No, that's not right. I didn't *find* something. I *made* something. A dragony something. By accident. But still. *I* made it. Just like you make stuff." Lucky pointed to the tiny, eight-legged machine with suction cups on its feet that was, at that very moment, washing the kitchen window.

"I can't say I know what you're talking about," Mrs. Hollins said, adjusting her glasses. "Show me what's in the lunch box." She said this like a real scientist. Scientists care about observations and data. Lucky could hardly contain her delight.

She opened the lunch box with a flourish and a smile. Her dragon sat on its haunches in the center of the box, looking up with large, curious eyes. *Her very own dragon.* There was nothing better than this. "Isn't it *wonderful?*" Lucky said breathlessly.

Mrs. Hollins sat down heavily on the polished metal chair and adjusted her thick glasses. "*Wonderful* certainly is a word that people on Earth use from time to time. Perhaps more often than they should." She put out her hand and encouraged the dragon to climb up. The dragon was slightly larger than it was before. Back at school, it was the size of a lima bean. Now it was just about the size of a grape. The dragon stood at attention on Mrs. Hollins's open palm, staring at her as she stared back. She encouraged the dragon to climb from one palm to the other, muttering in Old Countryish as she did so. Lucky knew this was for scientific observations, and was proud to have accidentally created a dragon so worthy of careful study.

"Good job, my friend!" she whispered.

"Why don't you pour the boiled water into the pot, dear," Mrs. Hollins said. She cast a side eye at Lucky. "You haven't *named* it, have you? The dragon, I mean."

Lucky felt a wave of guilt that nearly knocked her flat. *She hadn't named her dragon!* What kind of dragon parent was she? What else might she forget to do? She put two tea bags into the mechanical teapot and poured the boiling water on top. The mechanical teapot had stubby legs and extendible arms and a timer to make sure that nothing was ever oversteeped. Lucky set it on the table.

"I hadn't yet," Lucky said as casually as she could. "Of course I wanted to check with you. To see if it had a soul." This was a lie, obviously, but it would have been a good plan if she had thought of it. She stopped. Frowned. "Do dragons have souls?" she asked.

"Depends on the dragon," Mrs. Hollins said absently. She slid one hand into her pocket and pulled out a notebook and a pen and began writing in symbols that Lucinda knew to be in Old Countryish, but had no idea what they meant. "Dearest Lucinda, what is your favorite kind of cookie?"

Lucky was shocked that Mrs. Hollins didn't know. "Lemon," she said. It was what she asked for every single day.

"Fine, fine," she said, bringing the dragon almost to her nose and staring hard. She scribbled something else. "Bring me a lemon cookie. And also, can you please bring me that lens?" There was, next to the toaster, a very large magnifying lens on a metal stand. It was quite heavy, and Lucky needed both hands. Her biceps shook as she carried it over. Mrs. Hollins set the dragon on the table, right under the lens. Then she took a small crumb from the cookie and brought it to the dragon's tiny talons. The dragon shivered and Lucky shivered. Lucky felt its curiosity and delight. The dragon sniffed the cookie crumb and ate it. Lucky breathed in deeply through her nose, wondering at the bright scent of lemon. And lemon on her lips. And lemon on her tongue. And lemon forever. The dragon wiped its mouth. Asked for another bite with an outstretched paw. Lucky licked her lips. The dragon devoured the second piece and fell back to the table with its paws on its belly. A look of unmitigated satisfaction on its face.

Lucky sat heavily on the kitchen chair. She rubbed her tummy.

"Hmm," Mrs. Hollins muttered. She turned toward the mechanical teapot. "Tea, please," she said curtly. The pot didn't need a second command. Its mechanisms were old and it rattled as it moved, but it still pulled the cups in range and filled them with tea, and then extended its filament-thin hyper-arm outward toward the creamer, twining its tendril tip around the handle and positioning its suckers, then cautiously lifting it across the table, landing dollops of cream into the tea (and a few drops on the placemats along the way). "Nicely done," Mrs. Hollins said. The teapot seemed to shiver with delight. Its gears shone just a bit.

The dragon burped. Lucky did too. She had heard one time that burps are contagious. Or maybe it was yawns. Or maybe both.

Mrs. Hollins narrowed her eyes. "Lucinda, dear, you've had a long day. Surely you must be hungry. Have a cookie. Lemon is your favorite."

Lucky shook her head. "No thanks," she said. She yawned. The dragon yawned too. "I'm full."

Mrs. Hollins wrote it down.

Ever since Mrs. Hollins's house—with its inventions and laboratories and hidden rooms and unusual floors—appeared without warning next door to Lucky's house, Lucky regarded it with a combination of wonder and gratitude. She introduced herself to Mrs. Hollins right away. Mrs. Hollins, after her initial shock that Lucky noticed the house at all (no one else seemed to), muttered to herself that "there's always one" and then told Lucky that she might as well make herself useful, which Lucky did. Every day after that, Lucky helped Mrs. Hollins with the sweeping and the polishing of various scientific instruments. She fed the ancient bird and checked on the ancient fish and left crackers for the squirrels and walked outside to the tree where the owls lived to say hello, because everyone deserves a proper greeting.

Mrs. Hollins asked Lucky to stand next to the kitchen doorway. The old woman stood on a stool and, using a ruler to guide her pen, marked a spot on the trim showing how tall Lucky was.

"Why do you want to know how tall I am?" Lucky asked.

"Because I am a curious lady. And I do curious things." And she left it at that. Mrs. Hollins wrote something else down in Old Countryish. She didn't explain to Lucky what it meant.

They took the mechanical lift down to the sub-basement, where Mrs. Hollins checked on sentient metals growing in their glowing incubators. One was getting restless inside its warm womb, forming itself into a shiny hand one moment, and then a monster, and then a single eye.

"That's enough out of you," Mrs. Hollins said, tapping on the glass. The metal collapsed into a molten heap.

Lucky looked closely through the glass.

"How does it do that?" she asked. Her dragon peeked over the rim of Lucky's shirt pocket, and then dived for cover. He was a very frightened dragon.

Mrs. Hollins shrugged. "It's sentient. It can do what it wants." She gave the lump a narrowed look. "It can also do as it's told, no matter what its opinion is on the matter." The mass bubbled meekly.

Lucky moved a safe distance away from the mass, and let the dragon crawl out onto the table. The dragon sniffed around for a bit, but stayed close to Lucky's hand. Her dragon needed her. She knew this with a deep certainty. She looked at Mrs. Hollins. "If it's sentient, does that mean it has a soul?"

Mrs. Hollins startled. "Why no. What a mad idea! Lots of beings of Mind are lacking in Soul. Surely you've seen politicians on the news." Lucky hadn't, but decided not to tell Mrs. Hollins that.

"Well," Lucky said slowly, "how do you tell if something has a soul?"

Mrs. Hollins gave a hard look at Lucky, and then at the dragon, and then at Lucky's shoes, which were roomy now, and had begun to flop a bit around her feet. "An educated guess," she said. "And God help you if you're wrong." She looked back at the dragon, which was now the size of an apricot. "*Give it back*," she said sternly. The dragon ran up Lucky's arm and dived into the security of the pocket. Lucky didn't know what, exactly, the dragon was supposed to give back. The dragon whimpered. "I mean it," Mrs. Hollins said. The dragon sighed and then relaxed. Mrs. Hollins patted Lucky on the shoulder. "It's important to set expectations and boundaries," she said. "In all relationships. But, of course, you know that." Lucky pretended she knew what that meant. She followed Mrs. Hollins back into the mechanical lift. As they descended into the sub-sub-basement, her shoes regained their fit.

Lucky had never been in the sub-sub-basement before. The light was blue and green down there, as though they were underwater. Several screens that looked like portholes blinked on the wall. Mrs. Hollins had several such porthole screens on the main floor, maybe ten at most, but down here, they numbered in the dozens. Lucky gaped at them all. Like the upstairs porthole screens, each one here showed images of a laboratory. Most looked like normal labs, but some appeared to be submarine labs or in deep caves. In one, the scientists looked as though they were floating. Two showed animals in lab coats and three others showed scientists in hazmat suits with strange things, like extra heads or four arms or a fabric-covered, very large tail extending from the rump. Lucinda assumed it must be some kind of strange television show.

"Put the dragon on the table," Mrs. Hollins said. "I want to take its picture."

"What for?" Lucky asked.

Mrs. Hollins pointed at the porthole screens. "As you know, my colleagues are . . . well, they are all very far away. But they, like me, are a curious bunch. They will be very excited to see your wonderful dragon. Because of science."

Lucky nodded happily. She *loved* science. She scooped the dragon out of her pocket and set him down on the table. The dragon instantly began to cry, its silent tears pouring into a sizeable puddle. Lucky felt her heart would break. Mrs. Hollins didn't seem to notice. "Lucinda, darling, why don't you sit next to your dragon. I'd like you in the picture as well."

Mrs. Hollins wheeled her camera over. It was a giant thing, much different than any camera Lucky had ever seen. It swiveled on casters and its brass exterior shone with polish and elbow grease. Mrs. Hollins climbed onto the seat. She flicked the switch and sent the camera's mechanisms whirling.

"Hello, colleagues," Mrs. Hollins said. Instantly, the figures in the other porthole screens looked up in interest. They inclined their faces toward the screens. "This is Lucinda. She lives next door to me on Earth, er—I mean." She cleared her throat. "That is to say. We live on a block in a city that happens to be on the planet Earth, which is a normal thing to report in genial conversation, as it is the planet where we all live." Mrs. Hollins paused for a moment. Her cheeks grew red. "There are other normal and regular things that I might mention regarding fingers and toes and the color of the sky, but that is not why I've asked for your professional input. It seems that Lucinda has accidentally created a dragon. We have heard of such things happening, obviously."

Mrs. Hollins looked at Lucky. "It's because we're scientists."

"Oh," Lucky said, trying to sound knowledgeable. "Of course."

Mrs. Hollins returned to the camera. "But not for a long time. Indeed, after the last incident, I daresay that all of us assumed that we never would again. And yet, here we are. This young lady is entranced by the dragon, which is typical, and, Lucinda, darling, we all are very curious to hear the whole wonderful story of how your perfect dragon came to be. Please tell us everything from the beginning. Leave nothing out. Including, and this is important, *who else was in the room*. Proceed, dear."

Mrs. Hollins adjusted her glasses, recalibrated her camera lens, and inched the large contraption forward. The dragon dived for the side of Lucky's hand and grasped her skin in his talons, holding on tight. Lucky could feel it shaking. Every figure in every porthole screen pressed their faces to the glass, their eyes large with wonder.

Lucky told her story. She left nothing out.

Later that night, Lucky lay in bed, staring blankly into the dark. She didn't have her dragon. But Mrs. Hollins had said, and, Lucky conceded, rightly so, that the dragon was not housebroken yet, and that she had a very sick and delicate mother at home. What if the dragon wandered off at night? What if it grew? What if it scared someone? Could Lucky's mother's heart take it? Probably not.

Lucky wept at the thought of leaving her dragon and wept as Mrs. Hollins firmly took it out of her hands and closed the door. But now . . .

Her room was mostly dark. There was a streetlight outside her window, leaking yellow onto the floor. She knew if she went to the window, she'd see Mrs. Hollins's house, and the odd, multicolored lights randomly blurting from the cracks, like always. Lucky assumed this had something to do with being a scientist.

Mrs. Hollins was good at inventing things and solving problems. This was something that engineers *did*. Mrs. Hollins was building a terrarium. Mrs. Hollins was building a carrying case. Mrs. Hollins was going to solve the problem. Lucky trusted Mrs. Hollins, and knew she should be relieved. But with her dragon gone, she didn't feel much of anything. It was as though the arrival of the dragon was so monumentally *awesome* that all her feelings—past, present, and future—had been siphoned into it, leaving nothing else behind. Lucky lay in bed and did not move. She didn't sleep. She didn't worry. She didn't feel anything at all. She simply experienced the absence of her dragon like a missing limb—a phantom that ached. More every second.

The next day, Lucky sat on her mother's bed to say good morning. Her mother hadn't slept either. Her face was wet with tears. Normally the sight of her mother in such a state would make Lucky sick with worry, but today she felt nothing. She patted her mother's hand because it seemed the right thing to do. She felt no stab, no pinpricks in her ears, no anxiety at all in the face of her mother's sadness. She couldn't even remember feeling it. "Have a good day, Mom," she said as she left the room.

Before walking to the bus stop, Lucky knocked on Mrs. Hollins's door. She had never visited Mrs. Hollins first thing in the morning, but her need to see her dragon felt like a pull in her insides so strong she might turn inside out. And the closer she came to Mrs. Hollins's house, the stronger that need became. Through the porthole, she could see Mrs. Hollins standing at the table in the living room with two other people, both very, very old. This was strange—Lucky had never seen anyone visiting Mrs. Hollins before—but really, Lucky reasoned, it wasn't as strange as all that. After all, surely old people were friends with old people and visited one another all the time. Like Mrs. Hollins, they were both wearing lab coats and Wellington boots. Like Mrs. Hollins, they both wore thick glasses that enlarged their eyes. One of them had skin that was a faint purple hue. Lucky knew it was rude to stare, and figured it just had something to do with being old. Mrs. Hollins hobbled to the door, blinked through the porthole, and greeted Lucky through the intercom.

"Why, Lucinda! We were just talking about you. Come in. We have tea." She called to the living room while she pulled the velvet cord, "Mrs. Oleander! Why don't you get our Lucinda a cup from the cupboard, will you?"

The door rattled open. The dragon sat on the table under a glass bowl. *Her* dragon. Lucinda felt the space between them collapse like a rubber band after its been snapped.

"*I missed you!*" she found herself shouting, a sob ripping from her feet, through her body, and out her mouth. She scooped the dragon close. It was bigger now. The size of a plum. She kissed it and cuddled it and felt—well, everything. Every feeling that ever existed surged through her, all at once. She felt angry at Mr. Shaw for rudely giving her an F and she felt anxious about her father gone these many months and she felt awestruck at the beautiful morning and she felt worried and sorrowful for her mother and she felt hopeful that now she had a real friend just like other kids and maybe everything would be okay. She had so many feelings she felt like she might explode. The dragon seemed to expand with feelings too. It was now the size and heft of a large apple.

"Give it back!" shouted Mrs. Hollins. Lucky was so startled by the old woman's sharp tone that she instantly began to cry, and Mrs. Hollins rested her hand on her shoulder. "Not you, dear. You are perfect. As always."

Mrs. Hollins had never called her perfect before. Lucinda felt a smile unfurl that felt so large it might take up the whole room. The dragon felt suddenly heavier, but returned to its early plum size the moment Mrs. Hollins cleared her throat.

Lucky learned that the two old women—Mrs. Oleander and Mrs. Xenon—were friends and scientists from the Old Country. Mrs. Oleander only spoke a little English. Mrs. Xenon spoke none. They conferred in Old Countryish while Lucky whispered her love to her dragon. Suddenly, she heard the distant rumble of the school bus coming nearer.

"I have to go," Lucky said. "Can I bring my dragon?"

She already knew the answer.

"Not right away," Mrs. Hollins said slowly. "Not until we find the safest way. In the meantime, dear, will you please stand next to the doorjamb? I would like to see how tall you are."

"But you did that yesterday," Lucky protested.

"Fine, fine," Mrs. Hollins said, steering her toward the doorway and marking the spot on the trim. She didn't need a stool this time. Lucky could feel Mrs. Hollins's breath on the top of her head. It was very hot. She shooed Lucky out the door without showing her the mark.

Lucky ran to the bus stop—it seemed farther than normal. Perhaps she was just tired. She struggled with the entrance stairs, each platform feeling higher than usual. Lucky did not feel worried about any of it. In fact, she didn't feel much of anything. And as her bus rolled forward, the *not feeling* became so wide and so tall and so voluminous that Lucky couldn't remember feeling anything at all.

Lucky gave one last glance at her house and noticed that someone was knocking on her door. They could knock all day if they wanted to, Lucky knew. Her mother wouldn't be getting out of bed for hours. And even when she did get up, she was unlikely to answer the door. The knocker turned around, and Lucky's eyes started to narrow. It was Mr. Shaw. But, Lucky thought, Mr. Shaw never went to people's houses. As far as Lucky knew, he lived at school. The bus moved quickly. Lucky could observe only for a moment. She saw Mr. Shaw peek in the window. She saw him listen at the door. She noticed it, she thought, the way a scientist notices things. She simply observed the data. She took out her notebook and wrote the word *OBSERVATIONS* at the top of the page.

1. Mr. Shaw is at my house.

She didn't know what else to write. Is it still an observation when a scientist observes a subject who is, in turn, observing things? She wasn't sure.

At school, she took her breakfast tray, but didn't eat anything. She sat alone and did not notice that she sat alone. Her uniform pants and her uniform shirt were both too large for her—though they fit yesterday. Perhaps they stretched out. Wallace and the boy who always sits with Wallace made fun of her for wearing hand-me-down clothes. Normally, this sort of teasing hurt her feelings, or at least the incorrectness of the assumptions would have made her irate *on principle*. But not today.

In fifth period, she walked into the science classroom and Mr. Shaw seemed surprised to see her. "You're here," he said, his lips growing dry, like he'd seen a ghost.

"I always come to school." She did not feel confused at his confusion. She did not feel anything at all. She simply stated a matter of fact. Mr. Shaw walked around her, his eyes going up and down.

"Did anything . . ."

But he didn't finish the question because the bell rang and it was time to start. The project in the lab was almost identical to the project that produced Lucky's dragon the day before. Which was strange because Mr. Shaw never repeated class projects. But from the way he stalked the rows and hollered at the students, no one wanted to ask about it either. Lucky wondered if maybe she wasn't the only one who got an F the day before. The students, once again, measured and combined liquids and powders from beakers and vials that were only known by their labels showing the days of the week. The instructions were written on the board in Mr. Shaw's aggressively neat, regulated handwriting:

"SWIRL EIGHTY GRAMS OF TUESDAY INTO 142 MILLILITERS OF SATURDAY AND WAIT TEN SECONDS BEFORE GIVING IT A GOOD SHAKE. ADD NINETEEN GRAINS OF WEDNESDAY, ONE AT A TIME."

And so forth. Mr. Shaw said this was to help them learn how to follow directions with precision and care. They had to follow the instructions to the letter. Lucky held her breath, waiting for her project to explode again. She didn't hope for it—she didn't *feel* anything. But she did know, in an intellectual way, that two friends were better than one.

The explosion didn't come. No dragon appeared. She completed her lab perfectly. Both Anji and the boy who always sits with Wallace jumped back as their projects went bright and wild and hot. The floor shook and the beaker smoked. Lucky saw their eyes go wide and their hands shoot under the table. She saw them force their faces into something appropriately contrite as Mr. Shaw shouted his displeasure and grabbed the trash can, heaving the destroyed projects into the metal bottom and lugging it away.

Lucky didn't feel anything, but for the first time she *noticed* herself not feeling anything. She looked over at the boy who always sat with Wallace. Wallace kept tapping him on the shoulder, asking what he was looking at, but the boy who always sat with Wallace wouldn't say. She looked over at Anji, who had moved over to the corner. Her mouth was smiling. Her eyes were wet with tears.

"Interesting," Lucky muttered. Mrs. Hollins wanted Lucky to think like a scientist. She never said so, but Lucky could tell. And being a scientist meant observing everything. She pulled out her notebook and turned to the page that said *OBSERVATIONS*. And she began to write. She left nothing out. She described the look on Anji's face and the way the boy who always sits with Wallace absolutely refused to make eye contact with his friend. She noticed other things, too, and wrote them down.

5. The boy who sits with Wallace won't show his hands.

And

9. Mr. Shaw's neck veins are noticeably more bulgy than usual.

And

15. It smells like licorice and gingerbread and baby spit-up.

And

21. Mr. Shaw has called us soldiers ~~eight~~ twelve times.

"There is nothing worse than a soldier ill prepared to complete a mission when the mission presents itself. You have all been well trained, soldiers, and I know you'll be grateful for this training when the time comes to take the lead in your next great mission. DISMISSED."

She made up her mind to report all of this to Mrs. Hollins.

Mr. Shaw yelled at Wallace and told him to fan the smoke alarm. He yelled at Mari and told her to open the widows. He told Anji and the boy who always sits with Wallace that he would be emailing their parents. But everyone knew that wasn't going to happen.

After school, Mrs. Hollins's house looked different than it had earlier that morning. First of all, there were several odd-looking vehicles in the driveway. They were cars . . . *mostly.* One looked like a regular car except the cab had no doors at all. Just a hatch at the top. And the interior was entirely filled with water. Another—and this one she examined closely, carefully inscribing her observations in her notebook—had been fitted with folded up wings on either side and another had eight wheels instead of four—and each of the wheels was attached to the car with telescoping legs. Lucky ran her hand along the car's shiny chrome, and looked at the back where cars normally display their model name and the company who makes them. This car didn't. Instead, it read, PERFECTLY ORDINARY EARTH CAR in shiny silver letters. Lucky frowned. She had never heard of that kind of car before.

Another difference with Mrs. Hollins's house was the house itself—or rather the large, metallic fabric tent attached to the back of the house. The tent had two turrets, several alcoves, and even a flag displaying what looked like the Milky Way, fluttering in the breeze. Lucky knew she should feel curious. She knew she should feel confused. But she didn't *feel* anything. She didn't even feel guilty for not visiting her mother first.

She went to the front porch and knocked on the door. No one came. She knocked again. The door moved slightly. It wasn't locked. Or even fully closed. Lucky pushed it open and went inside. The ancient bird squawked and the ancient fish spun around in its watery world. Lucky reached in her pocket and pulled out a cracker for the bird, because she always brought a cracker for the bird. Then she took a pinch of fish food from the canister and gave it to the fish, because she always fed the fish. It was a small thing, but it made Lucky feel as though her skin fit a little better and her bones moved a little smoother and her head rested a little more surely on her neck. Her dragon was nearby. She could *feel* it. It felt good to feel something.

"Hello?" Lucky said as she peeked into the kitchen. A very old man and a very old woman stood over the kitchen table, examining the mechanical teapot. The very old man had what looked like a fancy stethoscope attached to his ears. He listened intently to the teapot. The very old woman had a magnifying lens like Mrs. Hollins's, but this one also had buttons and lights and controls and made a whirring noise as it got closer to the teapot. Both the very old man and the very old woman were dressed like Mrs. Hollins—a white lab coat and black Welling-ton boots and a floral cotton housedress. The very old man also had a tuft of chest hair and a beard oiled to a curl and point at the end. They scribbled notes on their steno pads.

"Hi," Lucky said. "I'm Lucky."

The very old man and the very old woman both had thick glasses that magnified their eyes, which widened farther in surprise. They said words to Lucky that she didn't understand, and then they motioned to Lucky to sit down. The very old man poured her some tea. The very old woman yelled some words at the top of her lungs. One of those words sounded something like "Hollins," but not exactly. Then she returned to the table and patted Lucky on the head, like she was a dog. At any other time, this would have enraged her. Instead, she felt only a twinge of something that could be a feeling, but she wasn't entirely sure.

There was a loud crash in a room very far away. The sub-sub-basement, maybe. Mrs. Hollins entered the room with a wide smile. "Lucinda!" she said brightly. "I believe I have solved your problem. Or one of your problems, anyway. The easiest one, I'm afraid. There are several harder problems ahead, but we will get to them in good time." She squinted her eyes. She put her hand on Lucky's forehead, and then put her fingers on her wrist. She spoke to the very old man and the very old woman in Old Countryish, using an explainy sort of voice that Lucky recognized, even if she didn't know the words.

Lucky tried to hold very still. Her teeth rattled and her bones began

215

to shake. Her dragon was nearby. Her skin vibrated. There was, she realized, a part of her that was dragon-shaped. Perhaps it had always been dragon-shaped. And with her dragon far away from her, she felt a dragon-shaped hole in the center of . . . well, everything. The universe. The house. Her very being. She would not be whole until she had her dragon.

"Eat," Mrs. Hollins said. She didn't wait for a response. She just shoved the cookie into Lucky's mouth. She chewed, but did not enjoy it. The very old man and the very old woman took notes.

The very old man asked Mrs. Hollins something in Old Countryish. "It's pronounced *drink tea*," she said. And then she muttered to Lucky, "He's been trying to learn English for one hundred and seventy-two years, and it still won't stick." She shook her head. "*Men.*"

"*Drreeenk too*," the very old man said gallantly, handing Lucky a steaming cup.

Mrs. Hollins rolled her eyes. "Come on, Lucinda," she said. "Let's have you meet the other scientists."

The tent attached to the back of the house had several towers fitted with a tall stack of monitors with casters at the bottom so they could be repositioned easily. Several scientists muttered in groups. Most of them, like Mrs. Hollins, were very old, and all were wearing cotton house-dresses and lab coats and thick Wellington boots. One had a third lens on his glasses over his forehead, which made it look like he had a third, blinking eye. Another had a snout and jowls like an elderly hound, but Lucky knew it was not polite to stare at old people whose faces have gotten mushy over time. Another had a growth that looked a little bit like a hawk's beak. And one man was quite green, but Lucky knew that they had traveled a great distance and that motion sickness can do that. Mrs. Hollins sat Lucky on a stool next to her podium and called the meeting to order in Old Countryish. The scientists all took notes.

Lucky didn't know how long this would last. She wanted her dragon. She didn't feel much, but she did feel *that*. The dragon-shaped hole at the center of herself seemed to vibrate and hum. She closed her eyes. She tried to focus inward. *Where are you?* she thought as hard as she could. And then—

Lucky?

Lucky's eyes snapped open. She scanned the room. No one else had heard it. The voice, for it *was* a voice, she was sure of it, wasn't coming through her ears. Rather, it seemed to come from her bones, from the air, from the empty space within her. The voice *was* her. And she was the voice.

Lucky? There it was again.

She closed her eyes very tightly. She tried to focus her thoughts.

Dragon? she thought.

Where are you? It was the dragon. She was sure of it.

I'm here. With the scientists. I have to tell them something, but I don't know if they will understand.

There was nothing for a long moment. Lucky felt the dragon-shaped space within her get a little bit bigger. Finally:

I'm lost, Lucky. I don't know where I am. I can feel you, but I can't see you. You're the only one I need. I can't be me without you.

And the dragon-shaped space grew a little bit bigger.

The scientists gasped. Two ran to Lucky, one taking her hand and the other pressing the back of her hand to Lucky's forehead. Everyone spoke at once, some in Old Countryish and some in languages that sounded nothing like it, but were for sure not English.

Lucky looked at Mrs. Hollins, who looked different than she had ever seen her. Her eyes glowed red, and her spiky, silver hair had somehow grown taller, and thicker, like actual metal spikes erupting from her skull. She gave a great yell in Old Countryish, that Lucky had no means of understanding, but she was fairly sure, deep in her guts, that the old woman had yelled, *Bring me the dragon!*

Two scientists scurried away. Very quickly three scientists pulled a low cart that had strapped onto it a large metal box. The box rattled. Lucky felt her heart leap. Mrs. Hollins took Lucky's hand. Lucky realized that Mrs. Hollins's fingers had an extra knuckle to them. Had they always been that way? She thought that maybe she should write it down under *OBSERVATIONS* but it didn't seem to be the right time. Mrs. Hollins leaned close to Lucky's ear.

"No matter what happens, darling Lucinda, your soul is indelible, unalterable, and utterly yours. I know what I'm saying doesn't make a lot of sense right now, but promise me that you'll remember it anyway, will you?"

Mrs. Hollins was right. It didn't make any sense. But Lucky promised anyway. The scientists opened the box, and Lucky felt a curious sensation deep in her solar plexus. She heard a deafening roar and she saw a bright light, and then the world went dark.

Lucky?

Lucky?

Lucky didn't know where she was. All she knew was that it was very dark.

I'm sorry, Lucky. I didn't know what to do. There were too many people and I was afraid.

Lucky squinted, her eyes adjusting to the low light.

You have been asleep. And you're . . . oh, Lucky, please don't be angry with me. I didn't mean it. I believe this is my fault, but I don't know why it is my fault. All I know is I need you, Lucky. I need you.

Lucky scanned the room. She looked up and saw a clock on the wall, its glass face reflecting the yellow glow of a far-away streetlight. She was sitting on a hard surface, next to a towering stack of what seemed to be large pieces of fabric. A chalkboard stretched across one wall. A faint light pulsed under a closed door. And next to the window was a row of desks. Lucky frowned.

"Am I in Mr. Shaw's classroom?"

I don't know Mr. Shaw. I only know you.

The dragon stood in front of her. *Lucky's* dragon. But he was larger now. He took up . . . so much space. Lucky shook her head, trying to clear it. The dragon's tail curled around his body, and he held on to the tip, pressing it to his cheek, the way a little child holds a blanket. His scales shimmered in the low light. His large green eyes overflowed with tears.

I love you so much, Lucky. I didn't know what else to do. I am very afraid.

"Why did you bring me here. Of all places?" She noticed the pulsing light in the back room again. She noticed that Mr. Shaw had written the class schedule for the rest of the week on the blackboard, and they were to repeat the same project every single day. He'd written *UNTIL THE PROPER RESULTS ARE ACHIEVED!* in very large letters. Mr. Shaw never repeated himself. He saw it as a sign of weakness. So why do so now? Mr. Shaw was at her house the other day. Why exactly? Lucky wasn't sure. She tried to think the way a scientist thinks. Observe the data. Right now, she was in Mr. Shaw's classroom, but what was she sitting on?

I brought you here because this is where it began. Or maybe this is where I began. Or we began. I came here because it felt right and I couldn't leave without you.

Lucky remembered learning that salmon always return to the exact place where they spawned so that they might spawn again. She knew that other animals behaved in this way as well—something deep inside compelled them to return to the ground of their making. Is that what her dragon was doing? Was he intending to . . . make more dragons? Since he was created out of nothing, maybe it was possible. She wasn't sure it was such a good idea if there were more dragons. She loved her dragon. But it was important to think like a scientist.

Lucky stood, shivered, and wrapped her body with her arms, only realizing at this moment that she wasn't wearing any clothes at all. She shook her finger at the dragon. She realized with a start that she had to crane her neck and look way up in order to see his face. How big even was he now?

"Did you steal my clothes?" she demanded. "It is not okay to steal someone's clothes." She knew she was responsible for the dragon's moral upbringing. It was a very large task, she realized.

The dragon bit its lower lip. *Your clothes are right there. They just didn't fit you anymore. You are . . . well, you got very small, Lucky. And I didn't know what to do.*

Lucky looked back at the towering stack of fabric and realized that it was a pile of her own clothing, extending far over her head. She also realized that she was standing on the surface of the lab table, and it seemed to extend very far in all directions. She frowned.

"How tall am I?" she asked.

I don't know how tall things are. This tall? The dragon measured with its hands, which did not help. Lucky stood up. She wasn't embarrassed being naked in front of the dragon, but she knew she needed clothes. She climbed up the tower and found her pants, which she knew had a bandana in the back pocket. It was still too large, but she was able to wrap and twist it and tie the corners to make a serviceable dress. Assuming she didn't get smaller. Or bigger. She wasn't sure how any of this worked.

"How long have we been here?" Lucky's mind raced. What did she know? What could she deduce? She needed Mrs. Hollins. She needed her mother. What if she shrank so much she disappeared? The dragon looked at her blankly, so she tried again. "How much time has passed since we left the scientists?"

I don't know about time. I only know you.

The dragon was not very helpful. Lucky needed information. She looked back at the pulsing light in the back room.

"Did you bring my backpack?" Lucky asked.

Do you mean this thing? The dragon held up the backpack. It was so much bigger than Lucky was. This did not seem like a good sign.

"Okay, you need to open it." This was harder to explain. The dragon's fingers were clumsy, and he didn't always know words like *zipper* or *strap*. Suddenly she stopped. She cocked her head and looked at her dragon.

"Wait a minute. Your voice is in my head. Did you put it there, or did I?"

I don't really know what a head is, the dragon said.

Lucky thought for a minute. Then she said, "Close your eyes," showing her dragon what eyes were. Then Lucky tried to get a picture in her mind, as clear as she could. Her mother on the couch. Weeping into her hands. Lucky's stomach hurt and her skin felt prickly. The dragon started to cry.

I'm worried about Mom, the dragon said.

Lucky nodded. "Me too," she said. "Okay, now pay attention." And she tried very hard to think at the dragon as clearly as she possibly could, visualizing opening the backpack and finding the notebook, and then opening the pocket and finding a pencil. And then going over to the pencil sharpener. That part was harder. The dragon's hands were large and clumsy, but Lucky hoped that he would get more agile, because she needed him to write some things down as well.

"Okay, carry me into the back room. I need to see what Mr. Shaw is doing."

The next morning, a very worried Mrs. Hollins went into the backyard to check on the owls, and found three dragons instead. The dragons were of varying sizes—one the size of a grizzly bear, another the size of a sheep, and the third the size of a bushel basket. There were three children as well. Also of varying sizes. The smallest one stood on the palm of her dragon, wearing a dress made of a bandana.

"YOU!" Mrs. Hollins shouted at the largest dragon. Then she yelled something in Old Countryish. "And you didn't even *ask*. You are taking something that does not belong to you, *without permission*."

"I don't think that's right, Mrs. Hollins," Lucky said. She had to speak very loud. Her small lungs and small vocal cords didn't project very far.

Mrs. Hollins put her face very close to Lucky's. "Oh, Lucinda!" she said. "I'm so sorry this is all happening. That dragon is taking—"

"No, Mrs. Hollins. That's what I'm trying to tell you. The dragon isn't taking anything. The dragon is *me*. It's my soul. Or maybe we have the same soul. I'm not entirely sure. There is a part of me that is dragon-shaped and a part of the dragon that is Lucky-shaped, and what I know the dragon knows and what the dragon thinks I think. We have the same feelings, because I think he *is* my feelings. Does that make sense? I've tried to be a good scientist, and I've tried to observe the data. And this is my conclusion." Lucky became very red in the face. She valued Mrs. Hollins's opinion and didn't want the old woman to think she was being foolish. Even if she was only three inches tall and standing on a dragon's palm wearing only a bandana as clothes.

Mrs. Hollins nodded very seriously. "Tell me what else you've discovered."

And so Lucky told Mrs. Hollins about the repeated experiments in her science class and how Mr. Shaw came to her house, which is why she gathered the other two kids. She told her about the lemon cookie and about the dragon-shaped hole in the center of herself and how when they were apart she felt nothing. She told Mrs. Hollins about how she taught the dragon to read files and open a backpack and write things down and that when she thought about her mother her dragon began to cry. She explained what Mr. Shaw was like in class and the strange symbols that he wrote on the wall of the back room and how the dragon had mostly written them down. She showed her notebook to Mrs. Hollins, whose eyes became wide, and then they crinkled in concentration. Lucky explained how there was a map of the city back there too, with pins marking her house and Mari's house and the boy who sits with Wallace's house, which was how she found them both.

"Actually, my name is Alfred," the boy who sits with Wallace said. He was the size of a medium-sized cat. His dragon cuddled him close. They were so happy together.

"It *is*?" Lucky said. She had no idea. She shook her head. "I didn't want Mr. Shaw finding them first, so I snuck into their houses and woke them up. It's easy to sneak in when you're this size, but it takes a long time. Especially since the boy who sits with Wallace—sorry, I mean Alfred—is hard to wake up." (*And he's not always very nice*, Lucky

222

thought, but she didn't want to say this out loud. Her dragon, of course, heard her perfectly, and gave Alfred a hard look.)

Mrs. Hollins nodded. "Everyone has been worried sick about you ever since"—she glared at the dragon—"yesterday's incident." Lucky's dragon's eyes filled with tears.

It wasn't my fault! I was scared! I don't think I like scientists.

"Come on, then. All of you. We'll decide what needs to be done."

Mr. Shaw paced at the front of the class. His face was blotchy and red. The veins on his neck bulged. Mari put her backpack on Anji's seat to keep anyone else from sitting there, and Wallace slumped in his seat and was the quietest that anyone had ever seen him.

"WE WILL CONDUCT THIS EXPERIMENT A THOUSAND TIMES UNTIL YOU HAVE IT RIGHT," Mr. Shaw bellowed.

"I WILL NOT TOLERATE FAILURE."

"THIS IS BIGGER THAN YOUR PERMANENT RECORD. STEP UP, SOLDIERS."

Analin started to cry. Marcus usually would have told her a joke, but even Marcus couldn't think of a single funny thing to say.

Lucky, Anji, and the boy who always sat with Wallace—or Alfred, she supposed she should call him—peeked from behind the bookshelf. They were all about the size of half-used pencils. Their dragons waited on the roof. Close enough to still feel them, but far enough to notice the ache.

Lucky? Are you okay? her dragon thought desperately at her.

"Not now, dragon," she whispered, and then blushed because she realized she didn't even have to say it out loud. The other two kids didn't notice.

"I love you too," Alfred whispered.

"What's happening?" Anji whispered.

"I'm not sure. Mr. Shaw is trying to make more dragons come out of kids. Were we always part dragons? Were our dragons living inside us this whole time?"

"Well, I knew it," Alfred said insufferably. Lucky gave him a withering look. He cleared his throat. "Well. I mean I sort of knew it."

Lucky shook her head.

"YOU HAVE CLASSMATES WHO ARE CURRENTLY AWOL. THEIR DERELICTION OF DUTY IS NOTICED AND WILL NOT BE TOLERATED."

"Is he talking about us?" Mari asked.

Alfred was about to scoff at her, but Lucky gave him a swift elbow to his shrunken ribs. Mrs. Hollins was supposed to be here by now. She had *said*. Lucky looked at the clock. It was nearly noon. This, Mrs. Hollins had explained, was important.

Marcus's beaker turned red, then blue, then white.

Penny's Bunsen burner started spitting out a purple flame.

Laurence gasped.

The door opened and Mrs. Hollins, flanked by five other scientists, strode in, followed by the secretary, the security guard, and the principal.

"I don't think you actually heard me," the principal said from the hallway.

"Hello, Lucan," Mrs. Hollins said mildly. "You look terrible." She added something in Old Countryish that Lucky couldn't understand but clearly made Mr. Shaw angry. His eyes were bloodshot, but became even redder than before.

"YOU'RE TOO LATE, YOU KNOW." Mr. Shaw's movements became jerky and odd, like the mechanics of his joints were catching. His red eyes flashed white. Then blue. Then they were red again.

"I don't think I am." Mrs. Hollins jerked her head toward the other scientists. "Colleagues?"

The scientists swarmed in. And the three very small children, each the size of a half-used pencil, hooked out of their hiding place behind the bookshelf and ran across the room. No one noticed them. Mrs. Hollins had told them exactly what to do.

The principal, still in the hallway, said, "Matthew, why did that woman call you Lucan?" When Mr. Shaw didn't answer, he said, "I am calling the police. Right now. Sheryl? Will you please call the police?" The secretary didn't move.

The scientists moved quickly through the room, extracting vials from the patch pockets of their floral housedresses and dipping them into the various beakers.

"ALL THEIR SOULS BELONG TO ME," Mr. Shaw yelled. "AND ANYWAY I ALREADY HAD THREE SUCCESSES AND YOU SAID THIS COULDN'T BE DONE. SO I WIN."

"Actually," Mrs. Hollins said mildly, as Lucky, Anji, and Alfred helped one another hoist themselves up onto Mr. Shaw's lab coat and climb the back of him like the side of a mountain. They each had a thumbtack tied to their backs like a sword in a scabbard. "You don't. I'm sorry, my dear. You were my finest work. But I never should have named you. One must never give a name to something that doesn't have a soul."

"There's an off-switch, you see," Mrs. Hollins had told the children, back at the tent. "Right in that divot at the base of a human's skull."

Alfred narrowed his eyes. His dragon did so as well. "But wait," he said. "Why specify human? Since we're all human, shouldn't you just say skull?"

Lucky smacked her forehead with her hands, and Mrs. Hollins rolled her eyes. "You aren't the brightest one in this group, but that is okay, dear. I'm sure you have other gifts."

Mrs. Hollins drew a diagram, showing where the thumbtack should go. "And then he'll turn off?" Lucky asked.

"Well," Mrs. Hollins said. "Hopefully."

Wallace's project exploded. The scientists didn't make it in time. So did Analin's.

"I WIN, I WIN," Mr. Shaw screamed.

Lucky? her dragon thought at her. *It's too dangerous. I'm coming down.*

"Not yet," Lucky said, realizing too late that she said it out loud.

Mr. Shaw flinched, and grabbed her in his palm. He grabbed Alfred in his other hand. He looked at Mrs. Hollins. "A THUMBTACK? YOU TOLD HER ABOUT THE THUMBTACK? TREACHERY!" His fist squeezed around Lucky's body, choking out the air.

The window shattered, and three dragons burst in amid a spangle of glass and light. Later, Lucky would remember that moment in several ways. First, she remembered the fear of dying. And the fear of loss. And the fear for her dragon's grief. And her mother's. She remembered the swirl of bodies and voices and the metallic screech of Mr. Shaw's voice and that her dragon became the size of a polar bear, and then the size of a buffalo and then the size of an elephant. He filled the room. He broke the room. She remembered colors and motion and falling plaster and screaming children and the abrupt bellowing of a soldier standing in the center of the room.

"YOU BELONG TO ME," Mr. Shaw screamed, his voice sounding metallic and rusty, and nearly grinding to a halt. "YOU ARE SO BEAUTIFUL AND YOU BELONG TO ME."

No, Lucky's dragon said in her mind. His voice was so big and so full of feelings, it seemed as though he held the whole world close to his heart. *I belong to me. And Lucky belongs to Lucky. And we belong together.* Out loud, the dragon shouted, "AND YOU ARE A VERY SILLY SCIENCE TEACHER AND NO ONE LIKES YOU VERY MUCH." It was the first thing he'd ever said out loud. Lucky was very impressed.

In Mr. Shaw's astonishment, his hand opened, and Lucky fell, grabbing onto the hem of his lab coat. She still had her thumb tack. The dragon screamed. Mr. Shaw screamed. The principal mumbled about this being "highly irregular" and "certainly the authorities are coming immediately."

Lucky climbed. The thumbtack was *so heavy*. She was so small now that Mr. Shaw barely saw her. She was getting smaller every second. The thumbtack grew heavier and heavier and larger and larger. Lucky shrank and strained as the dragon grew and grew. Finally, she found the spot at the base of Mr. Shaw's skull. She heaved the thumbtack, found purchase, and pushed.

There is not, as it turns out, a cure for what the scientists referred to as a Soul Split. But there were several accommodations to help the affected children. Mrs. Hollins arranged for meetings with the parents and guardians and teachers and social workers to help them make sense of this new reality. This proved difficult, as most people didn't notice Mrs. Hollins's house most of the time—despite the metallic tent and strange cars and crowds of unusual scientists going in and out in their lab coats and Wellington boots. People's eyes went fuzzy when they looked at Mrs. Hollins's house. Even Lucky's mom, who noticed it more than most people. So most of the meetings had to be held in Lucky's house instead.

Symposiums were scheduled and papers published. Lucky's mother welcomed the other parents warmly, and made sure there were ample snacks and tissues, because there were often tears at these meetings. The scientists staying in the metallic tent attached to Mrs. Hollins's house wrote colorful booklets aimed at assuaging the fears of worried parents. Unfortunately, the text, while informative, consistently referred to endragoned children as "perfectly normal human children, from Earth where we all obviously live," which wasn't exactly reassuring. Parents of endragoned children developed a permanent crease in their foreheads and palpable anxiety that could be felt the moment they walked into a room.

Except for Lucky's mom.

Once the team next door was able to get a better handle on the sizing problem, and halt Lucky's rapid shrinking (after the incident at the school, Lucky had been reduced to the size of a grain of sand—it was a miracle they found her at all), much of the worry about having all her feelings in the shape of a highly affectionate dragon were largely assuaged. The dragon was now the size of a small poodle, and would likely stay that way for the rest of its life. Lucky needed new pants, as she had lost about five inches, and her projected height would be less than it was before, but in the scheme of things, both Lucky and her mother agreed that it was better than being the size of a pencil. Or a grain of sand. And so life next door to the scientists returned basically to normal.

Better, actually.

Since her feelings lived in her dragon—a creature whom she loved more than anything—Lucky was able to observe them the way a scientist observes. This made it much easier to discuss vexing problems with her mother. It also made it easier to understand the people around her. Lucky had friends for the first time. She was no longer baffled by people. And people were unbaffled by her. And since her mother could see Lucky's feelings right in the open, it made it easier for her to discuss her own. And in doing so, her own pain and grief and confusion started to lose their weight and injuriousness. She started laughing again. And reading the mail. Lucky's mother painted dragons all through Lucky's room. And then she painted dragons in every room in the house. And then she painted dragons that she sold to other people, and made a fine living doing so. Indeed, years later, Lucky and her mother both said that the dragon was probably the best thing to ever happen to them.

Autumn slid into winter, which melted to spring. Lucky found herself going to Mrs. Hollins's house less and less. She had friendships to manage. And dragon playdates to arrange. And she and her mother and the dragon took weekly excursions to the museum or the library or the zoo. Over time, the less Lucky went to the house next door, the less Lucky thought about the house next door, the less Lucky remembered Mrs. Hollins at all. Finally, one day, while playing an epic game of tag with her dragon and the other kids in the neighborhood, both Lucky and her dragon found themselves in a backyard that they didn't recognize.

Are those owls? the dragon thought at her. *I love owls.*

"I also love owls," Lucky said. She scrunched up her forehead. "I used to check on owls. Do you remember?"

No, the dragon thought. *I remember lemon cookie, though.*

"Here," Mrs. Hollins said. She was holding a plate.

"Mrs. Hollins!" Lucky cried. She nearly tackled the old woman in a hug, her dragon squirming in the compressed space between them. "I've missed you!"

"I've been standing next to you for nearly thirty minutes. If you've missed me, perhaps you should get your eyes checked. Here. Have a cookie."

Mrs. Hollins stared at Lucky through her large, thick glasses. Her magnified eyes blinked. Then narrowed.

"You seem to be intact. That's a relief. And the dragon? You still haven't named it, have you?"

The dragon perched on Lucky's shoulder and curled its tail into her hair. She could no sooner name her dragon as name her right hand or her own eyes. Her feet were Lucky's feet, and her tummy was Lucky's tummy, and her dragon was Lucky's dragon, and that was that. "My dragon doesn't need a name," she said, her mouth full of lemon cookie. "We already know who we are."

"Who are you talking to?" Lucky's mother asked.

Lucky looked up. She was standing in her own yard. Her dragon absently played with her hair.

"Who?" Lucky asked.

"Who," said the owl in the tree. "Who, who."

Lucky swallowed. Her mouth was full of lemon cookie. "No one, I guess."

Mrs. Hollins watched the girl and her dragon and mother walk away. She shrugged, and called to the owls, who fluttered with her into her house. And then, after sadly waving farewell, she picked up her equipment, inventions, books, research, discoveries, and even her entire house, and simply took off. No one, not even Lucky, noticed as the house silently lifted upward. No one noticed as it hovered over the trees, lingering as the leaves rustled and the birds sang. No one noticed as it glinted against the edge of the sky. And no one noticed when it disappeared.

I MAKE MYSELF A DRAGON

Beth Cato

this body
frail
human
wrong
it does not fit my soul

I will make myself
a dragon

I will flay away my skin
word by word
split wide my seams
with invectives
that still echo
from childhood

I will reclaim those words
shape them upon the tines
of my freshly forked tongue
shred them with teeth
sharpened to ivory knives

those words
will be exiled
to the roiling acid
of my belly
to become the fuel
of my dragon's fire

my wings I will stitch
from the remnants
of my former self
the body that ill fit my soul
will gain new purpose
as it powers me
toward the stars

laid bare
I am muscle and verse
crimson anger in motion

I refuse to be a medieval beast
laying waste to villages
without sense of discretion
or direction
no
my regurgitated words aflame
will be an assassin's bullet

a strike between the eyes
my enemies never see coming

I will claim the magic
that has lain dormant
inside me all these years
I will accept that I
am someone more

someone ancient

powerful
someone worthy of
the scaled skin
that will clothe my new form
skin that is not
impenetrable
but strong and sensitive together

because although I
will be reborn a dragon
I intend to feel
with every nerve ending
set alight
I refuse to shun the world
that has so often shunned me
I will fly high and far
to find the souls
so like my own

for them
I will aim my fire

for them
accept the wounds
of barbed words—
the pain easier
to bear in another's stead

for them
I will offer respite
beneath the shadow of my wings
and the reassurance
that they, too
will escape
survive
triumph
that they, too
can awaken their dragon within

that together we
will know our own fire
know the fierce jagged shapes
of our own souls
still human
and yet forever more

THE EXILE

JY Yang

JY Yang (jyyang.com) is the author of the Tensorate series of
novellas, beginning with *The Black Tides of Heaven* and *The Red
Threads of Fortune*. Their work has been shortlisted for the Hugo,
Nebula, World Fantasy, and Lambda Literary awards, and the Tensorate novellas were an Otherwise Award (formerly known as the
Tiptree Award) honoree in 2018. They have more than two dozen
works of short fiction published on Tor.com and in *Uncanny*, *Lightspeed*, *Clarkesworld*, and *Strange Horizons*, among other venues. JY is
currently based out of Singapore. They are queer and non-binary.

The first time the dragon spoke to Linear, they had not yet made planetfall.
Their sentence had not yet commenced. Because Linear was the least
ranking of the priests on board the ship, and because it was their fate,
it fell to them to bring the deity the daily offerings. The temple was in
the underhold that lined the ship's belly, tucked under its beating heart
and humming spine. Pre-suited and fully helmeted, Linear climbed the
hatches, balancing the capsule of sweets and ashes in one hand. By the
time they reached the bottom deck, their free hand had curled into a
cramp.

Yare had no love for humans. Dragons rarely did. Some took to binding and veneration with a certain amount of resignation, even equanimity, but this one had fought hir strictures for the past hundred years with every warp and weave of hir being. And even though Linear said the right prayers before waking the temple doors each time, the animal fear of being instantly obliterated clung to them, a gluey clot in the hollows of their chest.

Inside the temple was water. Cold, pure spring water from the home continent, floor to ceiling, blue-tinged and unbreathable to the human lung. Water was a contradiction, both life and death at the same time. In their airtight suit, Linear waddled carefully into the temple's fluid interior, past elaborate and porous columns of bone and metal, down the gilded silver steps, toward the whale-skull altar in the center of it all. Light flickered in the periphery of their vision: piscine ribbons of intent, prowling the edges of the temple. Yare was hungry and resentful as ever. Hir hatred permeated the water, sending prickles crawling up the skin on Linear's arms.

Don't be absurd, Linear thought. *Zie can't possibly be doing that. It's just a trick of the body.* Yet Yare was a god, and who knew what gods were capable of?

Linear approached the skull and nestled the offering into one of its massive openings, saying the correct things at the correct time the way they'd memorized it. In the shallows of nighttime they often wondered if their impropriety was part of the reason Yare was so angry all the time.

The light ribbons swirled in the water, thickened, and coalesced into a shape. Axis like an eel, fins and scales a rainbow, a crown of white all loose in the water. Linear was familiar with this form of Yare's; they had seen it often enough.

But something went differently this time. Instead of solidifying into a serpent—the way dragons were always depicted in pictures and tales, the way they usually presented themselves to humanity—the deity's borders kept changing, shrinking into ever more compact forms, until what stood before Linear was a familiar shape. Human. No—not quite: humanoid. Bipedal. Absolutely not human. Eyes black, skin white, hair still that wild crowning halo. A rare form, one only fit to be witnessed by the most holy of the holy. Certainly not by a convicted criminal like Linear.

Yare blinked, and moved hir very bloodred lips. "So. I see it's you." Their voice, transmitted through water, was the sound of glass breaking over sand.

Linear bowed, unsure of what to say. Their rushed and deeply begrudged training taught nothing in the way of conversing with the gods. Yare in particular was known for being aloof. Zie never spoke to humans, instead letting hir desires be known through signs in the wind and water. How did one engage in small talk with a god? Linear didn't know, so they thought it best they kept their mouth shut. They'd been doing that a lot lately, trading their thoughts for silence. If only this lesson had been learned earlier. Keeping their mouth shut could have kept them out of trouble.

Yare said nothing for an uncomfortably long time, simply staring at the hunched-over form of the priest-penitent until they unrolled from their bow. The water danced between them. Nervous energy built in Linear's spine and bloomed into their body. Should they say something? Was this a test? Words bubbled haphazardly in their forebrain. Afraid of what might happen, Linear clenched their jaw to keep all those loaded syllables inside. The god's void-black eyes were a knife upon them, carving off pieces of flesh and will until Linear thought they would collapse inward.

There had to be a right thing to say. Which means that everything else would be the wrong thing to say, and so therefore it was best to say nothing at all. Eliminate that risk. Fear swirled in their gut, watery and treacherous.

The god spoke again. "We are to spend a long time together, you and I."

"Yes," Linear said, through the glass of their helmet. "Ten years."

"As each other's only company."

"Yes. It is our fate."

Hair tendrilled around Yare's face as zie moved. The dragon looked amused, and that sent more fear through Linear. A god's amusement was a dangerous thing. "Fate. You believe in that, don't you?"

"It's not a belief," Linear said, confused. "This is the path that was fated for me."

Yare laughed: a splintery, stuttery thing. A pinch grew in the space between Linear's ribs and their stomach. They shouldn't have said that. That was almost certainly the wrong thing to say.

Since when had they become someone so afraid of saying the wrong thing?

"I look forward to our time together," Yare said. Hir face split into a smile, revealing a zipper of bladed teeth. Behind that lay another sharply glinting row, and behind that yet another, so on and so forth.

Panic swept through Linear. They bowed vigorously, driven by crude instinct, then fled the temple. The water resisted their passage but they plowed through anyway. By the time they returned to the dry deck their pulse occupied their whole body down to the fingers and toes, and even when the last of the water glaze had sluiced off their suit, it had not returned to normal.

Linear made it back to the cloister deck on shaky limbs. The archpriest—a proud and senior man named Chase—took one look at them and said, "You were gone a longer time than usual. Something wrong?"

"No. Nothing." Lying was definitely the wrong thing to say, but it felt less wrong than telling the truth. Linear hid their unsteady heart like a frightened animal in their chest. No one needed to know what the dragon had said to them.

To Linear's relief, Yare did not manifest for the rest of the journey. The temple remained cold and silent when they brought the offerings each day. The water did not even stir. Linear knew Yare was there—the pressure of the deity's presence was unmistakable, and escape from the ship was impossible anyway—but zie chose not to show hirself. That suited Linear just fine.

The next time they saw the god was during the ceremony. By then they had landed on 9Xcil-5L. The prison ship nested on the purple horizon, a finned alien thing against the acid sky. The priests stood in rows, sashes bright over their ENV suits, chanting as the dais-bearers brought the crucible containing Yare to the silver edge of the ocean. Linear was the last in the processional line, backed up by a dozen guards. They watched the bronze cauldron slip under the mercury. For a while, nothing happened except the constant, toxic pelt of the rain. Then the reflective surface began to bubble, and as it frothed it turned clear, as though the poison was being boiled from it. White light punched up from the expanding crystalline depths. As Linear watched, they imagined they saw the sleek white shape that was Yare gliding through the newly birthed water. Hir new home.

"It is done," said archpriest Chase. The water deity was loose upon the world, free to bend it to hir will, in the way gods did. In ten years, humanity would return to the planet and christen it a new home, full of water to drink and air to breathe and land to till.

When the prison ship lifted from the surface of 9Xcil-5L, Linear was not on board. They watched the electric-blue take-off trail from the portcullis in their living dome, fastened to the rocky bones of the planet. Their long exile had begun.

The second of three times the dragon spoke to Linear, it was nearly a year later. By then the igneous land had begun to soften into soil and clouds amassed in the bruise-pink atmosphere with growing regularity. When they were not tending to the greenhouse or the upkeep of their dome, Linear spent their days walking the alien land, documenting these changes. In its native form, 9Xcil-5L had been geographically convenient, but environmentally hostile, as so many of these colony planets were. Temperatures below freezing for the most part, oceans liquid poison, atmosphere thin and sulfurous. It took a god to change something as vast as a planet. Yare brought water with hir, and water was the essence of life, water was the shaper of worlds. This barren rock was developing weather. An ecosystem. It was days yet before the blossoming of primitive life, but the vistas around Linear were taking on familiar shapes and colors. Their living dome sat on a plateau that overlooked the ocean, and in the absence of obscuring vegetation, Linear watched the months-long process of mercury being replaced by limpid gray, a widening swathe of crimpy surfaces that broke in soft peaks. In the controlled sanctuary of the living dome, Linear would strip off an ENV suit that had started to smell more like brine than burning vinegar.

The changes to the planet were memorialized by a host of machinery and drones, their sensors taking in more details (temperature, pressure, chemical composition) than human observation ever could. Still Linear recorded their daily explorations in their journal. *Went as far as the crescent basin today. Followed the river farther southwest.* Old-fashioned, ink on recycled pulp, pages they could flip through and words they could trace with their finger and reassure themselves: *Yes, this happened. This was real. I am here.* The writing was an anchor, ribbons fastened on branches, marking the undiluted passage of time in their solitude. *Thought I saw a gull today, far out over the ocean. Turning and turning in a wide, endless circle. What are you doing here, gull? Were you sent here in exile, like me?*

They had to be careful. Writing was almost like poetry, and poetry, the wrong kind of poetry, could get them in trouble.

The thing that beguiled Linear the most were the crystals. In the beginning they were barely worth taking notice of. Crystals grew everywhere Linear looked: geometrical inflorescences that sprang from the flint of the ground, some clear and some brightly colored. Linear assumed they were natural formations—like salt or minerals back home—and of no useful interest. But as weeks passed into months and the length of their sentence began to weigh upon them, they started paying attention to the most trivial of things in their environment. They began to notice patterns in the way these crystals grew. They

242

spread in whorls that reminded Linear of sunflowers, or the succulents that sprouted green and pink in Bryar's garden. This did not match any pattern of crystal growth that Linear knew. A hook upon which Linear's orderly mind snagged.

In the absence of any other thing that could possibly occupy them, Linear found themselves obsessed with the puzzle of these strange crystals. The more they looked, the less sense they made. At certain times of the day, when the distant blue sun was in just the right position, they could see that the crystals glowed with a soft light that pulsed in flickering patterns. What did this mean? The machines that accompanied Linear said the composition of the crystals was no different than the ones back home—silicon dioxide and feldspar and all kinds of minerals—and they, with their infinite wisdom and knowledge, said that there was nothing unusual about the crystals. But Linear could *see* that this was a lie. Were the machines lying to them? Or was this even beyond what science and machinery could understand? Linear prized a crystal sample from its cradle for further study, plucking out the heart of one strange whorl with pincer and pickax. Under the lights of the colony dome, the crystals' color faded, and then they turned opaque and brittle and crumbled into dust. Linear didn't know what they'd done wrong. When they returned to the spot where they'd uprooted the crystals, they found it empty, an open wound upon the land. All around it, the spiral of the crystals' kin had turned white as a grandmother's brow, as though in mourning.

In the days that followed, a cloying, inexplicable guilt slid around in Linear's guts. They would be wandering the desolate plains with no aim in mind when a welt of anxiety would strike them. They felt judged by the alien outgrowths, by the very ground itself. There was nothing rational about this, and Linear knew it. They were alone on this distant planet. There was no one and nobody here to cast judgment upon them.

No one except for Yare, of course.

Linear had not seen the god since they had slipped into the ocean on the day they arrived. At the start, they were relieved by this: it comforted them to think of the great depths that separated them and the dragon with their void-black eyes and rows of teeth. But loneliness had a weight, and the alien world seemed to grow in endlessness around them as time stretched on, greater and vaster than they ever could be. They found themselves spending more and more time by the water, staring out across the deckle-edged surface, imagining the sinuous form that tunneled through it in great coils.

As their torment grew over the mystery of the crystals, they started to think that perhaps the god would have some answers for them. But Linear was not really thinking about that—and maybe they weren't really thinking at all—when they swept the ashes of the dead crystals into a shallow dish and brought it to the ocean's edge. Their breath echoed in the tubes of their suit as they flung the white powder over the choppy gray. The ash floated for a brief second before it sank, dissolved, vanished. Linear stood by the chafing shore and waited for something to happen. For something to change. Time was meaningless in their exile. They waited for as long as it took them to start feeling stupid, for the point at which the lead of their uncertainty started to outweigh the swell of their hope. What had they expected to happen? Why had they expected anything to happen? This world owed them nothing, least of all closure. Their only job was to guide an invasion.

Linear turned to leave. As they did so, the ground under them rumbled, a development so unexpected they pivoted back in surprise. The ocean's surface boiled with unrest. As Linear watched, its meniscus rose in a great gray hump, which a white-haloed head pierced. Ocean sluiced off the sides of Yare's body as they rose ten meters upward and towered in the sky, alien and ineffable. One breath of wonder, one breath of terror. Then Yare leaned forward, hir scaly head the size of a house, and Linear froze.

The dragon spoke into Linear's mind. *Now I understand.*

"What? What do you understand?" Linear heard their voice reflected in their helmet and almost got startled; it had been so long since they'd spoken that they'd forgotten what they really sounded like.

This land. This strange world. The rocks feel your pain.

Linear blinked. The sky above them roiled black with clouds, just as it used to back home. Filaments of lightning seared bright veins in the growing tempest. They swallowed, not understanding what the god meant. "Pain? I'm not in pain. I'm not—"

I see everything. The rocks see everything.

"I'm just trying to get by. I'm not—I'm not what you said." Linear found themselves alarmed by the turn this conversation was taking. They just wanted to spend ten uneventful years on this alien rock, serving out their sentence without any trouble. No trouble, no surprises. They regretted coming to the water's edge. They regretted trying to find an answer. They didn't know what they were doing, they never did, what were they thinking?

You are afraid, Yare said. *You are lonely.*

Linear shrugged. Yare was right, and yet—who cared? What use did emotion have out here? There was no one but Linear the priest-penitent, and the alien planet, and an unknowable god who, not being human, could never understand the travails of humanity. Who would the emotion be for? Who would it serve? Better to keep it all inside. Expression was meaningless.

It is not meaningless, Yare said, as though zie could read their mind. *Expression is everything. A poet should know that.*

That last sentence struck something deep within Linear, and they recoiled as though physically wounded. They were stung, betrayed by the god trampling into such private, inflamed territory without asking. "How dare you," they said, even though Yare was a god and zie could do anything zie wanted. "It's none of your business. Don't talk to me."

Yare said nothing. Did nothing. Their maned, whiskered dragon's face was impossible to read. Adrenaline tightened Linear's chest and energized their hands and feet. Without thinking they turned and walked away from the god's presence. Away from the tempest they had woken from the waters they had disturbed. Back to their living dome, back to the silence of the tomb. They regretted doing this. They regretted everything.

As they walked, the god spoke in their mind again. *Thank you, Linear. Thank you for showing me what you did.*

Linear ignored hir. They wanted to shut the dragon's voice out, but they could not.

I have been struggling with my own questions. You have shown me the truth.

Linear walked faster. Ignoring it was all they could do.

Linear was not a poet. That had been Bryar: wild, unfettered Bryar with her words and her passions and her presence of mind. She was both a sun and a maelstrom, a burst of mad energy that could not, and would not, be contained. Into Linear's orderly, civil servant's life she had come like a bolt of weather, and Linear had been swept along, joyously and riotously. Bryar was not afraid of saying the wrong things, and in her presence Linear lost that deeply ingrained fear too. Bryar wrote poems about the shortcomings of the planetary government. They were popular, those poems. And then they got a little too popular, and then the uniformed men came for Bryar, and they came for Linear too.

The penalty for sedition was death by drowning. But the judge was magnanimous, and offered them a reduced sentence of ten years in exile if they repented. Bryar refused it. She would never compromise.

"Think of your families," said the judge. "Think of your parents." And so Linear, afraid of the watery depths, recanted. Repented. In a widely broadcast speech, they denounced the things they had said, the clumsy verse they had written. The script they read was given to them. It comprised exactly all the right things to say.

Sometimes when Linear could not sleep at night they would lie perfectly still in their exile's bed, and in those moments of disquiet, they imagined waters closing over their face. Imagined their lungs filling with cold liquid, holding down those hapless organs while they thrashed for freedom. Imagined the way Bryar's face would look under the surface as it contorted until it fell still. They liked to imagine that their lover had died proud and defiant, but their solitude and the weight of the alienness around them pressed down on their mind and body until black thoughts burst forth and spattered across their consciousness.

When the upset from their second conversation with Yare had receded to a gently lapping tide, Linear considered going back to the god and demanding that zie answer their questions about what happened in the water, right at the very end. What had Bryar been thinking? Did she hate Linear for what they did, leaving her to die alone? And was she afraid, right as her heart stopped and her consciousness was about to dim forever?

But they didn't call upon the god, even though they now knew how—a burning, an offering. Maybe the god wouldn't know. Or— more frighteningly—maybe they did. And they could tell Linear the truth. Just like that.

When Linear finally summoned Yare, it was the third and final time the dragon spoke to them. It was a week to the day before the anniversary of their arrival on the planet. A week to the day before Linear would send their annual report back home, to reassure their jailers that all was going well with the colony project. But not all was well. Not that Linear had noticed at first, their mind wrapped in misery and their body heavy, laced with melancholy. They spent each day drifting in a stupor that dulled their senses and obscured the changes creeping through the world around them. By the time they snapped from its fugue-ish hold, the sky had returned to the same electric violet it was when humanity first touched down on the planet. Almost like the tapestry of changes Yare made had come unraveled.

Linear stumbled out of their dome. On the ground, across the ground, the crystals had changed. Where they had lightly carpeted the surface like grass, they now towered, human height, a forest of glowing spikes Linear had to navigate as they shuffled across the land in disbelief. They had the sense of an immune response, a rejection of the invaders who were trying to transform the planet from inside out. Had 9Xcil-5L rebelled?

At the shoreline they found the ocean water still, familiar ripples in an unfamiliar world. Linear bent over, dipped their suit glove into the surf, and shouted for Yare.

Nothing happened. Of course nothing happened.

Linear returned to the dome. They needed ash, and the alien crystals were now too big for them to collect. Linear feared the mere idea of tearing one of those behemoths out of the ground. They may have acquiesced to that violation when it was Linear who was the giant in their world, but who knows how they might retaliate now?

There was one thing Linear could burn. It was the only thing. Linear prised their journal out of its cabinet and laid it on the laboratory bench. It wasn't real paper, but it was still pulp, and it could still burn. It contained all of Linear's observations, thoughts, and feelings, a whole year's worth, from the practiced diligence in the beginning to the half-effort incoherence they had deteriorated into. Linear had kept it as a record of their life.

They lit the tip of the burner and set it against the journal's black cover.

When it was over and the ash was cool, Linear filled a glass-walled dish and returned to the ocean. They flung the black powder over the seething water, and watched as the record of their life in exile sank beneath the waves. Then they waited, breath heaving in their chest as though they had just run marathons, moved mountains. Would Yare come? Were they even alive, if gods could be considered to be alive?

Water heaved and began to turn in an angry spiral a mile wide. Linear backed up, afraid that the whirlpool would somehow suck them in. From the eye of this exuberance rose an enormous, deadly figure. It was Yare, but this time in the human form zie showed to Linear the first time they spoke. Only magnified to terrifying scale: a mountain of a deity, rising from the waters.

Yare had changed. Hir face, hir skin was riddled with alien crystals, like zie had been infected, a host for parasites. Linear shouted, gesturing to the world around them with all its wrongness: "Did you do this? What is going on?"

The dragon spoke with all hir teeth. *Thank you, Linear. It was you, after all, who showed me the way.*

"Showed the way? What is happening?"

I have said. You presented me with the truth.

"What truth? What is this? What are you doing to the crystals?"

What I should have done. Did you know there was life on this planet?

"No. There's no life here. We surveyed the planet before. It's desolate, toxic, there was no water—"

Are those the only conditions for life? These crystals, as you call them, they are alive. They have thoughts and desires as you do.

"How is that possible?"

Your narrow mortal mind cannot comprehend possibilities beyond your own. But I can. I have spoken with them, I have understood them. The life on this planet, it has welcomed me. Our relationship is without chains. Without expectations. Here, in my new role, I am no longer bound by the strictures of your world. You see, I am their god now. I am the god of this planet, and I will act accordingly.

The meaning of the dragon's words seeped into Linear's bones. After staring at Yare's transformed face for this dizzy period, the crystal growth looked like it belonged, like it had always been there. "So all this is your doing, then."

Who else?

"I'll have to report this."

Yare tilted hir head. *Do you?*

"You can't derail the whole project just because there's primitive life here. I'm supposed to keep you on track. That's why I'm here. This is my job."

Why do you do it?

"My job?" Linear shook their head, as if they could shake the dizziness out of it. "Because . . . it's my job. I have to do it. I have nothing else to do."

You work for people who have caused you more pain than you could imagine. Why?

Linear shrugged. Why? They had never come up with a satisfactory answer to this question that haunted them in the liminal space between consciousness and dreams. Because they feared death. Because they felt helpless and following a path laid out for them was better than nothing. Because they didn't know what else to do now that Bryar was gone.

At their silence the god laughed. The sea around hir shivered, and every crystal in Linear's field of vision flashed a reddish yellow.

"You have to stop this," they said.

Yare blinked. *And if I don't?*

Linear breathed harshly and opened and closed their gloves. They stared at the frothing surface of the ocean. What then?

What are you looking forward to, at the end of your exile?

Linear's head snapped up, but Yare was already sinking back into the ocean, their piece said. Their curiosity sated. *What you do next is entirely your choice.*

"Wait," Linear said, but the dragon vanished between the waves. The last peak smoothed and the sky lightened. The deity was gone; Linear stood alone on the shore. "Come back," they shouted, but the words were empty echoes in their suit. Yare was not coming back. They were on their own.

Linear returned to the dome and stripped off their ENV suit, their mind blank, their hands following a set of instructions laid down a long time ago. They didn't stop with the plasticky suit. When they came to the layers of soft cotton underneath, they continued to peel. Shirt and trousers were followed by underwear. Finally, sated and naked, Linear went and sat on their favorite couch. Their gaze fixed, obliquely, on the blank wall across from them. Their fingers were so struck with cold no feeling was left in them, but Linear barely noticed.

What were they looking forward to, once their exile was finished? Once ten years on this lonely rock were over, their sins forgiven, and they were returned home. To do what? Pick up what remained of their life and carry on? Live in the little box erected for them by those in charge?

It had been easy to choose not to die, relatively speaking. Harder to live with the consequences of that.

Day turned into night turned into day, or maybe it was Linear's mind that was rising and setting. They dreamed of Bryar, a cloud of hair and warmth who lived in the water now, her eyes bright as ever, her lips still soft and red. She stood at the bottom of the ocean, in Yare's domain. "Come join me," she said. "It's lovely down here. And all is forgiven."

"Aren't you angry with me?" Linear asked. "Haven't I betrayed you?"

In response Bryar reached out and grasped their hands, tugging them down into the deep. Laughter swelled around them and caressed them, tangling in their hair and feet. Linear discarded their lungs; they didn't need them anymore. Bryar's teeth shone in the gray. "I've missed you so much. We're meant to be together." And it had been such a long, long time since Linear felt such peace in their heart. Down in the water with the woman they loved.

A missive was sent from 9Xcil-5L. The annual report, filed by the local priest-penitent in exile, was short and to the point. Everything was going according to plan. Nothing was wrong. The dragon deity was doing hir job as zie should. If anyone noticed that the report did not include the collated machine logs, the raw data, as it should, no one made a fuss about it. A small slip in routine, that was all. Everything was fine.

Linear was standing on the shore. Above them, the sky was purple; in front of them, the ocean stretched gray and full of promise. A forest of alien crystals surrounded them, pulsing with their own secret thoughts.

They started to strip. First the white shell of their suit, then the soft wrap of clinging cotton, and finally nails scraped cold skin as they pulled the last scraps of clothing off themselves. The atmosphere was not breathable, and they only had the well of their lungs to draw from, their final breath rapidly dissipating through their body. But it did not matter. Where they were going they did not need lungs. Linear stepped into the icy surf and found the ground beneath them solid, not yet broken into yielding sand. Out in the middle of the ocean glowed a white light, not warm but clear and crisp, and with the last of their oxygen Linear began striding toward it. They imagined, as the gray waters began closing over them, that in that light they could see a familiar and perfect set of teeth. There, right there: a pair of arms, waiting for an embrace.

EXCEPT ON SATURDAYS

Peter S. Beagle

Peter S. Beagle was born and raised in the Bronx, where he grew up surrounded by the arts and education. Both his parents were teachers, three of his uncles were gallery painters, and his immigrant grandfather was a respected writer, in Hebrew, of Jewish fiction and folktales. As a child, Peter used to sit by himself in the stairwell of his apartment building, making up stories. He is the author of fantasy classics *The Last Unicorn*, *A Fine and Private Place*, and *The Innkeeper's Song*. Peter has written teleplays and screenplays for the animated versions of *The Lord of the Rings* and *The Last Unicorn*, plus the fan-favorite "Sarek" episode *of Star Trek: The Next Generation*. His nonfiction book *I See By My Outfit* is considered a classic of American travel writing. A recipient of the World Fantasy Award for Life Achievement and the Science Fiction & Fantasy Writers of America's Damon Knight Memorial Grand Master Award, he is also a gifted poet, lyricist, and singer/songwriter. He currently makes his home in Oakland, California.

She was already on the 29 when I got on at Milvia, a couple of blocks from Berkeley High, where I teach. I have real trouble telling blondes apart—we didn't have many in the neighborhood where I grew up—

but this one I would know in the dark if I ever saw her again. It wasn't so much that she was, literally, breathtaking, but the way she went about it: her eyes looked absolutely black until a streetlight showed them to be an oceanically deep blue, and her rich, dark mouth bore the curl, the gentle twist of so much sorrow that it was painful to look upon, and harder still to look away from. She appeared to be— I'm terrible with ages—somewhere in her late thirties or early forties; she wore a heavy tweed overcoat over a nondescript sweater and slacks, with a blue kerchief tied loosely around her neck. Her hair was animal-colored, the dusty, tawny gold of a mountain lion's fur, or of a tiger's without the stripes. People don't have hair that color.

I took a seat a row behind her, on the opposite side of the bus. Beautiful as she was, it was the wheelchair that fascinated me. I'd never seen one remotely like it: one more button, one more knob or lever, and it could have been the dashboard of a Lamborghini; one more lighted dial, and it would surely have been the bridge of the *Enterprise*. I kept stealing glances at it over the cover of the book I was reading (my students tease me because I read a lot of memoirs of old jazz musicians and baseball players), and wondering what did what, where the batteries must be located, and whether she could actually take that thing out on the freeway. What was its top speed? Its range? I don't usually find myself speculating on the horsepower of wheelchairs.

I had stayed late for a departmental meeting that ran considerably overtime, as they always do, so rush hour was long over, and the bus was less than half-full, moving nicely as the traffic on Shattuck thinned out. But the bicyclists were out in force tonight, fluttering and wobbling like butterflies on all sides without ever paying the least attention to traffic flow, let alone traffic lights, and the driver had to slow down or stop half a dozen times between University and Durant. We had just made the turn onto Durant when he abruptly let go with a sizzling blast of what I think was Amharic and hit the brakes with all his weight, so that the bus stopped dead, on a dime, and the woman in the wheelchair was hurled to the floor. She never made a sound.

To do people justice—I don't always, being a history teacher—most of the passengers were gathered around her almost on the instant, asking whether she was hurt and what they should do to help. A couple of them had quickly gathered the two small grocery bags that had spilled from her lap and were awkwardly but carefully holding them for her. The bus driver was loudly urging everyone to stand back and give her air, and I remember an old woman who was all but drowning him out with her prayers to St. Martin de Porres, which doesn't make sense, because he's the patron of hairdressers, but there you are. I have *got* to ask someone about that.

The woman herself was the calmest of all of us. Tumbled onto her side, but already beginning to push herself into a sitting position, she said, "I am all right, I am not injured at all." It was a low, clear voice, with a slight hint of a French accent, and an even slighter trace of amusement. "Please, I'm sorry to delay everyone, but my legs do not work," which was indeed obvious from the boneless look of them as they sprawled out before her, with one bent across the other at the shin. "If someone could straighten them . . ." The driver did that, lifting her legs very gingerly, only gripping them at the ankles. "Thank you—I was such a fool not to be wearing my seatbelt. Now, if some strong young man could take me under my arms . . ."

I hadn't noticed that I was one of only two men on the bus; the other, sitting all the way in the back, was plainly younger than I and just as plainly stoned on something that he'd certainly be riding to the end of the line. Everyone else aboard was female, and smaller than I— which is rare—including the driver. I said, "You'll have to settle for an old gentleman with a bad back, but I'll do what I can."

Positioning myself behind her, I placed my hands as she directed, and pulled. You're supposed to crouch, of course, and lift from your legs, rather than risking your back—as I know to my cost—but I didn't have much choice, or much room to hunker down properly. I was able to raise her a little way, but not to any purpose, not even to the edge of the seat. She never complained, and no one laughed at me; and it shouldn't have been embarrassing, but it was.

"All right," I said. "Hold tight—here we go." I bent farther, managing a bit of a squat this time, got one arm under her knees, supporting her shoulders with the other, and, with the aid of a tidal surge of adrenaline, actually swept her up and set her down again in her wheelchair. A few passengers applauded, and I think I blushed, remembering the last time I had done such a thing with a woman. One's legs may go first, as they say, but vanity definitely goes last.

"There," I said. I snapped the seatbelt around her, and said, in a lower voice, "There you are, Melusine."

She froze for a moment in the chair—and why shouldn't she have? I surely had, feeling the ridged scales underneath those slacks. People were beginning to return to their seats, and the driver had already restarted the engine and was about to pull back into traffic. The woman and I stared at each other. I said, "Is Saturday still the day? That's tomorrow."

"I get off at Thirty-Ninth," she said. "Don't forget your book."

I went dutifully back to my seat, and for the rest of the ride—all the way to the end of College, where it bends right and joins Broadway—I really did do my best with Rex Stewart's essays on his life in jazz, because he was one of the surprising handful of musicians who could write well and without sentimentality about the old days. But all the time I kept the corner of one eye on her, and when she rang for the Thirty-Ninth Street stop, I stood up too. The driver came back and lifted a plate in the floor that became a ramp, and she rolled smoothly off and waited for me on the sidewalk. The bus pulled away.

"It's still Saturday," she said. "*Samedi . . . Sabado . . . Sabato . . . Samstag*. It has been Saturday for a thousand years. I have never known why." She looked up at me, and now her eyes were black enough to give meaning to the Dark Ages that bore her. "How did you know me? My legs will not change until midnight."

"But the tail is there now," I said. "I could feel it under the human, coming. I was raised on the old legends—you and Bisclavret, the poor werewolf, were my favorite bedtime stories. What on earth are you doing in California?"

She shrugged. "Immortals always end up in California, sooner or later, quite often as bedtime stories. You would be amazed at whom I have seen in Palo Alto alone, never mind Berkeley." The wheelchair's electric motor caught silently, and she started along Broadway, as I walked beside her, carrying her grocery bags. There was a breeze up, and she pulled the blue scarf over her cat-colored hair.

I said, "There are German stories about you, but you begin in France." She nodded without answering. "You married either Count Raymond of Poitou, or Guy de Lusignan, who fought in the Crusades—"

"Both. Raymond was far more handsome, but Guy . . . Guy was the better man, in the end." I could barely hear the last words.

"Well, you certainly had more children with him. I always imagined you living in the forests near Lusignan, watching over your family, even after you left Guy—"

"Gone." She spoke the word flatly, without drama or sentimentality, but it tolled tonelessly in her mouth. "The family—the castle itself—all, all gone. They marry, they migrate, they buy, they sell, they die . . . of my old blood, there are none left, no matter how their inheritors print my image on their stationery, carve it on their bed-and-breakfast signs. All gone but the one in Canada."

"Canada? Quebec?"

She nodded.

"Then why are you here?"

The wheelchair turned abruptly down a side street, and I kept pace. With her head covered by the blue scarf, she looked about eleven years old; but it was with an adult's dry humor that she answered me. "I may be immortal, but I have my limits. Too cold, and too northern—and what they do to my language makes me want to eat them to make them stop. No . . . at my age, your California is as far from home as I travel.

Besides, he is young, thank my stars. Ah, here we are."

We had arrived at one of the older apartment houses in this part of Oakland. Nineteen twenties would have been my guess: it was tall—a good five stories—which is fairly rare; it had a genuine doorman just inside the lobby, which is very rare; and the kind of architectural features—cornices, dormers, fanlights, and even dentils, for God's sake—that you don't usually see on any place you can get to by public transit. The doorman hurried out to welcome Mrs. Lusignan, as he called her, pronouncing it perfectly, and I followed her in under his instantly disapproving eye.

"Will you come in for coffee?" She smiled with a sudden startling tenderness, not at me, but at a memory. "Raymond discovered coffee in the Holy Land. He tried so hard to make it grow in France, but it never would."

The building actually had a penthouse, and she used a key in the elevator to get us to the top floor. I can't describe the apartment in any great detail, because I was so occupied in trying to deal with the notion of Melusine—the *real* Melusine herself—living in any apartment, in any building, in any century but the thirteenth or fourteenth, and in any locale but Southern France. But the walls of her living room—where she served our coffee, accompanied by madeleines that would have made Proust weep—were white, with an undertone of blue, and there were a lot of paintings and hanging tapestries, some surprisingly modern; most clearly as old as the books on her shelves. There was no loom visible, nor any sketchbook, nor so much as an embroidery frame; but there was a small keyboard, plainly meant to hook up to an organ of some sort, and I was reminded that aristocratic thirteenth-century ladies needed to have some demonstrable talent to entertain. Even if they could turn into a dragon at a moment's notice, and avenge themselves properly against people who couldn't.

Which reminded me . . . and I looked at my watch. Ten thirty, a bit before. She saw the movement and smiled, this time definitely at me, myself: a born professor, prematurely aged by the pointless pressures of his job, but with a magpie memory, completely unsystematized, for all sorts of myths, legends, and fairy tales. She said, "I have never harmed a human being in all my very long life. You would appreciate that statement more if you knew even one of the temptations that have been placed in my way."

"Good to know," I said lamely; and then, thinking it just as well to change the subject, "Do you need the chair all the time?"

"Only on Friday. Sometimes Thursday as well—lately, it varies." She sighed. "The children never had any trouble remembering to leave me entirely to myself on Saturdays. I don't think Raymond and dear Guy quite knew the days of the week, not really. And why should they have? That sort of thing was for women and priests, in those days."

"Yet you left them both without giving either one a second chance, and without ever looking back. I always thought that a bit harsh of you."

Melusine bridled somewhat. "I was simply too old not to see the end in the beginning. First, spying on your bath—then, the next thing you know, they are choosing your dresses, choosing their own mistresses, ordering the cook around, and demanding that you sing for their drunken friends when you have a headache. No, no, thank you, I offer no second chances, no atonements." Yet the last words were, though not regretful, touched with something close to wistfulness. She poured more coffee.

"When they died," I said, "when any of your descendants died, the legend was that you flew in dragon form around their castle towers all night long, weeping so that trees fell and rivers flooded. They still claim you in Lusignan."

"So they should," she answered, with a wry twist of that haunting, haunted mouth. "I am become a tourist attraction, like your time's theme parks and my time's holy relics—lies and pigs' bones, either way." She broke one of the madeleines in half and handed me my portion with the air of a queen granting a supplicant an earldom, or a monopoly. She said, "But I will fly once more only, whenever the last of my family dies in Canada. After that . . . after that I will be no one but a retired old Californian lady, living quietly on a side street with my books and my memories. Nothing more."

"Except on Saturdays," I said.

Her smile bared small, perfect teeth, remarkably white and just slightly pointed.

"Except on Saturdays. But remember, I am only half a dragon—the other half is as human as makes no matter. I know how to live here. Shall we have some wine?"

I am not a wine buff—an impossible, arrogant beer snob, yes—and I do not know how to describe the wine that she served me in crystal glasses that rang together for a toast as gently and distantly as wind chimes. All wine turns to vinegar beyond a certain age, no matter how fancy and expensive it is; and this vintage simply could not have been as old as she told me it was. But I have never had such wine again, which is a great pity, now that I know what wine is supposed to be. What wine is.

The earliest reference to Melusine that I have ever found dates from the late fourteenth century. The last woman I had been with was a university student (no, not one of mine, thank God; leave me a little honor, a smidgen of dignity). She seduced me—talk about falling off a log—and then told all her friends about it, and even put it up on the Internet. There has been no one since. Had been. Has.

I cannot tell you to this day whether or not I actually made love with Melusine, a creature perhaps far older than even the fairy tales tell us; perhaps as old as Lilith, as old as Ishtar or Isis. What I do know is that at some point I did lift her in my arms for a second time, and I did look down into a face fierce and beautiful, universes beyond my understanding of either word. There were dragons in her eyes; there were lilacs on her mouth; there were tiny thorns guarding the nipples of the round breasts so like those in erotic Indian bas-reliefs. And as for the legs—for yes, I am sure those sleek slacks came off . . . no, they were not human legs, not legs, really, not at all, and I did not care. I still have the occasional nightmare about them, but it was worth it. Whatever truly happened, it was worth it.

Obviously, I lost track of time. I didn't care about that, either. But I will swear that it was not yet midnight when she rose through my arms in another form, so swiftly, and with such power, that knife-edged scales sliced my shirt open, great claws put marks on my back that I bear to this day, and a desert breath like a sirocco, a khamsin, a simoom, hurled me halfway across the room, where I sprawled as helplessly as she had done on the floor of the 29 bus. She rose over me—half-human, quarter-human, what price fractions?—the face still her face, after a fashion; the arms that had at once cradled and commanded me now shrunken against her chest, all but hidden in the shadow of the great wings spreading from her sides. The legs had fused completely into a tail curled like some sort of wasp poised to sting. When she spoke, I could understand her, but her speech itself was agonizing to hear, as though there were scales on the words too, raking against my eardrums. I can hear them yet, even though she only spoke three.

"Open the window . . ."

I picked myself up and hurried to obey, lest she should speak again. She went through with a rush that did not knock me over again, but did set my torn clothes flapping absurdly, and my head almost literally spinning on my neck. The old-style fire escape outside the window crashed onto the street below. No one was hurt, that I ever knew.

She did not fly off immediately, but hovered outside the window, looking back at me. The tail unfurled fully for the first time, glittering metallically in the light of the risen three-quarter moon. There are ancient woodcuts and etchings of Melusine that show her with two tails, but one is plenty. From her matted mane, gleaming like chain mail itself, to the very end of her body, she must have been a full twelve feet in length; yet in part she remained recognizably, terribly human, just as Medusa must have done. Her face looked more like metal itself than like flesh, but the twist of great grief was on it, on her mouth, as visibly as it had been on the 29 bus. I was terrified of her, and of what we had been about to do—or had already done? My body told me nothing—but I ached for her, and toward her, as I still do. *Melusine . . .*

She lingered against the moon, heading northeast, for what seemed a very long time, before I lost sight of her altogether. There are so many images, so many book-cover paintings of dragons flying across the moon that I sometimes think they must favor being seen in that light, the same way that horses will gather on a hilltop just at sunset, to be silhouetted there. I'm sure it's deliberate. I closed the window, picked up the chairs and little tables that had been knocked over in her passage, washed our coffee cups, and let myself out. The doorman eyed me, but said nothing.

It took a good bit of googling and scouring the Internet for the next couple of days, but I finally found a few lines concerning a particular motorcycle accident near Quebec City. A French-language newspaper even gave some details of the funeral; but whether in English or French, there was no mention of a dragon's mourning the very last descendant of the oldest de Lusignans. But she was there. She would have made it there.

I have not seen her again, nor do I expect to, for all that I ride the same bus every day, and make a point of walking by her apartment building now and again. For all I know, she may have moved away, having no more reason to be in this country at all; though she did suggest that she might stay on, for the sake of the weather. But I do think that if she wanted me to see her, it would have happened by now. Still, I am not unhappy, nor haunted, nor even particularly wistful. I am more like the donkey in Chesterton's poem, who remembers having borne Christ into Jerusalem. I have also had my hour, "one far fierce hour and sweet," and who else can say that in the Berkeley High history department?

LA VITESSE

Kelly Robson

Kelly Robson (kellyrobson.com) grew up in the foothills of the Canadian Rocky Mountains. Her novelette, *A Human Stain*, won the 2018 Nebula Award, and her novella, *Waters of Versailles,* won the 2016 Aurora Award. She has also been a finalist for the Hugo, Nebula, World Fantasy, Theodore Sturgeon, Locus, John W. Campbell, Aurora, and Sunburst awards. Her most recent book is *Gods, Monsters, and the Lucky Peach,* which has been nominated for the Nebula and Hugo awards. After twenty-two years in Vancouver, she and her wife, fellow SF writer A. M. Dellamonica, now live in downtown Toronto.

March 2, 1983, 30 kilometers southwest of Hinton, Alberta
"Rosie," Bea said under her breath, but the old school bus's wheels were rumbling over gravel, and her daughter didn't hear. Rosie was slumped in the shotgun seat, eyes closed. She hadn't moved since Bea had herded her onto La Vitesse at six fifteen that morning. She wasn't asleep, though. A mother could always tell.

Bea raised her voice to a stage whisper. "Rosie, we got a problem."

Still no reaction.

"Rosie. Rosie. Rosie."

Bea snatched one of her gloves off the bus's dashboard and tossed it. Not at her kid—never at her kid; it bounced off the window and landed in Rosie's lap.

"Mom. I'm sleeping." Big scary scowl. Bea hadn't seen her kid smile since she'd turned fourteen.

"There's a dragon right behind us," she said silently, mouthing the words. None of the other kids had noticed, and Bea wanted to keep it that way.

Rosie rolled her eyes. "I don't read lips."

"A dragon," she whispered. "Following us."

"No way." Rosie bolted upright. She twisted in her seat and looked back through the central aisle, past the kids in their snowsuits and toques. "I can't see it."

The rear window was brown with dirty, frozen slush. Thank god. If the kids saw the dragon, they'd be screaming.

"Come here and look."

Rosie crawled out of her seat and leaned over her mother, hanging tight to the grab bar behind Bea's head. Her too-tight black parka carried a whiff of cigarettes.

Bea flipped open her window and adjusted the side-view mirror for Rosie. Behind the bus, a long, matte-black wing beat the air in a furious rhythm. The pale winter sun glinted on the silver scales that marked the wing's fore edge.

"Wow," Rosie said, her voice so low it was almost a growl.

Bea stepped on the gas. La Vitesse surged ahead, revealing the dragon's broad chest, rippling with flexed muscles. It lifted its taloned forelegs as if reaching for the bus, and showed them the barest glimpse of a lissom neck and triangular, snakelike head before it caught up to the bus and disappeared into the mirror's blind spot.

Rosie pushed her ragged bangs out of her eyes and leaned closer to the mirror.

"No fire. Why isn't it trying to roast us?"

"I don't know. Maybe it's breathing too hard," Bea said. "But, honey, you got to help me. Herd the kids into the front seats. Pack them in tight."

Rosie wasn't listening, though. She stared at the mirror, transfixed, watching the dragon's wing flexing from hooked tip to thick shoulder.

"Rose, please." Bea slapped the wheel with both hands. "Get the kids up front."

"Yeah, okay." Rosie straightened, then leaned over her mother again for one last look.

Even Bea had to admit her kid looked scary, especially lately, with her death metal T-shirts and her angry slouch. Not yet sixteen, but so big and tall she looked twenty. Add all that to the black eyeliner Rosie melted with a match and applied smoldering, and the spiky haircut she'd given herself in grade ten and kept short with Bea's only pair of good scissors, and yeah, Bea could understand why other mothers gave her hell for letting her kid look so rough.

Bea couldn't do anything about it. Rosie had always been more trouble than Bea could handle. But as long as she came home on the bus with Bea every day, nothing else mattered.

But Bea didn't like the way her daughter looked at the dragon. She wasn't scared, not even a bit. Maybe she was even glad to see it.

Bea drove the longest and most remote bus route in the school district. Starting at her trailer south of Cadomin, she headed north and picked up kids along the Forestry Trunk Road all the way past Luscar and the Cardinal River coal mine, then turned east on the Yellowhead Highway, and hauled the kids through town to drop them off at all three schools.

The round trip took five hours—two and a half each way. La Vitesse was a fast bus with a big V8 engine but Bea drove slow. She had to. The Forestry Trunk Road was gravel, heavily corrugated with washboard created by runoff from the surrounding mountains. The soft shoulders on either side of the gravel-road bedding could easily pull a vehicle into the ditch or off a cliff, and moose lurked around every corner—often right in the middle of the road. Bea had seen what hitting a big bull moose could do to a bus, and she didn't want anything to do with it.

So Bea drove slow. She was kind, too. School bus drivers were allowed to leave kids behind if they weren't outside on time, waiting by the road, but Bea never did. Bears were common fall and spring, and cougars hunted year-round. A kid waiting for the bus made a nice warm snack.

And lately, Bea worried about dragons, too.

Rosie herded the kids into the front rows, three and four to a seat. Too rough; Rosie was always too rough with other kids, but it didn't matter now.

"We're playing a game," Bea sang out in her best sunny voice and smiled into the rearview mirror. "Let's see how fast La Vitesse can stop. I'll honk my horn ten times. You all count with me. On the tenth honk, I'll hit the brakes. Everyone hang on tight. Brace yourselves, okay?"

In the rearview, hoods and toques framed twenty pairs of big, scared eyes. They knew something was wrong. Kids always did.

"It'll be fun," she said, smiling wider. "Ready?"

The kids counted along as she honked. She hoped the horn might drive the dragon off, but she'd already tried that and it hadn't worked.

On the tenth honk, they were on a good flat straightaway. Decent gravel, no potholes or washboard. Shallow ditches on either side, lined with slender young spruce. If La Vitesse skidded off the road, they'd be okay. The bus would stick, though; Bea had faith.

When she slammed on the brakes, one kid screamed. Several whimpered. The dragon hit the back of the bus with a hollow *thunk*. La Vitesse skidded but stayed square in the middle of the road. Bea shifted to first gear and slammed the gas. La Vitesse's engine roared, then screamed. Bea let the revs build and shifted to second, her foot flat on the floor.

In the side-view, the dragon lay crumpled on the gravel, wings canted like a broken tent.

Bea held her breath, flicking her gaze from road to mirror to road. Dead, she hoped. Let it be dead.

The dragon lifted its head and yawned. A tongue of blue flame licked from between its fangs. It clawed the gravel with the hinges of its wings and staggered to its feet. In the early morning light, its eyes sparked a keen and murderous ice-white.

*Bea had seen the first dragon in 1981, two years back, when she was bring-*ing home a bus full of soccer players after a tournament in Jasper.

She'd been cruising east along the Athabasca River, heading toward the Jasper park gates. The sunset light turned the mountains mellow orange, and the trees threw long, spear-shaped shadows across the highway. La Vitesse's speedometer was two fingers below the speed limit. The wheels hummed on the gently curving highway. Bea was thinking about making barbeque ribs for Sunday supper when she spotted the dragon perched on the massive cliff-edge of Roche Miette.

On the mountain high above the highway, the dragon's red scales gleamed bloody in the sun. It stretched its wings and beat them once, then pointed its narrow head at the highway below. It dropped off the cliff, kited low, and disappeared behind the trees.

When La Vitesse rounded the curve, the red dragon hunched spread-winged atop the dynamite-blasted rock face where mountain met highway, a bighorn sheep clamped in its jaws.

"Look," Bea squeaked. But the kids were making too much noise to hear. She floored the gas and watched the dragon recede in the rearview mirror. If she busted the speed limit all the way home, nobody noticed.

Twenty kids, and Rosie made twenty-one. The youngest not yet six, and Rosie the oldest at nearly sixteen. More than half of them were crying.

"Brake check all done!" Bea's voice was high with tension. She hunched in her seat and twisted from side to side, scanning the sky through the side-view mirrors. "The brakes are fine! La Vitesse is a good bus."

She patted the dashboard like it was a horse.

"Mom. They heard it hit us," Rosie growled. "Fucking tell them."

"A moose ran up the ditch," Bea said. "Gave us a little knock on the bum but we're fine."

The kids wailed louder. Tony Lalonde yanked his toque down over his eyes and howled.

"The moose is fine, too," Bea insisted. "Everything's okay."

But it wasn't okay. The dragon wasn't hurt. It flew a dozen car lengths behind, wings beating hard, mouth gaping. On every down-stroke, that blue flame licked the road. Was it hot enough to melt her tires? Probably. She couldn't afford to find out.

Behind her, Rosie stood in the aisle, surfing the bumps. When the dragon tore the emergency exit off its hinges and lunged up the aisle, Rosie would be its first victim. It would rip her daughter's head off and slaughter the kids one by one while Bea sat behind the wheel. She had to think of something.

"Rosie, honey," she said in the sweetest voice she could muster. "Come and drive the bus."

When Bea reported the red dragon to the Hinton RCMP, the Mountie at the front desk had just smiled.

"Imagination goes wild in the mountains," he said. "I had a coal miner in here the other day saying a giant black cat was lurking around his dragline."

"Yeah, okay, but have you been to Jasper lately?" Bea asked. "You know the bighorn sheep along the highway? The ones that graze under Roche Miette? They're gone. All of them."

The Mountie smirked. "Last summer a bunch of campers said they saw a Bigfoot at Jarvis Lake."

Bea gave up. He was from Toronto. What did he know? Nothing.

Bea and her family weren't coal miners and they sure weren't camp-ers. The mountains weren't terra incognita to her. She'd been born in the bush, like her parents and their parents and so on back all the gen-erations. Her ancestors lived in Jasper before it was a park, until they were kicked out and resettled in Cadomin. Those Rocky Mountain ranges were her true home, so when Bea said she saw a dragon, she saw it. No matter what some Mountie said.

"You want me to drive La Vitesse?" Rosie said. "Are you fucking kidding?"

From the back of the bus came a high-pitched rasping sound, like metal on metal, and if Bea had been unsure, she wasn't any longer.

"I'm not kidding. Take the wheel, please."

They exchanged positions awkwardly. Bea's ample hips didn't leave much room, but Rosie slid in behind her. What mattered most—after staying on the road—was keeping pressure on the gas pedal. Bea hung from the grab rail and stretched to keep her toe on the pedal, like a swimmer testing the water.

"Let go, let go, I got it." Rosie dug her shoulder into her mother's hip, hard.

"Okay, honey. Keep it above fifty, even on the curves. Floor it on the straightaways. And if you see anyone coming, lean on the horn and don't let up." Bea grabbed the fire extinguisher from the stepwell. When she stood, Joan Cardinal glared at her from under her glossy black bangs.

"I'm going to tell on you," Joan said, fully thirteen and fierce.

"That's okay, honey. You do that." Bea cradled the fire extinguisher like a baby. "Let's play another game. Here are the rules. Everybody stay in your seat. Don't get up. Hold tight to your seat buddies, stay quiet, and do everything I say. If you do, we'll stop at Dairy Queen on the last day before Easter break. My treat."

Every kid's mouth dropped open. Ice cream was the bus driver's secret weapon.

"Sundaes or cones?" said Sylvana Lachance, ten years old and already a master of negotiation.

"That depends on how good you are." Bea gave them a big motherly smile. "Now take off your snowsuits."

Rosie only had her learner's license but she'd been driving since she was ten. Out in the bush, all kids drove early. She'd learned on Bea's rusty Chevy Blazer, a four-speed with a sticky clutch, and had been driving it with confidence for years. Maybe the Blazer was nothing like La Vitesse, but Bea had no choice. She couldn't do anything about the dragon while stuck in the driver's seat.

Bea knelt in the aisle and stuffed her own parka inside Michelle Arsenault's tiny pink snowsuit, then padded the legs and arms with all the toques and scarves within reach.

"Who's got meat in their lunch today? Anyone?" The kids shrunk in their seats. "If you've got it, I want it."

Blair Tocher threw her his lunch bag. Bea ripped it open and tore through the plastic wrap with her fingernails. Peanut butter, that was fine. All animals liked that, right? She smeared the insides of the sandwich all over the snowsuit.

"Nobody's got baloney for lunch? Sausage? Spam?" She tried to sound normal, but her voice was high and shrill.

"Give her your lunches," came a growl from the driver's seat, where Rosie hunched over the wheel. "Do it or I'll take us into the ditch."

Bags rained on Bea's head. Pork sausage on thick homemade bread with mustard and a lick of golden syrup—that would be Manon Laroche's grandkids. Baloney and cheese on brown—could be anyone's. Cookies, apples, celery with Cheez Whiz, those all went inside. The meat she smeared on the outside, grinding the greasy dregs into the snowsuit's knit cuffs and fuzzy hood.

"Okay," Bea said. She hefted the snowsuit in one arm and grabbed the fire extinguisher with her other hand. Then La Vitesse hit a pothole and the whole world spun around her.

"Try steering around them, Rose," Bea called from the floor.

"We got a logging truck coming." Rosie's voice was strangely deep.

"The horn. Hit the horn, honey!" Bea scrambled up the aisle on all fours. "He's got a radio, he'll call for help."

She waved her arms as Rosie blasted the horn. High in the truck's cab, a man in a trucker hat and stubble. Sunglasses though it wasn't even full light yet. One hand on the wheel with fingers raised in a lazy wave while the other hand brought a white Styrofoam coffee cup to his lips for a sip. The truck flashed by.

"Did it work?" Rosie asked.

Bea ran to the first empty row and dived for the side window. She pressed her forehead against the cold glass and watched the truck disappear around a curve.

"No," Bea said. "He wasn't looking."

She limped up the aisle.

"I didn't turn on the hazard lights." She reached around her daughter and flicked on the hazards. She hit the warning lights too, the big orange traffic flashers front and back. Then she turned to the kids and took a deep breath.

On her left and right, all twenty kids, their precious little upturned faces. Tear-stained. Some contorted in fear. Most blank with shock. Her fault. She'd failed them all.

"It's a dragon," she said. "A big one."

Hinton didn't have a real library. Technically, the high school library was open to the public during school hours, but the librarian had ideas about the kinds of people who should be allowed to walk through the door. And in grade eleven, Bea had been banned. That might be sixteen years ago, but as far as she knew, she was still banned.

Still, Bea needed information and the library was the only place to get it.

After talking to the Mountie, she'd parked her bus at the hockey arena and walked over the playing fields toward the high school. Across the road, the pulp mill's stink-stacks belched rotten-egg vapor that drifted over the high school in a yellow haze.

She slipped into the library, walked softly to the reference shelf on the back wall, and pulled out *Encyclopaedia Britannica*, Volume 3. The entry on dragons was subtitled "mythological creature." She examined the illustrations. Clearly her dragon was the European type. Its snaky head and batlike wings matched the picture.

In European myth, it said, dragons terrorized entire valleys. After eating all the sheep, they'd start eating children.

Sheep. The sheep in the picture were fairy-tale versions, white and fluffy—nothing like bighorn sheep, with their sleek brown fur and curling horns. But the sheep under Roche Miette were gone. Did that mean the children were next?

"Bea Oulette."

Bea slammed the encyclopedia closed. Mrs. English watched her over the edge of her reading glasses.

"You're not allowed in here," she said. "You're banned."

Bea slipped the book back on the shelf and padded toward the door, keeping her eyes low.

"High school was a long time ago," she said softly as she passed the checkout desk.

"Not for me," the librarian snarled. "Don't come back."

Bea stood on a bus seat, reached high, and yanked open the rooftop safety hatch. It popped up easily—Bea kept the hinges well oiled. She steadied herself with one hand on the hatch's open edge and put her foot on the seatback, holding the greasy stuffed and smeared snowsuit between her teeth. With both hands, she shoved the hatch fully open.

Still awkward, but steadier now as she poked her head and shoulders through. Her hair whipped her face.

The dragon kited behind the bus. It scrabbled at the roof with its forelegs, raking its talons along the metal, looking for purchase. It lost its grip and fell behind, twisted in the air, then extended its long neck and beat its wings hard to catch up again.

All along the roof, long shiny marks gashed the paint and road dust. It was only a matter of time before it hooked a talon into La Vitesse.

Bea yanked the stuffed snowsuit through the hatch.

"Here," she yelled. "Do you want dinner?" She held the snowsuit by its waist and danced it, the arms and legs flopping. She pitched it at the dragon, then grabbed the hatch handles and slammed the hatch closed.

"Floor it, Rosie," she yelled.

But La Vitesse was already moving fast, and the highway intersection was on the horizon. No choice, they had to turn.

Bea lunged up the aisle.

"Slow down, honey! You won't make the turn."

"It didn't work." Rosie had her eyes on the side mirror. She wasn't even watching the road.

"Slow down now!"

Bea grabbed Rosie's shoulder and tried to pull her from the seat. The bus swerved. Rosie hunched over the wheel, gripping it with both hands, knuckles white, her whole body tense.

"Get out of the seat." Bea's voice rose, high and shrill. "Rosie, get out now."

A ripping sound of nails on metal. A gash of sunlight appeared in the ceiling over the left rear seat.

"That's a problem," Rosie said in a low, ominous voice.

"Slow down or we'll flip," Bea pleaded.

Rosie nudged the speed down a little. Bea grabbed two armfuls of kids from the seats behind Rosie and pushed them into seats opposite.

"Everyone on the right side." No time to be gentle. She grabbed arms and shoulders—whatever she could get a grip on, and then leaned in, pressing a seat full of the littlest kids under her belly. "Hold tight."

A popping sound. Bea twisted to look. Just above the smeared rear window, three talons punctured the bus's roof. The window itself was dark. The dragon hung from the back of the bus.

"Sundaes," Bea shouted. "If we make this turn, I'll buy you all sundaes."

"Hot fudge," Rosie said, and swung the wheel.

When she was a teenager, Bea took books from the high school library. Not often. Not every book. Just the good ones. But it wasn't stealing, not at first. When she started, she'd bring the books back. That's how she got caught.

First day of grade eleven, she was returning the books she'd taken home for the summer. Her plan was to slip them onto a shelf in the morning, make herself scarce, then sneak back in the afternoon like she'd never been there. But the load was too heavy. The books tore through the paper bag and spilled across the library linoleum, right in front of Mrs. English.

In the vice principal's office, Bea kept her eyes hooded and looked at the floor. Never confront them, that was the survival strategy. It's what her grandpa did when hunters crossed the ridge where he set up his sweat lodge. It's what her mother did when the grocery store manager followed her through the aisles. Eyes down, calm breaths, wait for them to lose interest.

Getting banned only kept her out of the library for a week. Mrs. English wasn't always watching. The student volunteers didn't care, and best of all, nobody else seemed to know what Bea knew. To steal a library book, all you had to do was sandwich it between two other books, say a binder and a math textbook, and hold the stack horizontal as you walked through the exit door. Held flat, the magnetic strip wouldn't set off the detector.

So Bea still had all the books she wanted, even though Hinton had no place to buy them but the drugstore's rack of boring bestsellers. She stocked up. After getting roasted by Mrs. English and the vice principal, she felt absolutely fine about it.

*La Vitesse's rear wheels screeched as they skidded sideways over the gravel-*coated asphalt at the Forestry Trunk Road intersection. One rear wheel parted from the ground. The chassis shivered like it was Bea's own flesh.

She clung to the seatbacks with her nails and wrapped her sneaker-clad foot around a seat strut. Under her belly, she pressed the littlest kids hard into their seat. As La Vitesse fishtailed, the dragon's claws ripped through the roof—four jagged rents lengthening in a clockwise curve as the dragon swung like a pendulum. A wing slapped the left rear windows, once, twice. A foot scrabbled at the glass, talons clacking in rapid staccato.

Warm wet spread across the thigh of Bea's jeans. One of the little kids was peeing himself. The dragon hung from the bus's side, talon tips hooked into the window seals. Its head whipped back and forth like a flag, bashing La Vitesse's side windows.

Under Bea, Tony Lalonde wailed. But if he could cry, he could breathe, and that was all that mattered to Bea.

The bus fishtailed onto the highway, spun across two wide east-bound lanes, and spat gravel across the median. The dragon's maw opened in a scream, but instead of sound—a lick of blue fire, transparent, like the propane flame from Bea's camp stove. Then it lost its grip and fell. One talon dangled from the window, ripped out at the roots, smearing ashy gore from its root.

Bea plunged up the aisle and scrabbled at her daughter's shoulders.

"Out of my seat, now," she demanded.

"This is almost over." Under the caked eyeliner, Rosie's narrowed gaze was flinty. "Take care of the kids. They hate me."

"Rosie. No."

"That's okay. I hate them, too."

No use. Bea had never been able to stand up to her daughter. But Rosie wasn't wrong. It was almost over. She turned to face the huddled kids.

"We're going to be fine." She gave them her best motherly smile. "Rose will drive us to the RCMP station. Five minutes."

Those little tear-streaked faces just about broke her heart. Theresa Lalonde held tight to her little brother. He sobbed into his big sister's sweater. Bea stooped over them.

"Did I hurt you, Tony? I'm so sorry."

"This is your fault," Theresa said. And she wasn't wrong. Bea had known about the dragons for months, and what had she done? Nothing.

"It's okay. Someone will rescue us," she said, but she knew it wasn't true.

Encyclopaedia Britannica, Volume 3 *was the first book Bea had stolen* in sixteen years. She hadn't lost her touch. All she had to do was wait for Mrs. English's smoke break. The teenage girls behind the checkout desk didn't look up when Bea walked in, or when she took the volume off the reference shelf. Bea walked through the anti-theft gate, the heavy book held flat at stomach level.

The book fit perfectly over La Vitesse's steering wheel. Bea read through the dragon entry twice to make sure she hadn't missed anything, but there wasn't much. European dragons were voracious. They slaughtered, consumed, and laid waste to the land until finally stopped by a great hero.

Bea had lived all her life in the bush, but she knew this much about the world: heroes were more mythical than dragons. They simply didn't exist.

"Slow down, honey," Bea said. *"Turn on Switzer."*

La Vitesse shuddered. Rosie had the gas pedal flat on the floor. They'd be in the RCMP parking lot in minutes. But first, they had to take a sharp right onto Switzer Drive.

"I said slow down," Bea repeated.

Rosie didn't slow.

"What are you doing?" Bea screeched as they blew through the intersection.

"Do you want it to grab us again?" Rosie said.

Rosie flipped the latch on the driver's-side window, stuck her hand out, and pointed the mirror at the sky behind them. The dragon was still following, ten lengths behind and high above the highway.

"We've got lots of room," Bea pleaded. She gripped her daughter's shoulder and pointed at the last access point to the service road, coming up fast on their right. "Slow down and turn."

Rosie shrugged off her mother's hand. "Too late now."

Tears sprung to Bea's eyes. "Rosie, baby. You can't do this."

The rest of the highway was a straight shot through Edson and on to Edmonton. Three and a half hours of bush. But Hinton had service roads lining either side of the highway, busy with gas stations and strip malls. Not much traffic this early in the morning, but someone must have spotted the dragon by now. They were probably already running to a pay phone.

Bea raced to the back of the bus. The glass was clearer now, its coat of grime smeared thin by the dragon's swinging body. A little red Datsun chugged along in the right lane. Bea caught a glimpse of the driver's shocked expression, their mouth open in a perfect O as La Vitesse roared past.

High above the highway, the dragon folded its wings. It seemed to hover in the air. Then it dropped toward the tiny car like a torpedo.

It hit with all fours like a pouncing cat, talons puncturing the flimsy fiberglass roof. The car swerved through the median and plunged across the oncoming lanes. The dragon rode the car like a rodeo cowboy, legs flexing, wings slapping the air as if it could lift the car right off the road.

"Brake, brake," Bea whispered. "Throw it—Oh, no."

Hinton's Husky station was the biggest in town, impossible to miss with the massive Canada flag snapping above. Big diesel pumps for the semis, four banks of regular pumps for the summer tourist traffic. And the Datsun was out of control. It missed the first pump but hit the second. The station went up with a *whump*.

Orange flames. Boiling smoke. And from the conflagration rose the dragon. Its wings fanned the flames with long, lazy beats.

"Go, Rosie!" Bea howled. Maybe they could get around the next curve before it spotted them. "Faster!"

Maybe the dragon would attack another car, blow up another station. Did she want that? No—it was horrible—but neither did she want the dragon on their tail again.

Then La Vitesse's horn blasted. One long, insistent, unending bellow.

"No, Rose!" Bea screamed.

The dragon's wings hitched. It flipped and turned, graceful as a swallow, scales shedding streams of smoke. Its eyes gleamed, two chilly points, square and level.

Bea lived in the bush. She'd seen plenty of cougars, and she knew this: when a predator's eyes focus on you, two orbs in perfect alignment, you are meat, meat, and nothing but meat. Whether you live or die is no longer in your control. Your fate lives between the claws and teeth of another.

"Honey, why?" Bea moaned. But there was no answer, never any answer with Rosie. She did as she pleased.

From the time her daughter was born, Bea's one goal was to keep her at home for as long as possible. With a kid as strong-willed as Rosie, that meant giving in, always. It also meant feeding her well. Tasty food, and lots of it. Though tiny as a baby, Rosie had always been a good eater. She'd grown big and tall—nearly six feet and still growing—with broad shoulders and big hands and feet.

The food was an important strategy. Bea knew from experience that, aside from weekend bush parties, going for pizza or fries with friends was pretty much the only thing a Hinton teenager could do to beat the boredom. Bea had been caught in that trap herself.

At sixteen, instead of getting on the school bus for the long ride home, she'd head to Gus's Pizza. Then she'd wait outside the IGA grocery and try to catch a ride home with a neighbor. But that didn't always work, so she started hitchhiking. The first two times were fine. But the third time, her social studies teacher picked her up. For half an hour, he'd lectured her about the dangers of hitchhiking, and then pulled over and slipped his hand into her jeans. That's how she got pregnant.

Bea didn't want that to happen to her girl. So if the poutine at the L&W was good, Bea's was better—the fries crispier, the cheese gooier, the gravy dark brown and chunky with lumps of salty hamburger. And that was just the start. Bea's nut-crusted elk roast was perfection and her

open-fire flatbread with homemade jam beat any cake. So when Rosie
got to that dangerous age, she never even thought about staying behind
after school. Why would she hang out with kids she hated and eat sub-
standard snacks when her mom's food was so good?

Rosie scared her teachers, but Bea didn't care. If her daughter sat
in the back of every class and did the bare minimum of work to pass,
that was fine with Bea. And if she stomped down the hallways with her
elbows out, glaring at the other kids from under her ragged dyed-black
bangs and wore the same two Slayer T-shirts for a year, that was better
than fine. Nobody would ever take advantage of her Rosie. Anyone
who tried never tried twice.

La Vitesse blasted east, the speedometer topping out, the dragon still chasing
them, and nothing ahead but open highway. Soon, they'd start climbing
Obed Mountain. The engine couldn't take it at speed. Bea had to do
something, but she was too scared to think. Scared of what the dragon
would do when the bus began toiling up that long, steep slope. And
also, for the first time in her life, she was scared of her daughter.

Rosie hunched in Bea's seat, her mouth set in a permanent sneer.
The remnants of her blue-black lipstick smeared her chin. Maybe the
biggest danger they faced wasn't the dragon. Maybe it was Rosie. Maybe
it always had been.

The kids knew Rosie was dangerous. They'd always known. Bea
made a habit of looking away when the kids scooted past Rosie's shotgun seat as if it were on fire. She ignored it when Rosie snarled at a tardy
kid, and when she snagged a treat out of one of their backpacks, Bea
treated it like a joke.

Bea knelt beside the driver's seat and put a gentle hand on her
daughter's thick wrist.

"Honey, whatever I've done, I'm so sorry. But take it out on me,
not the kids."

Rosie's brow furrowed. The bridge of her nose crinkled like she
smelled something rotten.

"Don't talk shit, Mom," she snarled.

Bea moved her hand up to her daughter's bicep and tried again.

"You've been angry for a long time, haven't you? And now you're in control. And you do have control. You're making all the choices. So make the right one, honey. Turn us around."

"Fuck, Mom, what do you think I am?" Rosie said. She took a deep breath and screamed, "Hang on!"

Rosie slammed on the clutch and brakes and spun the wheel. The momentum threw Bea down the stepwell. She hit her head on the door, hard. By the time she'd shaken off the pain and climbed to her feet, La Vitesse sat idling in the middle of Pedley Road, a gravel-top dead end with nothing along it but a few old houses tucked back deep in the bush.

"Good girl, thank you. I'll drive now." Bea laid a hand on her daughter's thick shoulder. It was solid as stone. Rosie's right hand strangled the steering wheel and her left stuck stiffly out the window, twisting the side-view mirror to scan the sky behind them.

"No," Rosie said quietly. "Stop touching me."

Rosie shifted the bus into first gear, then second. They rolled up the road. Over the soft crunch of wheels on gravel and the engine's low hum, the *whump-whump* of wide wings sounded, louder and louder. Behind Bea, the children sniffled and sobbed. Maybe Bea did too. She knew she should fight—but how? Bea had never hit anyone. Certainly not her child. Not ever. How could she have known it was a mistake?

"I'm sorry," Bea whispered. "I didn't know what I was doing. I was too young."

When Rosie answered, her voice was flat and emotionless. "Stop. I'm trying to think."

"I should have made you play with the other kids. I wanted to keep you home. Keep you safe. I didn't know what it would mean. That you'd be isolated. That it would be bad for you."

Bea leaned her left cheek against Rosie's arm as La Vitesse rolled toward the Pedley railway crossing. The lights flashed red under the white-and-black crossing sign. A train was coming, but Rosie was utterly focused on the side mirror, jaw clenched, eyes narrow.

The train's low horn sounded in the crossing pattern. Two short blasts, one long, one short. Bea put a soft hand on her daughter's fist where it gripped the wheel.

"We have to stop before the tracks, honey."

No answer. Bea climbed to her feet. The fire extinguisher lay in the aisle, beside a tiny sneaker that had slipped off the foot of a terrified child. A child who was in her care. A child she had to keep safe.

She hoisted the heavy extinguisher in her arms. Bea knew herself. Violence wasn't in her nature. She'd never raised a hand to anyone, even when she should have. Even when they were hurting her. Now she had to hurt her daughter. Had to. Lift the extinguisher high and drop it on Rosie's head. That's all.

But she couldn't. She put the extinguisher down and turned away.

The bus's front wheels bounced over the rails. The train raced toward them, a massive stack of silver metal topped by a curved glass windshield. Close now, so close Bea could see its wipers stuck at a low angle across the glass. Its horn screamed as it bore down on them with all its murderous weight and velocity. Rosie still had her hand out the side window, yanking at the mirror with her thick fingers.

Behind La Vitesse, at the bus's grimy rear window, a shadow reached out to wrap its wings around the bus. Then a wall of silver speed obliterated it.

Rosie couldn't get the bus door open. Not even with both hands and all her muscle and weight.

"Mom, how the fuck do you do this?"

"There's a trick to it." Bea slipped her soft hands over her daughter's and flicked the rubber thumb control on La Vitesse's spring-latched handle. She cranked the door open, just as she'd done a thousand times before, but never with such relief.

The train was still rolling past, brakes howling and throwing sparks. When it had cleared the crossing, Bea ushered the kids off the bus.

"You too," she told Rosie, and followed her daughter down to solid ground.

Bea wrapped her sweater around little Michelle Arsenault and lifted her up to settle on her hip. She wiped the child's nose with a crumpled tissue from her jeans pocket, then lifted Tony Lalonde onto her other hip.

At the railroad crossing, the tar-smeared sleepers and silver rails were painted with red-brown gore, thick and smoking. The dragon's head lay beside La Vitesse's right rear wheel. Bleeding pits marked the milky sclera of its eyes, and a blue liquid leaked from its fanged jaws.

Rosie heaved the dragon's head so it lay chin-down on the road.

"Where's the rest of it?" Michelle Lalonde whispered from under Bea's elbow.

"Here, in the ditch," Rosie said. She slipped down the icy incline and hefted a tattered wing, then dragged it up to the road and deposited it beside the dragon's head.

"That's not good meat," said Blair Tocher, eleven years old and an experienced hunter. "Smells like bear gone bad. You can't eat that."

"I think Rosie could," Joan Cardinal said.

Bea shivered, cold without her sweater, and her forearm was wet where she was supporting little Tony Lalonde against her body. His arms gripped Bea's neck and his little snot-smeared face burrowed into her.

"Is someone coming to help us?" he asked in a whisper.

"Soon, I think."

Far up the tracks, the train had finally stopped. The engineer would have already reported the incident. She couldn't hear the sirens yet, but it wouldn't be long.

Rosie dragged the dragon's torso from the far side of the tracks.

Its gut had split open, revealing a nest of mottled entrails padded with honeycombed tissue.

"The dragon you saw on Roche Miette was red, Mom." Rosie stripped off her gore-soaked gloves and dropped them on the ground. "That's what you said."

"That's right," said Bea. "And you didn't believe me."

"Then this isn't the only dragon." Rosie shaded her eyes with her hand and scanned the sky.

Bea nodded. "There must be one more at least."

Tony whimpered. Bea hitched him up higher on her hip.

"We're okay. We're safe," she told the kids. "Right, Rose?"

Rosie shrugged and drew a pack of menthols from her pocket. A cigarette dangled from her lips as she fished for her lighter. She glanced at Bea, furtively, as if she needed her mother's permission to light up in front of the kids. Bea almost laughed.

She'd thought there were no heroes, but she was wrong. Dead wrong.

"Go ahead and smoke, honey," Bea said. "You earned it."

A FINAL KNIGHT TO HER LOVE AND FOE

Amal El-Mohtar

Do I love you more when you roar or speak?

In flight, a shadow between me and the sky,
or bending your strength to nuzzle my palm, my cheek?

Do I love you more ridden or devouring? Unbidden or scouring
a countryside, an enemy fleet—do I love you more
in triumph or defeat?

Do I love you more by way of rivers, water-bearing, rain-making,
Heaven-born and sinuous as thrill?
or as fire-breathing, mountain-shaking,
livestock-thieving, treasure-taking
boundless hunger, clap of thunder,
hoarder of the world's delights?

Do I love you when you fight
or when you yield your scales to my flesh,

this weak mesh of blood and bone to your fires and your stone,
your riddles, your greeting—

do I love you most in parting or in meeting,
solid or fleeting?

Do I love you by your head or by your tail,
your wings or your teeth,
your hard armor above or your softness beneath?

Do I love you by your breadth or by your depth,
your vast size,
or perched upon my shoulder in surprise? Your eyes

are everything, are all the world,
tail and mouth meeting, unmaking, repeating
feeding and fed, mountain and bed,
I love you as I love the vast, unnamable, untouchable, impossible
star-sewn sky and a severed thread
or a poem in its stead—

I love you living
And I love you dead.

THE LONG WALK

Kate Elliott

Kate Elliott (kateelliott.com) has been writing stories since she was nine years old, which has led her to believe that writing, like breathing, keeps her alive. As a child in rural Oregon, she made up stories because she longed to escape to a world of lurid adventure fiction. Once she realized her only marketable skills were baking and typing she turned to writing for a living. She now publishes fantasy, science fiction, steampunk, and YA. *Unconquerable Sun*, her most recent novel, tells the story of a gender-flipped Alexander the Great in space. Other recent work includes *Black Wolves*, *Court of Fives*, and *Cold Magic*. Eager to explore new places, Kate has traveled to five of the seven continents and hopes to catch them all. In her spare time she paddles outrigger canoes competitively in the beautiful state of Hawaii and hangs out with her goofball schnauzer.

Her husband died in the night after a long illness. Asvi slept through it, exhausted by two years of his decline into wasted helplessness. Waking, she knew at once he had breathed his last. The bedchamber, with its curtained bed and painted wardrobes, felt one soul emptier, flown to the mountains of ever-lasting morning.

She didn't touch him, just swung her legs off the bed and got to her feet. Her body ached the way it always did now in the morning. She shuffled over to the closed window, feeling an almost choking need for fresh air despite the bundles of herbs hanging from the rafters to sweeten the smell of dying.

As she opened the shutters, she lifted her eyes to the horizon with a sense of relief. He'd been a good enough man, as men went. She'd been fortunate her father had arranged a match for her with a man who wasn't ruled by his temper, although more likely that had been an accident. Her father's main concern had been sealing an alliance that would worm him securely into the wool trade. Her husband had not complained much, had hit her only twice and even apologized for it once, and had generously allowed her to hire a second maid for the kitchen as she got older.

Dawn spilled light over a cloudless sky. The eastern mountains rose stark in the distance. She stood gazing at them for far longer than she usually had a chance to do. For the first time in her entire married life she had no one she had to tend to, no porridge to cook at dawn and meals to prepare for later, no child's clothing to mend that had gotten torn the day before, no invalid's bedpan to empty. No reason she was required to turn away from the splendid vista that had hung beyond her reach for her entire life.

Sparks drew long to become dancing threads of gold and silver and bronze. The dragons were flying over the peaks and spires of the Great Divide, as they did at dawn and dusk, too big not to see and too far away to see properly. But they were always magnificent and deadly. Like the eastern massif, they were a barrier no one could cross.

The latch of the bedchamber door rattled softly before the door cracked open.

Feloa spoke in a whisper. "Mistress? Are you awake? Your son is concerned because you're not in the kitchen yet."

Asvi turned as the door opened farther on well-oiled hinges. An older woman took a step into the room. She was dressed in a drab gray-green skirt with a work apron tied over a faded blouse.

"He's dead," Asvi said.

"Ah." Feloa's gaze flashed toward the bed, whose curtains were tied back for the summer months. The shape lay under the blanket like the topography of a broken hill. A white sleeping cap hugged the unmoving head. "Shall I tell your son? He is the master now."

A great lethargy settled on Asvi. Even to think of dressing seemed as impossible as climbing the eastern mountains to look over the wilderness of demons said to lie beyond the stony peaks.

Feloa's eyes widened. "Mistress, you must sit down."

She steered Asvi to the dressing table and its birch-back chair. Asvi sat obediently. The mirror was shrouded, since vanity could never be tolerated in a house where the master was dying.

"Stay there, mistress."

Feloa walked to the bed and held the bedside glass with its water over the dead man's nose and slightly parted lips, now tinged blue-gray. When it was clear he was no longer breathing, she set down the glass and went out. Asvi heard her descending the stairs, heard voices in the entry, heard the front door close. Maybe she dozed, because the next thing she knew, Feloa was back.

"He's gone to the temple, mistress. Let me help you dress before he returns with the priest-magistrate."

Asvi pressed a hand against Feloa's sleeve. Words welled up from an urgent spring.

"Feloa, I won't let them cast you out to take the long walk."

Her lower lip trembling was the only visible sign of emotion Feloa allowed herself. "Mistress, you have always been kinder to me than I deserve."

"Have I?" Asvi muttered as an utterly unanticipated anger boiled up from her gut in response to Feloa's submissive words.

A surge of energy agitated her. She had to get out of this room or she'd suffocate. Maybe she'd already suffocated and these last years had been her wandering in the desert of perdition that was the only fitting reward for unfilial sons and disobedient women.

She stalked to the wardrobe to fetch the brown mourning dress every bride was given on her wedding day, to be worn at the death rites of men. Brown was the color of widows and fatherless girls. In the ancient days of old, when the people had lived in a far-off land, before they'd boldly journeyed to these shores, any woman obstreperous enough to outlive her husband would be buried with him. From earth, into earth, so it was proclaimed at the temple on every Twelfth Day as a reminder of the way people had once lived more purely and closer to the gods. The temple was more merciful now. And there were the dragons to think of. The dragons to assuage.

But of course she was safe from that. She had sons.

After unfolding the dress, she pulled it on over her shift, needing Feloa's help to do up the back buttons. Women like Feloa had to make do with front-buttoned mourning dresses. For all that he poured his profits straight back into the business and never into fripperies or conveniences for his household, her husband had insisted on certain niceties for his wife that would be visible to others.

Feloa shadowed her downstairs and into the kitchen, where Bavira had already folded up her sleeping pallet and stoked the fire.

"You sit down, mistress," the girl said. "I'll make the porridge."

Since her husband was no longer alive to complain if his morning porridge hadn't been made by his dutiful wife's hands, Asvi sat. But it chafed her to sit. Her mind was filled with fog, and yet her body was restless.

She rose. People would come to pay their respects. They had to be fed: ginger pancakes, buns filled with red bean paste, fruit tarts, spicy meat paste, flat loaves of faring bread baked with salty cheese because it was the traditional food of travelers. She would add sage and parsley to give the bread a more pleasing flavor.

She pulled on her kitchen apron and by rote began assembling the ingredients she'd need. Just two months ago she'd brought a tray of one hundred folded pancakes filled with sweet cream and early season berries to the memorial of her last uncle, youngest of a gaggle of brothers.

"Mistress, you should rest," objected Bavira anxiously from where she stood by the porridge pot.

Feloa said, "Let her be. The work comforts her. She likes it best in the kitchen."

It was true enough. Meklos could have hired a cook, but he preferred to be seen as a man so successful that his wife would never allow another woman's hands to make food for him. Since it was bad luck for a husband to set foot in a wife's kitchen, the kitchen had become her treasured domain. Her whole heart and attention could fall into the food. Batter to be mixed. Dough to be rolled out and braided. Rosebud cakes to be decorated. Savory pinwheels to be rolled up, sliced, and baked.

"Mother! What are you doing?"

Her eldest son appeared in the kitchen doorway. When little, Elilas and his brothers had spent plenty of time in the kitchen with her, but now that he would inherit the headship of the house, he hesitated, not wanting to bring ill luck to the home he'd lived in his whole life. His wife, Danis, pushed past him, easy with him as Asvi had never been with her own husband.

"Your mother wants everything done right with the food, just as she always has," Danis said, coming to the table where Asvi was kneading dough. "Dear Mother, I am sorry to interrupt you. The priest-magistrate has come. You must attend him in the parlor for the ceremony of crossing."

Asvi's hands stilled, fingers laced through the comforting texture of dough.

"Oh," she said in a low voice.

"I've sent a servant to the tea shop for a full tray, but you should have been in the parlor to greet him," said Elilas with his usual hint of impatience.

Feloa had been making pancakes. She took the pan off the top of the stove and came over to the table with a damp cloth to pat flour off of Asvi's face and wipe her hands clean. "I'll finish the kneading, mistress."

The ceremony had to follow its proper course.

Asvi took off her apron, then paused at the door. "Do the pancakes first. Bavira, bring the last tray of sesame dumplings for the priest."

"Mother! He's waiting!"

The parlor was a formal room used only for entertaining visitors and decorated to impress with lacquered chairs, embroidered couches, a polished side table, and a glass-fronted cupboard to display the delicate cups and saucers used for important guests. The priest-magistrate was standing with hands folded behind his back, studying her husband's collection of precious demon eyes, hard gleaming spheres like gemstones. To hold one in your hand could kill you, but each of these was encased in a net of silver thread to confine and dampen its toxic magic.

"Your Honor," said her son.

The man's cold and forbidding presence was leavened by a warm baritone voice. "Widow Meklos, may you follow your husband in peace as you followed your father in obedience and follow after your sons with a nurturing heart to care for their needs."

She inclined her head, glad she did not have to speak. What was there to say? The words were part of the rite once used in the old country when a widow was drugged and buried alongside her dead husband. Who was a woman, after all, except through the men who recognized her as part of their lives? Asvi, daughter of Hinan. Asvi, sister of Astyan, Nerlas, Tohilos, Elyan, and Belek. Asvi, wife of Meklos. Asvi, mother of Elilas, Vesterilos, and Posyon.

The priest went upstairs with her son to examine the body. Once he was out of the parlor, she went to the cupboard and took out cups for the men.

Danis came in, carrying the tray of sesame dumplings. "Dear Mother, will you not sit down? I'll set out the tea things . . . ah, here is the tea."

A servant hurried in carrying a covered tray, which he set down on the side table next to the dumplings.

"Thank you, Herel," Danis said graciously.

He touched fingers to his forehead, ear, and heart, and left the parlor. With the practiced movements of a woman who has had the leisure, as a girl, to learn such niceties, Danis set the cups on saucers and the saucers on a tray painted with flowers. Then she tipped the lid of the heavy teapot just enough to inhale the scent with a satisfied nod.

"Feloa will bring up hot pancakes when they return, but don't expect the priest-magistrate to eat any," Danis went on, watching Asvi with a wary eye as if expecting her to collapse at any instant. "We can eat them once he's gone. We're not required to starve!"

"Will you promise to keep Feloa on, Danis?" said Asvi in a low voice.

"Keep her on?"

"Households often turn out older women who are servants and hire in younger ones."

"Such a course is advised as a matter of economy. A younger worker can get more done. An older worker should return to her family to rest."

"She has no male kin. She was never able to marry and have sons. She's served me well all these years. I would not want to see her forced—" The thought caught in her throat like a bone that could not be swallowed.

Danis nodded with a sober expression, never one to pretend she did not understand an uncomfortable truth. "You want me to promise we will not turn her out and force her to take the long walk."

Asvi swayed, grasped the nearest chair, and sat. A sweat broke out down her spine, as if she were sitting with her back to a hot fire.

Danis sat next to her, taking hold of both her hands. "Father Meklos did well. His sons are good stewards of the business. We can keep her on."

"Even if she grows too old to do much work?"

"She's a good cook, better than me. Cooks can work a long time. Elilas does not care if his meals come from his wife's hands. Nor do I! Did you never tire of cooking, Dear Mother?"

"No." She shook her head. "I like the kitchen. Nothing ever turns out quite the same two days in a row. And there's no one looking over your shoulder if you want to try something new. You won't keep me out of the kitchen, will you?"

Danis smiled sadly. "Dear Mother, everyone in this household knows we are blessed with the food you make for us. Once the rites are finalized and Father Meklos is buried, we'll move you into that nice room in the back that looks over the garden. That way there are no stairs for you to climb. You can easily go to the kitchen whenever you want."

"I can't see the mountains from there."

"Of course not. That will be a comfort, won't it? Imagine waking up every morning to see the eastern peaks. Then you never have to think about dragons hunting and demons clawing their way along the ground through the poisonous fog." She shuddered theatrically.

"Won't Elilas take that bedroom?" For generations the tower room had been the bedchamber for the head of the household.

"No. I don't want to sleep there. We're going to turn it into a schoolroom for the children. I feel sure the sight of the mountains will scare them into concentrating on their studies. Elilas and I will stay in the chamber we have now. It's small but I like it. I've convinced him to extend it with a sitting room and courtyard so I can invite over my friends." She squeezed Asvi's fingers. "You can sit with us, of course. We embroider, and read aloud last season's plays and all the most current poets."

Asvi had never had the chance to learn to embroider, only to mend. Her father hadn't wasted any money educating his daughter, although her brothers had taught her the letters. She tried to imagine Danis's elegant sitting room and her fashionable friends quoting plays and practicing dance steps, but it was a room she viewed from afar, not a place she could inhabit.

"Oh, dear." Danis released her. "I'm talking too much, and you're the one grieved, Dear Mother. Not that I'm not grieved as well," she added, too quickly. "But Father Meklos was so ill and in so much pain, I can't help but be relieved he's shed of it. His illness exhausted you. Maybe you can rest now."

What was rest, if not death? Rest didn't sound at all appealing, any more than did a tidy room overlooking the garden walls.

Footsteps sounded in the passage outside, brisk and demanding. The men had returned.

Elilas helped her stand and held on to her arm a bit too tightly, so she couldn't go to the tea tray, as if he thought she didn't understand how things had changed in the house. Instead, Danis poured with a skill Asvi admired, giving a rhythm to the pattern of warming the cups with hot water, emptying out, and pouring in the amber-colored tea in a perfectly curved stream. So graceful. So beautiful. Like Danis herself, a prize on the marriage market the year Elilas had convinced his father to pay her staggering bride price by explaining how such a bride would enhance the household's status in the wool trade.

Asvi recalled the first time she had poured tea in the place of her husband's father's wife, after the old man's death. Her hands had shaken so badly she'd spilled, and then spilled again at hearing the disapproving hiss made by Meklos's mother. Ever after, she'd dreaded visitors for fear of disappointing his mother or him. Danis's confidence felt not like a slap at her own incompetence but instead like a long-sought escape. Elilas's proud smile toward his lovely wife was echoed by the priest-magistrate's appreciative nod.

Danis served the men first and afterward brought a cup to Asvi and sat beside her. The magistrate sipped; Elilas sipped; the women sipped.

Once the magistrate had finished his first cup and allowed Danis to pour him a second, he began.

"I will send over the acolytes to take the body to the temple for preparation. Because it is high summer, the crossing ceremony must be held tomorrow instead of after the traditional five days of reflection. You have brothers, do you not, Headman Elilas?"

"Two still living. One is in the militia, stationed at Fellspire Pass."

"Courage to him," said the magistrate. "A brave sword who through his sacrifice secures peace for us all."

Asvi squeezed her hands together, thinking of gentle Posyon and how he'd comforted her when she wept to see him sent off to the frontier from which there could be no return. But she said nothing. It was not her place to speak.

"The other supervises our warehouse in Farport."

"So too far to return for the ceremonies in time. Very well. You can send him the proper offerings to make." The man turned his cool gaze on Asvi, measuring her and, she was sure, finding her wanting. Her father had been a sheepherder who sought a better market for his wool. His child wasn't worth much on the marriage market, but she'd been sixteen and a good cook even then. For ambitious Meklos, who revered his distinguished mother, the monopoly on her father's excellent wool and connections into sheepherding clans farther up in the foothills was the bargain he'd been after. He'd doubled his family's business on the strength of it.

"You'll pay the walk tithe for your mother, I presume?" the magistrate added, lifting an eyebrow in query. "We discussed the amount upstairs."

Elilas's hesitation startled her. She looked up to find him staring meaningfully at Danis. "It's higher than I expected," he mumbled.

Danis gave Elilas a scalding, scolding look and expelled a huff of exasperated breath, enough to make him grimace.

He said, "But of course the family will pay it, Your Honor."

"Let's settle it now, then, rather than wait for tomorrow. I find it's easier that way."

"If you'll accompany me to my father's office."

"Your office now, Headman."

"Yes, of course. If you'll accompany me to my office."

The men went out. Danis set down her cup so hard the impact chipped its base. She glowered at the cup, painted with miniature scenes of women walking nobly into the dagger-toothed maws of massive dragons. "These are so dreadfully old-fashioned. I'll replace them all."

"But they've been in the family for generations," said Asvi in surprise. "They were purchased from the temple."

"Yes, I can tell. I can get a good price for them in the market, unless you want them, Dear Mother."

"Why would I want them?" Asvi muttered.

"Why, indeed! You have good taste, not that the old man ever let you have your way in clothing or decoration. No wonder you like the kitchen. It's the only place he never interfered with you."

Asvi did not know what to say in answer to this plain speaking, so she said nothing. Saying nothing was always safest.

Danis rose. "I'd best go look in on the men or that thieving priest will squeeze another hundred out of our treasury. Eli is a canny trader, but he's so unbelievably naïve when it comes to the temple. My father says—"

She broke off and leveled a hard look at Asvi, then smiled as one might at a well-loved but rather simple child. "Never mind. It's been a difficult time for all of us. I blow hot and cold and can't hold my tongue. Dear Mother, forgive me."

"You've always been kind to me, Danis."

Danis bent to give her a kiss on each cheek. "You welcomed me when most humbly born mothers would have set themselves against a woman of my exalted background coming into their life. For your modesty and graciousness I will always be grateful."

She went out.

To sit in the empty parlor was a luxury Asvi had rarely experienced. She savored it now, knowing it would not last long. The demon eyes stared at her from the glass cupboard. People said their eyes never stopped seeing, even when they were dead, not once they had been wakened by a glimpse of prey. The eyes were Meklos's pride and glory. People respected him for having the courage to keep such a collection within his own house. He had liked to handle them while wearing gloves, entertaining visitors with ghastly descriptions of how each had been acquired. The physic who had treated him over the last two years had informed the dying man that he'd been poisoned by handling the eyes. Yet toward the end Meklos had whispered, in a tone of thick and almost erotic passion, that even so, this withering and painful decline had been worth it, to have seen what he had seen. These claims were nothing more than the ravings of a dying man, the physic had explained to her, and Meklos had never described his visions.

She never touched the eyes. Once, as a girl, up in the foothills, she'd seen a living demon as it plunged in to attack a herd of sheep, its eyes blazing with a venomous light as an acrid, ashy mist poured from its upper mouth like spilled tea to scald and slay the terrified sheep as well as her favorite brother, boiled alive. Just as its blazing eyes saw her, just as it turned toward her to boil her, too, a dragon had come diving out of the clouds with no warning except a stinging pressure of hot wind. The great beast had marked her with a single, slow look, like honey oozing over a wound. But it didn't care about her; she was nothing, just a human girl, of no more interest than the bleating sheep. It clamped its gleaming claws over the demon and carried it away into the heavens. If she'd had wings, she'd have flown after it right then, before the weight of the world trapped her on the dull earth.

Through the open door she heard Elilas make polite farewells to the magistrate. The front door closed, leaving the two in the entryway.

In a low voice, barely heard through the open door, Danis said to her husband, "They're corrupt, the whole lot of them. He'll pocket half and give the rest to the priest-adjudicator."

"What can we do? They rule the prince, and the prince rules us."

"We shall see."

"Danis!"

"Shhh. You know I'm right. I can't believe you hesitated like that. Your own mother!"

"It's a lot of money, and she's old."

"'She's old!' Is that what you'll say about me someday?"

"You! Of course not. You're—"

"I'm splendid and elegant and just disreputable enough to be respected by everyone, not mousy and browbeaten and obedient, and born in the foothills among the sheep, to boot! Your father was bad enough, treating her like a servant and never appreciating the inventive and delicious meals she cooked his whole life. Have you any idea what a treasure she is? I would trade any cook in this city for her. Even the prince's cook. What do you think of that? And never a word of complaint about having to sleep in that horrible room up in the tower all these years next to the whining, selfish man who complained if she added any scrap of flavoring to his bland porridge."

"Danis!"

"I'm just repeating your own words, darling. Don't try to throw them back in my face. He browbeat you, too. No wonder your brothers fled as far away as they could go once they were of age. You're just fortunate I took a liking to you."

His voice softened to a teasing tone. "Why did you take a liking to me, my sweet?"

"That would be telling," she said with a laugh. "Come now. Give your poor mother the bracelet before the magistrate decides to come back and squeeze more coin out of you. He saw your hesitation. You know what they say at the temple. *Times are hard, and the dragons need offerings.*"

"I would never!"

"You would never, right up until you would."

"Vesti and Pos would never forgive me."

"As well they should not. We would lose all face in the community if we let her be taken for the long walk. Did you even think of that?"

"Of course I wouldn't let her be taken, my sweet. I was just shocked at how much he demanded."

"Because he is ruled by greed and free to take what he wants because the prince protects the magistrates because they protect him. If we have a fourth boy, I'll pledge him into the temple and with my tutoring he'll shake things up!"

Elilas laughed nervously.

"Enough of this, darling," Danis added. "It's settled, and she's safe. Let's go back in."

Their footsteps approached. Asvi folded her hands in her lap and said nothing as they came in. She liked for people to assume she was as hard of hearing as Meklos had been the last few years. Elilas entered the room and crossed to her. He stiffly held out a bracelet of polished obsidian and carnelian beads strung together on a silver chain.

"Your family vouches for you, Mother. With this tithe signified by this bracelet, we take on the responsibility of caring for you even though you can no longer bear sons and are too weak to ease the burdens men carry in this harsh world."

A flash of ire twitched at the corner of Danis's eyes as she gave a sardonic smile. But she said nothing and made no retort. What retort could there be?

In the entry hall, Herel began admitting visitors who'd come to pay their respects. The first were the neighbors along the street who had seen the magistrate arrive and depart. As word spread, more arrived. Bavira brought a tray of pancakes, quickly consumed, and Danis sent out to a bakery for five trays of rosebud cakes. It seemed blasphemous to Asvi to serve cakes bought at a shop to visitors in her own home. But she was just too tired, and anyway it was no longer her place. Danis would make such decisions from now on. A stronger mother-in-law would have ruled her son's wife, as Asvi had been ruled for years, but no one ruled Danis. Asvi could not imagine even trying.

Her youngest brother arrived with a pair of actors in tow. While much of the family still lived and herded in the foothills, he was a city man now, a playwright educated with the money brought in by their new trading connections. The bright gold sash slimming his torso and his hair plaited to look like dragon scales gave him the flair of a man of fashion. He greeted Elilas first, of course, then lingered longer, speaking to Danis in bent-headed confidences, before coming over.

"You should do your hair differently, Asvi," he said with a brotherly kiss to her cheek. "This style is so outdated and never suited you any-way. Let me see it."

She gazed at him blankly, trying to sort out what "it" was. For an instant she could not even recall his name.

Belek! As a girl she'd had most of the household chores and the childminding to do, with her mother ill for long stretches after each of her pregnancies. Little Belek had just learned to walk when her father had taken her downslope to try his luck with her on the marriage mar-ket in the flatlands.

Belek took hold of her wrist and examined the bracelet. "Those are fine-quality beads. They'd have lost face if they'd not paid the tithe for you."

"He's my son!"

"Sons have discarded mothers before this. Or lost them through no fault of their own."

They exchanged a look, for, however little they understood each other's lives, they shared the knowledge of how their father had lost his own mother in this way, as he had reminded Asvi constantly as she grew into marriageable age. His father—Asvi's grandfather—had died when her father was still a boy. He'd been eldest of the surviving children and thus the one responsible, since, at sixteen, he was considered a man. His mother had no surviving brothers or father, and her male cousins lived too far away to care. When he hadn't had enough to pay the tithe, his mother had been taken by the temple and sent up the long walk into the eastern mountains as an offering to the dragons, who were all that stood between the human settlements and the demons. He'd never seen his mother again, of course. He'd never forgiven himself for not being able to save her.

"I'd scrape together the money no matter how many loans I'd have to take out," Belek added. "People like us can't afford to be shamed as uncaring hill folk who chain their daughters to the cliffs for the dragons to take."

"No one ever did that. Young women are far too valuable to throw away!" exclaimed Danis, gliding up beside him with a sly smirk on her bountiful red lips. "It's just a story playwrights tell because nubile youth plays well on the stage."

She solicitously fussed over Asvi, pouring her a fresh cup of hot tea and arranging and rearranging a platter of tiny rosebud cakes on the table set to Asvi's right. Strangely, Asvi noticed that Danis's elegantly slippered foot had somehow come to rest against the side of Belek's expensive leather shoe.

Over her head, Belek quoted a few lines to Danis from what was evidently a new play he was working on. "'Why do we chain ourselves to the yoke of the old land when we stand on soil budding with fresh blooms?'"

"Tendentious."

"How about this? 'On what secret paths does the soul tread toward its beloved?'"

Danis raised an eyebrow, quirking up her mouth until he flushed.

"Ai! Belek!"

He looked up from his rapt contemplation of Danis's skeptical expression. A man wearing the ostentatious clothes of those who want to flaunt their money had just entered the room. The fellow beckoned to Belek with the expectant obliviousness of an individual who always gets what he wants.

"Oh, good, I was hoping he would come, since he's expressed interest in bankrolling the next production," Belek remarked to Danis, and left them.

Before Danis could follow, Asvi grasped her hand and tightened her grip until Danis bent close.

"Are you well, Dear Mother? I know this must be an ordeal. You need endure only a little longer."

"Are you lovers?" Asvi whispered, thinking of how devoted her son was to this woman whom she'd never really understood.

"Lovers?"

"You and Belek?"

Danis laughed merrily as she glanced toward the two actors, handsome men with fine features and dashing smiles. "No. I'm not his type. But I do have a secret, Dear Mother. I help him write his plays."

"Women aren't allowed to take part in the theater. It would be indecent."

"An antiquated custom held over from the old lands. I know you won't tell."

She withdrew her hand from Asvi's grip as a flood of new visitors swept in. Everyone carefully did not see her; it was considered impolite to greet the widow until after the crossing ceremony was complete, since she was legally dead the instant her husband died. Anyway, she'd been seated in a corner out of the way, as easy to overlook as a modest wooden stool set amid an ostentatious stage set.

Danis, secretly writing for the theater!

The thought, blending with the constant flow of visitors in and out like the rush of waters, reminded her of the time she had traveled to the sea as a girl. Her father had taken her the twenty days' journey to the harbor city of Farport, where Meklos had been supervising the family's farthest warehouse. At that time, Meklos was still a fourth son, a man who might consider a sheepherder's reasonably pretty daughter as a marriage prospect because his older brothers hadn't yet died and left him to be headman quite unexpectedly.

She had watched ships shear away across the water, sails beating in the wind like wings lightened by magic. A handsome sailor, one of the far-traveling Aivur with their skin the color of pale spring leaves, had winked at her. He'd smiled when he was sure he had her attention and told her half the crew of the ship he sailed with were women, that a strong girl like her could take a chance on adventure.

Adventure!

But her father had already told her she needed to marry to benefit the family so her younger brothers could have a better life than his own. So her mother, weak from so much childbearing, would never be forced into the long walk if her father died before his wife did.

Three days later, she'd been wed to Meklos, and her father had a foothold in the wool trade. On the strength of his new alliance, Meklos had been allowed to move back upriver to his inland birthplace. Her second son, Vesterilos, lived now in Farport with a foreign-born wife and a growing family, tending his share of the wool trade. He and his father had never gotten along, so he never visited, only wrote terse reports, appended with long descriptions of the grandchildren for her, along with occasional gifts of spices from overseas.

The murmuring voices of women standing by the side table jerked her attention back to the parlor. They were tasting the cakes with appraising bites.

"These aren't as succulent as I'd expect in this household," one sniffed with a snide look toward Danis, half the room away.

"Are they from the shop? Young people these days have no respect for hard work."

"She can afford to get everything done for her, can't she? I pity Meklos's widow. Such a drab creature. She'll never see the inside of this parlor again."

"Have you ever tried to speak to her? That hills accent!"

"She won't have the backbone to stand up to a council member's daughter, even one who is so much of a frippery she might as well be a tart. If you know what I mean."

They laughed together, as if their shared disapproval tasted sweeter to them than the cakes did.

A flash of comprehension swept through Asvi like a blast of wind off the heights. If she walked out of the room with its crowded, busy, chattering, important people, no one would stop her, because they would not notice her leaving. The gathering would proceed in exactly the same manner. She could set a stick in her place and it would do.

She stood.

For one breath in and one breath out she did not move. She ought to stay. Her mind knew her duty. But her body was restless.

Like the merest touch of a breeze, she wove her way through gaps between clusters of people, all the way to the door. Stepping past the threshold took no effort at all. No one called after her. A constant swell and ebb of conversation floated out of the parlor to push her like a current along the path her feet remembered best: down the main corridor toward the back of the house.

As the noise grew muted, her steps slowed. A strange reluctance wrapped around her like invisible vines as she approached the door to the kitchen, the place she had always taken refuge. She would live in the downstairs room and come here every morning from now until the day she was too weak to manage the work. After that she would lie abed until she died in a room with no view of the sky.

Through the partly open door she heard Feloa giving directions to Bavira. They did not need her. Danis would send out for more cakes from the shop. Anyway, a widow did not cook for the crossing ceremony of her dead husband. That would be like a ghost serving food to the living: nothing but trouble. Once Meklos's soul had crossed, and with the tithe paid, all would go back to what it had been, except it would never again be what it was. Her marriage to Meklos had obliged her to serve him. But he was dead, and that meant she was legally dead and therefore only able to remain among the living if her male relatives paid a tithe to the temple.

But what if she did not want to remain among the living if living meant trudging onward as a shadow within the life she'd led? She hadn't been unhappy, precisely. Her father had told her often enough that her dutiful obedience had brought good fortune to the family. But her brothers were secure, her sons were grown, and her father was dead, his gentle gaze no longer leashing her to the earth.

Bars of light and shadow in the passage ahead warned her that a few more steps would bring her to the door that led out into the garden. She did not precisely move with volition but rather more as if drawn on a thread she hadn't the will to untangle from her limbs. A plain hip-length cape with a hood hung from a hook on the wall. She slung it over her shoulders as she often did in the mornings. The outside door was ajar wide enough to allow her to slip through without touching the latch, so it wasn't as if she actively opened it. Three steps took her down onto the garden walk and to the neat beds of herbs and flowers she'd planted over the years.

She paused at the bench where she often sat outside in solitude, beside four bricks she'd planted upright in a bed of lilies and chrysanthemums. The three daughters and one son who'd not lived past infancy hadn't been old enough to earn a temple burial, so she had secretly rescued the bodies before they could be tossed into the night soil wagon and had buried them in the garden. Bending, she kissed her fingers and touched each brick with the same tender grief with which she'd given each infant their farewell before she cast dirt over their faces. But she did not linger.

The thread tugged onward. The elderly gardener was working beyond a latticework screen that set apart the audience garden where visitors could take tea and conversation amid plants chosen for their appealing fragrance and attractive appearance. The old man did not look up. For all she knew, he'd not been told he had a new master. The change would make little difference to his routine, after all. Men were not sent on the long walk. They were never a burden, and anyway the dragons did not want them.

The big bar and thick lock on the garden gate had been set aside. She heard the wheels of a cart. A young man appeared carrying a large covered tray.

"Is this the way to the kitchens?" he asked her without preamble, mistaking her drab clothing for that of a servant.

Her voice had failed her some time ago. She pointed down the walk and stepped aside to let him pass. A second young man followed with another tray, then a third and a fourth, striding with the vigor of youth and destination. When they had passed, she found the gate into the rear courtyard, where deliveries were made, standing quite open as it usually never did.

There was no one else in the courtyard. The back gate into the alley gaped wide. It was easy to keep walking, to leave the compound and continue down an alley that ran along the back of households that belonged to other prosperous trading clans.

The alley split at an intersection. She paused, imagining the layout of the compound of their clan, and the neighboring houses, and the nearby streets as if seen from above as a dragon would see, if dragons ever flew over the city. Where did a person go, when they went out with no obligation tying their hands? Because it was the most familiar place she could think of, she headed toward the market.

Fruits, vegetables, grains, spices: each had their own lane under the arches of the east market that lay close to her home. The movement and color of the morning's business swirling around her made her feel like the wind, unseen but present. It wasn't until she reached the spice lane that a voice caught her in its hook and reeled her to a halt.

"Mistress! Here you are! A little late today. I have your usual box ready. I even have a fine packet of dried alsberry, early this season. I saved it especially for you."

The spice seller was a hearty man who had recently succeeded his father in the trade. He was voluble, chattering on about his second wife's pregnancy—her first—without needing anything from Asvi except nods and smiles.

Suddenly she was stricken by curiosity. "How much does it cost?" she asked, feeling the weight of the box in her hands as she took it from him because she was unable to say no.

He chuckled to cover a wince of discomfort. "You needn't trouble yourself, Mistress. I'll send my eldest son over to collect from Master Meklos. It is the very errand I used to do before my good father crossed. You're a fortunate woman. Your husband never haggles over your expensive tastes!"

He turned to a new customer, leaving her standing with the box.

Should she go home with the spices? Or shop first for vegetables, grain, and fruit? Should she plan the evening's meal, even though she could not cook it?

A cold sensation seeped against her right foot like the pressure of death's chilly breath. When she glanced down, she found herself standing in a tiny puddle of liquid—she hoped it was water—saturating the silk of her indoor slippers. The spreading stain—what a waste of good silk!—catapulted her into movement. Carrying the spice box by its strap, she wove her way through the hum and bustle of the market to the lane where footwear was sold. She passed elegant stalls selling city shoes and city boots and fetched up in a quiet section where a rustic couple were shaping the hardy styles worn in the highlands. Even the shopkeepers' hills accent felt well-worn and comfortable, though she heard in their long o's and sharp ch's how her own speech had been shortened and softened by so many years in the city. They treated her well; they could still hear the hints of her childhood in her voice.

Because no one knew Meklos was dead, and the short cape covered much of her widow's dress, it was easy to direct them to collect from the household of such an illustrious merchant. She walked away shod in sturdy wool boots, following the melody of wind chimes. Meklos hadn't liked the sound, which she associated with the ever-present voice of the wind on the slopes of the high hills where she had tended sheep as a girl, when the sky was her roof and the wind her companion. Here at the northwest corner of the great market arcade a person could see the east gate, open for the day. Chimes hung on either side because demons hated the high metallic tones and would hesitate to charge past them. The guards wore tiny chimes sewn to their brimmed hats. They stared straight ahead, not seeing

314

her as she walked out of the gate into the outer ring of the city, although they cast measuring gazes at young women about their daily errands.

All household compounds huddled safely inside the high stone wall of the city proper, while the expansive outer ring of gardens was protected by a wooden palisade. The stockyards and tanneries lay in Tanners' Town about a league away, because the beasts attracted demons. She walked past gardens on the eastern road toward the Morning Gate of the palisade. The crossing temple, where the dead set out for their final journey to the mountains of morning, blocked her view of the gate.

Built of bricks and capped with a massive dragon's horn at each of its four corners, the compound had two entrances: one for the priests and one for the dead. No one else was allowed to enter, or leave, because the dead held within their transitioning flesh the seeds of lightning and disruptive magic. Demons fed on blood and magic—blood because it held the power of life, magic because it sprouted out of death. The priest gate, closed, faced toward the city walls.

Four young women hurried past her. By their faces she could guess they were sisters, around the ages of her own sons with perhaps ten or twelve years between oldest and youngest. As a bell began to clang on the other side of the compound, first one and then all the women broke into a run, three sobbing brokenly and one urging the others on.

The bell rang the weekly call for the long walk. Asvi hastened her steps, caught by the urgency of the young women. Following them around the far corner of the temple brought her in sight of the palisade's Morning Gate.

Seven death wagons waited in a column, driven by priest-drovers and escorted by a cohort of priest-guards. Hook-mouthed, four-eyed, six-legged ghouls stirred restlessly in the traces, heads yearning repeatedly toward the canvas-covered wagon beds that concealed corpses. The seventh wagon was yoked to a quartet of stolid oxen who had heads lowered and shoulders bunched. Three elderly women huddled in the bed of the ox-drawn wagon. Another eight women waited by the wheels in their brown widow's garb. Those eight were healthy enough to walk, although their heads were bowed and their hands folded with womanly resignation.

It was to one of these women that the sisters ran. They crowded around her as the first wagon jolted forward, headed out on the long walk. What bright, sorrowing faces they had! How concerned they looked, desperate and grieving! As Asvi walked closer, drawn by their tears, she saw how threadbare their clothing was, how their mother's widow's dress was a faded, much mended hand-me-down, buttoning up the front, the kind of dress bought at the ragpickers by a bride who can afford nothing better.

"We tried, Mama. We tried," cried the eldest. "But we couldn't raise enough. The priests kept raising the fee when they saw how desperate we are. What will we do without you?"

The second wagon moved in the wake of the first. The other women sidled away from the commotion, looking frightened. A woman's grief was meant to be shared in private, not in so public and audacious a way.

"There, there, my girls." The woman touched each of her daughters with tenderness. She might have been a good ten years older than Asvi, or maybe she had just lived harder on the edge of want. Struggle and deprivation aged a person, too, as it had aged Asvi's mother, who at least had died in her own bed with her children beside her. "I know you did your best. The priests say women go ahead to make a comfortable home for those who will come after. I will be waiting when you make your crossing many years out, gods willing."

The third wagon pulled forward as the young women wept and their mother comforted them. So had Posyon tried to comfort her, when he was the one forced to leave behind those who loved him.

A sensation as powerful as the beating of furious wings flamed in Asvi's chest. She tugged off the obsidian and carnelian bead bracelet. Without plan, more like leaping off a cliff, she strode up to the little group as, with a grinding of axles, the fourth wagon moved. She slipped in among them with two fingers to her lips, for silence.

"Here." As the young women gaped, surprised at her intrusion, she grasped the older woman's arm quite rudely and yanked the bracelet onto her wrist. "You need it more than I do."

A startled gaze raised to meet her own, brimming with tears. "But Mistress, this is yours."

"I know what I am doing." All the years of bowing before Meklos's demands fell from her shoulders like a weight dropping. She felt almost dizzy with the sense that the walls had fallen away at long last. The fifth wagon jerked forward with a sharp command from its drover. "This is what the gods intend for me. You belong with the family who loves and needs you. Go. Hurry, before the priests notice."

She slung the cloak off her shoulders and slid it over the other woman to conceal her clothing.

"Make ready!" called a guard as the sixth wagon shifted and rolled. He hurried over to them, gaze sharp and lips pursed with disapproval. "You should already have made your preparations. Leave-taking is not allowed at the gate."

"It was just one last kiss for my sister and the daughters I'm leaving with her." Asvi spoke so brusquely the poor young man took a step back, surprised at her vehemence. The lie fell easily from her mouth. She'd never had a sister, nor any daughters who had lived past three summers. She nodded at them and walked away without looking back.

As the last wagon began to move, another priest-guard came running up with his spear and net to scold the walking women. "Hurry! We must make Eldaal Temple before dusk, and we're getting a late start. If you get tired you may sit in the wagon. But there isn't enough room for all. You'll have to switch out."

He did not glance at Asvi nor did he notice anything strange about her presence there. She was just another valueless old woman, exactly like the others.

She walked briskly through the double-walled palisade gate and past its guard towers, its chimes and lanterns that would be lit when night fell. Beyond the barrier lay fields and orchards tended by farmers who lived within the walls after sunset. The sky was blue, striped with high, thin clouds. It was warm but not hot, a pleasant day to walk if you liked walking.

She had grown up walking along the hills, so the steady rise of the road did not trouble her. Avoiding the last wagon with its passengers and their inevitable questions was easy. She did not fear the harnessed ghouls, who had no interest in living flesh and wouldn't even go after lambs. The wind breathed a slow song across fields of barley and dry-soil rice. In the distance, she spotted the threads of dragons curling around the peaks. A woman began to cry.

Her fear had fallen away when she'd taken off the bracelet and given away the cape. Posyon had gone to the edge of the world. Why not her? She would see the mountains up close, as she'd always yearned to. She'd finally follow the dragons into the clouds.

Midday passed, accompanied only by the tinkling of the chimes hanging from the guards' hats and the spokes of the wheels. Alerted by the chimes, people working in the fields did not look their way, since it brought ill fortune to stare at the long walk. The corpses were too freshly dead to speak. The guards ignored their charges. The women were too much strangers to one another to speak of their own lives. Perhaps some had even loved the husband or brother or son whose death left them vulnerable. Their silence felt charged with despair.

In the early afternoon the wagons took a short rest in the shade of a row of mulberry trees. One of the guards handed out faring bread. She could not abide bad food caused by carelessness or cheapness.

"This is sour and undercooked," she said to the priest-commander, showing him how spongy and dense the bread was. "Surely we are not expected to eat inedible food for the entire journey."

Her bold comment startled the man.

"We cook as we go," he said in a stern tone, mouth pursed with disdain. "We haven't the leisure to please our palates. Unless you think you can do better."

"Of course I can do better."

He snorted, turning away as he called for the drovers to get the wagons moving. "We must make Eldaal Temple before sunset."

They walked.

The temple was set away from the road behind a screen of thorn-gast trees. No one lived here. Countryside temples were built as refuges since demons might attack day or night. The corpse wagons and the oxen were sheltered in a shed protected by chimes, and the ghouls corralled in a stockade surrounded by ground glass. She ignored the open door that led to a dim barracks where the women sank exhausted onto hard pallets. Instead of resting she took her spice case to the kitchen.

Two guards assigned kitchen duty had started a fire in the hearth. She ignored their surprise when she walked in and began looking through the bags and baskets of provisions.

"Simple fare can be well made," she instructed them, setting them to work as she had done with her sons when they were boys. Barley flour mixed with nuts and a pinch of alsberry was soon baking for the next day's faring bread. She chopped up cabbages and onions to cook with oil, garlic, ginger, and star anise. The priest-mage came in to set out lamps lit by the magic slowly bleeding out of the corpses. He lingered, inhaling the scent as she whipped up a savory batter for pancakes fried in oil to go with the cabbage for the evening's meal.

Everything was eaten, down to the last bite. The two guards, now smiling and genial, cleaned up while she set beans to soak for a hearty morning pottage. The commander came in wearing a frown.

"People need strength," she said to him, thinking he was about to complain about the beans or the pancakes or the cooling bread.

He said, grimly, "The food tasted well, mistress."

Then he remembered she was dead, no longer deserving a living woman's title of respect, and he flushed.

She said, "I'll cook every night, with your permission. I am sure you priests are powerful enough that you'll take no harm in eating food cooked by a ghost. By the amount of provisions, I am guessing it will be about seventeen days' journey."

"That's right," he said, startled again. "It usually takes seventeen days to the bridge into dragon country past which no man can follow."

Seventeen days. She took it as a challenge instead of fretting. Each night she concocted a different style of meal from the staples. Even the women grew more animated. Several who clearly had never had enough to eat began to gain strength instead of wasting away.

The third night she heard a guard complaining to the commander outside the way temple's kitchen door. "Your Honor, the ghouls are growing weak. Usually one or two of the women have died by now."

"They're not women, boy. They're ghosts."

"Yes, Your Honor. Should we forbid one of the ghosts from eating? The eldest, perhaps? She can't even walk on her own."

The commander sighed. "I don't want to risk it."

"Risk what?"

"I don't know about you, but this is the best food I've had on the long walk in all my years supervising it. Feed one of the corpses to the ghouls."

"But the dead are meant for—"

"Do as I command. Don't mention the ghouls again."

With shaking hands, she finished preparing a stew of tubers sweetened with pears. The priests ate with gusto, and the women gratefully, but although the meal was as tasty as the ones that had come before, this night it tasted of ashes in her mouth. All that night she barely slept thinking she heard the ghouls slurping on decaying flesh and crunching on bones. But at least all the women woke up the next morning and set out with the wagons. She counted them five times, to make sure.

The fields gave way to uninhabited scrubland that turned into pine and spruce forest in which they walked in a rare sort of peace, unable to see the mountains. The women exchanged names and began to speak of commonplace things.

After days in the forest, the landscape opened up again as they emerged past the tree line onto a high plateau of short grass and frail summer flowers. The mountains rose in fierce majesty, gleaming in the crisp air beneath the sharp sun. This close, she could see a rippling halo of shining dragons winding around the peaks like elongated clouds painted in a rainbow of colors. Sometimes the dragons would dive steeply, then pull up, rising laboriously with a blurred object clutched in their gleaming claws.

A new silence fell, weighted as with lead.

The procession reached a fork in the road, one branch turning north and the other turning south. Ahead, the plateau was split by a cleft running in a line north and south without any visible end. The eastern massif rose beyond the crevasse. The six corpse wagons continued north toward a distant temple placed at the fissure's edge. Its wall bristled with horns, chimes, and corpse-fire lanterns burning with the waxy gleam of magic.

The commander himself, and the two guards who had helped her in the kitchen, accompanied the seventh wagon straight ahead along a rutted path. The oxen plodded toward a line of ghostly trees grown along the crevasse in the manner of trees growing alongside a river, fed by its moisture. As they approached, the uncanny appearance of the trees grew evident: paler than milk, almost translucent, like no trees she had ever seen. The women clustered close behind the wagon as they trudged in its wake. What else could they do? There was nowhere to run. Even Asvi felt a chill like doom whispering off the wraithlike trees. Branches stirred as if tasting their approach.

"What will we do?" whispered a woman whose living name had been Vicara. She was often frightened, and cringed at every unexpected noise. "Will it hurt when they eat us?"

"Hush," said the one who'd been called Bilad. She never smiled. "Our sacrifice keeps the city safe. We prepare a home for those who come after us."

They all looked at Asvi.

"Why did you do it?" Bilad asked the question at last.

"I want to see the dragons."

They sidled away from her, as if she were a dangerous influence, malicious and wild. But there was no escaping the crossing: these twelve old women, even if Asvi and several of the others really weren't so very old, not like aged Kvivim, whose family, the elder had told them in a frail whisper, could have afforded the tithe for her but didn't want to pay it for a woman who could barely walk. Maybe a different death would have been preferable, but Kvivim had stubbornly clung to life and Asvi admired her for it.

The respite was over and the end was nigh.

They walked toward where the trees grew thickest, spreading out to either side for some distance along the crevasse until the wood petered out into a few last stragglers.

In front of the central grove stood a massive gate of white wood shaped as a dragon's gaping mouth. The trees crowded up on either side like brambles too thick to penetrate, forming a barrier that blocked anyone from going into the forest unless they entered through the gate.

The drover halted the wagon. The guards used ropes to drag open the gate, not touching it with their hands. A gleaming silver-white path led straight from the gate's gulletlike opening into the shadows under the trees.

The priest-commander raised both hands, palms up to entreat the heavens. "So is it said, that in the first days after landfall, a fog rolled down out of the mountains of morning, and in it dwelt a ravage of demons. Again and again they descended, ravenous and insatiable. No sacrifice assuaged them, not even the offer of daughters in a marriage of blood. Only when the dragons came did the demons retreat. Ever after, according to the covenant of the new land, the dragons took their tithe in return for protection. By your sacrifice the world lives."

Dutiful Bilad went first through the gate's open maw, assisting old Kvivim. The others followed, but the commander tapped Asvi's arm with his staff of command to hold her back.

In a low voice he said, "The temple here could use a cook. It's so isolated, no one will know." He gave a sly tilt of his head back the way they'd come.

The other women had all crossed by now. They halted on the other side, surprised as the guards set their strength to the ropes and began to haul the open gates shut.

"Asvi?" Bilad called, sounding scared now that she wasn't with them to steady their hearts with her food.

She thought of Danis's words. What could the priest do to her now? Once she crossed, he could not follow.

"You do need a cook, but it won't be me. My father did not raise me to act so dishonorably. I will not let others shoulder the burden on my behalf. But you'd know all about that, wouldn't you? Your own magistrates cheat people, demanding more than they can pay and keeping the extra money for themselves. You would cheat the tithe by keeping me back to gratify your own belly. It's a disgrace you feed such poor food to the women you send here. They deserve better on their journey."

"Why waste food on people who will be dead soon?" he snapped.

"You are not a good man. No wonder the dragons don't want the curdled taste of the likes of you."

She turned away from his reddening face and slipped through the opening just before the guards slammed the gates shut.

"What was that about?" asked Bilad.

"I told him the priests ought to serve better food on the long walk."

Several of the women laughed nervously. No one moved. The trees sighed, and in their rustling whispered regret, despair, exhaustion, fragility, worthlessness, fear, pain, defeat, surrender. The sun began its slow descent across the vast expanse of the sky. Looking out over the land falling away westward was like being able to see into forever. But they didn't belong to that world anymore.

She turned her back on the life she'd lived and set off along the trail. Her limbs felt wooden, graceless, heavy, but the lure of dragons pulled her on.

The others reluctantly shuffled after, deeper into the disturbing silence. Although the branches had no leaves, the trees' eerie canopy nevertheless blocked the sun's rays. They followed the trail as along a path wrapped in an intangible shroud that sucked away all noise and most light. No birds sang or insects buzzed. Not a single flower bloomed although it was midsummer.

In the dimness, it was just possible to see strange shapes warping the trunks with bulges and decaying mounds. Now that Asvi walked through the wood, she saw these were not ordinary trees. They too were ghouls, akin to the creatures who had pulled the corpse wagons. They grew out of bodies, eating the flesh and building a scaffolding out of the skeletons to stretch toward the everlasting sky.

Their presence troubled Asvi like a boil burning hot in her gut. What if they reached out with their swaying branches to yank her into their midst? They flourished because they fed on the dying flesh and abandoned magic of discarded women.

Were these trees what it really meant to feed the dragons? That women walked so far and suffered so much fear and exhaustion only to become food for ghouls? Why not just feed the doomed women to the hauling beasts and be done with the façade of ceremony? The false promise of noble sacrifice?

Bitterly her heart soured and raged. It wasn't fair or right. Danis had been correct about that. Maybe Danis would find a way to change things back home as Asvi could never have done.

Yet the part of her mind that measured ingredients and portions nudged her fear and anger aside. There weren't enough trees to account for all the years and generations of the long walk. The women hadn't all died here, short of their unseen goal.

"Keep walking and don't stop or pause at all." She herded them onward when their steps lagged as they stared around in fear and despair.

Light marked the end of the trail's tunnel. A gulf of brightness awaited them, so fierce it was hard to look as they came closer. A person could drown in such light. Her heart beat faster. Her steps picked up as if she were going to meet the long-sought lover she had never had.

She emerged from the trees at the edge of a cliff face, a sheer, dizzying drop-off overlooking a staggering height. What she had thought from a distance must be a shallow fissure was a crevasse far too wide to shoot an arrow across and so deep she could not see its bottom. Thorngast ran like a fence along the far cliffside, and behind them grew beech, sycamore, and fir. Beyond the treetops in the most incongruous manner imaginable rose a watchtower. Threads of smoke rose from chimneys, marking a fort or settlement impossible to see from this distance and angle.

"There's someone living over there but no way across," said Bilad, coming up beside her.

Vicara fell to her knees, too drained even to weep. "What do we do now? Must we walk back into the trees? Is that the death that awaits us after all? To rot on the earth like discarded trash? Not even anything glorious?"

But Kvivim said, "Look! Demons!"

Because she was so bent over with age, the old woman was looking down into the crevasse. Gleaming colors churned far below within a sea of changeable fog caught in the fathomless abyss. Lean shadows flicked through the fog like fish swimming in murky waters. At first it seemed the demons were swimming away, but then the shapes flashed around and swarmed back toward the cliff face. They had scented the women.

A long, sinuous body rippled through the mist, colors shining in its wake. It was many times the length of the longest of the demon shadows. Its head, like a spear's point, thrust up out of the fog, scales gleaming with the variegated colors of polished amber. Slender whiskers whipped, tasting the air. Then it plunged back beneath the surface and drove forward, coming up behind the demons and swallowing them whole.

Its body vanished from sight, diving deep into the obscuring fog.

"Gods bless us," whispered Bilad.

The fog settled to become a still, opaque skin. Then it began again to churn as something huge ascended toward the surface. The dragon emerged out of the fog headfirst, the rest of its massive body following after. It coiled skyward in a spiral, leaving a trail of color in its wake.

All the women fell to their knees except Asvi. She stared with a hand pressed to her heart as the dragon flew on shining wings up out of the crevasse's depths. It rose past them, so bright she had to shade her eyes, then swooped down to hover impossibly in the air more like a delicate hummingbird than a massive beast. Its eyes were great round brass sheets slit with lozenges of pure black. Its wings thrummed with the beat of a drum through their hearts. It opened its jaw wide and wider still until the lower part of its muzzle slammed into the edge of the fissure with a weight that shuddered through their feet.

Vicara leaped to her feet and turned, taking a step to run back into the wood. The path was gone, vanished, only a wall of deathly trees waiting to consume them. Bilad grabbed Vicara's arm and dragged her to a halt.

"Wait," said Asvi.

The dragon's gleaming body elongated, stretching out and out across the gulf until the tip of its tail caught the far side and hooked there. Impossibly, through the gaping mouth appeared not a dark gullet simmering with banked fire but a translucent veil whose shimmering curtain gave onto a bridge made by the dragon's glistening back.

"I can't," said Vicara. "I'd rather die here."

Asvi looked into the eyes of the dragon, but the slits had closed. The creature had gone utterly still, almost lifeless. Its body created a solid span arching over the chasm to the shore beyond, which was dragon country, a place men dared not walk. Once across, no one could return.

Yet, even though to think of this was a fearful thing, curiosity tugged at her, like wondering if a new spice would flavor the food or if it was poison. She had grown so far beyond the first step she had taken out of the parlor that she didn't at first recognize the shod foot—her own!—as she set it down onto a surface hard as tile.

If she looked back she would not go forward, so she did not look back. The span of its back had no railing. An acrid wind curled up from the depths to tug at her skirt and hair. Even stretching out her arms to either side, she could not measure the breadth of its torso. Where its spine should have lifted up along its back, there was instead a dip, like an inverted spine, as if she were in truth walking down a monstrously long gullet whose wall was invisible to her gaze. When she reached the mid-point she dared look to either side along the length of the crevasse. To the north, appearing like a child's toy blocks, stood the temple tucked against the edge of the chasm. Glittering metal ladders linked down to caves hewn into the rock face. To the south, even farther away and visible only because of a rainbow spill of magic like a waterfall pouring down from the cave mouths into the fog, stood another temple. This was also what they meant when they said the dead protected the living, the secret knowledge the priests held to themselves and with which they ruled over the prince.

The crevasse was a barrier but not enough of a barrier. Temples had been built all along the course of the chasm. The magic unwoven from the dead kept most of the demons out. What the magic could not repulse, the dragons hunted.

The other women reached her, moving together as they had come to do over the days of the journey. Their fear propelled her on, and yet as she walked with them, she slowly, by degrees, fell to the back of the group and then behind. A thread of yearning still tugged her toward the peaks so impossibly far away. As they came down the last part of the span she saw a gap in the line of trees that, like a railing, guarded the cliff's edge. Beyond the gap lay a village.

A village! Of all the ordinary things, this was the one she had not expected to see.

The height and angle of the span, and perhaps the magic within the dragon itself, gave her a strangely clear view of the distant town. No walls surrounded it but rather a peculiar arrangement of moats, chimes, and intimidating pillars that resembled the bony remains of giant rib cages. The watchtower overlooked it all.

People hurried up to the ledge where the span met the far shore. They were ordinary women, older but hearty and healthy-looking, with outstretched arms and welcoming smiles, people who have reached a safe haven and, having prospered there, are glad to open their doors to new refugees.

Vicara began to snivel, again. For once she was the one who led the way, hastening along the last bit of the span until she collapsed onto firm soil. The others followed, laughing and weeping. Kvivim said, "I feel better than I have in years!"

But Asvi's feet slowed and halted before she reached the end of the bridge.

"Asvi!" called Bilad, waving at her from the safety of the other side. "There's a whole town here, built by the women who survived the long walk. A place we can live in peace! And we never knew!"

A hidden refuge. A safe haven at the end of the long walk.

Her shoulders dropped as she exhaled, letting go of the fear and the tension. It seemed too good to be true and yet . . . and yet . . . a pinch constricted her heart.

Was this all? A secret hideaway, concealed from the priests with the puzzling complicity of the dragons? It was an unexpected reprieve, certainly, but she couldn't shake the feeling she'd been handed a basket of barely edible weeds.

It was better than being eaten alive by dragons, wasn't it? It was better than dying in a cloud of toxic boiling steam spat out by a demon. Better than dying on the road and being fed to ghouls, or sitting under a canopy of trees that grew by absorbing the essence of living things. She'd take a room, with a bed, and she'd cook, as she always had. It would be a satisfying life in that way. She'd make do with what food-stuffs they had available, just as she always had. Maybe in the dragon country there would be a way to get a message to Fellspire Pass, wher-ever it lay up in the massif, marking the only route to a distant country on a treacherous road winding through the wilderness of demons.

Even thinking this, she could not move her feet to walk on into this new life. Her heart weighed like a stone.

A low tone rumbled through the span beneath her feet. Words thrummed up into her flesh, not quite spoken, not quite heard.

"What is it you seek, sister?"

"I wanted to see the mountains," she whispered.

"And you will, if you wish it."

"Must I stop here?" she asked.

"This is not the end of the journey. Just a way station as you gather strength."

"Can I not travel on right now?"

The dragon's laughter was a rumble like the earth shaking. "Very well."

A sonorous sound rang in the air, its complicated resonance vibrating in her flesh as if the dragon itself were a bell giving warning. The women at the end of the span shepherded the new arrivals away from the edge. Asvi's companions were guided toward the village down a wide avenue lined by double-branched dragon horns twice the height of the tallest of the women. They called to her, but she did not answer.

The dragon spilled life back into its stony span. Its tail unhooked from the far shore. Its head lifted toward the sky. Asvi felt herself trapped deep in the hot, sulfuric gullet, airless, suffocating. Just as her life had been before.

Then the dragon turned itself inside out, or outside in, and abruptly Asvi found herself braced on the back of its mighty neck as it flew east toward the mountains. She grasped for the whiplike ends of its horns to hold herself steady. The wind stung her face, and her hands hurt from gripping so hard, and yet exhilaration thrilled through her heart.

They passed over the town. Its neat brick buildings were laced with star-crown vines. Gardens blazed with summer blossoms and ripening vegetables. A central plaza ringed a fountain in the shape of a dragon's skull pouring water from its orifices. People waved without alarm, as if they saw dragons fly close overhead every day and welcomed their presence. In the watchtower, women stood guard as if it were the most ordinary thing in the world for women to do. If only Danis were here to see it. But of course Danis would never be forced out onto the long walk, would she? She was protected; she was safe, if living that life could be called safety.

A white stone path led eastward. Soon it split into three paths, each of which led to another village, and then three more each after that, splitting again like the delta fan of a river spreading wide. These villages were smaller clusters of houses, work sheds, and gardens set around a central plaza. Each was ringed by fences built of giant bones—dragon bones—and moats filled with what looked like heaps of glittering crystal sand gleaming hotly under the sun. A draft rose from the mounds, thick with a drowsy scent of glorious summer solitude amid the rocky pastures of her youth. One of the mounds looked recently dug out. Its pit was streaked with the remains of a slick, torn membrane withering to dryness under the sun.

As they cleared the last of the villages, they flew onward, eastward, upward, over the tufted grass and stunted woodland of the plateau. Gnarled juniper was overtaken by scrub thorn-gast tangling in elongated veins across the land. Grass gave way to spiny, fernlike plants and blooms whose petals undulated in the wind like tongues licking the air.

A ripple of movement caught her eye. The dragon shifted course until they flew over a group of eight hunters running as in pursuit of prey.

Hunters! How had hunters crossed the chasm?

Farther ahead, an unseen creature thrashed a trail through the tall grass, accompanied by puffs of glimmering mist that she recognized as the exhalation of a demon. When she looked back, amazed at the boldness of the hunters, she realized they were women, armed with spears, bows, courage, and resolve. Where had these women come from? They were manifestly not the weary, discarded widows and servants sent on the long walk. They were hale and strong, fleet of foot and tireless. Delicate two-pronged horns not much more than a finger's height grew out of their temples. Their skin, as dark as Asvi's own, had an uncanny sheen, as if they did not precisely have skin as she did but something more like soft scales.

When they looked up, they hailed the dragon with a whistling keen that dug into her flesh and throbbed in her bones as if it were meant to cut her open.

"Who are they?" she asked, even as the rumbling of the wind swallowed her words.

"Our sisters," said the dragon, and kept flying, leaving the hunters behind.

Up they rose, as the peaks slashed into the sky ahead, growing larger, impassable. Asvi became dizzy, gulping in thin air, shivering as the temperature dropped until she felt packed in ice. But the dragon's heat rose to keep her heart warm and her courage kindled.

They flew along avalanche-strewn slopes, across blinding ice fields, and past the peaks with their jagged teeth. Beyond lay a rugged plateau cut into pinnacles and canyons and flat-topped mountains. This massive upland ended in a stark escarpment, like the edge of the world. Spinning its way down on a thread of bronze light, the dragon came to rest on a flat prominence of bare rock where the mountain massif came to its abrupt end. With a turning, inside out or outside in, the dragon curled in on itself, shrinking into a denser shape.

Into a woman, clothed in bronze-brown skin. Two-pronged horns grew from the woman's head, in a shape exactly like those of the dragon. Asvi stared at her, struck speechless at the change.

The woman gestured for her to look east.

The escarpment ran roughly along a north-south line. The mountainous massif they'd just flown over rose west behind them like the shoulders and back of a huge beast. The drop of the escarpment's cliff face was too great for Asvi to measure. Here and there, waterfalls cut notches and funnels into its side. Falls of rock had accumulated into mysterious patterns at its base.

East lay an impossibly wide landscape shrouded in shifting mist, the distant horizon hidden by haze. Here and there the mist would shred, revealing a glimpse of meandering river or a forest whose moon-pale branches were surely those of ghoul-trees. Amid the ghostly pallor of the woodland the occasional solitary tree stood out for its startling color, as if grown from a precious gem. There were other sights as well: a city whose elegant ruins sprawled between the fork of a river; a towering bluff carved with the giant shapes of noble figures, crowned and robed, who didn't quite look like men; a road paved in white stone, leading to some far-off realm, although from this distance the route appeared empty and untraveled.

These glimpses emerged and vanished within the ever-winding mist.

"Is that the land of demons?" Asvi shivered in the cold wind that howled across the height.

"Once we lived there and hunted there together with many other beings. Then the demons came."

"Where did they come from?"

The woman tilted her head to one side as if listening to a voice Asvi could not hear. "The ancestors do not know. But in their relentless way, the demons have slowly driven us back to these mountains. We thought our kind were doomed because the demons destroyed our nests. We could no longer brood our young. Then your people came from over the sea."

"Did we drive you out of the lowlands? Away from the ocean?"

"Oh, no. You do have not that kind of power."

"What difference do we make, then? The demons kill us, too."

"Yes. So we have observed. At first we thought you also were vermin, small and weak and with the native cunning and cruelty necessary to small, weak creatures if they wish to survive. But your kind wields a magic we cannot."

"The magic the priests use to keep demons out of our land?"

"They harness death. But we can harness life."

"Then why do you demand the sacrifice of women like me?"

"We ask merely a chance to harvest what is already being thrown away."

Asvi thought of the chasm that separated the uplands from dragon country and how the priests evidently did not know about what lay beyond. She thought of quiet villages and tidy lives, of women standing sentry duty in watchtowers as if it were commonplace and perfectly normal for women to take on tasks that were elsewhere considered suitable only for men. She remembered the hunters she'd seen, with their budding horns and their youth and vigor. The outlying villages surrounded by bone fences and heaps of sand radiating heat under the summer sun. The strange vegetation never seen in the lowlands where people lived.

Maybe she should have gone with the Aivur sailor who'd offered her adventure so long ago. Maybe she should have settled into the room by the kitchen and accepted its boundaries for the rest of her life.

But what use are regrets? She was here now. There was no going back to what might have been. Anyway, here at the edge, she was glad to have seen this much.

"Did you bring me here to eat me?"

"Eat you?" The woman laughed. A deep echo of the dragon's belling call shivered within her mirth, a reminder of how exceedingly large and powerful a dragon was. "I have not tried human flesh myself, but the ancestors say it is sour and either too greasy or too gristly. I brought you here, sister, because you asked to travel on."

"Is this the end of the journey?"

"You tell me."

Asvi again looked east over the wide wilderness and its hidden contours. A thread of fog had undulated out of the undifferentiated tangle of mist and was crawling up the face of the escarpment toward the very spot where she was standing.

"They never rest and will never rest until we have destroyed every last one."

The woman stepped back just as Asvi heard a scrape of claws and a hiss of breath like the boiling of a kettle. A thick smear like an oily cloud of white slithered over the lip of the cliff and solidified into a demon. Once before, she had stood this close to a demon. It was about as big as she was, with six tentacle-like legs, a pair of lipless mouths, and a stack of pipelike tendrils clustered atop its dome of a head that pumped a steady stream of stinking mist into the air. Rearing back, it braced itself on its four hind limbs as its forelimbs waved to taste the air and find her scent.

Run.

If you run, they will chase you, her father had taught his children. Her brother had panicked and run. But even if you didn't run, it would still see you.

Its head swung around, getting a fix on her. The dull round nodules in its head lit as if fired from within to an almost blinding blaze of garish color, like molten gems. The eyes had woken and would not sleep until they had fully absorbed every last fiber of its prey.

It opened its upper mouth and spat toward her. Too far to do real damage; still, the spray of mist spattered across her face, raising welts as she put up her hands too late to shield herself. Only then did her shock evaporate as a vision of her scalded brother flashed in her mind's eye, how he had writhed in the grip of an unspeakable agony, unable even to cry or moan. Maybe it would have been better if the demon had eaten him to cut short the torment of his slow dying.

The demon slid closer to her, gurgling as it readied a bath of acid in which to boil her alive, so she couldn't move while it sucked her dry.

The dragon—she hadn't seen it change—dived from above and behind her. Too late the demon sheared away, making for the cliff. The dragon's claws fastened over the demon's hindquarters and lifted it as the demon spat harmlessly toward the receding ground. The dragon flew in a spiral upward into the cloudless blue of the sky. From that great height, it dropped the demon. When the creature hit the base of the escarpment, it cracked like stone into shards.

Asvi's legs gave way. She collapsed onto her knees, hands shaking, breath coming in gasps. Yet it was exhilarating, too. So easily the dragon had disposed of the deadly beast.

With a scuff, the dragon landed many paces away from her. The air shimmered, drawn in and drawn out, and the woman with horns walked over to her, dusting off her hands.

"We were not the only beings who retreated, or died, when the demons invaded," she remarked as she came up to Asvi. She indicated the wilderness. "When we became too few to keep their numbers in check, the ancestors made peace with the inevitability of our obliteration."

"Until my people came from over the sea."

"All beings in the world are woven with the weft and warp of the world's magic. But each may wield it differently."

"Do dragons weave?"

"No."

"Then how do you know about weaving?"

"She who gave herself to the sands was a weaver in a town called Gedaala. Do you know that place?"

Asvi clambered to her feet, even as she knew she had no weapons that could defeat this creature standing beside her and chatting with her in the most unremarkable and yet utterly astounding way. "I have heard its name spoken in passing, but I don't know it. Do you?"

"I grew up there. I lived there and worked there as a weaver. I was sent on the long walk. I crossed into dragon country, thinking I was meant to die there. I lived for a time in the company of others like me."

"In the village I saw? The one that those I came with were being led to?"

"Yes. When I was ready, I went into the sands. Now I am as you see me."

"So you do eat us!" She took a step away, caught herself retreating— do not run!—and held her ground.

"We do not eat you."

Having flown with a dragon and seen the edge of the habitable world had given Asvi a new and exciting tincture of bravery. She thrust out her chin boldly. "This woman you claim to have once been. What was her name?"

"Merea."

"If I called you Merea, would you answer?"

"I am Merea."

"You are a dragon."

"I am Merea, and I am a dragon."

"But the woman named Merea is gone. You consumed her, did you not? Devoured everything of her except to use her form to speak to me. Is that what the sands are? A nesting ground?"

"The sand is what remains of the ancestors, the grains of their flesh and the sparks of their memories. Your bodies and your minds cook within the heat, if you will. And out of this, we are transformed and reborn."

"So it is no different than it ever was. After our labor and our lives are used up down there, we are sent up here. You use up the last scraps that are left of us." Anger made her heart ache. Disappointment bit like betrayal. Maybe it would be better to leap off the cliff and dash herself to death on the shores of the demon wilderness. At least that would be her choice.

The woman looked at the ground with a sigh, then up again. "Shall I tell you of my life? How my family sold me to a weaving shed when I was still a child? How I sat on the ground chained to a loom for years and years, never seeing daylight except through the open shed door? Was fed too little? Abused by those who owned me? How my hands became broken by the work so I was no longer useful to them? Or to any family, because I was too ill to bear sons and keep a husband? How I hobbled, in pain, up the long walk? I did not weep, you know. I believed I deserved nothing more. And yet the sky amazed me. I had forgotten the world could be beautiful."

Asvi bowed her head. Her breath felt tight in her chest, and she wiped away a tear. But it would not do to let sentiment obscure her vision. "And then what happened?" she asked coldly.

"Do you know what I found in the village? I found peace. I found people who treated me with respect. I was happy there for many years. I sat in the sun when I wished. I took on such work as I could with my ruined hands."

The woman held them out now, strong dark hands with a glimmer of scales and dusted with the dry, flaking residue of the demon she'd just killed. Yet they were human hands, too. Hands that had labored for long years to enrich someone else. Hands used up until they could give no more, and thus discarded.

"And then," she said, meeting Asvi's gaze with the hard, challenging light of her luminous eyes, "then I chose the sands."

"*Chose* them? Or was forced to choose them?"

"Do you think we force your kind to join with us? That any dragon wishes to be born out of coercion and captivity? Those who come to our country may live out their lives and die by their own rites. If that is what you wish, Asvi, then the village's peaceful round of life will be the end of your journey."

Asvi raised her eyes to the west, as if she could see back into the room where she had woken up with her husband dead beside her, as if she could look down along the promise to her father fulfilled through all those years. Sparks drew dancing threads of gold and silver and bronze over the peaks and spires of the Great Divide, where dragons flew.

"What if I want wings?" she whispered.

Merea smiled sadly, softly. "Sister, you have always had wings. They were stolen from you long ago. Now they wait here with us, when you are ready."

CUT ME ANOTHER QUILL, MISTER FITZ

Garth Nix

New York Times bestselling novelist **Garth Nix** (garthnix.com) has been a full-time writer since 2001, but has also worked as a literary agent, marketing consultant, book editor, book publicist, book sales representative, bookseller, and as a part-time soldier in the Australian Army Reserve. He has written numerous books, including the Old Kingdom series, beginning with *Sabriel*; the Keys to the Kingdom series; *Frogkisser!*; and many others. His most recent novel is *Angel Mage* and coming up shortly is *The Left-Handed Booksellers of London*. He also writes short fiction, with more than sixty stories published in anthologies and magazines. More than six million copies of his books have been sold around the world, and his work has been translated into forty-two languages.

"Cut me another quill, Mister Fitz, if you would be so kind," said Sir Hereward. The sometime knight-artillerist's hands were blotched with ink rather than the more usual powder or blood, and the quill he was gazing at ruefully had lost its point entirely.

"That is your second within the hour," said Mister Fitz, who was perched upon the neighboring desk, rather than at a stool like Sir Hereward. But then the sorcerous puppet stood only three feet, six-and-a-half inches tall on his carved wooden feet. "Can you not sharpen your present pen?"

The scrivening room was dusty and dark. A single arrow-slit in the far side failed to admit much in the way of daylight, and there was only a single candelabra of three branches on Hereward's desk, though the candles it held were pure beeswax and quite bright as candles went. Mister Fitz, of course, could see very well in the dark, and in fact the blue-painted pupils of the eyes in his pumpkin-sized papier-mâché head had a faint glow of their own.

For the purpose of keeping their activities secret from the general populace, their chosen place of work was high in the southwest tower of the Archon's palace. There were guards in the chamber below, who fetched and carried whatever documents Mister Fitz requested from the chancery over on the eastern side of the palace.

Both the knight's and the puppet's desks were laden with thick rolls of faded yellowish vellum, and knight and puppet each had a roll unfurled before them, revealing them to be tax records. They were making lists of selected names drawn from the roll on sheets of more modern, clean white paper. Sir Hereward's page was rather spoiled by blotches, though his fist was otherwise neat enough. Mister Fitz's list was impeccable and much longer, and any scriptorium would have enlisted him at once, though scriptoriums were not what they once were, since the advent of printing a century or so before.

"You have the sharper knife," grumbled Sir Hereward. "Furthermore, my present quill is too brittle and second-rate to take more sharpening, and it has slowed me abominably."

"How many names have you writ?" asked Mister Fitz. He took a tiny triangular knife from some hidden sheath behind his head and expertly shaped and slit the end of a goose feather, the blade so sharp it parted the quill without any resistance at all, as if the puppet sliced the air. "A noteworthy number, I hope?"

"Certes! Nine . . . no . . . ten that are possible. And you?"

"Sixty-two," replied Mister Fitz dryly. "As the complete census, across twenty-nine rolls, contains in my estimation in excess of eleven thousand personages, your progress and contribution to our task will clearly be minuscule."

Sir Hereward got up from the desk and bowed to the puppet.

"Most excellent calculation, good puppet," he declared, waving his hand in a series of descending flourishes. "What I doubt is the method overall. Why do we not simply walk through the city and look for anything that might suggest the presence of the dragon? If there is a dragon."

"The records I found in the Library of Karrilinion strongly support the presence of a dragon here, and more importantly, its treasure," said Mister Fitz. "But we will not find it by walking around. This dragon has managed to hide here for at least three hundred years, suggesting it is not entirely foolish. Unlike others I might mention. I know your expertise is with gunpowder and shooting off guns and so forth, but even so, I trust you have heard or read something about the extra-dimensional invaders commonly called godlets?"

"A little, I suppose," grumbled Sir Hereward. "What has that to do with anything?"

Mister Fitz's question and Hereward's answer would have surprised and perhaps amused anyone who had significant dealings with the duo in the past, since Sir Hereward and Mister Fitz were agents of the Council of the Treaty for the Safety of the World and, as ever, were engaged in their seemingly eternal quest to rid the world of exactly those illegal godlets and other proscribed extra-dimensional invaders Mister Fitz had just mentioned. But neither the Archon of Nikandros nor anyone else in the city-state knew this. Or so Hereward fervently hoped.

"I shall enlighten you," said the puppet.

Sir Hereward sighed and slumped back onto his stool, not needing to feign his resignation. Mister Fitz had been his nanny long before becoming his companion in arms, and the sorcerous puppet very frequently lapsed into the didactic persona of Hereward's school years.

"The beings commonly called dragons are a peculiar class of extra-dimensional entity. They can assume a variety of physical forms, given sufficient raw material to do so, including the classical winged reptilian, but also that of a man or woman," continued Mister Fitz. "When they take the shape of an everyday person, their otherworldly essence is cloaked and hidden, and so would appear neither more or less than any other citizen of this fair city. In other words, there would be nothing for us to see. No horns, no tails, no strange eyes—"

"Yes, yes, all right," said Sir Hereward, but this did not stop Mister Fitz.

"They do not necessarily have a predilection for consuming young maidens, nor do they flamboyantly display their hoards. They do not breathe fire, at least not when hiding in mortal shape. They do not—"

"Enough!" cried Hereward, holding his hands up in surrender, accidentally splashing a large drop of ink on the original roll, requiring immediate ameliorative work with sponge and knife.

"So walking around the city would achieve nothing save the gratification of your senses, which I perceive is the true reason you wish to do so, and also why you play the laggard at this work."

"Oh, very well," said Sir Hereward, giving up on his efforts to remove the ink stain as hopeless. "How about we leave this musty alcove to look into the first seventy-two we have, a goodly number to begin, I say."

"Because as soon as we do, word will spread of our activities," said Mister Fitz. "This should be obvious even to you, Hereward. If the dragon hears rumor the Supreme Archon has sanctioned investigations into all those who possess a stock of gold amounting to more than ten thousand staters, they may well flee to some previously prepared retreat, before we are ready to pursue them. And as I need not remind you, I am sure, locating that retreat is our chief consideration, for that is where the dragon will have amassed their *primary* treasure—"

"Which the Archon is going to confiscate," interrupted Sir Hereward. "I still think we should have held out for more than a quarter share. After all, we found the tablets at Karrilinion—"

"We? And a moment ago you suggested there is no dragon."

"All right! All right! But my joints grow stiff and I have aged a year in the two days we have spent here already. Let us divide and conquer, as Narbonius declaimed in *The Death of Many.*"

"You know the historical Narbonius divided his forces and they were defeated piecemeal?" asked Mister Fitz. "When Kidenses wrote the play, she chose to change the actual events."

"No," admitted Sir Hereward. "I mean, the play is the thing. Who remembers the history?"

"Narbonius was a fool," grumbled Mister Fitz. "He was well advised, but chose to disregard what I . . . that is to say, I have read that he turned against his advisors."

"Ancient history!" said Sir Hereward. He scowled at Fitz and changed the subject, his voice growing louder. "I wonder if we renegotiated—"

"Six hundred and seven years ago," mused Mister Fitz, but he had lowered his voice, almost whispering to himself. "Four months and three days. Shortly before noon. Battle was joined thereafter and Narbonius slain shortly after sunset, an arrow in the back as he fled the field."

"As I was saying," declaimed Sir Hereward. "A quarter share seems little recompense for not only bringing news of this dragon, but also all this busy work here—"

"I have cut you a new quill," said Mister Fitz. "Pray continue more speedily."

Sir Hereward sighed, took the quill, and returned his attention to the roll in front of him.

"You know that once we start examining all these rich people, there will be an uproar," said Sir Hereward. "They'll presume the Archon plans a new tax. There will probably be a revolt."

"There will be no fuss," said Mister Fitz. "If you had bothered to listen when I explained matters to the Archon, the list of those possessing a sufficient stock of gold is only the first step, an indication, if you will. Once we have those names, we must cross-index them against the registry of births, deaths, and disappearances, to discern any unusual pattern of inheritance. This, I expect, will deliver only two or three people to look into more closely. The Archonate is to be commended on the excellence of their records."

"You were nattering away for hours," said Sir Hereward. "It was very dull. Besides, the Archon doesn't like me."

"I doubt the Archon has any feelings for you one way or another," said Mister Fitz. "She is a very sensible woman. Pray, do get on with the task."

Silence reigned in the chamber, save for the occasional sound of a pen scratching a new name, until the great bell in the central tower began to sound the turning of the sun, when it reached its zenith and began to fall again. Or as those in the North called it, noon.

"We should have just done this in the chancery," said Sir Hereward, flinging down his quill again. "An airy, well-lit chamber, all records close at hand—"

"And many of the clerks young women for you to attempt your charms upon," interrupted Mister Fitz. "We are better here, in seclusion, where none may know of our task, or suspect the existence of a dragon's treasure."

"I'm not convinced there is a dragon after all!" announced Sir Hereward, rather loudly.

"Shush!" snapped Mister Fitz, with a meaningful glance at the door. While it was of solid oak, it had swollen from disuse and occasional inundation due to the inadequate roofing of the tower against the monsoonal weather of Nikandros, and did not properly close. There was a three-finger-wide gap at the bottom, so it was quite possible the two guards could hear every word, even from the chamber below, and definitely could if they had crept up the steps to eavesdrop.

"What? They're the Archon's Chosen, aren't they?" blustered Sir Hereward. "Fine soldiers. Loyal. Not to be swayed by thoughts of treasure."

"Hereward. I have told you before, we must keep this matter close, you need to curb your natural tendency to conversation. Now, the sooner we press on, the sooner finished."

Hereward mumbled something.

"What was that?"

"I merely wondered how long this current task might take," said Sir Hereward. "Not in so many words."

"A reasonable request," replied Mister Fitz. "By my computation, presuming only a slight increase in your contribution, we will be finished with the tax rolls in another eight days, and can then move on to the cross-indexing, which will require nineteen to twenty-one days—"

"A month!" roared Sir Hereward. "A month stuck in this dark, mildewed chamber! I can't do it! I need air and light . . . I . . . I need a drink!"

"Sir Hereward!"

But the knight-artillerist paid no attention to the puppet. He stood up, knocking his stool over backward, and stormed to the door. He wrenched at it uselessly once, then again, before finally getting it open. Mister Fitz watched him with his strange, painted blue eyes, but said no more. Sir Hereward grunted something and went down the steps at a dangerous speed.

Mister Fitz waited a moment, hopped down, and went over to push the heavy swollen door closed with an ease at odds with his small stature and the limbs of thin, polished wood beneath his loose scholar's robe, which was the same color as the stone of the tower. The door shut, he crossed the chamber, picked up a leather satchel, and swung it over his back, before swiftly climbing up to the single-arrow slit, those same slim wooden fingers piercing the mortar between the stones like hammered iron pitons. Reaching the window, the puppet lifted the hood of his robe over his pumpkinlike head, and climbed outside.

Sir Hereward, taking the more conventional steps, arrived at the landing below where the two guards were stationed. He almost collided with one of them, who had either been listening or perhaps merely looking up, curious as to the source of the commotion. She stepped lightly out of the way, and Sir Hereward slowed down to stand between the two guards, his fists clenched, nostrils agape, breath snorting, all too like a fractious bull.

"Is there some trouble, Sir Hereward?" asked the woman. Her name was Aryadny and she was the senior of the two guards, and far more dangerous in Hereward's reckoning than Zanthus, despite the other guard being younger, at least a foot taller, and considerably heavier, in muscle not fat. Both wore the close-faced bronze helms, gilded scale mail, and plated leggings of the Archon's Chosen, and both carried short-staved demi-halberds, but Aryadny also had a punch misericorde at her belt, and she moved with the sinuous grace that suggested frequent use of the narrow-bladed weapon. She was more of an assassin than a soldier, unless Sir Hereward missed his guess.

"Your pardon," said Sir Hereward. He took a deep breath and let it out slowly. "That clerkly puppet irks me! I swear his blood is ink, and of course his head *is* made of paper!"

Aryadny laughed.

"A dry stick, sure enough," she said. "Very different to the musical puppets I've seen. They are full of japes and jokes, and sing and play most beautifully."

"I'd like to see one of them," said Zanthus wistfully. "Do you think old . . . whatshisname . . . Futz . . . would give us a song?"

"No," said Sir Hereward. "A crow could sing better. A stone would! Whatever ancient sorcerer put him together made him solely to burrow in books and scrolls, and write damn fool lists of no consequence."

"You make an odd pairing, Sir Hereward," said Aryadny. "I mean, a mercenary officer, skilled with cannon and the like. Why do you truckle under an inky old puppet?"

"I don't truckle," protested Sir Hereward, but with good humor. "As you said, I am a mercenary. In high standing in the western kingdoms, I'll have you know. Ask anyone."

"The western kingdoms lie a thousand leagues distant," said Aryadny.

"What's that to do? In any case, I work with Fitz because he pays very well, and has a nose for . . . let's say a nose for even better pay. I aim to raise my own company of great guns by next spring, and that will not come cheap."

"It's true we offer the best prices on bronze or iron guns in the known world," said Aryadny, with a look that suggested she now understood Hereward's motivation for being in Nikandros far better than she had a moment ago. "My cousin's a cannon-founder, a master of the Guild, should you wish an introduction. Doubtless he would offer attractive prices for a man known to be in the Archon's good graces."

Hereward nodded thoughtfully.

"I may well ask that of you, once our work is done," he said. "I thank you. But right now I *need* a drink to wash the dust from my throat. Can you suggest a tavern with good wine for a discerning soldier such as myself?"

"Sign of the Black Sun," offered Zanthus.

"I think Sir Hereward would prefer the Windflower," said Aryadny. "It has the superior cellar. Perhaps even wines from the western kingdoms."

"Whichever is the closer will serve," said Sir Hereward.

"Or you could simply visit the buttery within the citadel, close by the gatehouse," said Aryadny. "We serve our noble visitors a pleasant *zinthen*, a wine you may know."

"Oh, aye, a white grape, somewhat sour for my taste," said Hereward. "But it would quench my thirst, which I confess is mighty. Yet if there is a finer vintage to be had . . ."

"Then the Windflower should serve you well," said Aryadny. "It lies on the wall between the Upper Third and the Middle. From the main gate of the citadel, you should cross the great court and take the varden marked with the bronze statue of a bull—"

"The varden?"

"Our name for what you might call an alley, or perhaps a lane of steps," said Aryadny. She continued with a long list of directions that Hereward kept asking her to repeat, though he had them memorized on the first recitation.

He had also closely studied the map of the city Mister Fitz had purchased before they took ship at Sarg Sargaros, so Hereward already knew what a varden was, and had a good idea of the layout of the city.

Nikandros was built atop a wedge-shaped stone mountain that formed an island off the coast of Er-Nikandros. The narrow point extended several leagues out into the sea, and atop this was the Archon's citadel, fourteen hundred feet above the water. As the arrowhead broadened and descended toward the mainland, it was filled in with the houses and shops of the rich or at least well-to-do. This was the Upper Third, though in fact it occupied less than a quarter of the city's rambling acreage. A high wall separated the Upper Third from the Middle, which was terraced into five main sections, the lowest terrace some five hundred feet below the wall.

A great crevasse—bridged at over a dozen points—separated the Middle from the Levels, the generally flat outer area dominated by forges, foundries, and the metalworking industry that was the source of Nikandros's wealth. The Levels extended to the base of the arrowhead, where the peninsula joined the mainland, and was enclosed at its extent by an ancient wall and beyond that by more extensive and modern defenses of ditch, bastion, and ravelin, all suitably equipped with fine cannon of the city's own making.

Because it was built into and upon a mountain, the streets of Nikandros were generally narrow and involved a lot of steps. But only the broadest thoroughfares, and there were few of these, were known as streets. Most of the ways were very narrow, never went in a straight line, zigzagging back and forth as the slope required, and these were known as vardens.

The other thing Hereward already knew was that a dark, steep, constantly turning varden was the ideal spot for ambush and murder. Though there were plenty of places like that within the citadel as well, Hereward thought, and he hoped Mister Fitz was right about certain aspects of the plan they had set in motion.

"So I turn right at a barber's with the tree in the tub by its door?" he asked.

"No, left at the barber's, which has the sign of a copper comb," said Aryadny. "After that, right at Pharem's fruiterer—*she* has the tree in the tub as a sign."

"Ah, yes," said Hereward. "I fear all the scribing in that little room has mazed my mind. Left at the barber's, with the copper comb, right at the tree in the tub, go straight on and down the steps with the rotten railing—I'll be careful of that—and then when I get to the courtyard with the old cannon, there are various vardens, and I take the second from the left."

"No, it's the third varden from the place of various vardens!" exclaimed Aryadny.

"I can just ask directions," said Hereward. "And if I see some tavern on the way, perhaps—"

"No, no, the Windflower's wine is far superior to anywhere else," said Aryadny. "You know, I think I should accompany you."

"What! You can't—" Zanthus started to say, but Aryadny held up her hand.

"I'll send up Mennos to take my place," she said. "After you, Sir Hereward."

"I will be able to collect my weapons?" asked Sir Hereward. He had surrendered them when they first arrived at the citadel, but he didn't want to go wandering about the city without being fully armed. Or that was the impression he wanted to give.

He had a dagger in each boot, of course, another up his left sleeve, and the locket he wore around his neck did not contain a portrait of a loved one, but rather opened to reveal a very small moon-shaped blade, sharp as a razor.

Then there were also the curious gold earrings he wore, shaped like long bones. They were hollow, with little holes drilled through them. Charming little pipes the length of his little finger, a solid weight of near pure gold. Not exactly weapons, but they had a purpose.

"Your baggage is held at the main gate," said Aryadny. "Of course, if going into the city, you may take up sword and pistols. Though you will not need them, provided you stay out of the worst parts of the Levels."

Still Hereward did not move. Aryadny shrugged and went ahead, sweeping down the stairs with the ease of a native Nikandrosite, for whom steps were more natural than a level floor. Hereward did not immediately follow, taking a surprisingly large silver flask from the pouch at his belt to indulge in what appeared to be a long swig.

"You cannot wait for the wine, Sir Hereward?" asked Aryadny politely, looking back up the steps.

"This is a medicine," replied Hereward, wiping his mouth. The smell of powerful brandy rolled off his breath. "A nasty concoction for an old wound in . . . in my hip . . . that niggles at me betimes."

"I trust it will not grow worse," said Aryadny. "You are not troubled by all our steps?"

"Not at all!" declared Hereward, bounding down after her. He immediately stumbled, recovering himself just in time to avoid cannoning into Aryadny, though she had stepped aside in any case. She was very light on her feet, further confirming Hereward's assessment of her as an assassin.

"Or perhaps a little," confessed Hereward. He belched brandy fumes and started off again, more slowly. "It is true I have never been confronted with such an array of stairs and ramps and steep changes of altitude."

"Nikandros is unique in many ways," said Aryadny. "But then you are also a novelty to us, a visitor from so far away. Do you really think there is a dragon here?"

Hereward pretended surprise, stumbled again, and clutched at the wall to save himself.

"What . . . why . . ."

"We are the Archon's Chosen," replied Aryadny. She paused to open the door at the base of the stairs, admitting welcome sunlight. "Naturally we have been informed of your purpose here."

"I see," said Sir Hereward, following her out into the narrow courtyard that led from the isolated tower to the palace proper. "I had wondered if you'd been told. I am not personally convinced there is a dragon, but Mister Fitz has found old documents that purport otherwise, and I have to confess that clerkly old puppet is very good with documents. And he has found dragons before."

This caused Aryadny to almost stumble herself, on perfectly flat paving stones.

"He did?"

"Without profit to us," grumbled Sir Hereward. "I had to kill it before it could lead us to its hoard."

"You killed a dragon?" asked Aryadny. "Might I ask how this was done?"

Her tone did not so much suggest curiosity as disbelief, but not in an offensive manner.

"It's easy enough when they're in mortal form," said Sir Hereward, puffing out his chest and assuming a rather pompous manner. "Though 'tis true they cannot be slain with any ordinary weapon."

"How then?"

"Fitz is a clever fellow, for all his other defects," said Hereward. He stopped to take out another, smaller flask from his pouch and drank from that as Aryadny waited patiently. "He found me something that would do the job."

"Some particular weapon?" asked Aryadny. "I confess I did wonder about one of the items in the small arsenal you brought ashore."

"Ah, noticed it, did you?" asked Hereward, tapping his finger with his nose, apparently forgetting he held the small metal flask. He flinched as its stopper almost went up one nostril.

"I would say it is unusual for an artillerist and exponent of gunpowder weapons to entertain the use of something so outmoded as a crossbow," said Aryadny. "I think anyone would have noticed that."

"Well spotted, well spotted," said Sir Hereward. He took another drink as Aryadny opened the door at the other end of the courtyard. "But it—*hic*—isn't the crossbow, as such. No, the secret lies in the quarrels!"

"The quarrels?" asked Aryadny. She frowned. "I do not recall seeing any."

"They're in a case," said Hereward. "A case, made special, lined with lead to keep them quiet."

"Keep . . . the quarrels quiet?"

"They've got imps in them," confided Hereward.

"Imps!"

"That's what I call them," said Hereward. He returned the small flask to his pouch and fished around for the larger one, removing it with an air of triumph. "Fitz found them—the bolts, I mean. Dug 'em up somewhere. They talk. Mutter. High-pitched little voices. Imps. Apparently that's what it takes to kill a dragon. Worked on the other one, anyway. Oh gods, more stairs."

"There are always more stairs in Nikandros, Sir Hereward," said Aryadny. "This is something of a secret way to the main gatehouse. I would like to look at these imp-haunted bolts, if you don't mind."

"Didn't think we came up this way," said Sir Hereward. He tripped, fell against the wall and rebounded with the air of a man who thought the wall was at fault for being there. Somehow he didn't drop his flask.

This stairwell was very narrow, the ceiling was low, and unlike the fine stonework everywhere else in the citadel, the passage that stretched down and down and down, lit only by the occasional torch in a bracket, was the original rock of the mountain, rough-worked, as attested by the many chisel marks.

"No, this is a direct passage. We generally prefer our visitors to take more pleasant paths," said Aryadny. "But I fear this is a long stair, and dull, without windows or outlooks. Perhaps you would tell me how you came to slay your . . . ah . . . first dragon. Where was this dragon, as it happens?"

"Oh, far off," said Hereward. "Can't tell you. The puppet, he swore me to secrecy. Might go back and search for its gold someday. Only when he found out about the dragon here, that had to come first. He says it will have a much bigger hoard!"

"Why is that?"

"Oh, the one we got was youngish, or so Fitz told me. Only a hundred or so. The one here is much older. Least that's what the puppet says. Busy old fool."

"You think the puppet is wrong?"

"Oh, probably not, but his ways are tiresome," complained Hereward. He paused on a step to vigorously shake his flask, sighing as he heard no answering gurgle. "Won't let me drink. He found the other dragon without all this fussing about with musty old tax rolls. Shepter's Blood! How many more steps are there?"

"It is not far to the gatehouse now," said Aryadny. "It is a shame you could not find your first dragon's hoard. Was there a great area to search?"

"Half of . . . half of the county," said Hereward. "You said there was good wine near the gatehouse? The buttery? I've a mind not to bother traipsing down any more stairs. My hip, you know."

"Oh, yes, the buttery would be much easier," said Aryadny. "And you won't need to pick up your weapons."

"Fine, fine," said Hereward. "Lead on."

"I am leading on," said Aryadny, in a puzzled tone. "We're almost at the lower door and then it is but a hop and a skip to the buttery, so to speak."

"Good," cried Hereward. "I *need* a drink! *Many* drinks!"

But Sir Hereward drank only two glasses of very sour wine before collapsing face-first on the table with a lengthy, snoring grunt. Once planted, he concentrated on breathing noisily through his mouth, and began a meditative exercise taught him long ago by his mother, one of the Mysterious Three who ruled the Witches of Har. His sense of himself retreated into a deep, inner place, where he could observe his own body but would not immediately react to any stimulus.

He lay there for a minute or two before he felt Aryadny prod him hard in the ribs with the pommel of a dagger. It hurt, but he did not let himself flinch, instead simply stopping his breath for a moment before letting out a donkeylike snort of the kind someone dead drunk might make at sudden pain.

Next, Aryadny's clever fingers cautiously opened his pouch, taking out the contents. He heard coins on the tabletop, followed by the soft whirr of the stopper being unscrewed from his large flask, followed by a deep sniff.

"Strong stuff," Aryadny said to someone else, who chuckled. "I'm surprised he made it down the narrow back stair."

"Talking all the way," said the other person. A man, whose voice Hereward had not heard before.

"You got it all?" asked Aryadny.

"I hear, I remember," said the man. "She'll be interested, for sure."

"Go recite it to her then," said Aryadny. "I'll get this drunken blowhard taken back to the guest chambers."

"What about the puppet?"

"He scratches away in the tower," said Aryadny. "Very single-minded, sorcerous puppets. He'll keep reading and making notes until he's stopped. Go on."

Almost as if he watched it happen from some distance, Hereward felt himself lifted up by strong hands. He made no effort to hold his head up. It lolled backward and he almost choked on his own tongue before someone lifted his neck and he was able to take another gargling breath.

"How'd he get so sodden so quickly?" muttered an unknown woman, one of Hereward's bearers.

"I'd say he's a drunkard who's been holding out," said Aryadny. "Until he couldn't. Knocked back at last three gills of a fierce spirit."

"Surprised he isn't dead," muttered another voice. "We'd best lay him down so his vomit goes out, not in."

"Yes, you had," said Aryadny sternly. "*She* will want to see him later, I'm sure."

"Where are you going?"

"To get his weapons. He has sorcerous quarrels that must be destroyed. Go on, you have your orders!"

Hereward waited in his trance state for a good hour after he was carefully placed on the floor of his guest room, arranged so that he would not choke and die. It was surprisingly restful, and in a disassociated way he wondered why he had not kept up with all the daily meditations he'd been taught by his mother and aunts and Mister Fitz, though of course he had many other daily exercises to pursue. Sword work, shooting with carbine and pistols, wrestling, sleight of hand, trigonometry and ballistics . . .

When he heard the bell from the central tower strike the third hour of the falling sun, Hereward opened his eyes and looked about the room. It was the pleasant guest chamber he'd been assigned. It had a window with nine panes of glass that looked out to the sea; a plain but more than serviceable bed with a feather mattress; and a chest for clothes. The door was shut, and there was no one else there, so he carefully got to his feet and sat on the bed.

"How travels the bait?" asked Mister Fitz, climbing in through the window. He shut it behind him carefully, then sat atop the chest, his leather sewing bag on his shallow lap, so the sorcerous needles within would be close at hand.

"Slowly," answered Hereward. "I am fairly sure it is not Aryadny, but she is certainly in the employ of the dragon."

"She would not have left you if she was the dragon," said Fitz. "They cannot resist the lure of another dragon's hoard; she would have made you give up all you know. And she would have taken the earrings."

"There was someone else, slinking behind us on the stair," said Hereward. "Some sort of spy, ears flapping. He has gone to tell 'her' everything I spoke of."

"Then matters will be soon in train," said Mister Fitz. "You have done well, Hereward."

"I trust *you* will be prompt," said Hereward. "And what if she has minions hard by? Aryadny is a killer if ever I saw one, and she will be swift with that misericorde."

"No dragon would chance a mortal hearing the whereabouts of a hoard," said Mister Fitz with calm certainty. "She will question you somewhere undisturbed by others."

"I hope you're right," said Hereward. He made a face and wiped his mouth with the back of his hand. "I also hope I never have to drink any more of their disgusting wine."

Mister Fitz did not answer. His perfectly round head rotated on his neck like a globe upon a well-oiled stand, and his leather ears pricked up.

"Someone comes," he said.

Hereward dropped to the floor, stuck his fingers down his throat and managed to regurgitate up a loathsome, alcohol-stinking puddle near his mouth. He drew back from it, wrinkling his nose, then gasped as Fitz pushed his head completely into the vomit before hiding under the bed.

The door opened, and several people marched in.

"Faugh! What stench!"

"Clean him up and get the cordial down him," instructed Aryadny. Hereward felt himself lifted up onto the bed, a cloth was wiped across his face, his mouth was forced upon, and a stream of something even viler than Nikandrosite wine was forced down his throat from a skin under pressure. He coughed and gasped and opened his eyes.

"Sir Hereward!" bawled Aryadny, close to his face. "You have an important audience! The cordial will clear your head."

Someone clapped an open hand against his stomach. Hereward breathed in and inadvertently swallowed the foul brew. He knew what it was from the taste alone—oil of gnashtur mixed with the juice of erskberries—even before he felt the horrible, hollowed-out sensation which rapidly spread through his entire body. While it had the virtue of removing drunkenness, it also delivered an immediate, peculiarly nasty kind of hangover. Very unfairly in Hereward's case, since he had no more than one swallow of brandy from his trick flask, a mouthful of stomach-lining moklek milk from the small flask, and the two glasses of wine.

"Urgghhh," he gasped. "What?"

Three of the Archon's Chosen were standing over him. One gripped his left arm, the other the right, while the third stripped his boots from him, quickly followed by his belt, pouch, and dagger, and then his coat and shirt, along with his other knife. The large pendant on the necklace at his throat was examined, found to be a blade, and removed as well.

Fingers plucked at his ear, but stopped as Aryadny spoke.

"Leave the earrings. They're gold. She'll want them."

Hereward roared and struggled as his undershirt was lifted, and kicked at the third man, sending him reeling him back.

"Have no fear, Sir Hereward!" soothed Aryadny, who was standing by the door. "We merely wish to ensure you have no hidden weapons."

"How dare you!" roared Hereward. "I'm a guest of your Archon!"

"Be easy," said Aryadny. "Allow him up, gentlemen."

Hereward staggered to his feet, and swayed in front of Aryadny, his shift billowing about his knees, his stockings around his ankles. No one noticed the wide garter on his left leg which had also fallen, after all it was only a piece of cloth. The men who had held him down stayed close, but it was Aryadny he watched, her and that thin dagger.

"I shall explain two possibilities to you, Sir Hereward," said Aryadny, smiling. "The first is that you allow us to blindfold and lead you to an audience, which I assure you will be of profit; the second is we beat you a little short of senseless—for you will need to talk—and carry you there, and doubtless it will be of less profit. I give you the choice."

"Bah! The Archon will hear of this," said Hereward. "I choose the first of your so-kind alternatives. Who is it I am being taken to meet?"

"You will see," said Aryadny. "When the blindfold comes off at our destination."

They blindfolded the knight and led him quickly out into the hall and immediately through a secret door that Hereward had not known existed in the opposite wall, into a space where they were crammed together while Aryadny opened another door, from the sound of it one with a complex or little-used latch.

"Head down," she instructed. "Pull his stockings up. There are steps, Hereward, lift your feet. Up."

They climbed for some time. Hereward counted steps, for form's sake, rather than any real need. At the two hundred and six mark, they stopped and he felt the warmth of the late afternoon sun on his face, and saw the edge of its light stealing in around his blindfold. From these things, he deduced they were outside, and atop one of the towers of the citadel—and he had a very nasty feeling everything was about to go hideously wrong.

"Leave us."

The voice was a woman's, and sounded calm and even kind. There was a general shuffling around Hereward; the hands that had held his arms were gone, and he heard his captors walk away and a door shut.

"You may remove your blindfold."

Hereward pulled the blindfold off. It was very bright, and he lifted his hand to shield his eyes. He was not atop a tower, as he'd thought, but on a demi-lune or miniature bastion outthrust from the mountain of rock at its highest and most narrow point, with the sea below, the sky above, and all of Nikandros behind it.

The woman who had spoken, who for a moment he'd thought might be the Archon herself, was not. Which was a relief, because if she had been the Archon, the whole plan would have turned toward disaster. This woman had the same air of authority, and was similarly middle-aged, dark-haired, and olive-skinned, but she was older than the Archon. She sat on a carved stone bench and was eating olives, spitting the pips over the railing to fall the fourteen hundred feet to the sea.

As Mister Fitz had said truthfully earlier, there was nothing physically obvious to indicate she was a dragon, but Hereward had no doubts as to her identity, even before she spoke.

"You have found what you are looking for," she said. "Or rather, part of what you seek. I am the dragon of Nikandros, but you will never have my treasure. Nor will you slay me. Your 'imp-infested quarrels' have been taken to the great smelter in the Levels and melted down, the pathetic entities within released. Your life is naturally forfeit. However, if you will tell me where you slew this other dragon, and where its hoard might lie, I *may* spare you."

"That seems a fair offer, milady," said Hereward. He sat down on his bottom, extended his legs, and pulled off his stockings, including the wide garter on the left.

"What are you doing?" asked the dragon. "If you hope to fashion a garotte, you are even more of a fool than I anticipated."

She put down the olive she was about to eat and stood up.

"Oh, no, milady, they were uncomfortable," said Hereward. He stood up, slipped the broad garter—an armband really—over his wrist and up on to his bicep. Then he tugged the earring from his left ear, lifted the small bone to his mouth and blew upon it. No sound came out, not even a butchered single note.

"Are you mad?" asked the dragon. "Or still drunk?"

"I might be still drunk," admitted Hereward, backing up to the door. Reaching behind him, he tested the ring to open it and found it wouldn't move.

"Even in this weaker human form, I can rip your heart from your chest in a trice," said the dragon, flexing her hands to show him some long and very disturbing fingernails. "But I will start with something softer and more easy to detach if you do not tell me what I want to know. Where is this other dragon's hoard?"

Hereward made a whimpering noise and blew on the golden bone again.

"Your eyes," said the dragon. "I will pluck them and eat them like those olives. What was the dragon's name?"

"I don't know. Mister Fitz knows," said Hereward. He gave up on the door and edged along the wall. But there was nowhere to retreat in the small demi-lune. There was the locked door behind, or over the walls to certain death far below.

"Sorcerous puppets are notably resistant to torture," said the dragon. "They simply don't care. Whereas you, I am sure, care greatly."

"I do, I do," said Hereward. He lifted the golden bone in his hand and blew on it for the third time, without result.

"Is that little golden pipe meant to do something?" asked the dragon. She tilted her head. "I sense no magic in it. Only gold, leavened with a tenth of silver."

"Yes, it is meant to do something!" declared Hereward. Unwisely, he added, "Distract you."

"From what?" asked the dragon, and then she moved incredibly swiftly, flinging herself down as Mister Fitz appeared over the wall, leveled one of his sorcerous needles, and unleashed a bolt of blindingly violet sorcerous energy.

Unfortunately, through a space in the air where the dragon no longer stood.

Hereward dived to the floor. Black blotches were floating in his vision, but he managed to see the dragon roll hard against the stone bench, even as Mister Fitz leaped onto it, readying his needle again. But the puppet lost his footing as the dragon heaved herself against the solid slab. With the shriek of stone on stone, it slid aside to reveal a deep hole, the entrance to some secret shaft. The dragon threw herself headfirst down it, legs flying.

Hereward caught her foot, but he could not hold her. She was far heavier than any normal person her size, and gravity did the rest. The dragon slid down the hole and Hereward followed.

The escape passage was an oiled slide, a narrow tube. After the initial short drop, it ran at a forty-five degree angle for a hundred feet or so before it suddenly corkscrewed down in a series of giddying turns.

Hereward gripped the dragon's ankle with one hand, and with the other touched the garter turned armband, gabbling out the necessary recitation, coupled with shrieks and cries as he was flung about by the sudden turns and the dragon managed to land a kick.

"In the name of the Council of the Treaty for the Safety of the— ow—World, acting under the authority granted by the Three Empires, the Seven—curse you—Kingdoms, the Palatine Regency, the Jessar Republic, and the Forty Lesser Realms, I—arrgh—declare myself an agent of the Council. I identify the dragon manifested as Harquahar-Drim-Jashar—ow—a listed entity under the treaty and an enemy of the World, and the Council authorizes me to pursue any and all—damn it—actions necessary to banish, repel, or exterminate the said entity!"

The dragon screamed something back at him and kicked him again, but it had little effect. It hurt, of course, but she couldn't get the leverage to deliver a decent blow while they were sliding so swiftly.

Hereward tried to look behind to see if Mister Fitz had jumped after him, but he was falling too fast, sliding up and down and around the well-oiled escape tube. He desperately hoped the puppet was very close indeed, for even with the activated brassard providing some minor physical protection, the dragon probably *could* rip his heart out when they arrived wherever this slide ended up.

The ending up happened rather more suddenly than Hereward expected. One second he was being flung around another corkscrew turn, and then in the next the slide slanted steeply upward to check the velocity of the sliders, went slightly down again, and spat the dragon and Hereward out onto the floor of a vast cavern. This was well lit by many small holes in the ceiling and upper third of the walls, allowing the afternoon sun to poke dozens of brilliant fingers in to light up what would otherwise be a dark and dismal cave.

Hereward rolled away as soon as he landed, and sprang up, not quite as easily as he'd intended due to the oil he was covered in. But he managed to stay upright and be as ready as he could be to fight the dragon.

But she did not instantly attack him, as he expected. Rather she stood staring at the center of the cavern, where the sun's rays flickered over a scene of destruction. Dozens of empty chests were thrown together in a pile, surrounded by a nimbus of at least a hundred flat and flaccid leather moneybags, their drawstrings loose and every which way, looking like a mass beaching of sea-stingers cast upon an unforgiving shore.

"My . . . my treasure!" she wailed. "My gold! My lovely, lovely gold!"

She turned on Sir Hereward and hissed, revealing long, daggerlike teeth he hadn't noticed before. They were even more disturbing than her talonlike fingernails.

"Where is my gold?"

"The Archon took it earlier today," said Hereward, backing up. His eyes flickered from side to side, looking for a weapon, and also, rather hopefully, to the escape slide. But he couldn't see anything useful, not even a stone, and there was no sign of Mister Fitz. There were probably trapdoors that closed behind the first escapee, or something of the sort. Any well-planned escape slide would block pursuers. He'd been lucky to hang on to the dragon.

"The Archon?" asked the dragon, as if she couldn't believe it.

"Mister Fitz and I were never interested in the treasure," said Hereward, hoping to keep her talking rather than ripping his heart out. "Only in you, Harquahar-Drim-Jashar."

"What? Who?" asked the dragon. She had half turned to look back at the empty chests again. Her shoulders sagged, and she seemed older somehow. In fact, she looked just like a shipwreck survivor. Hereward had seen this kind of shock before. He'd been shipwrecked himself.

The knight touched the brassard on his arm. The arcane symbols glowed more brightly, the violet light harsh in comparison to all the rods of soft golden sunlight slanting down from outside.

"You are a proscribed entity, Harquahar-Drim-Jashar," he said. "We are agents of the Council of the Treaty for the Safety of the World."

The dragon turned back to him. She frowned in puzzlement.

"Who? I'm not Harquahar-Drim-Jashar."

It was Hereward's turn to droop slightly.

"W-w-hat?" he stammered.

"I'm not Harquahar-Drim-Jashar," said the dragon. She stepped closer, but did not raise her taloned hands, and her teeth appeared to have retracted to more normal human dentition. "My name is Jallal-Qreu-Kwaxssim. I am nowhere near as old as a Jashar. They're ancient."

Hereward stepped back, glancing at the slide exit again.

"I see you have to answer to a puppet," said the dragon, stepping closer again. "And belatedly I recall stories of scarred women who slay godlets and the like. But you are a man. And surely, this is all ancient history, and I am not who you are hunting, anyway."

"I don't answer to a puppet," protested Hereward. "And not all the agents are women—Oh!"

Mister Fitz came flying out of the slide, a sorcerous needle cupped in his hand, its blinding light contained. He landed easily, skidded far less than Hereward had, though he was just as oily, and spun about. Fierce light bloomed as he opened his fingers to unveil the needle.

Hereward dived away from the dragon, but she had already launched herself toward him. He felt her snatch the earring from his right ear; there was a flash of sorcerous energy, immediately followed by the harsh rumble of falling rock. He crawled away on his belly and elbows, blinking away afterimages of violet light and coughing up stone dust. All the

while desperately hoping the dragon wasn't about to land on his spine and wrench his heart out through his back.

When the heart-ripping didn't happen after three seconds, he rolled over and pushed himself up, to look frantically in all directions for the dragon, who was not immediately visible. Hereward could see only Mister Fitz, standing in the middle of the cavern, his head tilted back, no sun-bright needle in his hand.

"Did you get her?" he gasped. The object of Mister Fitz's sorcerous blasts was to unstitch the dragon's connection to this universe, which would banish her back to the dimension from which she had trespassed. If he had succeeded, there would be nothing left.

There was nothing left, Hereward was relieved to see.

Until Mister Fitz pointed up.

Sir Hereward narrowed his eyes, looking toward all those tiny, sunlit holes in the cavern's upper walls and ceiling. A golden dragon in the classical reptilian guise, though only the size of his little finger, folded her shimmering wings back to shoot through one of the holes. She spread those wings on the other side to catch the sea breeze that came every afternoon to blow the foul smoke of the foundries on the Levels far from the city.

Hereward and Fitz caught one more slight glimpse through another hole as she spiraled upward and away.

"I didn't know they could shape themselves so small," said Hereward. He looked at the empty chests. "Why bother with all this, then?"

"She would have to give up nearly all of her energistic energy to take so small a size, and with it went much of her invulnerability and combative prowess," said Mister Fitz. "Though not banished, she will not prey on any more large, blond-haired men for a considerable time, presuming she is ever able to amass sufficient gold to grow. So I suppose we have not entirely failed."

"What!" exclaimed Sir Hereward. "You never mentioned . . . I thought it was young maidens—"

"Hereward," said Mister Fitz, adopting his didactic voice. "As I am not an entertaining puppet, you are not a trained actor. Our plan depended on you presuming yourself to be not immediately at risk. Need I say more?"

"You could have told me," grumbled Sir Hereward. "By the way, she said she wasn't Harquahar-Drim-Jashar, she's Jallal-Qreu-Kwaxssim."

Mister Fitz's head slowly rotated to fully face the knight.

"Hmmm," he said, after a long, drawn-out moment of silence. "I need to check that name. It was most likely an attempt at misdirection. Though occasionally *two* dragons will join forces . . ."

But he spoke to the air, for Hereward was already looking for the way out.

HOARD

Seanan McGuire

Seanan McGuire (seananmcguire.com) writes things. It is difficult to make her stop. Her first book was published in 2009; since then, she has released more than thirty more, spanning multiple genres, all through traditional publishing channels, and has been awarded the Hugo Award three times and the Nebula Award once (so far). We're not entirely sure she sleeps. We're also not entirely sure she isn't a living channel for the corn, green grow its leaves, shallow grow its roots. When not writing, she enjoys travel, spending time with her cats, and watching more horror movies than is strictly healthy for any living thing. Keep up with her online where she posts many, many pictures of the aforementioned cats. Seanan would like to talk to you about the X-Men, Disney parks, and terrifying parasites. She can be bribed with Diet Dr Pepper to stop.

Jasmine forgot her lunch again. It sits on the counter like a brown paper accusation, her name written on the curled-down flap in black Sharpie. Its six sibling bags have all been collected by their respective owners. Jazzy is my youngest, sweet and shy and still a little unsure that she really gets to stay. If I were still in the burning and pillaging business, she'd represent a virtual village of people who needed to be set on fire. Sadly, the modern justice system, while still as inefficient and unbalanced as any process from the past, doesn't leave a lot of room for vengeful arson.

More's the pity.

She gets disruptive when she gets hungry. She'll be embarrassed if I interrupt class to drop off her food. But maybe that's a good thing, for Jazzy. She's still having trouble accepting the idea that we really want her here. Acts of aggressive affection have been successful with some of my children in the past, and it's not as if love is a limited resource. Not when spent wildly. The only time I've known love to become limited is when people place limits on it.

Human children. Of all the things I could have devoted myself to in this terrible new world, it had to be human children. I suppose it's no different than humans keeping venomous snakes in their homes. Sometimes we have the most love for the things that could destroy us.

The house is so empty during the day. Charles finally started college this term, and he'll probably be moving out soon; my children always do, sooner or later, once they hit the point of feeling self-sufficient. They're damaged enough by the time they end up remanded to my care that all the work in the world won't make them comfortable feeling like they need to depend on someone else. The rug has been yanked out from under their feet again and again, leaving them uncertain of their footing. They leave me, but they stay in touch, all of them. The corkboard next to the fridge is a collage of Christmas and birthday cards, wedding invitations and birth announcements. They don't forget where they came from, or that, while I may not have been their first childhood home, I do my best to be their last.

I pick up my cereal bowl and coffee cup, carrying them both to the sink, where I rinse them before placing them in the dishwasher. Everyone cleans up after themselves unless they're sick or otherwise incapacitated. Finals week counts as incapacitation for our seniors. During the week of tests and the week of study beforehand, they're waited on hand

and foot by their younger siblings, very few of whom complain, since they know they'll get the same treatment in time.

Collecting Jasmine's lunch, I head for the door. I'm almost there when the doorbell rings. I half stumble before stopping myself and looking around the living room. It looks like seven children and teens live here, yes: the rug is threadbare, the shelves are a mishmash of books and board games. Nothing is newer than it absolutely has to be. I replaced the television three years ago, after Peter lost his temper and punched the old one. I docked his allowance for six months to pay off his debt to the household, and he apologized to all his foster siblings at the end of his punishment, even though most of them were genuinely thrilled by the upgrade. The old television had been on its last legs before his assault, after all. Despite the clutter, everything is clean. I am a good guardian to the children in my care.

Satisfied that there's nothing about the environment that could be used to damage my family, I proceed to the front door.

The social worker on the porch is unfamiliar to me. He's wearing a cheap suit—I swear those things are standard issue with the job—and fashionable glasses, and he's studying the faded paint next to the door like it holds all the secrets of the universe. I clear my throat and he transfers his gaze to me.

"Patricia, ah, Dracan?" he says, tone implying that it's a question, even though it's a pointless one. This is my house. I am the only adult living here, although some of my current crop of children have come of age according to human law. Who else would be opening my front door?

"Yes?" I hold up the lunch bag in my hand. "I was on my way out. We don't have a home inspection scheduled for today. How can I help you?"

Home inspections can come at any time. They're less common than they were in the beginning. The agency is accustomed to me now; they no longer look at me and wait for the other shoe to drop, bringing chaos and broken hearts in its wake. There *is* another shoe, but it's not one of the ones they expect. I don't abuse the children in my care. They come to me bruised and bleeding, often on the verge of aging out of a system that was never equipped to truly help them, not in the way they need, and I give them what they need to flourish. I'm a gardener of sorts. I plant and harvest futures.

The man reaches up to adjust his glasses before he says, officiously, "I've recently arrived at this office, and I had a few questions for you."

Of course he did. The new ones always do. I swallow my sigh as I place Jasmine's lunch on the nearest end table, where it won't be swept out of sight and forgotten, and I take a step back, making space for him to enter the house. His eyes never stop moving, sweeping over every surface, taking in every detail and filing it away, ready to pass judgment on what he's sure is somehow a hidden house of horrors. His mind is already made up. I can see it in his stance, which has never varied down all the ages of Man. He thinks he knows better than anyone else what is good and just and right, and has no room in that knowledge for such as me.

"Please, have a seat." I gesture broadly to the couch, which is plush and overstuffed, and large enough to hold four active teens at the same time. It will swallow him and make him small. Small enough, I hope, that this goes painlessly and without any of the problems that have historically attended such visits.

He stays where he is, not accepting my admittedly grudging hospitality. I try again. "Can I get you anything? A cup of tea or coffee? If that's not to your liking, Andrea made lemonade this morning, and the boys haven't had time to drink it all yet."

"Before school?" His tone is suddenly sharp. "Shouldn't she have been worried about getting ready?"

So that's how this is going to be. I abandon the idea of things going gently. "The bus comes at seven thirty," I said. "Andrea shares her room with Brittany and Kim. Kim has nightmares from a previous foster home, and wakes up screaming by five most mornings. Andrea got up when Kim woke her, and wanted to make lemonade so that she could have some when she got home from school. She prefers it after it's had time to settle a little."

"These nightmares. Have you reported them?"

"I assure you that the agency is fully aware. Kim sees a psychiatrist every other Wednesday afternoon, and we hope she'll eventually be able to sleep through the night." I look along my nose at him, frowning. "If you check her file, you'll see that this condition was documented well before she came to me." Seventeen years old and thin as a rail, shivering on my porch, with everything she owned in a busted suitcase that looked like Goodwill would refuse to accept it. It took six months before she stopped cowering every time one of her foster brothers came into the room, and another three before she was able to speak to one of them in anything above a whisper. I don't know what happened to her before she came to me, and I don't press. That's what her psychiatrist is for. If I had answers for my unspoken questions, quite a few people might have to die, and again, the human justice system frowns on that sort of behavior.

"I see." The man—who has yet to give me his name, and best believe I've noticed; it's a small slap to the face, not the large one I'm sure he's gearing up to, but it still stings—finally sits. As I had hoped, the couch all but swallows him, boiling him down to one of the children in my care.

Jasmine was probably the last straw for some bureaucrat somewhere, sitting in a windowless office and making choices about the future of their own kin and kind. She's only twelve, four years below my usual cutoff. I watch for children on the verge of aging out of the system, the ones most likely to be angry at the world thanks to their treatment, the ones losing hope. Foster care will keep them with me until they turn nineteen, if I'm willing to accept responsibility for legal adults, and some of them stay on longer than that. My eldest was Angelo, who stayed until shortly after his twenty-fifth birthday, finishing community college and finding the girl who would be his wife before he struck out on his own. A few more would have stayed that long, if they hadn't felt a vague obligation to clear out and make room for kids like they'd been, kids who really needed the space.

Jazzy, though . . . she's young enough that someone probably flagged her file as a candidate for adoption, and thought it strange when I inquired about her. Never mind that she's been in foster care since she was five, or that humans have strange ideas about what they look for in children. Glasses and gapped teeth and a formal diagnosis of both dyslexia and ADHD tends to move kids into the "someone else's problem" bucket. But all those things were why I'd known she was meant to be *my* problem from the moment I saw her picture. There was no reason to leave her in a series of unsuitable and potentially dangerous homes until she was old enough to have a room with me. Not when we had the space.

Even if I'd known, for sure, that bringing her home would bring this man's shadow to my door, I would have done it. This is where she belongs. Even before she came here, this was home.

He looks at me, eyes sharp, and says, "You've fostered quite a few older children, Ms. Dracan. An almost unrealistic number."

"Is there a question there?"

"Why?" He shakes his head. "You don't adopt until they're legally adults, and even then, not always. Why do you do this?"

"I offer to adopt all my children, when they reach legal age," I say. "Before that, they might feel trapped, like saying no would put them on the street. I don't want any of them to feel obligated to stay with me, and they don't all. Some of them pack their things and leave the day the law says that they're allowed, because they don't want to steal resources from kids they assume must need them more."

And I cry every single time, because for a while, they were mine. They were my children, and this is where they will always, always belong. Here. With me. With their brothers and sisters and me. This is their home.

"I see," says the man from social services. He adjusts his glasses again. "Ms. Dracan, surely you understand that what you've been doing here is highly irregular, and not normally tolerated by the people in charge of the foster care system. Children are not cats, to be hoarded by unmarried women with houses that feel too big for them."

"Have there been any complaints about the way I care for my children?" I ask. "Or is the absence of complaint the cause of your suspicion?"

"Ms. Dracan, this isn't personal." He stands. "We simply think it might be better if the children were temporarily removed from your care, to ensure their safety."

This isn't about their safety. This is about a flawed system that has never worked the way it was intended, running up against the unyielding stone of my commitment. I smile at him, slowly, and hear the clicks echoing through the house as every door and window locks itself.

"Did you ever wonder," I ask, "where the dragons have gone?"

He doesn't have the common sense to look alarmed. "Flights of fancy will not change the situation."

"They were everywhere, once, blackening the sky, and then they disappeared. Oh, human heroes slew a certain number of them. It took time to learn to handle swords and armor. But the dragons were so vast, and so strong, that there's no way a handful of knights could have stolen the sky from them."

"Ms. Dracan—"

"The gold thing was a bit of a red herring, I'll admit. You see, dragons hoard. Every dragon collects something. Gold and

373

jewels were easy before humans developed a concept of money. Most went for more ephemeral things. Spring breezes. Butterflies. Sunsets. Tattered innocence in need of a place to recover." This time my smile shows my teeth, which are sharper and whiter than they were a few minutes ago. The smell of sulfur is starting to seep into the air. My uninvited guest is beginning to look nervous. Good. He should look nervous.

"We learned to hide. We learned to build our collections through legitimate means. We learned to be better. We never gave up our wings."

He has time to scream exactly once before he is devoured.

After, curled around the living room, careful not to crush the couch, I use one claw to delicately flip through the papers in his briefcase, the ones he didn't bother showing me. As I had suspected, he came on his own, sure that he had discovered some terrible predation upon the children I care for. No one will tie his disappearance to me. It will take several days to get the smell of sulfur out of the curtains, but it's not as if this is the first time.

I fold myself back into a human guise, rubbing out the kink the process always leaves in my neck, and head for the door, pausing to pick up Jasmine's lunch.

It wouldn't do for my little girl to go hungry, after all.

THE WYRM OF LIRR

C. S. E. Cooney

for Carlos Alberto Pablo Hernandez

1.

new to the isles, me

not cityfolk-fast; don't hop just any wyrm to ride it, hooked
in, hanging from iron scales, pay the ferrygrubs till pockets grow holes, no
I still mostly
    mosey

        landlard, slugfoot, molassestoes
          you've heard the names

                but I like my neighborhood
red brick, cliff-like, crumbling, not many balconies, but the windows,
the
windows are worth the view:
    archipelagic rails like slug-trails stretching sea to sea

               and the Wyrm of Lirr . . .
                  lightning on the tracks

2.

friendly, out by the footbridge
lots of community activity, young families
daycare teachers, their charges
mostly toddlers I see, sapling-
green
squealing jamboree, waiting
waiting for the dragon

3.

onrush, she comes—from out the east, from out the Sound—scream they!
scream they happy when that she-dragon comes! stomp-stomp-dance, cement
over rails. run to chain link, cling like wizard monkeys. wave, wave at dragon!

OLD LADY LIRR! WYRM OF ISLES! SEE ME! SEE ME!

stop too, I. admire the Wyrm. tour guides call her oldest, finest. foundling
    of sewers, service-bound to those who saved her. ah, endless
    indenture. see cityfolks ride her, hair flowing, coats blowing, iron
    hooks sunk in, sunk into iron scales. how fast on beast-back they
    ride. brutal commuters.

4.

old lady lirr, I whisper—sister,
    I, too, am foundling out of place and time
    scarred and bent, I
        see you: three-fathoms tails, green-flash eyes in
            dark or daylight, eleven noble heads bent to rails
                back and forth you slither, slave to schedules
                    ancient serpent
              had I come to city younger, stronger
    might have tried to free you, split fists against their iron hooks, let them
laugh

let them laugh to see me try

      but do you even know ought else than blackdark tunnels

      under estuary rivers, will ever understand enough to shuck off

        brinetrash, brash hooks, warrior commuters

      and climb

        climb the frozen

          sky?

5.

but last night, last night!

pushing my cart of laundry bags and frozen pizzas, sack of plums, some onions

    limping

      from a blister, all this walking, walking

    came across that footbridge, handspan of cement, slug-green rails

         running

      all across the archipelago

    stop

    stop to watch the four-year-old, lonesome girl, fierce black curls

    mouth of

    sorceress

      daddy on his cell phone, half-turned, muttering, but she

        she pays her sire no-sir-never-mind, sites

         downrail, one arm out

         beckoning:

    COMEDRAGONCOMEDRAGONCOME!

old lady lirr, more scar than scales, obeys—always obeys—

    was coming this way

      anyways

        rattles under footbridge

          sparking

        spitting

        sorceress, she's planned for this

memorized
      her maps like ABC's, knows
         schedules like her
           1–2–3's, switches arms, salutes
                the beast
        wide stance, red maw, white teeth, and
      arcs a feral scream

      and such a scream!
such a
     scream
     as I have longed to scream!

sound and size of it, seed
   of
      power
        impotence and indignation
          dragon
             screams in answer
           and so scream I, so scream we
        three together
     caught up in the child's dream:

6.

up, serpent!
wake!
shake rails, shake wheels, shed the lot—
commuters, iron hooks, life of service, all.
up, snake! up, dragon!
Wyrm of Isles, be free!

up cracks she
mighty and with snapping wings, then—

out, out
to sea

7.

Honored Members of the City Council,

As a newcomer, perhaps it is not my place to—

Recently, I have begun investigating the disturbing history of—

I am here to petition on behalf of Dragon 87 (Archipelagic Line) for immediate release into—

Included herein are five hundred signatures from in and around the Borough of—

Very respectfully—

THE LAST HUNT

Aliette de Bodard

Aliette de Bodard (aliettedebodard.com) writes speculative fiction. She has won three Nebula Awards, a Locus Award, four British Science Fiction Association Awards, and has been a Hugo finalist multiple times. She is the author of the Dominion of the Fallen series, set in a turn-of-the-century Paris devastated by a magical war, which comprises *The House of Shattered Wings, The House of Binding Thorns,* and *The House of Sundering Flames.* She is also the author of the short story collection *Of Wars, and Memories, and Starlight.* She lives in Paris.

Xuân Thao's world was the hunt—her muscles spasming from running, her breath fire in her lungs, and in the distance, the screams of the masters' birds.

The masters had let her loose in the gardens, still dripping from the fluids of the genmod berth—a day ago, a lifetime ago. Beside her were others, lined up on the polished metal surface of the gardens. She'd caught a glimpse of Auntie Man's exhausted, gray face, and Auntie Cam Huong—the small and slight woman who always slipped Xuân Thao extra rations from her own stash—who'd held her gaze a fraction longer than necessary, grimly smiling: from one elect to another, one shell-thrall to another. Around them were the masters' trees: skeletal shapes, the branches of which were razor blades, casting barely any shadows on the harshness of the ground.

Xuân Thao had wanted to ask about what had happened during her sleep—how many days it had lasted, where her daughter was—but the masters' voices of power had choked words in her mouth and sapped the strength in her knees until all she could do was bow.

Their faces had shimmered, sprouting scales and teeth as they moved, the way they always did. In the sharpness of their antlers shone their names—a reminder for their servants and pets who couldn't tell one master from another as they shifted between shapes like water.

Lianlei. Ongjié.

Elect, Lianlei had said, the tip of her serpentine body wrapped around Xuân Thao's legs, leaving a trail of fire on her ankles. She'd moved away from Xuân Thao to touch the other elects in turn, her absence almost making Xuân Thao's legs collapse. *Prove that you are worthy of leaving with us*, Lianlei went on.

Ongjié's smile had been fractured, his fangs shining like sheened oil. *Run*, he'd said. *Get to the doors.*

Xuân Thao ran, away from the entrance and the masters. Under her feet, the ground of the gardens curved upward; if she lifted her eyes, she'd see the infinitely receding spheres, dotted with trees that bore the liquid fruit the masters so loved to share among themselves, sipping on their glass openings as they decided which of their shell-thralls should be genmodded, which of them had failed, and which of them needed to be recycled for blood and organs. Shells, the masters called them. Easy to break, easy to put back together, easy to discard.

Not her.

She was alone; the others lost a long, long time ago: looking at each other by unspoken agreement and stumbling in three different directions, hoping to split the hunt. Hoping for one more chance to survive, no matter how slight.

Xuân Thao stumbled on a branch—bit her lip so as not to cry as it stabbed her through the thin soles of her shoes. The sounds of the hunt were getting closer—the beating of wings filling the air, the masters' laughter merging with the endless tides of pain in her gut and lungs. Outlive the hunt and leave with the masters, or die. There was no other choice.

A sound boomed in the air, starting like a bell-toll in the shell-thralls' pagodas, but then deepened and expanded until it seemed to underlie the room like a booming, rising heartbeat. Xuân Thao fell to her knees, her hands desperately scratching at her skin, desperately seeking to pull the sound out of her—*ancestors, please watch over me, please keep me safe . . .*

The sound came again. The gates. Xuân Thao couldn't see them from the gardens—she wasn't even sure they were in the palace—but it meant the last of them were closing. That the masters would be leaving this world forever; and what they couldn't take with them, they would savage and tear apart.

Khuê . . .

For a brief moment she saw her daughter in her mind's eye: ten years old and holding her favorite writing brush against her chest, her face creased in that familiar stubbornness that refused to give way, the same one Xuân Thao was so afraid would get her killed one day.

Mommy . . .

No, she wouldn't think of her daughter, or she would never get up.

She pushed herself up, muscle by muscle—every movement sent a fresh jolt of pain, and her lungs were still afire—and started running again.

Ahead, the trees gave way to a field of saplings as sharp as impaling spikes. And something . . . something was off. Xuân Thao set off through them, acutely aware that the slightest stumble would send a spike through her foot, incapacitating her. Shadows moved across the surface of the sphere: the hunting birds, the sound of their wings echoing like thunder.

They couldn't be far away. She had to keep running, but her muscles were seizing up. And there was no refuge, no hiding place she could find.

No.

That wasn't true. Slightly to the right, there was a sapling a little larger than the others—no, not a sapling. An opening in the gardens' spherical surface, a door that had to be barely large enough for her to slip through. And she shouldn't have been able to see that far, but now that she'd noticed it, she couldn't tear herself away. The genmods? She didn't know what the masters had sought to engineer, the endless tinkering with their thralls' bodies until organs were spat out as incompatible. They wanted their thralls to be more like them—less easily broken, less easily felled by disease—though of course they'd never uplift them all the way, would never turn them into their equals. What would have been the point of losing their own playthings?

Xuân Thao turned, slightly—shouldn't have, because she saw that they were close enough for her to see Lianlei's eyes—the scales shining faintly behind the sclera, the elongated, beating pupils, the dark amusement in them.

Prove that you are worthy of leaving with us.

The door didn't seem to get any closer as she ran—weaving her haphazard way between saplings, stumbling and catching herself just in time, thorns slicing the palm of her hand until the floor beneath her became stained red, the color irising and pulsing like a beating heart.

Something grabbed her from behind—Xuân Thao fell backward, kicked, with a strength she hadn't known she possessed, feeling cloth and flesh tear from her back, and kicked and kicked again, striking a welter of razor-sharp feathers and talons—one or two hunting birds, trying to grab her again, trying to feast on her blood.

Time blurred, stopped. Xuân Thao found a prayer to her ancestors on her lips, even as the world froze and changed around her. One moment she was standing in the midst of saplings, fighting the birds; the next she was free of them, and standing on the threshold of the door with nausea flooding through her.

No time. She stumbled through, drawing the panels shut as she did so—and the last thing she heard was Lianlei's laughter: not malicious or frustrated, but the good-natured one of a parent satisfied with a child's first words.

*Beyond the door, everything was dark for a moment. Time stretched, ago-*nizingly slowly. There was nothing but silence. No masters, no birds, nothing—no, that wasn't quite true, because something moved in the shadows.

A master.

No time to turn, or flee, and the door had closed. Xuân Thao sank to her haunches, tensing for the words that would hold her submissive.

Footsteps, coming her way. Not the masters' serpentine shapes, though they would sometimes turn human, just as they sometimes took their names from the humans they'd subjugated. These steps were not brash or assured, but slow and deliberate. They couldn't possibly be the masters—

A hand, reaching down. Xuân Thao took it without thinking, and the other person hauled her to her feet without any hint of weakness.

She stared, gape-mouthed, at them.

They were tall, with long, dark, flowing hair spread in a mane around the nubs of antlers, and scales dotting their cheeks and the backs of their hands—and everything about the way they stood spoke of ar-rested movement—of stretching and flowing, effortless and graceful, under the waters of some river or lake.

"Rồng," Xuân Thao said, before she could clamp her lips on the words. The masters had spirits serving them, of course—so lowly, so insignificant in their view that they never even attempted to genmod them, but she hadn't thought . . .

"My name is Vu Côn," the dragon said, amused. The pronoun she'd used to refer to herself was feminine, and encompassed all the years be-tween her and Xuân Thao. Her face was dark. "You're in shock."

All Xuân Thao could find in the scorched desert of her mind were the old prayers, the beseechings Mother and the other aunties had passed on to her—asking for the crops to be blessed, for sickness to depart the house, for treasures as numerous as the raindrops of the monsoon—the prayers Khuê so loved to sing in a halting voice, mouthing each of the words as if they were unexpected treasures . . .

Something clinked and stretched as if in answer to her words—a chain of woven silver, each link a different word in the masters' language. The chain passed between Vu Côn's legs, hobbling her. It then climbed to her chest, where it buried itself—shining, faintly, along the length of her rib cage before disappearing. It pulsed, slowly. Vu Côn's face was frozen in an expression Xuân Thao knew all too well: pain that she struggled to hide.

"I'm sorry," Xuân Thao said.

A short, bitter laugh. "Don't be," Vu Côn said. The chain was dark, and its pulse was slowing down. For a moment Xuân Thao caught a glimpse of other, squatter and uglier words at the heart of the masters' language, as if someone had tried to draw other letters by reusing their outline. Then it passed, and the chain was silver again.

"What brings you here, child?" Vu Côn asked.

Hiding. Running. The sound of the birds' wings, filling the air, and of distant screams, and the memory of the masters' burning touch binding her legs. Xuân Thao's legs trembled. She realized that her heart was beating fast enough to burst out of her chest. The words came out, before she could swallow them whole. "The hunt. I got away . . ." She turned then. Behind her was a faint outline of the door she'd gone through, and the even fainter sounds of something heavy hitting it, again and again. Silver traceries twined around the door's outline, words in that same squat language she couldn't quite identify. She heard, distant and muffled, Lianlei's voice urging the birds on, telling them about the feast they would have.

The feast.

Her arms ached where the birds had torn into them. Her knees felt weak and wobbly. They were driven and culled, and in the end, nothing but carrion fodder.

Vu Côn's eyes didn't leave her face. "They will come in here, eventually." Her hand strayed to the first link of the chain, the one over her chest. "And when they do . . ."

Then she wouldn't be able to say no to whatever they asked. Xuân Thao had seen it, all too often, the way power was used to turn them against each other. The way that *ky lan* would trample thralls to death, their faces contorted in pain; that crab spirits would tear out chunks of flesh, weeping tears of blood and nacre. Words, again, crowded themselves in her throat, like barbed blades. "Please."

The chain clinked, darkening again. Vu Côn's twinge of pain was barely visible this time. "I don't answer prayers anymore, child." On her hands, the same contorted words, swiftly disappearing. "I'm not *allowed*."

Because they'd bound her. Because she wasn't a spirit anymore, but their servant. And because she'd not been meant to interfere with the hunt. "The chain—" Before she could stop, Xuân Thao touched it. It was cold, not the masters' metallic touch, but the deeper and wetter cold of icy winters, of storm clouds. *Ancestors, watch over us. Give us your blessings: the pearls of the dragon king's palace, the never-ending rains, the bliss and felicity beneath the waves . . .* Where her fingers touched it, the silver tarnished, and the squat, ugly words grew larger. They almost looked familiar—and then the world shifted, and she saw they were another form of the letters engraved on the ancestral altars in the thralls' quarters. Her fingers burned from the cold. "Grandmother," she whispered.

Vu Côn's hands gently prised hers, finger by finger, free of the chain's links. "I already told you, child. The time for prayers is past. The world has new minders now."

Not minders, masters. People who'd taken everything from it, and who were abandoning it now. She ran a hand along her arms, feeling the marks of needles there—remembering the sound of Ongjié's voice like a lash, opening up a myriad thin cuts on her skin with every word.

Prove that you are worthy.

Xuân Thao bit her lip. She looked at the formless darkness behind Vu Côn: a faint suggestion of a dome, endlessly mirrored above them, its arc becoming the floor of another room from which grew the shadow of a tower, all the endlessly expanding geometry of the palace that made so little sense to outsiders.

There was a door. It was halfway across the dome, caught in that uncertain space between a hatch, a window and a gate. "Where does it lead?" Xuân Thao said.

Vu Côn's face was set. "The laboratories."

Xuân Thao didn't know that area of the palace. She didn't know most of the palace: most of her time had been spent between the shell-thralls' quarters and the genmodding berths, and sometimes, when the masters had been feeling indulgent, in the corner of the gardens where they had their feasts. "They said I had to get to the doors."

"The gate they're leaving through?" Vu Côn shook her head. "No, that's outside the palace in the scoured lands. They must mean the palace doors." She gestured toward the narrow door. "Just before the laboratories, there'll be a corridor on your right. It leads to the great hall. It's the nearest palace doors."

"Thank you," Xuân Thao said. She was about to leave, but then stopped. "Those who don't leave with the masters . . ." Her daughter, Khuê. The spirits, like Vu Côn—there were no spirit elects, because the masters didn't think them worthy of being uplifted.

Vu Côn's laughter was harsh. "Perhaps they'll remember to break our chains before they leave. Or perhaps they'll just leave us to starve here, in the ruins of their splendor."

Outside the palace were the scoured lands: the Earth that the masters had played with until they broke it, the charred remnants of grass, the wild plagues that had devastated the animals and the plants, shriveling the rice in the paddies and the fruit on the trees. The masters had said they'd repopulate the Earth with better things, but none of their creations had ever thrived outside the palaces. There was nothing to look forward to, but—

"Better to die free," Xuân Thao said, and thought again of Khuê, who wasn't chained, whom they would leave behind. And, slowly, "I have a daughter. She's not elect."

"And you think I could watch over her?" Vu Côn didn't need to say she couldn't watch over herself.

"She could free you, if they don't. If you find her in our quarters. Her name is Khuê. Tell her I sent you." She didn't know if she'd ever see Khuê again—if she'd ever see her daughter's face scrunched up as she drew the shape of buildings and people on brittle paper, retelling and transforming the stories Mother and the aunties had passed on to her. It didn't matter.

Vu Côn stared at her. The antlers were flickering again into existence around the mane of her hair, and in her eyes was the darkness of storms. "You. They chose *you*."

Xuân Thao shrugged. "I'm not like them."

"Not yet," Vu Côn said, and her voice was harsh.

Xuân Thao laughed. "Never. Do you truly think they would create their own equals?"

Vu Côn opened her mouth again, as though to say something else—a comfort, a warning?

A harsh and resonant sound against the door she'd entered through. Its panels bent, taking for a moment the outline of a serpentine body, and then it righted itself again, though its handles were singed and the filigreed decorations twisted and charred. The words sharpened, became painful to hear, as if Lianlei's voice were driving nails into Xuân Thao's ears—just as Lianlei had slid the needles into Xuân Thao's face and hands before the genmod berth, slowly and methodically, soliloquizing about mortals' incapacity to feel true pain and therefore true emotions, and then turning Xuân Thao's way, her gaze an unbearable weight that pressed down on Xuân Thao's shoulders and chest until the breath choked in her throat.

All of it can be changed, child. Be thankful that you have been chosen.

No time. Xuân Thao ran toward the door.

The world tilted and changed: the door and Vu Côn's figure falling away from her as she ran, the little jolt in her ankles and knees as the walls became the floor and gravity reasserted itself. The door remained tantalizingly far, and her worn shoes slid on the smooth surface of the sphere. The world slid by—she turned and saw Vu Côn at a distant angle from her, and the door snapping into kindling, Vu Côn falling to her knees, head bowed, as the hunting birds' cries filled the air.

No.

She turned, again, to the door. It was too far away, and she had no time. Except . . . Except that some dark, deep part of her knew what to do. She reached out, stretching and expanding and moving muscles on sheer instinct. A tearing out, and the world once more contracting and tilting, and she was on the threshold of the door, falling into it.

Xuân Thao was on her knees in a long corridor, vomiting. She needed to get up. She needed to run again. They would follow, and this door wasn't barred or closed. She paused then—why had the other door been closed?—and then she got up, and forgot those thoughts.

She'd never been in that part of the palace before. The walls were transparent and opened up onto a darkened sky, except that each section of wall had a view on a different moon—one of them pockmarked, one of them the shape of a flock of ravens, one of them large and red with an eye like a New Year's Eve lantern, and on and on until it seemed there was no end to it. The floor below was also transparent: she stood on a deep and sweeping dark with pinpoints of scintillating light. When she moved, the floor flexed, like a taut cloth under an acrobat's weight. She took one, two shaking steps—the floor was going to break if she went too fast, if she was too heavy. Was this just another test of theirs, to see how long she could survive in a vacuum?

"Elect." Lianlei's voice, wafting through the darkness of the door. Too close.

Run, Ongjié had said. *Get to the doors.*

A corridor on the right, and the great hall, Vu Côn had said.

Xuân Thao took a deep breath, and ran, her eyes on the walls. The moons shimmered and twisted and became dragons wrapped around stars, trees growing out of planets, stars that were hairpin wounds, with filaments of white hair streaming out of a hole in the fabric of the heavens. Under her, the floor flexed, every step the beginning of a fall that was suddenly and heart-shatteringly arrested.

Behind her, the beating of wings. She ran, and the universe fractured and contracted, and that odd tearing in her chest came back, a nausea that grew and grew until it seemed to entwine with her heartbeat. Her legs hurt, but she ignored the pain. She had to get to the doors. She had to survive, one way or another.

She turned into the corridor almost without noticing it—half ran, half jumped in a much smaller space that was an endless corkscrew of pillars diverging into infinity—and then that space was gone, too, and she stood, panting, in the middle of another sphere.

This one was so large she could barely see its curve. As she moved deeper into it, lines of gold and silver began to follow her: pale and shimmering traceries on the floor that clung to her feet, an odd buzzing feeling climbing up her ankles. When Xuân Thao finally stopped, breathing hard, the traceries raced on, toward the wall of the sphere— and reared up, snakelike, in the middle of empty space, curving into a perfect circle that gradually irised open, revealing only darkness.

The palace doors.

Almost there.

Xuân Thao took one, two faltering steps. The pain in her chest flared up, unbearable. No. No. She put a hand on her own chest—felt the panicked beating of her heart, the way her legs wobbled, unsteady and weak. She could do this. Only a few more steps.

Ahead of her, distinct and sharp, the clink of a chain.

When she looked up again, Vu Côn stood in front of the doors. Not the woman she'd seen in the laboratories—the one who'd held up a hand to help Xuân Thao stand, the one who'd told her where the doors were—but a huge and serpentine shape with iridescent scales, a mane of streaming hair in which danced the oily colors of the sea.

There was some distant similarity of shape between the masters and the dragon—they were both reptiles—but as unalike as a deer and a human, simply vastly different species. In the air was a sharp, unpleasant smell of churned waters, and the tight feeling in the air before the storms, droplets of seawater stinging Xuân Thao's abraded skin and eyes like needles driven into wounds.

"Vu Côn." The words burned in her throat.

The dragon didn't speak. Her eyes were dark and wet, and the chain around her massive neck shone in the darkness, contracting with her own heartbeat. It vanished somewhere in the darkness, under the scales of her belly.

"Elect."

Xuân Thao sank to her knees, even as Lianlei's own coils slid to wrap around her—a cool touch that smelled of sheened oil and the tang of molten metal, climbing into her throat until she seemed to choke with it. She couldn't hear the hunting birds anymore, but did it really matter?

"You did well." Lianlei's voice sounded amused.

"A failed experiment," Ongjié said. His voice made traceries of gold and silver tremble on the floor. *"Weak."*

"Of course," Lianlei said. "They always are, in the end." She sounded frustrated.

"Not worth staying for." Ongjié shook his head.

"Of course not," Lianlei said. "There's enough data here for another cycle of genmodding." She shook her head, and Xuân Thao felt its wind like lashes on her skin. "Enough to guarantee us a higher status with the council. Wasn't that what you hungered for?"

Ongjié laughed. "That would be a start."

A booming sound, in the air, deepening and expanding, burrowing under nails and muscles, an unbearable urge to run toward the gates, to tear out her own skin and bones until they no longer resonated.

"Time," Ongjié said.

Lianlei snorted. The wet, burning coils around Xuân Thao tightened. "There's always time left. Do you want to leave business unfinished?"

A silence, from Ongjié—except that the sound came again, unbearably loud. Ongjié twisted, his scales shimmering with the reflection of golden light, his eyes lidded and an unsettling, unusual expression on his face. When he spoke again, his voice was a fraction less assured. "More data? I think we have all we need, and the council gives us little choice. If you can bear it, finish here. I'll see you at the gates." He twisted again, and flew toward the palace doors. Vu Côn stood, stubbornly unmoving, until Ongjié spoke a word of power. The chain contracted, and Vu Côn didn't so much move as was thrown aside. Luminous blood pearled from the links of the chain, pooled on the floor.

"Servants," Lianlei snorted again. The hunting birds weren't gone: they were nesting in the sharpness of her antlers, perching on them as if they were branches, their clawed feet and leg feathers merging with the bone.

A touch of something cold and sharp on Xuân Thao's skin: the tip of Lianlei's tail, raising her head to meet her gaze. Her eyes were translucent, the scales of her fluid, shifting body visible as a faint underlay beneath the sclera, and her smile all razored teeth. "Such a shame," she said. "I had such high hopes for you, elect."

Xuân Thao said, speaking through the oily feeling choking her, "The others—"

An amused snort. "None of them measured up, either." The birds stirred, and Xuân Thao saw that their beaks were spattered with blood. "But they provided us with enough."

More data.

Auntie Man. Auntie Cam Huong. Xuân Thao remembered Auntie Cam Huong's frail hand, the dryness of her skin as she handed her rice cakes—the smell wafting up to her, and Khuê sleeping with her head on Xuân Thao's lap, a contented smile on her face. *Ancestors, watch over them. Enlightened ones, lead them along the right path, again and again until there is no rebirth.*

Let them be free.

Lianlei shook herself, her serpentine body sprouting more legs and arms and armored spikes as she did so, her coils withdrawing from Xuân Thao—a moment that felt like the drawing of a breath. Lianlei turned, briefly, to Vu Côn, who still stood barring the way to the door. "Kill her," she said.

The chain pulsed like a diseased heart. The dark words at the heart of each link vanished, and Vu Côn moved, lithe and elegant and with a faint thunder like the noise of a storm—maw outstretched and open, her teeth filling Xuân Thao's world.

Time slowed down and stretched. Xuân Thao found herself reaching out, and the world folded itself again, and she stood panting, behind Vu Côn, a mere stone's throw from the doors.

Lianlei was coiled upon the smooth floor. The birds in her antlers stirred, looking at Xuân Thao. The chain shone again, a harsh white light that *burned*, and Vu Côn made a roaring sound, taut over pain. Lianlei cocked her head, and the dragon turned around, fluid and elegant—diving for Xuân Thao again.

Everything was pain and nausea. Xuân Thao felt, again, the world tear—sidestepped, faster than she should have, and found herself on her knees, struggling to breathe. Something brushed past her: Vu Côn's huge mane, followed by the coldness of the dragon's scales, the seeming endlessness of her body, everything glittering with the colors of nacre and smooth, translucent jade.

Ancestors, how beautiful she was. Xuân Thao pulled herself up, every breath burning, and found the old prayers again in her throat. *Ancestors, give us rain like scattered pearls, fish running through our fingers with salted water, as small and as numerous as grains of rice . . .*

Vu Côn turned. There were tears in her eyes. On her chest, the chain turned dark, but still held her tight. "You forget," the dragon said, and her voice was the thunder of the storm. "The time for prayers is past."

She dived again. Xuân Thao sidestepped, exhausted—saw Lianlei's dark, amused gaze, and knew for a certainty that this—this capacity to skip across the surface of the world—was what the masters had injected into her—was what Lianlei was watching, dissecting and measuring so that she'd know what to inflict on the thralls that came after her. Too slow. Unable to jump for long distances. Too exhausted by such a small effort.

Xuân Thao threw herself to the floor—too slow, too weak. Vu Côn's maw closed over her—held her, motionless and trembling. Xuân Thao's arms flopped, out of control, and her head was upside down, blood rushing to it, slow and heavy, and no matter how she kicked and struggled she couldn't bring herself up, she had no hold, no way to make anything right . . . Her vision blurred, became redder, everything smaller and tighter and twisted out of shape, tantalizingly out of reach: Lianlei's huge shape and the malice in her gaze, the glimmering distant surface of the sphere, the darkness of the doors slowly irising itself shut again. The dragon's fangs still held her, lightly grazing her skin, lines of fire promising to turn into crunching, tearing pain—a long, stretched, agonizing moment before they closed, before it was all over. Except that Xuân Thao wasn't the only one trembling—she could feel Vu Côn's own heartbeat, the doomed struggle against the chain and the masters' words.

You forget.

"Finish it," Lianlei said, but as she spoke the palace shook again with the call for the masters to leave. And, as Vu Côn's muscles tightened in one last immense effort to resist Lianlei's orders, Xuân Thao, dangling from the dragon's jaws, saw the golden traceries on the floor shrivel, and Lianlei twist and contort, and she remembered Ongjié's troubling expression.

Pain. He had been in pain. Just as resisting their orders caused Vu Côn to writhe in agony, so did the masters' resisting the call.

The time for prayers is past.

Pain.

They were leaving. They had left, and only Lianlei remained.

They were *weak*.

Xuân Thao gathered herself—every scrap of strength, every hoarded bit of endurance—and pulled again, desperately. Nothing happened. She'd burned herself up like a lit candle, using powers she didn't understand, and at any time Vu Côn was going to follow the orders she'd been given . . .

And then the universe twisted and shifted, and she was elsewhere—in the darkness under Vu Côn's belly, kneeling on the first links of the chain. Her legs, scraped by Vu Côn's fangs, burned, but she paid them no heed. In her mind ran the old prayers like a litany of beseeching, the ancestors and the enlightened ones, and the spirits that walked the earth and the underwater kingdoms.

Give us the enlightening stillness at the heart of the storm, the wet, cold breath of life emerging from the river, the songs of the city beneath the waves . . .

Her hand closed over the darkened chain. The words at its heart, the strange, twisted alphabet, grew sharper and sharper. Pain spiked through her palms, and blood dripped warm and pulsing. The words became distinct enough to read, expanding outward, pushing the links of the chain closer together.

Fish. Gate. River. Storm.

And a last one like a pagoda drum beating in her heart, spreading to her whole chest until everything felt sharp and raw.

Rồng.

Dragon.

The chain shattered.

The links merged into each other, the masters' words completely extinguished by the darker words—and then even these disappeared, their outlines squeezed together until nothing remained but a jumble of blackened letters that fell to the floor amid the silver and golden traceries.

Vu Côn stretched—her body, swinging, sent Xuân Thao sprawling to the floor—but before she could even start to pull herself up, coils wrapped themselves around her: not holding her as Lianlei had once done, but loosely circling around her in an impenetrable wall.

Lianlei screeched. Her body sprouted fangs and scales, and the shadow of another head, and the hunting birds flew away from her—shrinking and multiplying and losing shape as they did so, becoming a cloud of gleaming needles. It sliced through the air, opened up on both sides, and reached out to imprison Vu Côn. Xuân Thao braced herself for the pain. But Vu Côn reared, speaking words in an achingly familiar language, and the fragments of the chain on the floor lifted themselves, along with the golden and silver traceries—weaving themselves into a thin lattice that imprisoned the needles in midair.

The call boomed again. Lianlei twisted—this time the pain on her face was clearly visible, her antlers becoming nubs, teeth and sharpened, brittle arms sprouting along her body, her tail splitting and forking and then becoming single again. Xuân Thao breathed slowly, carefully, feeling the echo of the call in her own bones. She needed to run toward the gates. She needed to throw herself on the masters' mercy, to be made whole again—to be lifted and blessed again . . .

"Leave," Vu Côn said. Her voice was again taut. She was free, but free didn't mean healed. And keeping the needles from shredding them both was costing her.

Lianlei looked back at them, head cocked—large and luminous and weighing Xuân Thao, finding her wanting—and abruptly Xuân Thao was back at the exit of the genmod berth, warm fluids dripping from her eyes and nose and mouth and fingernails and a hundred other places on her body, drained and exhausted and nauseous and knowing she would be theirs even in death.

Her hands shook.

None of them measured up, either.

Her hand, straying, found Vu Côn's scales. Coolness shot up her arm, wrapped around the wounds on her fingers and palms. They sealed themselves, one by one, leaving only faint scars on her skin. She felt Vu

Côn's heartbeat resonate through her, fast and panicked, the dragon's entire weight braced to shelter her.

Something, long stretched past endurance, snapped within her, just as she had shattered the dragon's chain.

"Leave," she said, to Lianlei. She looked the master in the eye. "Or will you die here with us, in the ruins of the Earth?"

For a while, she held Lianlei's gaze. She'd expected malice in the scaled, translucent sclera, but there was nothing but pain and anger—the utter certainty of the masters that the world and everything within belonged to them, that all creatures had been given to them as their playthings—that everything they held, they would hold forever.

"Leave," she said again, and her voice barely shook.

At length Lianlei tore herself away. She threw back her head, her mane stretching into razor-thin wires that tore gashes into the floor of the sphere, the palace itself shuddering and vibrating. "Very well," she said. "So be it, then." And turned, without a word, to face the palace door. It stretched itself open for her—a long, agonizing moment that seemed never to end. When she dived through it and the doors closed, Xuân Thao finally allowed herself to relax—except that none of it felt real or justified, the magnitude of it too large to grasp.

A last, distant call that resonated in Xuân Thao's bones—she fell to her knees then, her hands clawing at her skin, shaking with the effort of not pulling herself up, of not following Lianlei to the gates—and then it passed, and with it came a curious and unsettling finality, a faint taste of dread and something sharper and more wounding.

She pulled herself up, shaking. Vu Côn's large, scaled body was wrapped around her: the dragon watched her for a while, and then slowly uncoiled herself, shrinking back to the shape of the woman Xuân Thao had first seen, with the scales on her skin and the nubs of antlers, and the glimmers of the river's reflections in her long, flowing hair.

"Grandmother—"

Vu Côn's hands wrapped around hers, held her until a pleasant, comforting cold spread to her entire skin. "Younger sister," she said, shaking her head. "Sshh. It's all right. They're gone. Forever."

Gone.

Forever gone.

Xuân Thao opened her mouth, and realized she was shaking. Of course the masters wouldn't come back to the earth they'd devastated and ruined. Nothing of interest there anymore. "The gates . . ."

"We will hold them closed, if needed. And we will rebuild what they broke." Vu Côn's face was hard. "Come. Let's find the others."

Vu Côn was in her dragon shape again, and Xuân Thao clambered, awkwardly, between the spikes on her spine. So many words crowded themselves in her mouth: the scoured lands, the palace, the broken world the masters had left behind where nothing might be fit for their survival, too damaged to ever be rebuilt. Too many weighty things she couldn't give voice to.

She felt unmoored and light-headed, with that same unfamiliar feeling in her chest, something she couldn't place or name. But, as they rose, flying through the empty corridors of the palace—under the dome and through the gardens, and over the smaller, squatter shape of the thralls' quarters—as she stared down at the milling, uncertain crowd there and saw her daughter's dark, familiar face looking at her, and let out the breath she wasn't even aware she'd been holding, she finally realized.

The hunt had ended—and whatever happened next, the future was their own.

WE CONTINUE

Ann Leckie and Rachel Swirsky

Ann Leckie (annleckie.com) is the author of the Hugo, Nebula, and Arthur C. Clarke award–winning novel *Ancillary Justice* and its two sequels, and the fantasy novel *The Raven Tower*. She has worked as a waitress, a receptionist, a rodman on a land surveying crew, and a recording engineer. She lives in St. Louis, Missouri.

Rachel Swirsky (rachelswirsky.com) holds an MFA from the Iowa Writers Workshop, where she learned about both writing and snow. She recently traded the snow for the rain of Portland, Oregon, where she roams happily under overcast skies with the hipsters. Her fiction has appeared in venues including Tor.com, *Asimov's*, and *The Best American Nonrequired Reading*. She's published two collections: *Through the Drowsy Dark* and *How the World Became Quiet*. Her fiction has been nominated for the Hugo and the World Fantasy awards, and twice won the Nebula Award.

Something was wrong.

Jacq could tell. It was a thrum in the rock. Even human as he was, even though he didn't understand dragon speech, he knew.

Auntie grunted with effort as she backed into their chamber. The enormous stacks of wood under each of her forearms shouldn't have even slowed her down, but her scales were dull with exhaustion.

Jacq stumbled out of his fabric nest. "What's going on?"

"What's that? What's that?" Auntie replied in an old woman's voice. She couldn't really speak human, but she liked to chat like a parrot, repeating things she'd heard.

"Is everything okay?" Jacq said. "Why are you back in the hive? Did I lose track of time? Is it night?"

Auntie flapped her wings at him to be quiet. She began piling the wood by the wall.

"What are you doing?" Jacq pressed, but she pushed him away.

When she was done, Auntie turned to him. She fanned her ear webs, and the spikes along her spine and tail rose expectantly.

In various voices, she said, *"Damn dragons. I think they're pretty. How can those things fly?"*

She gave him a meaningful look, but all Jacq could see was how fast the milky tissue which had appeared last week was spreading over her eyes. The inky quickness behind them was still there, but it was disappearing.

"Are you bringing stuff here from the storerooms? Are you allowed to do that?" Jacq said. "I don't know what to do!"

Auntie gestured eagerly with her head toward the wood pile. *"Shit! Shit! Get in the shelters!"*

"It's . . . for me?" Jacq asked.

He stepped toward the wall. Auntie shuffled approvingly, claws ringing against the floor.

He laid his hand on the wood. "Okay . . . thanks."

Auntie's wings snapped open with an excited clap. Jacq's stomach twisted. Her wing edges were shredded as if they'd been snagged on huge rocks and ripped free.

Jacq rushed toward her. "What happened! Are you okay?"

She nudged him back with a wingtip. *"What are those things? Give me the scanner! I think they're pretty."* She patted him in place with her tail, and went back into the hive.

Over the next few hours, Auntie brought back a dozen loads of cargo: fabric, dried grass, bark, and other useful things. Whenever Jacq tried to help, she pushed him back into the chamber until he finally stopped trying.

By the time Auntie finished, her scales were tinged with gray. She folded her tattered wings and sat, breathing heavily.

"I know something's wrong," Jacq said.

She blinked at him, inner and outer eyelids moving in separate rhythms. In an exasperated, male voice, she said, *"They'll eat the goddamn sheep."*

Sometimes it made Jacq so angry that Auntie could talk to him in a hundred different strangers' voices, but never communicate a word of her own. He snapped, "I wish you could just talk!"

Both sets of Auntie's eyelids opened.

She stared at Jacq with the intensity he sometimes suspected meant she was trying to talk to him in her true language, whatever that was, something different from postures and colors and imitating human words. Sometimes, there was something that felt like a portent; sometimes, the rock beneath him trembled as if with intangible breathing.

Abruptly, Auntie rolled him up in her wings and hoisted him onto her back. She hadn't carried him like this in years, not since he'd hit puberty. Something was *so* wrong.

Jacq's stomach roiled as she carried him through the hive's slanting corridors. Briefly, he had the urge to tear free, but after a moment, he was surprised by how comforting it felt—the smell of the fine scales under her wings, the crackle of her joints, the thump of her steps.

Filtered through the veiny, purplish membrane of Auntie's wings, the hive looked misty and distant. A passing trio of dragons—Gatherers, like Auntie—began as a blur. Nearing, they came into dreadful focus; they looked even more haggard than Auntie, eyes sealed shut with saplike clumps, patches of hide hanging from remnant forelimbs.

Jacq squeezed his eyes shut. He thought of the Gatherer dragon he'd seen last week who'd gone into the snow with what should have been a treatable gash in her side, but which must have killed her in the cold. Something wasn't just going wrong. It had been wrong for a long time.

Dizzily, he thought, *And it's not going to get better.*

Collector dropped Child at the edge of the fermentation pit, *rolling him* forward over her shoulder and swallowing a grunt of pain. When she'd first found Child alone on the hillside, making loud distressed noises, his face hot and salty-wet, she had lifted him easily into the embrace of her wings. He had calmed and then slept as she'd carried him back to the hive. He'd been much smaller then, but even when he'd grown larger, she'd had no trouble lifting him. Now, with the next hatch nearing its last molt, the effort she'd just made to bring him her gift had bruised her phalanges and left her joints sore and stiffening.

Well, it didn't matter. "*Damn dragons,*" she said, and nudged Child gently toward the edge of the pit. She felt her ear webs opening out in anticipation, and perhaps just a little worry.

Shivering in the sudden cold after having been wrapped warmly in her wings, Child looked down into the pit. He made a series of little puzzled noises, and looked at Collector with an expression she had learned was confusion.

"*What's that,*" said Collector reassuringly. "*We should go home! How? We can't even get back to the orbiter anymore.*" Behind her, faintly, she felt as much as heard the comforting hum of the hive, faltering here and there, but still her sisters, still near.

The other human in the pit stared up, silent now, though it had shouted and struggled all the way up the hillside, tightly wrapped as it had been in Collector's weakening wings.

Child's eyes dilated, and he waved his forepaws in the air, making distressed noises now.

"*Damn dragons*," said Collector. She wished there were some way to really communicate with Child, to tell him her thoughts. To explain. But he seemed mostly deaf despite his pretty mammalian chittering. And he seemed not to be able to smell much at all.

Child made another distressed sound. He covered his eyes and snout with his forepaws for a few seconds, and then released them again, huffing. He made more noises, clearly unhappy.

What was the problem? Was he afraid of the new human? Collector had worried that might happen, or that neither of the two humans would smell right to the other. In the hive that would end in injury or death. But humans were different. Weren't they?

She looked down into the fermentation pit. The new human sat, still staring up, one forepaw wrapped around a lower extremity—the limb was badly swollen, definitely wounded, and Collector hoped again that it was the sort of injury that would heal on its own. The new human was larger than Child had been when she'd found him, and differently shaped. Perhaps it was further along in its development, an instar Child hadn't reached. Or perhaps it was a different caste.

It hardly mattered. Collector didn't have time to be fastidious.

Maybe she'd failed. Brought the wrong sort of human. Failed to help Child as she'd intended. Down in the fermentation pit, the new human began making noises of its own.

"*Shit*," said Collector, though so far the sounds she made seemed not to soothe this one.

And, well, maybe she couldn't blame it. It was injured, apart from its own sisters (horrifying thought), and no doubt frightened—most humans Collector had seen had fled the moment they'd realized she was nearby. And this one was sitting atop a layer of bones and rotted viscera, feathers, and fleece, the remains of animals that no one in the hive could eat without a good, long aging. Child had never liked the smell.

As recently as a month ago, the aroma of fungus and rotting sheep would make Collector's gizzard contract in anticipation. But Collector hadn't been hungry in days. Never would be again.

Child laid his forepaws on Collector's snout, and made louder, more insistent noises. Liquid welled in his eyes.

Maybe Child couldn't really talk, but she'd heard those particular noises before, when Child didn't want some food she'd offered him. Why . . . ? Oh.

The new human was sitting in the fermentation pit. Collector usually fed Child things unfermented—fermented food made him sick. But he must have understood somehow what the pit was for. He must be afraid Collector had brought the new human here to eat it!

Really, sometimes she was sure humans actually thought about things. They were almost like people sometimes. This was good. Her spines softened, and her ear webs quivered with relief. "*Not food, not food,*" she said, repeating back the sounds he'd just made. Despite the ache in her muscles, she brushed Child with her wings. And she wished, oh, she wished there was some way to just explain.

The girl in the pit was older than Jacq by a few years, maybe just turned adult. It was hard to tell. It had been a long time since he'd been close to another human.

A really long time. That docked nose. Those comical ears. The hairs pricking out of her skin.

"Fuck!" the girl shouted. "Help me out!"

Jacq broke out of his daze. "Oh. Uh, right. Just a minute."

The words came easily, and Jacq realized it was probably a good thing he'd kept talking aloud to Auntie all these years, even though she couldn't understand him.

The pits weren't that deep, but the girl's leg was injured, and she kept making things worse by trying to jump. Jacq finally located a rope in the adjacent storage cell, and threw down one end. The girl tied some impressive knots to help heave herself up until Jacq could pull her the rest of the way.

Her smell was an overwhelming wave even in the already foul cavern. Her face was sallow with pain and sweat. Bits of sheep hide and rotting meat stuck to her skin and clothes. She breathed heavily as she slumped onto the ground, propping herself against a disposal box.

Jacq pressed the back of his hand over his nose. "Did you fall into the hive?"

"What!"

Jacq removed his hand to shout, "Did you fall in?"

The girl looked disgusted. "Do you think I'm stupid?"

"I don't understand why you're here."

"A dragon threw me in!"

"To the hive?"

"To the pit. First, she kidnapped me—wrapped me up like a spider with a fly! Then she carried me here, and dumped me in."

"Wrapped you in her wings?"

"Yes!"

Jacq gestured to her leg. "Because she found you injured?"

"Look," the girl said. "Call me Stel. You're . . ."

"Jacq."

"Fine. Jacq, I'm a picker, okay? My clan spends the cold season near here. We just set up camp, so I slipped off to go looking for scraps in my old scouting spots. One of them is at the old Landing site . . . Well, maybe I went farther past the radiation warning signs than I should have. By the time I realized, it had been a while. I was scrambling over stuff to get back and . . . I admit it. I tripped. I probably looked like a great catch, separated from my herd."

"She wouldn't have eaten you."

"Why was I in a food pit?!"

"I don't know. She . . . wanted me to meet you? Something is wrong. They've been acting weird. The whole hive. Auntie especially."

"*Auntie?*" Stel asked, with a look of disbelief.

Jacq made an impatient noise. "She's bringing me stuff. She's getting sick . . ."

"Isn't that normal when there's a hive collapse?"

The silence was flat.

Jacq said, "I don't know what you mean."

"The hive is in shutdown. They've laid a new queen. You must be able to tell. Haven't you seen the dead workers? There were at least three on the way in."

"I haven't seen . . . anyone dead . . ." Jacq said, but he could remember the dragon with the fatal gash who'd gone into the snow.

"You *live* with dragons," the girl said. "Do you know *anything* about hives? How did you end up here? What clan are you?"

Jacq stared past her. "What's going to happen to the hive?"

"It's going to collapse! Hive. Collapse." She clapped her hands together to illustrate. "All the old workers and warriors and whatever are going to die to make room for the new ones. It's kind of neat, actually. It's part of their reproductive cycle, every few centuries."

Jacq didn't move.

Stel made an exasperated noise. "Whatever! The point is, I'm getting out before that happens! You, too. I can't leave you here. What are you, fifteen?" Stel clapped again. "Pay attention to me!" she said. "It's time to leave before everything dies."

Everything dies. *The message had been passing in the base thrum of the* hive since the new queen hatched. *Everything dies.* You *will die, but other life will continue and new things will come.*

Collector labored up the hillside, a bundle of mite bark clutched in her forehands, pushing her way through the pain as she would have pushed herself through a too-small corridor. Bracing, sliding, pausing, twisting, breathing. Her body was done, but she had more to finish—the duties she had postponed while she dealt with Child.

Collector had always been the odd one of her Gatherer sisters. Not that they didn't love her—she had always been one of them, part of them, another voice in the song that lent the world order and purpose. No, she had loved her sisters, and they had loved her. And she loved to gather for the hive, loved going out into the open to find food or materials for building or digging, or whatever the hive seemed to need.

But she also loved to look at and collect things no one seemed to have any use for—the quivering, gelatinous underside of a wideleaf; flakes of corroded metal from the abandoned human hive that gleamed when scrubbed; stones shot through with sparkling crystal. Then there'd been the tweeting, feathered creature with the injured wing. Its body seemed more similar to human than dragon, and Collector had exasperated her sisters by trying to explain why she'd kept it, fed it till its wing healed, and fed it still when it kept coming back. She'd tried to explain her idea about animals and plants and how they were related and how they weren't, how lately there seemed to be two kinds of life in the world that were, if not inimical to each other, somehow starkly different.

Her sisters all said she had too much work in her joints—she could never be still; when she was done with hive work she had to make her own.

She stopped, peered down at the pitifully small bundle of mite bark. She had found barely any—there seemed to be less and less of it in recent months, though perhaps that was just because she no longer ranged so far from the hive, or else her dimming vision. But there seemed to be less in her hands than just moments before. Slowly, she turned to find, once she'd stared fixedly enough, a trail of brownish-blue strips reaching back in the direction she'd just come from.

There was no excess work in her joints now. Still, the hive needed every bit of what she'd gathered. She would have to go back and pick up what she'd dropped.

So, first there had been that flying, feathered thing, and then there had been a trio of leaf-creepers that had delighted her with the way their segmented bodies would change color from pink to brown to green to blue, and she'd loved to watch them slide around, their cilia waving sinuously.

And there had been the water worm she'd kept in a bowl in the back of an empty egg cell—she'd bred mudhops to feed it, until her sisters had complained about the constant buzzing.

None of them had been like Child. Child seemed to return her affection. He could manipulate things with his so-dexterous paws—tying sticks together, stacking stones, weaving leaf stems. Sometimes his chittering seemed almost to be speech. Sometimes she was sure that he was actually speaking to her, like a person would. He was different.

She was glad for it. She was glad that things were different, and would continue even after she was gone.

As a picker, Stel had a sharp sense for adapting materials. She interrogated Jacq about what he could grab, and figured out how to make a cart they could use to get her out of the hive. Apparently, once she was outside, she'd be okay; her clan had a signal point nearby.

It wasn't hard to gather what they needed. They divided the labor, Stel molding sap while Jacq worked with the wood.

"*How* did you end up *here?*" Stel asked.

Jacq cringed. Stel made him uncomfortable with her bluntness, and her volume, and her humanness.

"Auntie found me."

"Found you where?"

"Near one of the radiation patches."

"Why didn't your parents stop her?"

Jacq hesitated. "They weren't there."

"And no one found you?"

"No one was looking."

Stel shook her head in dismay. "How old were you?"

"I was pretty small."

"Like, under ten?"

Jacq shrugged.

"Under five?"

Jacq looked at his hands. "I had a fever."

"Okay, but why—" Stel cut off. Her eyes went wide. She slapped the ground with excitement. "Wait! Are you from the *city*?"

Jacq shrank away, but he didn't like to lie. "Yeah."

"You're from Landing? Really? You really grew up in the city?"

"Yeah."

"Oh, wow," Stel said. "Oh. *Wow.* We heard they were sending people out by the end, but I thought it was old people and babies."

Jacq's knuckles whitened as he gripped a plank. He kept his voice blank despite wanting to shout in her face. "It was a bad fever."

"So they sent you out to die? Why? To save *food*?"

"There wasn't enough," he said tightly.

"Wow. Just wow."

Jacq threw down the wood with more force than he intended. The *smack* finally got Stel's attention, and she shot him a guilty glance.

"Oh. Uh, sorry," she said. "I guess maybe that's hard to talk about."

Jacq shrugged, picking up a new plank.

"Uh," Stel said. "I guess, maybe I should tell you. They died. The people in the city. Things got worse, with the food and the radiation. Some of them left, even toward the end, but the ones who stayed died. Um. A lot of the ones who left died, too. They were pretty sick, and they didn't know how to find the clans. We would have helped. We tried."

She paused, watching for Jacq's reaction. He said, "I see."

"I guess . . . maybe . . . it's revenge . . . ?"

"I had a baby brother."

"Ah. Yeah."

Jacq said nothing, letting the conversation sink into silence like a stone into a lake. Stel fidgeted, increasing discomfort visible on her face.

Words finally burst out in a rush. "It's so weird to think, like, there's a ship that's traveled so, so far, all the way from Mars. By another star! And it's been made into a city, and it's been there for like five hundred years—I mean, it's really old! Then there's a storm, and something happens to the old engines underground, and boom, no one can live there anymore, even though they keep trying, and dying. It makes you think, like: What else can get destroyed? What else can just go boom, and you lose everything?"

"It was an earthquake."

"Huh?"

"An earthquake, not a storm."

"Oh. You remember?"

Jacq shrugged.

"So, uh, yeah. The dragons found you and brought you here?" Stel asked.

"Just Auntie. She took care of me."

"Before or after throwing you in a fermentation pit?"

"Will you stop?" Jacq asked. He wanted to sound cold, but his tone was plaintive. "She saved your life, didn't she? Isn't that important?"

Stel's mouth shut on whatever she'd been about to say. She looked down, embarrassed. "I made a stupid mistake. I shouldn't have needed rescuing. Everyone always tells me to be more careful."

"Maybe you should."

"You're right," she said quietly. She cleared her throat, and when she spoke again, it was with overloud confidence. "Well. It's good I got here. At least I can get you out."

"I'm not going anywhere."

"I don't think you have a choice. Every dragon you know is going to die. The new ones might not like you."

"Humans would be new to me, too," Jacq snapped. "Newer."

"Yeah, but *new* dragons *don't* like humans breaking into their hives. *We* won't murder you just because you don't look like you belong in our camp."

Jacq's lips thinned. "As long as you have enough food."

She paused. "Okay, yes, fine, humans can be crappy. But I promise you, our clan takes in strangers. You can stay with my family if you want. There's an empty mat. My brother—"

For the first time, Stel balked. It was more than embarrassment; she looked as though she had swallowed something living, something that was flailing its way down her throat.

She wiped her eyes with the back of her hand. "Well, anyway, there's a free mat."

Jacq thought of Auntie, and the hive, and the people before them who he could usually put out of his mind.

His throat ached. "Thank you. Truly. But I live here."

"They'll hurt you!"

"No. They'll know me."

Waving away his objections, she leaned urgently toward him. "We could look for your brother. Not everyone died—that means there's a chance! I *know* you must want to find him. I *know* how you feel. You can't stay!"

She was so red and vulnerable and hurting. Almost crying, because of him. The first human he'd seen in years.

"Okay," he lied. "I'll go."

The queen was dead. Collector knew from the oppressive silence, and the smell that drifted from the center of the hive, the last cry of the old queen—Collector's queen—as she struggled weakly against the newly molted Warriors. Her own daughters.

That was the way of it. That was life. The new queen would feed on the body of the old, would grow large and strong and lay the eggs that would, someday, hatch her own death.

Collector had known all her life that it would come to this: herself among the last of her sisters, her eyes clouded, her wings tattered, her queen dead. She had always expected to die in the course of her duties to the new hatch, her lifeless body disassembled by the Cleaners and piled in food storage. Still serving the hive, even in death. If she had never been eager for it, nor wished it to come sooner, still it had always seemed right and fitting.

She hadn't realized that it would be so lonely.

She hadn't realized that her stiff and weakening joints would hurt so much. The sudden absence of her queen had struck her like a thunderclap—or like its opposite, a shocking, painful, empty silence. The newly molted hatchlings—the Warriors, the new Egg Tenders moving about the hive, few now but increasing daily—smelled familiar, but were somehow blank and alien to her.

They greeted each other with caresses of their spines and low, humming songs. But Collector they ignored, as though she were invisible, inaudible, unaromatic. She might as well have been already dead.

Well, in any way that mattered, she already was.

She had done her best for her sisters, and even for the new dragons. There was little else for her to do now, little other reason to live.

She had done her best for Child, too. The new Warriors were zealous, even vicious in their protection of the hive, of their own newly hatched sister queen, but after so long in the hive, Child would smell familiar to them. At worst, they would ignore him. The new Egg Tenders might or might not feed him, but Collector had left plenty of food, enough to last him until the new hatch was established, and Child had become, she hoped, just an accepted feature of the hive.

She thought of when Child had been smaller, and she'd carried him in her wings like an Egg Tender might carry a dragon larva. Oh, he had been irresistible as a larva; so strange and soft and sometimes almost dragonlike! Had she done wrong to bring him here, away from others of his kind? He likely would have died if she'd left him, tiny and alone and crying out as he was, and maybe long enough gone from his own hive that even if he found his own way back, he might be rejected.

Which was worse, to be dead, or to be alone? Collector was beginning to think that being alone was worse than death.

But Child wasn't a dragon, no matter how intelligent he seemed sometimes, and besides, Collector had brought him another lost one.

She'd worried the new one might injure Child, or even kill him, but so far it seemed only wary and skittish, not aggressive. That was good. That was promising.

She'd done what she could. She hoped it was enough, that he would not be alone, wouldn't feel this yawning emptiness, as though the hive, the forest, the world—the universe—was suddenly dead and empty. His own existence bare, painful, and pointless. Tedious. Exhausting.

A brace of new Warriors prowled around and past her, giving her no attention at all, the blood of her own queen slick and black on their jaws.

So tired. She was so tired.

Jacq pushed the cart through the deserted corridors, Stel complaining as it stumbled over ridges and ruts on the floor. There were things lying by the walls; Jacq struggled to fix his gaze straight ahead, but he could still see the shapes from the corners of his eyes, wings and limbs and sometimes whole dragons slumped on the ground.

They broke through into the light of one of the grand, outer chambers. Columns of sun pierced through small, round windows in the ceilings. Stel exclaimed with surprise, and stretched her hand toward the nearest one as they passed. Jacq laughed and pushed her closer to it.

The clap of unfolding wings made them both jump. Jacq came up short, unintentionally jolting Stel as the cart bumped to a stop.

A dragon scraped her claws against the ground by the chamber exit as she came farther into the room. She was a Warrior—a healthy one— with red eyes and red lacquered scales that were shinier than any Jacq had seen before. There were no nicks in them, no variations in color— none of the imperfections that were so common among the dragons he'd grown up with that Jacq had never even noticed them until now, in their absence.

Her immature head crest flopped to one side, only partially grown in. Her dual pairs of eyelids, not yet fully separated, stayed slightly closed even when her eyes were open.

Stel yanked back her hand, and shrank toward Jacq. "Shit. I didn't know they grew up so fast."

Jacq snapped, "It's fine."

"Is it?"

The Warrior lowered her head to squint at them. Her tail curled into the air, spines rigid. She rolled her weight onto her back legs, and tensed the claws on her forehands, not yet attacking, but prepared.

Once, when Jacq had been little, an unfamiliar Warrior dragon had managed to enter the hive. For weeks afterward, he'd heard the angry shrieks of his own hive's Warriors in his dreams. Eventually—days later? Months?—he had finally managed to banish the insistent memory of the invading dragon being literally shredded like cloth. And the more unsettling memory that followed, of the Cleaner dragons carefully, patiently gathering those shreds, grumbling angrily all the while, and carrying them to the food stores.

"Yes," Jacq said. "It's fine."

He pushed the cart forward. It rattled across the ground, echoing between wide, empty walls. The dragon moved to block their path, stretching her wings to extend her reach to at least twice Jacq's height. She stared intently, her unseparated eyelids shuttering in a rhythm he associated with puzzlement.

Jacq moved in front of the cart. "You know me."

The dragon whuffed in a breath. She looked puzzled, but withdrew slightly, seeming mollified.

Jacq gave Stel a satisfied look, and moved back behind the cart. The dragon's head swung back downward as she slitted her eyes at the new human. The dragon's nostrils flared. A deep, warning rumble began in the rock.

"Fuck. Fuck, fuck," said Stel.

Jacq moved in front of the cart again. He didn't take the time to see how the Warrior responded, just started shoving the cart back where they'd come from, hoping the dragon would leave them alone if they

418

weren't trying to get out of the hive. The Warrior was young. She might get confused.

"Is she following?" Jacq asked.

Stel craned her neck, searching. ". . . No."

"Good."

Spotting a niche in the wall, Jacq pushed the cart inside for long enough to turn it around the right way.

"That dragon was smelling us to see if we belonged," Stel said.

"See," Jacq answered, huffing. "I'm safe."

Stel's attempt to whisper back came out as a shout. "Maybe! For now!"

Jacq glared at her.

"You think this means you can stay here, doesn't it?" she asked. "What if it wears off? What if you only smell like that because you live with your Auntie?"

"I don't know! Stop asking!"

Stel kept talking over him. *"And what about me?* Am I basically just fucked? The first time a dragon smells me, they're going to rip me apart? I mean, I guess it's fan-freaking-tastic they know who *you* are, but what the fuck am *I* supposed to do?"

Breathing heavily, Jacq pushed the cart back into the corridor. "I think that's why Auntie put you in the fermentation pit."

"Shit! So we should go back there?"

"Probably, but I don't know the way from here." Jacq turned the cart down the right of a forked path. "I just hope Auntie is home . . ."

Collector had lain down somewhere—she wasn't sure exactly where. She hadn't had enough strength to choose her spot, to make sure she'd be out of the way, or at least somewhere that would make less work for the Cleaners. The new Cleaners.

She didn't care. Everything was gray light—she could no longer close her eyes all the way—and faint, murmuring noise. Besides the pain in her muscles and joints, the only distinct sensation was the cool smoothness of the floor under her jaws, the stone and smooth-packed dirt she'd stepped on, thoughtless, all her life. Now it was the center of the world, the whole world, the only thing keeping what remained of her life from being nothing more than exhausted pain.

She was ready to go. She'd thought there would be nothing more to do than acknowledge this, and let go somehow. But it seemed she was bound fast to life in some way she didn't know how to break. She didn't, pitifully, have the strength to die.

A shadow came over the grayness of her vision. Something brushed her snout, warm and familiar-smelling.

Child. Distressed—she could hear it in his breathing, in the way he smelled salty-wet, that fluid that would run from his eyes when he was particularly upset. Like the day she'd found him, small and alone.

Where was the new human? Had it hurt her Child? Was that why he was here, weeping, unhappiness in his voice and his scent?

Collector roused herself enough to blink away some of the gray, to taste the air more carefully. Child knelt beside her, one forepaw on her snout, as he'd done when he'd been small and she'd held him close in her arms for warmth and comfort. The new human sat—or crouched? Collector couldn't quite tell—behind him.

It was not the source of Child's distress.

Collector was the source of Child's distress. Oh, poor Child. "*Damn dragons*," she tried to say, but nothing came out, only a weakly huffing breath.

Her sisters were dead. Her queen was dead. Child must be the only being in the world now who cared about Collector.

All his life, at least since she had found him on the hillside, she had been the only being who had cared about him. And now she was leaving him.

She summoned all her remaining strength and raised her head. Just a bit. Just enough to brush his wet cheeks with her spines, to let him rub his forepaws under her chin. He made more sad noises, and the new human crept closer. Child seemed to speak to it, and it reached out with its own forepaw.

Lacking the breath to chitter, Collector tried to rumble in her own language, through the rock. It was so terribly hard, but she managed to thrum weakly. *Continue.* She knew Child couldn't understand, but she rumbled as clearly as she could anyway. *Continue.*

Child picked up her nerveless forehand with both his forepaws. His grasp was tight, as if, with that strange canniness, he'd sensed what she meant. Beside him, the new human reached out and gently stroked one of Collector's spines. Good.

Good.

Collector's vision darkened again, all gray and darker yet.

*Jacq stared at Auntie's body, unable to move. Weeks of illness and starva-*tion had tattered her body, but at least she'd still been intact when she died. They were going to rip her up now. There was nothing he could do.

"Dragons live for centuries," Stel said in quiet awe. "She could have been five hundred years old. As old as Landing. She could have seen the first people who ever lived here."

Jacq slipped Auntie's claws out of his hand, and laid her forepaw on the ground.

The new, red Cleaner dragons turned their attentions to the body. Thankfully, they dragged it into the corridor before beginning their grim work. Jacq tried not to listen, but the noises were wet and organic and he could hear them through his hands. Stel put her arms around him and tried to comfort him while he cried.

The Cleaner dragons finished outside. There were the sounds of movement, and then there weren't.

Jacq pulled away.

Stel said, "You don't have to stop crying."

He shrugged.

A new Gatherer dragon ignored them as she entered the chamber, seeming much more puzzled by the piles of cargo against the walls. She went to inspect them one by one, tail tapping behind her. Collector was being replaced, already, just like that.

"I don't want to make you rush," Stel said gingerly, "but we don't know how long my scent will last. We should go soon."

Jacq dried his face with his hands. "We can go now."

"Are you sure?"

"Yes."

"And can I ask you something?"

Jacq shrugged. "Yeah. Sure."

Stel tapped her fingers anxiously on the edge of the cart. "Don't get mad."

"Okay."

"No, seriously, don't get mad. Okay?"

Jacq took a moment to meet her eyes. "Yeah," he said. "Okay."

"Please," she said. "Leave with me. I don't want you to die."

*Five hundred years ago, in the city they'd built out of their ship at the land-*ing site, an old woman looked up and saw a dragon in the sky. Its iridescent scales caught the sun, and shimmered with lavender, indigo, and violet.

Behind her, other colonists scrambled and shouted. "What's that?" "Give me that scanner." "Shit! Shit!" "Get to the shelters!" "How can those things fly?" "We should go home!" "How? We can't even get back to the orbiter anymore." "They'll eat the goddamn sheep!"

Her son shook his head in awe. "Damn . . . *dragons!*"

The old woman stared at how the dragon's wings glowed in the morning, shot through with sun as if they were leaves. "I think they're pretty."

Seven years ago, an eight-year-old boy shivered through the night, hunger distending his stomach, and fever licking like fire at his joints. Dis-

422

connected memories cut through his consciousness like shards of glass, bleeding sensory scraps: the simultaneous screams of his brother and father as they took him, the kicks in the stomach from someone who thought it was okay because he was going to die anyway, the burst of light disappearing when they shut off their lantern and left him alone.

Through the dawn, through the dreams, a hazy form came nearer and nearer, murmuring gentle phrases that seemed more delusion than reality. *"What's that? What's that? Shit. How can those things fly?"*

Now there was the girl with the docked nose and comical ears, whose family had a free mat, and who knew what it was like to lose a brother.

Jacq said, "I'll go with you."

As they made their way out, the hive rock thrummed beneath them: *Everything dies. We continue.*

SMALL BIRD'S PLEA

Todd McCaffrey

Todd McCaffrey (toddmccaffrey.org) wrote his first science fiction story when he was twelve and has been writing on and off ever since. A *New York Times* bestselling author, he has written more than twenty books, numerous short stories, and one animated screenplay. His works include his science thriller *Ellay*, his alternate history *The Steam Walker*, and the first-contact story *The Jupiter Game*. In 2016, he teamed up the award-winning Winner Twins (Brittany and Brianna) to form McCaffrey-Winner. Together they created the ongoing Twin Soul series, beginning with *Winter Wyvern*, currently with twelve books in print.

Jing-Wei told her stomach not to bother her. She would feed it when she could. It rumbled in discontent, and she gave it a sour look: *Stupid stomach! Did I not say I would feed you when I* could?

But I'm hungry noowwww! her stomach seemed to grumble.

Jing-Wei shook her head and pressed on, convinced that in a few moments her legs would voice their woes. Probably, they would say: *"We've been walking for aaages!"*

If it is not for me to complain, it is not for you to complain, either, Jing-Wei told her body. She pressed on. The path was climbing upward. Perhaps that was a good thing.

Jing-Wei was not the largest person in her village—indeed, her name meant "small bird"—but she was the only one who went. She was the only one who *could* go—the rest were fighting the demons or had already lost the battle.

She rehearsed what she would say: *Oh, great masters! Please hear my plea! My village and valley are beset by demons and without your aid all will die!*

No, that wasn't good enough, she thought to herself, absently wiping a bead of sweat from her brow. The air was thick with steam, but at least it was not the freezing hail that had battered the valley's crops and driven the bravest men to cry at the torture inflicted by the demons. Of course, the demons liked to hear such things; it encouraged them.

Lau De had warned the others not to moan so, but they had paid no attention to her. When the hail beat her down and they found her body in a ditch, they had said, "See! The witch is dead! She was no match for the demons!" Why they hadn't said, "Oh, we are such fools! Here was a wise woman and we did not heed her!" Jing-Wei didn't know, except perhaps that they *were* such fools.

And so, the last witch in the village had perished along with their crops. As if in celebration, the freezing hail had stopped and the harsh heat had begun. The village went from sopping, icy wetness to hot, crackling dryness.

The villagers were starving; the valley was dying. The demons were winning. And soon they would feast on the corpses of those too weak to move.

Unless Jing-Wei could get help. She tried to get others to come with her; she begged her best friend, Mei-Xing, whose name meant "beautiful star," but she was too afraid. "My parents say I can't play with you," Mei-Xing had told her in a small voice, her eyes cast to the ground.

"I don't want to play!" Jing-Wei had snapped back. "I want you to come with me, so we can free the village of demons!"

"If I can't play, what makes you think I can come with you?" Mei-Xing asked crossly. "My parents say there are no demons. It is just the weather. They are going to pray to the god of spring for aid and we will be saved."

"I saw the demons, Mei-Xing!" Jing-Wei told her. "I saw them just like Lau De herself!"

"My parents say Lau De was moon-touched," Mei-Xing said with a frown. "They say that she was touched by all the moons in the sky and that was why she was blinded at night and fell into the ditch, hit her head, and drowned."

"There was a hailstone the size of her fist right where they found her!" Jing-Wei exclaimed, unable to believe that her friend hadn't understood the import of *that*. "It was the hailstone that killed her. The hailstone sent by the demons because she knew them for what they were."

Mei-Xing absorbed this silently. Finally, she repeated, "My parents say I can't play with you."

Jing-Wei had even less luck with the boys, but she only asked them because everyone said a little girl was not supposed to travel alone.

"You are a silly girl, go away!" Zhang Chen told her, grabbing a clump of cold, wet dirt from the drying river and throwing it at her. Jing-Wei was small, but she was fast, and dodged the clumsy boy's clod easily.

"I must help my parents in the field," Yang Dingbang apologized.

"Your name means 'protect the country' and yet you won't help?" Jing-Wei asked in astonishment.

"It's just a name," he said, with a melancholy shrug. He made a shooing gesture at her and smiled, saying, "Fly away, little bird!"

"*Small* bird!" Jing-Wei corrected. "Get it right, you oaf!"

Yang Dingbang's smile remain fixed. "Fly away!"

In the end, Jing-Wei had not flown, although she could easily imagine how her arms would have complained if they were wings: *I have to lift all of you up into the sky and you won't even feed me? How horrible is that?*

Fortunately, Jing-Wei had only arms, and they weren't complaining . . . much.

Her arms started to complain not long after because the climb had become so steep that she had to use them to haul herself up the densely wooded hillside.

I will not cry! I will not break! she told herself forcefully, as her legs tried to stop moving, and her chest couldn't stop heaving with the effort, and her stomach was an empty hole inside her.

Another step. Another foot.

The air was wispy with fog as she climbed higher. She shivered, realizing that she had left the dense, humid jungle beneath her, leaving the sweat to chill on her skin. There were fewer and fewer trees and no undergrowth to slow her down. Now all she had were rocks and a steady drizzle of cold rain falling over her through the breaks in the treetops.

But there! Just above her she could see the pass, flanked by two mountains. Soon she would see what was on the other side. And she knew, just *knew* that this time she would find what she was looking for.

Oh, great masters! Please hear my plea! My village and valley are beset by demons and without your aid all will die!

She reached the crest of the hill, crawled through the saddle between the mountaintops, and stopped, looking down at the expanse spread before her.

It was beautiful: the valley unfolding below her. Beautiful with verdant grasses and tall trees.

Jing-Wei's heart fell—it was just like the last three valleys she had seen. She would have to go through it and climb the mountains beyond. Her lips trembled at the thought. Wasn't there a limit to how far she could go?

She forced her legs to carry her forward, looking for any signs of something she might put in her mouth to silence her stomach.

As she reached the end of the saddle and prepared to descend into the valley below, a shape moved in front of her. It was a lion, and it looked just big enough to eat a small bird like herself.

It sat on its haunches and regarded her silently. It was a girl lion. Jing-Wei knew that the males had manes—"Just like peacocks, always strutting!" Lau De had told her when she had spoken of far-off places and strange creatures.

At least it isn't an elephant, Jing-Wei thought. As if to torment her, behind the lion a large shape loomed up. She saw the large ears, heard the slow lumbering thud of its movement, and her eyes grew wide. "Lions will eat an elephant if they can," Lau De had told her once on a dark night when they were guarding the village. "But sometimes they become friends."

Friends. The word echoed in her head. She started moving forward, her hands open but by her side. She looked up at the elephant and back to the lion.

"It's only me," Jing-Wei said. "I'm a little girl from a village beset by demons, and I need to ask for help in the cave of miracles."

The lion took two steps toward her. The elephant thumped up a moment later.

"I heard a song about you," Jing-Wei offered, telling her heart to stop racing, her lungs to stop pulling in air so fast. "Would you like to hear it?"

The lion took two more steps forward.

Jing-Wei licked her lips.

"Lion, lion, eyes so bright
What do you see in the night?
Elephant, elephant far away
Do you hear what we all say?"

They looked unimpressed.

"Okay," Jing-Wei said. "I made that up just now." She looked at the lion. "Did you like it?"

The lion took two more steps forward.

"My surname is Li and my personal name is Jing-Wei and I am far from home, looking to help my village as it is beset by demons," Jing-Wei told them, her lips trembling with sorrow. She looked at the lion. "I am only little and I haven't eaten in three days, so I would make a very poor meal, if that's what you are thinking." She looked at the elephant. "I don't know how you got so high but you walk farther with each step than I can run, and I envy you that." She glanced down at her legs and gestured toward them. "I have only these little sticks of legs and they are very, very tired from all the walking." She looked up at them again, and tired as she was, her eyes filled with tears. "But can't you see my village needs help? I am the only one who can still see the demons. The others are all lost, praying to the wrong gods, or they've just given up and are preparing to die." She took a ragged breath. "Please, won't you let me pass? Please let me find the cave of miracles?"

The lion moved to one side, and the elephant stepped forward. Jing-Wei's eyes widened in growing horror as the elephant grew larger and larger as it came up to her. She closed her eyes in fright.

"Please! I have to help my village!" she mumbled in terror. The lion roared, and Jing-Wei trembled. She heard the soft thuds of the lion stalking toward her.

And something inside her snapped. She opened her eyes, crouched down, brought her hands in front of her, ready to fight. "If you eat me, I will claw you from the inside!" she roared. "I will fight my way out of your belly, rip you asunder, and *then* I will find the cave of miracles and save my village!"

"Or you could just climb on my shoulders so that I can lift you up onto the back of my friend," the lion said.

Eyes wide with wonder, Jing-Wei did as the lion said. She found herself comfortably perched between the wide shoulders of the huge beast, which turned and began lumbering down into the valley below them. The lion, with a growl that might have been a chuckle, loped off to disappear into the forest.

"The lion *talked*," Jing-Wei said to herself in surprise. "I didn't know lions can talk."

"They can't," the elephant replied. "Only demons can talk."

Demons? Jing-Wei's mind trembled at the notion. "Where did she go?" Jing-Wei said.

"She went to get you some food," the elephant replied.

"If only demons can talk . . ?"

"Yes," the elephant replied, "I'm a demon."

I'm riding a demon! Jing-Wei wailed in her mind. She made herself as small as possible on top of the elephant's huge back, waiting for whatever end would come. Tears streaked her face, but she did not cry out loud for she would not give the demons the pleasure of knowing they had destroyed her.

A soft sound caused her to open her eyes, and she looked around to see the lion with a wicker basket in its mouth standing behind her on the elephant's back.

"You must eat," the lion said after she lowered the basket onto the elephant's back near Jing-Wei.

"So you can eat me?" Jing-Wei asked in a small voice, all she could muster in her despair.

"Well, certainly, if you do not succeed in your quest," the lion allowed. "But you'll need food for strength. Your journey was long, and the longest part is in front of you."

"In front of me?"

"In the cave of miracles," the lion said. "You are here to plead for your village, are you not?"

"Yes," Jing-Wei admitted. Suddenly beyond all caution, she added, "But you're a demon—why should you care?"

"Not all demons are the same," the lion told her. "Isn't that true with people?"

"Yes," Jing-Wei agreed slowly. Her stomach rumbled loudly, and the lion chuckled.

"Eat, little bird!" she said, nudging the basket toward her. "You're no good to either of us starving."

"Small bird," Jing-Wei corrected absently, looking at the basket and eyeing the contents warily. "Is the food poisoned?" The lion shook her head. "Or enspelled?"

"It is safe and good for humans to eat," the lion told her. "Chicken and ginger over rice."

"Any garlic?" Jing-Wei asked, moving carefully to grab the handle of the basket and creep it toward her.

"Of course," the lion agreed. "And vegetables. Fresh." The lion nudged the basket closer to the child. "There's warm tea, too."

Jing-Wei opened the cloth that wrapped the insides of the basket and discovered that the contents were exactly what the lion had said.

"Lion, what should I call you?" Jing-Wei asked in a small voice.

"I am a lion. Why do you ask?"

"Demons have names and I have manners," Jing-Wei told her primly.

"Well, then, well-mannered child, you may call me ATO Nightingale," the lion replied.

"ATO? Is that Japanese?"

"It's an old, old word that has no meaning anymore," the lion replied, mouth wide, displaying many bright white teeth. "It means Assistant Tactical Officer."

"It is important?" Jing-Wei asked. When the lion shook her head, Jing-Wei persisted, "To you, at least?"

"Very much so," the bass voice of the elephant snorted. "She'll never let me forget it, not even after a thousand years!"

"And you, kind elephant, what should I call you?"

"I am PO Knightsbridge, little one," the bass voice replied. "PO means Petty Officer, which means the ATO—who holds the rank of lieutenant—outranks me."

"She tells you what to do?" Jing-Wei said. The elephant bobbed his head up and down.

"Well," the lion—ATO Nightingale—mumbled, "I *do* ask for your opinion, Brandon."

"Oh, we're on a first-name basis again, are we, Paula?" the elephant said.

The lion said nothing, looking meaningfully at Jing-Wei. "Eat, child. We'll be there soon enough."

"I asked your names that I might thank you for showing such kindness to one so lowly as my poor self," Jing-Wei said, bowing her head to touch the rough skin of the elephant's back. "I, Li Jing-Wei, do give you thanks for this fine meal."

"Taste it first, before you say that," the elephant said with a deep rumble.

"You are welcome, little one," said the lion. "Eat up, life's always best on a full stomach."

Jing-Wei bowed once more and sat, cross-legged, on the elephant's back, untying the bundled cloth and laying the meal out in front of her. The rice was in a separate bowl. There was a strange container that held the hot tea and had a cup on top. The hot chicken, ginger, garlic, and vegetables were in another container. She found some odd metal things, but fortunately had no trouble identifying some very nicely fashioned chopsticks.

She drank a sip of tea—it was heaven! And then she could hardly contain herself as she transferred warm ginger chicken to the rice and gobbled it down.

She burped—and blushed—not certain if she was being rude to her animal hosts or expressing the highest of praise. She raised the last of her tea in the cup in a salute to the lion and drained it gratefully.

"I'm ready to die now," she said quietly. "My stomach thanks you for this last meal."

"Don't be so quick to plan your funeral," the lion told her. "The valley is wide and we've got hours yet before you get to the cave of miracles."

"Have you been there?" Jing-Wei asked in amazement. "Do they let animals inside?"

"It'd be hard to stop us," the elephant said with another bass chuckle. "And humans are animals, too."

"Really?" Jing-Wei asked. "Are we just like chickens and pigs?"

"No more than an old man is just like a baby," the lion chided her.

"Are demons human, too?"

"That depends on the demon," the elephant rumbled.

"Most aren't," the lion said. "They're native to Jade."

"Our planet under the Jade Emperor?" Jing-Wei said.

The elephant snorted and the lion looked amused, her amber eyes gleaming.

"Something like that," the lion allowed. After a moment, she continued, "What do you know of how you came here?"

Jing-Wei blushed. "I am told that my father and mother wanted a child and they did—" She found she couldn't continue, she was so embarrassed.

"Not that!" the elephant rumbled loudly. "She's asking how humans came to this planet. Do you know that, child?"

"Lau De said that long ago the emperor flew in a sky chariot across the night sky and brought our forefathers here," Jing-Wei said, glad to be on less worldly matters. "But the chariot was assaulted by the lesser demons and the demon Murphy—"

"Murphy!" the elephant bugled. "Poor lad never gets a break!"

"Go on," the lion urged Jing-Wei.

"—and crashed in the mountains," Jing-Wei said, pointing to the distance and then frowning as she realized that they were now *in* those mountains.

"Here, in fact," the lion agreed.

"The emperor and all the lesser gods were grievously injured, beset by the greater demons, but they managed to fight them off and plant man on the planet, blessed be their memories," Jing-Wei finished.

"We would have left if we could have," the lion added in a sad voice. "We didn't want to fight with another intelligent species."

"It was their planet. If they had just let us leave, we could have found another," the elephant agreed.

"We made a peace—"

"Hmph!"

"—and we honored it," the lion said.

"But the people forgot and expanded wherever they could," the elephant said. "And so broke the treaty."

"Both sides broke the treaty, there is blame on both sides," the lion said.

"Are you saying that my ancestors were wrong?" Jing-Wei asked, trying to hide her horror at the thought. "That they stole our valley from others?"

"That's what we'll find out," the lion said.

"And we'll punish their children and their children's children for their deeds?" the elephant asked, shaking his head. "Is that the right way?"

"Should we continue to break the treaty instead?" the lion asked. "And if we do, how will we survive?"

"You're a demon, aren't you?" Jing-Wei asked. "How can you die?"

"We can be killed, just as easily as a human," the elephant said sadly. "There used to be hundreds of us. Most of us died protecting the treaty or defending humans."

"And now?" Jing-Wei asked. "How many are there now?"

"A few," the lion said in a whisper.

Jing-Wei's eyes grew wide. "Just you two?"

The elephant shook his head.

"Look up," the lion said. Jing-Wei did just as a giant shadow crashed toward her. With a shriek, she flung herself into a small ball on the elephant's back.

"Shahbaz!" the lion cried. "You didn't have to scare her so!"

"But it's fun," a voice replied.

"You can look up, child," the lion said. "It's just Shahbaz."

"The bird?" Jing-Wei said, daring to open her eyes. A giant bird was perched on the back of the lion. Who was sitting on top of the elephant. Beside Jing-Wei.

"An eagle," Shahbaz corrected, grooming his feathers with his beak.

"And you're a demon, too?"

"I'm no demon, child," the eagle scolded. "I'm just as human as the other two."

"So, you're a demon," Jing-Wei concluded.

"Words, just words," Shahbaz grumbled.

"But if you are all demons, then what is in the cave of miracles?" Jing-Wei asked in a small voice.

"Memories," the lion said. "Just memories."

"And power," the elephant added. "Lots of power."

"At least until the captain returns," the eagle said.

"If he returns!" the elephant rumbled.

"PO! You shouldn't say such things!" the lion chided.

"With all respect, ma'am, it's been what—nearly a thousand years?" the elephant said. "They could have gone to Earth and back five times or more!"

"The ship was damaged," the eagle said judiciously.

"And the demons attacked when it took off," the lion said. "It could have slowed them down. They could have stopped for repairs."

"Or they could have been lost and will never return," the elephant said.

"We agreed on all that already, I don't see why we're rehashing it," the lion said.

"Because it's one thing waiting for help and another taking care of our descendants," the elephant said. A moment later, he added, "Ma'am."

"What else can we do?" the lion said miserably.

"We lost Sens fifty years ago," the elephant said. "By the law of averages, we won't last another two hundred years. And what then?"

"This is a conversation that should not involve a child's ears," the eagle said to the others.

"My ears are just as good as yours!" Jing-Wei protested to the eagle. She peered closely at the bird. "Where *are* your ears?"

"He doesn't have any," the elephant rumbled. "Which means that your ears are better than *his*."

"And your ears are the best," the lion said testily. "But the point remains."

"How many people have come to the cave of miracles?" the eagle asked. "How many since Sens?"

"In my village, the cave of miracles is a myth," Jing-Wei said. "I only know about it because Lau De told me."

"Who is Lau De?"

"She is the witch who took me in when my parents died," Jing-Wei said, trying her best to sound matter-of-fact. "She was the last witch of our village."

"I told you that witch idea wasn't going to work!" the elephant rumbled.

"And what would you say?" the lion asked. "That we're the avatars of lost astronauts?"

"First you'd have to explain avatars, then astronauts, and by the time you're done, they've either died of old age or fled in fright," the eagle said.

"You talk a lot," Jing-Wei said. Silence fell and she bowed her head. "I mean, it seems so to me."

"Out of the mouths of babes!" the eagle cackled.

"I am not a babe!" Jing-Wei protested. "I am small for my size."

"And how old are you, little one?" the lion asked.

"I'll soon have seen the five seasons six times," Jing-Wei said.

"That'd make her coming up on seven," the eagle said after a moment. "And she walked all the way here on her own."

The three demons were quiet for a long while. Finally, the lion said, "You should rest now, child. We'll wake you when it's time to eat again."

"Tomorrow?" Jing-Wei asked in surprise. She didn't think that the cave of miracles was all that far away—particularly as fast as the great elephant was striding.

"No," the lion said with a chuckle.

"How many meals do you eat in a day?" the eagle asked, peering down at her.

"One," Jing-Wei said.

"Most people eat three," the elephant said.

"They must be huge to eat so much!" Jing-Wei cried in awe.

"Well, at least bigger than you, that's for certain," the elephant agreed.

"Rest," the lion said. "And when you wake, if you're hungry, we'll feed you."

"I'll keep watch," the eagle said.

"And check on our guest," the lion said. "I don't like leaving it alone for long."

"It?" Jing-Wei asked, sitting up and suddenly alert.

"You are not the only guest to come into our valley," the elephant rumbled.

"You caught a demon?" Jing-Wei guessed. The lion nodded, while the eagle leaped into the sky and flapped quickly out of sight. "You caught a demon and you didn't kill it?"

"It is hard to talk to the dead," the lion said.

"You can talk to the dead?" Jing-Wei said in awe.

"No, child, the LT is just being humorous," the elephant told her.

"'LT'?" Jing-Wei repeated.

"It's short for lieutenant," the elephant explained. "Have you heard that word before?"

"The king's men, some of them are lieutenants," Jing-Wei said, eyeing the lion warily.

"When did you see them?" the lion asked.

"They come to collect tithes for the king," Jing-Wei said in a small voice. "Once a year. And sometimes they take people, too, to the war."

"And you don't like them," the elephant guessed.

"When they come, we don't eat," Jing-Wei said. "And the prettiest girls and the strongest boys—we try to hide them."

"Lovely," the lion murmured.

"You can't be everywhere, LT," the elephant said. "And at least they've still got monarchy."

"About what we'd expect, given everything," the lion agreed. "Still . . ."

"Like you said, ma'am, you can't talk to the dead," the elephant said.

"Things were better when the emperor ruled?" Jing-Wei guessed.

"The captain was never—" the lion began patiently.

"Things were better," the elephant said. The lion's amber eyes glowed with a fire that was quickly extinguished.

"Sleep, child, you need your rest," the lion said. Noiselessly, the lion leaped down beside the elephant . . . and padded into the jungle. "I'll patrol."

"She's right, you know," the elephant said. "You should rest."

Jing-Wei curled up into a ball, settled herself between the elephant's slowly moving shoulders, and closed her eyes.

Sleep overwhelmed her and brought her wondrous dreams.

"Have you figured out where this valley is, then?" A voice echoed in her ears.

"It is about thirty klicks from our base," another voice, the lion's, replied.

"Thirty klicks, no matter which way, is within the treaty," another voice—the elephant's—said.

"If it's to the east, that'd put it at the front lines," the eagle's voice said.

She was in the cave of miracles. Lights like rare jewels surrounded her, lighting ghostly images of people dressed in strange clothes. There were hundreds of them. Most looked like ghosts. *Were they all ghosts?*

"And our guest?" the first voice asked.

"We're trying to communicate, but we've had no luck so far," the lion replied.

"Which is odd, considering that we had no trouble communicating before," the first voice said.

"Captain, if I may—" the eagle spoke up.

"Yes, Chief Buhari?"

"We still don't know much about their organization, about how they communicate among themselves," the eagle said. "It's possible that this demon never learned our language."

"Which means that it knows nothing of the treaty," the captain said.

"Exactly, sir," the eagle agreed.

"Which means we've got a whole new ball game," the elephant rumbled.

"And the plan of 'educating' observers seems to have failed," the captain said.

"I don't know, sir," the lion said. "I know it was my plan, but I think that the fact that this child tells us that the demons targeted the village witch may mean that they've been more effective than we imagined."

"It's not their effectiveness I question, lieutenant, it's their survival," the captain said.

"Yes, sir," the lion said. "I see your point."

"There has only ever been a few of the colonists we could ever trust with the truth," the captain said.

"Sir, we never really told them everything," the eagle said.

"I know," the captain's voice agreed. "But we had good reason."

"You mean that if we told them that their best hope is to rely on the avatars of dead spacers, I'm sure they would never agree," the eagle replied.

"That doesn't change the fact that we're failing," the elephant said. "We're down to three functionals and we don't know how much longer we'll last."

"So you're saying that we must recruit more," the captain said. "From among the population."

"From the witches and those we can hope to trust with the truth," the elephant said.

"I think we should start them young, when they're not set in their ways," the eagle said.

"You want to start with this child," the captain said.

"She's the only one who's made it here in the last century," the elephant said. "If we're going to recruit, she's our only candidate."

"Except for the demon," the lion said.

"Yes." The captain's voice was frosty with disapproval. "Keeping it is a treaty violation, lieutenant."

"We haven't decided on keeping it, sir," the lion defended herself.

"But until we can communicate with it, we think it's dangerous to just let it go," the eagle said. "After all, it knows where our base is."

"And if we lose this, we've lost everything," the lion said in agreement.

"I agree," the captain said.

"Sir, sir!" a new voice cried out in alarm.

"What is it?"

"The girl—she can hear us! She's about to—"

Jing-Wei opened her eyes and remembered her dream. "We're here, aren't we?"

"How—?" the lion said.

"Where's the captain?" Jing-Wei asked, looking around a huge cavern that was just as she'd dreamed it. Except there were no ghosts, only the three animals. In the distance she spied a large ball of blue light that flickered to brilliant whiteness in a pattern that seemed like ripples on the water when a stone was bounced on it. She pointed to the ball. "The demon's in there, isn't it?"

"Lieutenant, how'n the hell does she know so much?" the elephant asked.

Jing-Wei ignored him, realizing that she was on the ground, on soft blankets just as she'd dreamed. She got up and moved toward the blue bubble. She approached it and reached out a hand.

"Wait!"

"I've never touched a demon," Jing-Wei said. To the bubble, she said, "Are you the one who killed our witch, Lau De, my teacher?"

"It can't be," the eagle said. "We captured it weeks before you arrived."

"How many weeks?" Jing-Wei asked. "The demons started their worst attacks about two weeks ago."

"About two weeks ago," the elephant said, nodding toward the demon.

"That's data we didn't have," Shahbaz the eagle said to the lion, who had a horrified look on her face.

"So, is this demon important to them?" the elephant asked.

"And how is it important?" the eagle added. "It could as easily be an escapee as an envoy."

"Did you kill Lau De?" Jing-Wei said, looking through the blue luminosity that held the demon at the dark shadow that was the demon itself. Her face hardened as she continued, "Let me tell you about Lau De. She raised me when my parents died. She raised me like her own. She raised me to know about peacocks and lions and elephants. She told me the stories of the great dragons, the most powerful beasts in the sky. She taught me to look up to the stars and wonder at the beauty that surrounds us all.

"And then you demons killed her," Jing-Wei finished, surprised by her own tears. "You murdered her with a hailstone and left her to drown in a ditch by the *shivelrat* weed.

"Is that all you demons are? Murderers?" Jing-Wei asked. "Do you care about us at all?"

"Child—" the lion said slowly.

Jing-Wei shushed her with a backward-flung hand and a shake of her head. "Demons have taken my laughter, my happiness, and given me in return only bitter tears."

Inside the blue jail, the demon turned a shadowy green. Was that remorse or exultation?

"You want to kill us all?" Jing-Wei shouted at the thing. "Very well," she said, thrusting her hand through the blue barrier. "Start with me. I am no one now. You have taken all that I ever was."

"Wait!"

"No!"

"Lieutenant, she's breached the barrier!"

The words were flung at Jing-Wei, but she did not hear them as she entered the blue energy that held the demon.

"Kill me," Jing-Wei said, now peering at the green ball shape that was the demon. "Because I have sworn to kill you. You killed Lau De, you destroyed my village. You should die!"

Life, the word sprang into her head. *Kill ends life?*

"Yes," Jing-Wei said. She did not stop to wonder how she could hear the demon in her head. She moved toward it, wishing she had a knife or something that could kill demons. Lau De had said there were ways but that no one in the village had the tools.

Life is good, the demon thought inside her. *No more life is bad. We want more life.*

"You killed Lau De," Jing-Wei said. "Do you take our lives for your own?"

Some do, the demon thought. *Are afraid. Don't know. Don't want to try. To change.*

"Jing-Wei?" The lion's voice came muffled through the energy barrier. She sounded worried. "Are you all right?"

"The demon speaks in my head," Jing-Wei said.

"It does?" the elephant boomed in amazement. "And you understand it?"

"Of course!" Jing-Wei shouted back.

End life bad. Life forever. End . . .

Jing-Wei got the impression that the demon was looking for a word and could not find it, finishing instead with: *not life.*

"When you kill, people are gone forever," Jing-Wei said.

Gone forever, when kill? the demon said in her head. She got the impression that the demon meant that it would be gone forever when Jing-Wei killed it and that people were gone forever when the demons killed them.

"Gone forever," Jing-Wei agreed.

Forever is now, the demon said.

"Stupid demon!" Jing-Wei swore, diving toward it. She hit it and flew backward, stung by something that bit her and left her skin feeling odd.

"What did it say?" the lion cried, loud enough that Jing-Wei heard her clearly.

"It said that 'forever is now,'" Jing-Wei repeated.

"That doesn't make sense," the eagle muttered. "How can that be?"

"Sounds rather Zen," the elephant said. "Like everything is in the moment."

"Did it say anything else?" the lion asked.

"And why did you fly back like that?" the elephant added.

"Are you okay?" the eagle said.

"It said lots of things about life and death," Jing-Wei said. "And I flew back because it bit me. And I'm going to kill it."

"Bit you?" the lion repeated.

"We read a surge of static electricity," the eagle reported. "It might have just zapped her."

"Why didn't you kill me?" Jing-Wei asked, flexing her hand where the bite had hurt the worst.

No kill. Kill is forever. Life is forever.

"Life isn't forever," Jing-Wei said. "People die."

Not we people.

"We've killed you, I know we can," Jing-Wei said, wondering if, perhaps, there was no way she just on her own could kill *this* demon.

Yes, the demon agreed. *Many people are dead.*

"You killed my people," Jing-Wei said.

Your people? We people. The demon seemed confused.

"We're people," Jing-Wei said.

"Oh! Semantic mismatch!" the lion cried. "Jing-Wei, it may be that the demons think that they're the *only* people!"

"Well, then they're stupid!" Jing-Wei snapped back. "Tell me how to kill it."

"We don't want to kill it," the eagle told her.

"That's because you're demons, too," Jing-Wei shouted, showing her despair. She was trapped with a demon she couldn't kill and she'd been led here by demons who were going to eat her. She was doomed, her village was doomed—Yang Dingbang, his brothers, sister, and parents; Zhou Mei-Xing, her only friend, and her stupid parents; Zhang Chen and all the others . . . doomed.

"This is supposed to be the cave of miracles! Why won't you help me?" Jing-Wei sobbed. She drew a deep breath and shouted with all her might: "Oh, great masters! Please hear my plea! My village and valley are beset by demons and without your aid all will die!"

"Oh, great masters!" the demon cried in a young boy's voice. "Hear my plea! I am the last child and I have no one to play with. The solid ones come and destroy my friends, dig up my plants, destroy my toys, and they won't listen! My parents are gone, lost in a battle I don't remember. My sisters are weeping for there can be no more children and the solid ones will overpower us. We are dying. We want peace. They will not listen. Oh, great masters! I call on you for justice! For compassion! For love!"

"What?" the three animals cried from outside.

"Do you have a name?" Jing-Wei said, turning to the shape now wreathed in blue and looking like the shadow of a very dirty boy. "I am called Li Jing-Wei. My name means small bird."

"I have many names," the boy shape replied. "So many that I don't remember them all. But your words . . . they are strange and hard to repeat. What name would you give me?"

"What name do you want?" Jing-Wei asked. "I was not given a choice. I was too little when I was born."

"I was little, too," the boy shape replied. "But I need a name that you can use, a new one. One that your mouths can shape and I can distinguish from the others."

"Did you kill anyone in my village?"

"No," the boy shape replied. "The others, when they thought you took me, they would have attacked."

"Why didn't they attack *here*?" Jing-Wei demanded. She turned to the shapes outside the bubble. "Did you cause the demons to attack my village?"

"No," the lion said. "We didn't know about it until you came here."

"My people would have gone for the nearest solid ones," the demon said. In a different tone, it continued, "Are there many who have died?"

"More than I can count!" Jing-Wei said, waving her hands at him twice.

"What does that mean?" the boy shape asked.

"Many," the lion said. "We count each finger of our hands and each toe of our feet and we get twenty."

The blue boy looked ill. *Kill is forever.*

"Yes," Jing-Wei agreed. "Forever."

"You would kill this one?" the blue boy asked, waving a hand at himself.

"You didn't kill any of my people, did you?"

"No, I did not," the boy said. "But if I hadn't come here, they wouldn't have died. I'm sorry."

"Sorry won't bring them back!" Jing-Wei cried, her hands balled into tight little fists.

"We can't bring them back," the lion called. "But we can make sure that no more die."

Forever? No.

"Why not?" Jing-Wei asked. "You say you live forever—why can't we make this last forever?"

You do not last forever, the demon said. *You are solid. You will stop one day, entropy will destroy you.*

"Is that what happened before?" Jing-Wei asked. "The ones who signed the treaty, are they all dead?"

We fight. We forget. We can die. We cannot be reborn.

"No one can be reborn," Jing-Wei said.

"So, not a practicing Buddhist, then," the elephant rumbled softly to himself.

No new ones. No "children."

"You said you were a child!" Jing-Wei protested.

Last child. Last in forever. No new children. Soon all will be gone.

"He says he's the last child," Jing-Wei said. "How can that be?"

"They seem to be beings of pure energy," the lion said. "They may have forgotten how they created themselves."

"Their numbers are dwindling, they're dying out," the eagle said.

"And we're helping them along," the elephant rumbled sadly.

"You're dying?" Jing-Wei said to the demon.

Can't die. Can't be born.

"What the animals said," Jing-Wei said irritably. "There are no new people for you?"

I am the last child.

"So why did you come here?" Jing-Wei asked.

To ask for help. Cave of miracles.

"He came to the cave of miracles to ask for help," Jing-Wei said. "He wants us to help them learn how to make new baby energy people, like him."

"We don't know how!" the eagle cried in anger and frustration.

"Can't you learn?" Jing-Wei asked. She turned to the blue boy. "We don't know right now. We could learn over time."

"People die," the boy said. "Ending is forever."

"How about I call you Fai?" Jing-Wei said suddenly. "It means 'beginning'—because we must begin something new."

"I can be Fai," the blue boy agreed. "Can I be Li Fai, so that we are related?"

"How does he know that?" the elephant asked from outside the blue energy bubble.

"He's accessing our databases," the eagle replied. "Check your monitors."

"Can we stop him?" the lion asked.

"It's probably already too late," the elephant said after a moment. "It looks like he's accessed about fifty percent of our records."

"It tickles," Fai, the blue boy, said. "Most of the memories fade. I was looking to see if I could remember . . ."

"How to make more of your people?" Jing-Wei guessed.

"No," Li Fai said. "I wanted to know if we could touch."

"Touch?" Jing-Wei repeated. She looked at the blue boy, flinched in memory of the strange pain she'd felt when she'd reached out for him earlier, and shook her head.

"Would you try?" Li Fai asked. He reached a blue hand toward her, stretching his fingers out until the index finger was closest. "Just a finger?"

Jing-Wei bit her lip. "Welll . . ." She reached forward. Her finger touched his and suddenly—

This is what it is like to breathe! This is what it is like to feel blood *flowing, a* heart *pumping!* Li Fai exclaimed in wonder.

You are like the lightning, like the flash and the boom! Jing-Wei responded. She moved forward, grabbed his hand in hers and pulled him tight against her. *You are power! You are*—Words failed her. She doubted anyone, no matter how old, could find them.

And suddenly Li Jing-Wei was no more. Li Fai was no more.

Together, Jing-Wei told the boy. *We do this together.*

Yes! Yes! the boy cried eagerly.

We tell my people and your people what will be, Jing-Wei said. Harshly, she added, *Those who don't listen will be destroyed.*

Destroyed? A note of doubt.

No one can hurt another.

But us? The boy didn't like that.

Only if they don't listen, Jing-Wei said. *We will make them listen.*

How?

We must become the biggest, scariest, most powerful being. We will listen, we will love, but we will not allow harm, murder.

You can do this?

No. We can.

How?

My name means small bird, the Jing-Wei half responded. *We will become the largest beast in the sky, the most powerful.*

What beast is that? the Fai half asked, accessing the data banks and bringing forth images and facts on known flying creatures.

I will show you.

"Lieutenant!" the elephant rumbled. "The field is collapsing!"

"We're taking a huge energy hit," the eagle added. They could hear the generators in the back of the cave whine with an immense strain.

And then the noise was gone.

"What happened?" the lion demanded. She glanced at the force field but it was gone. So were the demon and the girl. "Where are they?"

"Look up!" a voice called down to them. The three animals looked up.

"Oh . . . my . . . stars!" the lion cried in awe. "You're so beautiful."

"Why, thank you," the beast said. In a slightly different voice, it added with a note of wonder, "Am I?"

"You're a dragon!" the elephant rumbled.

"A dragon is a mystical creature of great power," the beast replied in a stilted tone. Again, in the different tone, it added, "Of course, silly!"

"Jing-Wei?" the lion asked.

"And Fai," the beast said in a boy's voice. In Jing-Wei's voice, it continued, "We are here."

"What are you going to do?" the lion asked, glancing up at the gossamer, rainbow-shaded wings of the dragon as it hovered elegantly above them.

"Learn," the boy's voice answered. Jing-Wei's voice continued, "But first we're going to my village and telling your people to stop!"

"Of course," Li Fai agreed. "We will tell your people that the *mamokh* grass and the *kerdveydza* bush are where we store our memories and keep our connection to the planet. They must stop rooting them up and destroying them, so that we can remember that we are at peace."

"I never knew that!" Jing-Wei's voice exclaimed. "I'm sorry that we took away your memory."

"We could not tell you—we'd lost the grass and the bushes that kept those memories," Li Fai replied.

"So we will tell the villagers and they will stop," Jing-Wei said.

"With your permission," Li Fai said, the great dragon head bowing to the animals beneath it.

"How can we stop you?" the elephant wondered.

"Words work," Jing-Wei's voice said, with a hint of her usual irritation.

"Can I come along?" the eagle asked.

"Only if you can keep up!" Jing-Wei's voice cried. And the dragon was gone, darting out of the cave of miracles. Its luminescent body lit the night sky and it gave a strange cry—a chorus of two voices echoing perfect joy.

We have to eat soon! Jing-Wei thought, even as the ground disappeared beneath them. *Oh, my wings! They're going to start complaining any moment now!*

The demon Li Fai snorted in amusement but said nothing. Together, the two beings in a dragon's body raced the moons to the village of the small bird.

THE DRAGONS

Theodora Goss

One day, the dragons came.

It was on a Tuesday, she remembers. It was
the sort of thing that would happen on a Tuesday,
which is an unsatisfying sort of day,
not the beginning of the week, nor the middle,
without the anticipation of a Thursday.
A troublesome sort of day.

And there they were, sitting on the back porch railing,
where she had hung boxes for geraniums
that summer. But now, since it was November,
there were no geraniums—only dragons, quite small,
the size of a Pomeranian or Toy Poodle,
but of course with scales, which shone with a dim sheen
in the gray light of a rainy Tuesday morning.
Seven of them—green, blue, red, orange, another orange,
a sort of purple, and a white one that seemed smaller
than the others, the runt of the litter. It shone opalescent.
They were damp with rain, and obviously

too young to be out on their own. Had someone abandoned them,
the way people sometimes leave dogs at the edge of the woods?
Or were they feral, born to a wild mother?

She couldn't just leave them there. As soon as they saw her,
the white one started a piteous baby roaring
and the green one joined in, showing the interior
of its pink mouth, like a geranium with teeth.
But when she opened the porch door, they just sat there,
staring at her with iridescent eyes.
What did dragons eat? She had no idea,
so she put half of last night's Chinese takeout
in a bowl outside the porch door.
The rest she put into another bowl, inside
the open door, then went to get ready for work.
By the time she returned, in her suit and sensible pumps,
they were curled up on the sofa, already asleep,
except for the blue one, which hissed at her, not in anger,
she thought, but simply to let her know it was there.
The bowls were empty.

They continued to be trouble.
The orange one burned a hole in the carpet, or was it
the other orange one? They were so similar,
initially she could not tell them apart.
But eventually she learned to distinguish them
by their quirks and personalities—
one was just playful, the other more mischievous.
She gave them all names: Hyacinth (that was the purple),
Orlando, Alexander (after her brother,
who was a software designer in San Francisco
and sent her pictures at Christmas of his apartment

decorated with plastic poinsettia).
Ruby (a little too obvious, but it suited her),
Dolores and Delilah (the orange ones),
and little Cordelia, the runt, who affectionately
clawed apart her favorite afghan
while trying to climb the armchair into her lap.
She tried calling the ASPCA
and the local veterinary clinics, but no one was missing
a clutch of dragons. The receptionist at one clinic
thought she meant geckos.
What in the world was she supposed to do with them?
The nearest shelter said it had no facilities
for dragons, sounding a little incredulous
over the phone. Meanwhile, they scratched the furniture,
got tangled in the hangers while creating
a nest in her closet of scarves and panty hose.
She could not leave out a pair of earrings, or coins
in a jar for laundry and parking—anything shiny.
They would begin to hoard it, hissing at her
when she approached to take back her watch or car keys.
Her bills for Chinese takeout
were astronomical.

She took sick leave when Orlando and Alexander
both caught pneumonia and had to be nursed back to health.
(She finally found a vet who would treat dragons,
a younger guy trying to establish a practice.)
"I'm not sure about dosage," he said, as he gave her
a prescription for antibiotics. "About the same
as for a golden retriever? But it's just a guess.
Aren't they getting a little big, for a place
of this size?" And she had to admit he was right.

Now when Ruby curled up next to her
as she watched *Casablanca,* the red dragon
took up half the sofa. Her sort-of-boyfriend,
Paul, who worked in the tax and bankruptcy group,
started complaining. She understood his perspective—
the dragons had never liked him. Hyacinth
always bellowed when he came over, Delilah
peed on his baseball cap, and Dolores chewed
a corner of his briefcase. "They're dragons," he told her.
"They're dangerous—what if they bite someone? You'd have
a lawsuit on your hands. I really don't know
why you keep them around."
Probably because they were warm at night,
piled on her bed, with Cordelia's silky muzzle
tucked under her chin. Whenever she got home
after a long day at the office, they greeted her,
trilling in unison. They never told her
that her hairstyle didn't fit the shape of her face,
or she really should lose a few pounds, unlike her mother.
They never asked her to file incorporation
documents yesterday, or talked to her
for an hour about baseball while she was trying to listen
to NPR. Anyway, who would take them,
all seven of them? Dragons don't make good pets,
and she hated the thought of separating them.
They needed each other.

Finally, she moved to a lighthouse in New England.
She saw the advertisement—*Lighthouse keeper*
wanted. Must be willing to live on an island
off the coast of Maine, near Portland. Competitive salary.

The ferry comes twice a week. She can take it to Portland
if she wants to, but it brings everything she needs,
from light bulbs to chocolate chip cookies to art supplies.
Sometimes she goes, just to get Chinese takeout.
The dragons have learned to fish and fend for themselves.
She watches them flying up in the sky like kites
when she goes on her morning walk, collecting shells
and bits of seaglass. Mostly they stay outdoors,
but Cordelia still sleeps in the bed beside her at night,
stretched out on the blanket. She has not grown much larger
than a Great Dane, although Alexander is now
the size of a Volkswagen Beetle. On sunny mornings
she finds them lying on the rocky shore, like seals,
shining in the sunlight. On rainy days, there's a cave
on the other side of the island, although Dolores
curls up in the lighthouse itself, around the beacon.
On stormy nights, she's seen them guide a ship
to shore, which seems an unusual behavior, but dolphins
do it, so why not dragons?
She's started painting again, the way she used to
when she was a teenager, before her father
told her to focus on something more practical.
Her canvases sell in a gallery and on her website.
Mostly, she paints the dragons—rolling around
in the waves, lying on the shore, cavorting above
in intricate arabesques, as if they knew
she was sketching below, showing off for her.

She doesn't make as much money
as she did at the law firm. But then, on the other hand,
she has dragons.

DRAGON SLAYER

Michael Swanwick

Michael Swanwick (michaelswanwick.com) has received a Hugo Award for fiction in an unprecedented five out of six consecutive years and has been honored with the Nebula, Theodore Sturgeon, and World Fantasy awards. He has also lost more of those awards than any other writer in the history of the field. He has written ten novels, more than one hundred fifty stories, and countless works of flash fiction. His most recent works include *The Iron Dragon's Mother*, which completes a trilogy of stand-alone fantasies begun twenty-six years earlier with *The Iron Dragon's Daughter*, and a collaborative novel, *The City Under the Stars*, co-written with Gardner Dozois and finished shortly after his old friend's death. Swanwick's share of the novel is dedicated to him. Swanwick lives in Philadelphia with his wife, Marianne Porter.

Every road and open doorway is a constant danger to a man of wandering disposition. Olav had stood on the threshold of his cottage one spring morning and the road had looked so fine that he couldn't resist setting foot on it, and the next thing he knew, it had carried him to the sea. There he chanced upon a merchant ship in need of a new hand. He learned the sailoring trade, fought pirates, killed a kraken, grew a beard, pierced an ear, and one memorable night won a handful of rubies at a single turn of the cards and lost them all to a barmaid who doped his ale. Two years later, he was shipwrecked off Thule and briefly married to a witch-woman who had blackwork tattoos on her face and had filed her teeth to points.

The marriage did not last, however. One day, Olav returned from the hunt with a red hart slung over his shoulders and found his wife coupling with a demon she had summoned up from one of the seven hells that lie at the center of the world. He slew them both, threw the fire pot onto the thatched roof of the witch's hut, and left his memories burning to his back.

So it was that, having nothing better to do, Olav set out on foot to see what lay to the south. Always there was something interesting just a little farther down the road. Always there was good reason not to stay.

To the south it was summer. It seemed to be always summer there. Like water, he flowed downhill, taking up whatever work came to hand, staying with it long enough to fill his pockets, and then proceeding onward, ever onward. He chopped wood, built walls, twisted cord into rope, and rode as a guard in a small caravan traveling across the desert, which one night was attacked by brigands who set about killing everyone, women and slaves included. He accounted for five of their number before realizing there was nobody left to defend save for one brown-skinned merchant's son and so scooped him up, sat him on the horse behind himself, and escaped.

Olav came away from that adventure with an excellent horse, a serviceable bedroll, a saddle that had seen better days, and the merchant boy for a servant.

The caravan trail led at last to a standing stone atop a high barren ridge, at the foot of which were low scrub forests and beyond them, at the horizon, a line of blue that might be ocean. The stone was carved with runes that made no sense to Olav. But Nahal, his boy, spoke up. "It says all the land beyond belongs to the free port of Kheshem." He pointed. "It's there, where the Endless Mountains touch the sea. The harbor is small but the mountains go inland many hundred *baridi*, so all trade must pass through it."

"You can read these squiggles, then?"

"My . . . I was taught how."

"What else does it say?"

"That the Khesh of Kheshem welcomes all honest men. But evil travelers will be tortured and put to death."

Olav laughed. "Well, I guess we'll just have to take our chances."

They rode down toward the sea. Kheshem lay nowhere in sight, but there was the tang of salt marshes in the air when they made camp. Nahal gathered wood and built a fire while Olav quested out into the twilight and returned with a brace of hares. He sparked the fire to life using a chunk of flint from his pouch and the hilt of his knife, then gave the tool to the boy to dress and section the meat and prepare spits. Finally, he took back the knife and cut them a pair of quarterstaffs. "Have you had weapons training?" he asked.

"Some."

"Then come at me."

Nahal seized the staff with both hands together and swung. Olav easily sidestepped the blow and rapped the boy's knuckles, making him drop his weapon. Smiling, he said, "You know nothing. So we'll start by working on your stance."

By the time the fire had died down to coals and they could begin cooking, the two had worked up a sweat.

Later, after they had eaten, Olav said, "Tell me, boy. What do you think of thieves?"

"When I am grown, I will kill them all!" Nahal's scowl was so fierce that Olav had to turn away to keep from laughing. "They will beg for mercy and I will show them the mercy they gave my family!"

"Hmm. That's too bad. Because we're low on coin and there's no guarantee that I'll be able to find honest work in Kheshem." Olav did not add that no man is more than three meals away from brigandage—the boy would someday discover that on his own—nor that it had been sheer chance that he had come upon the hares and great good fortune that the stones he threw at their heads had found their marks.

"You could sell Bastard."

"But then how would we travel?"

Nahal said nothing.

"I put the question to you because the greatest danger to a thief is treachery. If you're going to tell anyone about my activities, then I'll drop you off at the city gate to make your own way in life, and practice my thievery elsewhere. But if you wish to stay with me, you'll need to keep silent."

Sullenly, Nahal said, "I'll do what I have to in order to survive."

"So do we all, boy. So do we all."

At night, they shared the bedroll, fully clothed save for their boots. As he was drifting off to sleep, Olav felt the boy's chest moving with suppressed sobs. He pretended not to notice.

With sleep came dreams: Olav and Nahal were sitting by a campfire at the verge of a dark and moonless wood. There came a crackling noise in the underbrush. "Who's there?" Nahal cried in a panicky voice. Olav felt not particularly concerned because he had a sword and knew how to use it better than most.

Mocking laughter echoed through the forest—deep as oak, hard as steel, supple as a stream bouncing down a rocky mountainside. It was like nothing Olav had ever heard before, and it filled him with supernatural dread. Bastard, his steed, whinnied in terror, and would have bolted if he hadn't been hitched to a tree.

Olav seized a brand from the fire and was on his feet. "Show yourself!" he cried.

"Ahhhh, Olav," rasped an inhuman voice. "Thinkst thou I am afraid of thy little man-spark? I, who have walked unshod in the furnaces of the earth?"

If Olav had been blinded by the murky darkness of the forest before, he was doubly so now, with the flaming brand held before him. Nor, with the stench of smoke rising from the brand and that of a hundred campfires permeating his clothing, was his sense of smell of any use. But his hearing was still good, and he thought he knew roughly from whence the voice came.

"If you're not afraid of me," he growled, "then why are you hiding?"

"Beware such questions," said the voice in the darkness. "For now I *come!*"

With a howl, the creature charged. And in that same instant, Olav flung the brand into the brush before him. The weather had been dry, and the brush went up in a flash of flame.

Swiftly, then, Olav leaped atop Bastard, pulling Nahal up after him. With a sweep of his knife, he cut the reins. His horse reared up and then ran, fleet as the wind, with the fire to his back. Though it left him without gear, Olav abandoned his camp to the spreading flames without a second thought. For, as Bastard was rearing up in the air, he had felt grasping claws trying to seize his leg, and as they leaped away, he glanced back to see a misshapen form, black against the fire, still striving to reach him.

He rode through the night, with all the world burning behind him, as fast and furious as ever he could, and awoke in the morning beside the cold campfire, aching and sore.

The port of Kheshem curved about its harbor and sprawled up the mountain slopes, a labyrinth of golden-roofed temples and high, slender, ivory-tiled towers intermingled with low mud-and-wattle tenements, the walled pleasure gardens of the wealthy, sturdy stone warehouses, public squares, guildhalls, and the occasional shipyard, lime kiln, or knackery, all of it laced together by wide, granite-slabbed avenues and narrow alleys that smelled of spices and tar and camel dung. On his first day in the city, Olav took a great chance and played the cutpurse in a crowd that had gathered, ironically enough, to watch the public evisceration and beheading of a thief. The day's haul was such that he bought the two of them a rich meal with wine and then a long soak in hot water at the private baths. When Nahal, face slick with grease, fiercely declared himself in no need of such fripperies, Olav lifted him, struggling, into the air and dropped him in the bath. Then, wading in (himself already naked), he stripped the wet clothes off the boy.

Which was how Olav discovered that Nahal was actually Nahala—a girl. Her guardians had chopped her hair short and taught her to swear like a boy in order to protect her from the rough sorts with whom traveling merchants must necessarily deal.

The discovery made no great difference in their relationship. Nahala was every bit as sullen as Nahal had been, and no less industrious. She knew how to cook, mend, clean, and perform all the chores a man needed to do on the road. Olav considered buying cloth and having her make a dress for herself but, for much the same reasons as her guardians before him, decided to leave things be. When she came of age—soon, he imagined—they would deal with such matters. Until then, it was easier to let her remain a boy.

At her insistence, he continued the lessons in weapons use.

Nahala despised her new master. But merchants, however young, must be pragmatists. She knew that there was no good alternative. Few orphaned children survived to adulthood in the city and the common fate of those who did and were female was whoredom, which did not appeal to her. Also, Olav never beat her and only cuffed her with reason; as masters went, he was a good one. So there was that.

Most of all, Nahala was learning to fight, and this, she knew, would be invaluable to her when she was old enough to return to the desert and cleanse it of the vermin who had killed her family.

Sometimes, however, Olav had nightmares and Nahala would have to leave her pallet to shake him awake. Possibly because of those nightmares, he was drinking a lot. But what worried Nahala most was his spending. So one day, instead of wandering the city in order to learn its winds and ways (the higher up, for example, the richer the houses; the lower, the filthier the water), the prices food could be haggled down to, the rates charged by the money changers, and suchlike, she sewed together a bag out of discarded scraps of cloth and headed downhill toward the pebbled strand at the edge of town.

She was halfway to her destination when a ragged boy placed himself in her way, hands on hips, and jeered, "Hey, Stick!"

Nahala fell easily into a balanced stance and slid her hands so that her staff was in a defensive position. "Yah?"

"Seen you around a lot lately, strutting like a rooster. I guess that thing means you think you can fight?"

"Try me."

With a war yell, the boy ran at her, fists wild.

One end of Nahala's staff dipped almost to the ground. She thrust it between the boy's legs, then hopped to the side while simultaneously shoving the upper end forward, as if the staff were a lever.

The boy went facedown in the dust.

When he tried to get up, Nahala rapped one knee with the staff. Then a hand. Then the other knee. They were gentle blows, though she knew from experience how they stung. They would not break any bones. *If you have to fight, fight to kill,* Olav had told her. *Or else just give your enemy a little warning. All that stuff in between only makes your foe meaner.*

"Do you give up?" Nahala asked.

"King's palm," the boy said. Then, "Name's Sliv."

"Nahal."

"Where you goin' with that bag?"

"To the beach to gather pebbles. Wanna come along?"

"I guess."

Which was how Nahala and Sliv became friends of a sort. Not close ones, however, but wary allies.

When Olav returned to their room after a prolonged bout of wenching, Nahala had arranged two handfuls of pebbles in neat rows on the table that, along with a pair of simple but sturdy chairs, were the result of an extra coin's rent a month. When Olav saw them, he said, "What's this?"

"Pretend each pebble is a drachm. This is how many you had on our first day in Kheshem." Nahala swept four back into the bag. "The feast." Another two. "The baths." Six. "The room." One. "A week's feed and stable for Bastard." Two more. "A woman. Wine. Wine. Wine. Another woman." Item by item, the pebbles dwindled, until there were but fourteen. "This is how much remains."

"I could have told you that by looking in my pouch." Amused, Olav slid three more pebbles away. "You forgot tonight's woman. I gave her an extra coin because she . . . Well, anyway, now there are only eleven."

"Rent comes due in three days, both for us and the stable. Plus, we have no food. Nor any work. The old men who sit by the docks and watch the boats say that only smugglers will be risking their ships until the Sea Lords and the Khesh make peace, and smugglers trust no one they're not related to." She swept the last pebbles into the bag. "It's time we left Kheshem."

Olav rubbed his beard. "Yes, well, about that . . . I have been having dreams these past few weeks—nightmares—I'm sure you've noticed. There is something coming for me out of the desert. Something powerful. Something no man wishes to face. It cannot enter the city—too many wizards here, too much power. But if I leave, it will find me. So I must stay. It seems that I have no choice but to resume my career as cutpurse."

At which exact instant, the darkness to one side of the room swirled, lofted upward, spread outward, and gave birth to twin pinpricks of light—a pair of eyes, both hard and unblinking. Stepping out of the shadows, a man in wizard's black robes, with a ruby talisman hung on a chain about his neck, said, "That would be unwise."

Nahala shrieked and fell back against the bed. Olav grabbed at his side for the sword he had removed upon entering the room.

The wizard held up his hand. "Let me tell you what will happen if you do. As you are cutting purse strings, an incense vendor will happen to glance your way. Her shout will begin a hue and cry and though you bolt and fight like a demon, you will be run down and overwhelmed. I have just returned from your execution, a week from now. First you were flogged. Then your arms were broken. Then your abdomen was sliced open and, seizing your intestines—"

"Stop! I have seen enough executions to know what happens." A shrewd look came over Olav's face, though to Nahala's eyes it looked feigned. "But why should I believe your wild story of seeing things that have not yet happened?"

"Tell me this. How did I learn the exact moment you decided to try your hand at thievery again? By bribing the guards to let me interview you while you awaited execution and then walking back in time to your room just now. But I will give you stronger proof than that." The wizard put one hand on Olav's shoulder and with the other clutched his amulet.

They disappeared.

They reappeared.

The magician was unchanged. But Olav's face was ashen and his eyes were wide with horror. He seized a chair with one blind hand and crashed down onto it. "Wine!" he gasped. "There should be some left in the jar by the door."

While Nahala poured, the wizard spoke: "You killed eight men, trying to make your escape. Two of them were of the Harbor Guard and heavily armed."

"I . . . have no memory of that." Olav drank deeply. Then, looking thoughtful, "Still, I regret it. A man will do evil things in the heat of passion. But I could wish to have killed fewer."

"All the deaths have been unmade, as has your execution." The wizard gestured and coins rained down upon the table. "They call me Ushted the Uncanny. I have decided that a more decorous title would be Ushted the Protector. But to achieve that honorific, I need a servant whom I know can kill."

"He acts like a great wizard," Sliv said when Nahala saw him next. "But he's not. Most towns have two or three wizards. Kheshem has dozens

and every one of them is better at it than Ushted. If it weren't for that time-walking stunt of his, he'd be in a small village somewhere selling poisons, love potions, and balms to cure warts." Sliv had wanted to spend the day spying on the blood huts at the edge of town, where menstruating women went to spin and exchange gossip until their bodies were clean again. Somehow he'd conceived the notion that they did so naked. But Nahala had distracted him with the idea of instead exercising Bastard by taking turns riding him as he swam in the otherwise idle harbor. Now they sat dangling their feet from a dock, talking.

As an afterthought, Sliv added, "The balm for warts is a good one, though. I've used it myself."

"How do you know so much about Ushted?" Nahala asked.

"I'm his apprentice. Any other wizard, I'd be set for life. But none of them will take me. I've made the rounds and asked." Sliv spat into the water. "Someday, when I'm grown, I'll cut his throat, chop up his body, and take his amulet. Then everything he owns will be mine."

Nahala wondered, not for the first time, why boys' fantasies were always so violent. But she said only, "Be sure to do it in such a way that no suspicion falls upon you."

Sliv looked at her in surprise, as if his pronouncements had never before been taken seriously—which, she realized, was probably true. Then he said, "If they come after me, I'll just go back to before they do and run away."

Olav, meanwhile, was finding his new life as the wizard's hireling an undemanding one, though it did nothing to assuage his nightmares. At first, he was occasionally summoned, in the twilight hours, to wait motionless in an alleyway off a courtyard for bravos to set upon a wealthy citizen hurrying to get home before nightfall. At which, he would leap out with fierce cries, chasing off most of the assailants and cutting down any who loitered. The victim was always happy to send Ushted the Protector a lavish gift in gratitude for saving his life.

Later, however, as the number of assailants, never great to begin with, dwindled and those who remained grew warier, the game darkened. Olav would be sent to a rich man's mansion to smash in its door and murder its master. Always, just as he was arriving at his target's domicile, Sliv would come running with the news that the man had been shown his own death and agreed to pay generously for it not to happen.

In this manner, for a season, Olav prospered and his benefactor even more. Twice Ushted moved his alembic-filled elaboratory uphill to larger and more splendid quarters. Olav stayed where he was, but frequented a better class of courtesans. All those deaths, both the permanent ones and those that were unmade, seemed to weigh increasingly heavily on him. But he never spoke of them, nor did Nahala ask.

"It's here."

Nahala had set up a slab of wood against the far wall and was practicing her knife-throwing when Olav suddenly spoke. He had been lying on his pallet, staring at the ceiling for hours while the knives flew, landed with a solid *thunk! thunk!*, and then were freed to be carried across the room and thrown again, over and over. The knives were one result of their newfound prosperity and, though they lacked the filigreed decoration Nahala's magpie heart yearned for, they were well-made weapons. They would kill. "What's here? she asked idly.

"My destiny." Olav rolled over then, and went to sleep.

The next day, an earthquake toppled several towers and opened a chasm in the mountainside high above the city. News spread swiftly that something had made lair therein, where it could watch over the roads leading to the city from either direction. From there it sallied down to attack not just caravans but also the wagons bringing food to the city and even lone riders, feeding upon horses, camels, merchants, and farmers with equal ease, and defiling the goods and foodstuffs they brought with flame and smoke.

The flow of food into the city ceased and, though the Khesh ordered the granaries be opened to Kheshem's poorest, prices soared. There were riots. These were easily quelled by the military, but everyone knew there would be more.

A troop of soldiers was sent to deal with the menace and did not return. A hero with perfumed hair and oiled mustachios marched into the cavern, bright sword in hand, and did not emerge. In his wake, an assortment of fools and scoundrels also disappeared, along with the schemes they had assured all would win the day. The citizenry began to wonder why the city's wizards did nothing to counter the beast.

"My proud brothers have power but not force," Ushted said, "and they will not work together." He was talkative by nature. Merchants knew how to handle such men; whenever he came to see Olav, Nahala kept his wine cup filled and her mouth closed. "Against a brute that splinters bones and wagons with equal ease, their subtlety is useless. But I, Olav, have you. Together, we shall do what no others dare and accept no reward for doing so."

Olav had raised his cup to his lips. Now he set it down untasted. Nahala had noticed that he drank lightly, if at all, in his master's presence. "That makes no sense."

"Every despot likes to think he inspires selfless obedience. When I have proved myself to be exactly such a subject, the Khesh will welcome me into his court. And that is an opportunity beyond avarice." Ushted stood. "Sleep well tonight, for in the morning we go up the mountain."

The next day, the wizard walked out of the shadows to report that he had just seen the menace slain only hours into the future. So, sitting astride Bastard, Olav left the city and started up the mountainside. With him went Ushted the Protector, Sliv the apprentice, and Nahala, who had neither title nor any desire for one.

Nahala had woken up feeling strange that day, detached in a manner new to her experience. It was not until she felt a drop of blood trickle down the inside of one leg that she had thought: *Oh.* She was now, she supposed, a woman. It seemed a terribly inconvenient time for it to happen. Quickly, she had torn a strip from the bottom of her sark—it was cut long, so she could grow into it—folded it in the manner her mother had foresightedly taught her, and staunched the bleeding. But the sense of estrangement stayed with her as they walked.

Bastard struggled slowly up the mountain trail, while the others trudged after him. Ushted was uncharacteristically silent. Olav was quiet too, but sullenly so rather than in his usual manner, less like a hero headed for certain victory than one on his way to die. Every now and then, Sliv, who swaggeringly carried Olav's spear slung over one shoulder, threw her a strange look. It was a morning, it seemed, for odd behavior.

Once, when they had lagged far enough behind not to be over-heard, Sliv flared his nostrils and muttered, "What's that smell?"

"It's just the mountain sage in bloom."

"Naw, naw, it's not that. I know that smell . . ." There was a terrible light in his eyes. "I know that smell and it ain't no sage." He pointed an accusatory finger at her. "You're a girl!"

"Woman," Nahala said, trying to invest the word with menace. She had never felt less like fighting. But she took a step backward and angled her staff. "Ease up, Sliv. You and I are friends."

"Girls can't be friends. Girls are only good for one thing."

If you have to fight, fight to kill. Olav had told her that. Nahala's knives were in sheaths strapped on either thigh, but there was no need to draw them. All she had to do was wait for Sliv to lunge at her, aim the tip of her staff at his eye, and lean in hard.

For a moment, the potential for violence crackled in the air between them. Then Sliv spat at her feet and turned away. The others were far ahead, and Nahala, perforce, had to run to catch up.

As the mountain dwindled above them and the sky grew larger, Bastard became increasingly restive and hard to control. When he re-fused to go any farther, Olav alit and tethered him to a tree, saying, "You were wondering why I brought the horse. This is why." It took Nahala a breath to realize that this was directed at her, that he was still teaching her. "The monster is near. We must be ready for it." Turning to Sliv, he said, "Hand me my spear."

Without being told, Nahala untied the shield from Bastard's harness and held it ready to be taken from her.

"Everyone, wait here," Olav said.

"No," said Ushted. "We all proceed. This I have already seen."

Olav shrugged. Again he led, and shortly thereafter, a twist in the trail took them to the mouth of the cavern, their destination. The rock lining it was raw and broken, and scattered on the ground were similar shards, as from an explosion. In a voice louder than Nahala had ever heard emerge from him, Olav shouted: "Abomination! Come forth to meet your doom!"

The creature that flowed forth from the cavern darkness was shaped like a monstrous lizard and taller by half than Olav himself. Its substance was so black it glittered in the sun, looking for all the world like the foul-smelling liquid that bubbled from the ground in the distant desert wastes and defiled any water it touched. Throwing back its head, it opened a mouth lined with teeth like ivory daggers.

In a dulcet, womanly voice, the apparition said, "Ohhhh, Olav. Sweet, sweet love, at last you have come to me! Long have I yearned for this moment. Great indeed will be your torment before you finally die."

Olav's spear sank. Then it rose again. "So it's you. I suspected as much. Well, I killed you once, and if I must, I can kill you again."

"Wait!" Ushted stepped to Olav's side and pressed a lozenge to his lips, murmuring, "Take this. It will give you strength."

Olav swallowed. Then he cocked his arm, ready to throw the spear. Jaw grim and eyes a-glare, he looked the perfect hero. As the firedrake reared up before him, he cried, "Attack—and let the blood fly where it may."

Then he fell flat on his face.

For a breath, no one moved. Then the creature bent its head to Olav's side, sniffing at his body and nudging it like a cat. When Olav did not move, it *screamed*. Its neck spasmed and its tail thrashed, and its taloned legs dug into its own torso. It slammed against the rocky ground, over and over. With enormous violence, it tied itself into a knot, tighter and tighter, until it was as smooth as an egg.

Malodorous black fluid drained away from the egg, flowing back into the cavern shadows, leaving behind a human figure, a woman whose skin was as white as maggot flesh.

The woman's long leather skirt had witch-knots dangling from its hem. Her breasts were bare and three bright stones shone between them, hung from black cords about her neck. When she spoke, Nahala saw that her teeth had been filed to points. Shaking a finger at Ushted, she cried, "You! *What have you done?*"

Both Nahala and Sliv were trembling with fear, for the woman was no less dreadful than the lizard had been. Her hair rose up as if underwater, swaying like a hundred slim eels. Ushted the Protector, however, displayed not the least concern. "I have made your husband useless to you. You want him awake and aware and able to suffer. I can undo his stupor. But if I do not, he will die in his sleep. Painlessly."

The woman's eyes were bright with rage. "Why would you do such a foolish—and for you, fatal—thing?"

"You have three talismans upon you. One grants you passage from the fires at the center of the world to its surface and back again. That one I disdain. The second allows you to fly vast distances, supported by the winds. Tempting, but not to my taste. The third, which allows you to walk in time, however . . ." He drew the amulet from beneath his black robe. "I know you will surrender because I already hold it."

"It is true I can walk in time. Perhaps I will take a stroll to just before you poisoned my husband."

"If you do, I will similarly go back to this morning and Olav will not come to you. Game lost. But you won't—I have been here before, and I know." Producing a small silver knife, Ushted the Protector made a long cut in his palm. Blood welled up. "Here is our deal: I will bring Olav back from the brink of death in exchange for the amulet and your promise that as soon as you are done with him, you will leave and never return." He proffered her the knife, hilt-first.

Disdaining the offer, the witch-woman slid a hand across her sharpened teeth, opening a gash in it. Black ichor oozed out. "I have no interest whatsoever in your city or yourself or, when my vengeance is done, the lands of the living. It is an easy promise to give and easier to keep."

"Then I will descend the mountain a hero."

They clasped hands. Blood and ichor mingled. Then Ushted the Protector crouched by Olav's body and, turning the head away from him, stuck a finger down the warrior's throat.

When Olav was done vomiting, Ushted cleaned his hand with the hem of his robe and, standing, said, "He will come to within the hour. Do with him then as you wish."

The witch hissed in anger and looked upon him with absolute loathing. Nevertheless, she removed one amulet from her neck and held it forth.

Ushted the Protector shook his head. "Give it to the boy." Sliv looked startled. "As you did long, long ago, when I was him."

Nahala looked from Sliv to Ushted and back again, mentally erasing the wizard's beard and imagining the boy's face grown lean with maturity. How could she not have seen before that they were one and the same person?

Avarice burning on his face, Sliv accepted the gem.

Turning a disdainful back on Olav, the witch, and the cavern, Ushted the Protector said, "Follow me, the both of you."

Numb, Nahala did so. Sliv, filled with elation, skipped ahead, and fell behind to hold up his amulet to the sun, and ran to catch up again. The cavern disappeared behind them. "This is mine to keep?" he asked. "For as long as I live?"

"Obviously."

Sliv glanced sidewise at Nahala. "And the girl?"

With a shrug, Ushted the Protector said, "She is yours. Unless, as she did the first time around, she manages to slip away from you on the way down the mountain."

Nahala stumbled over a rock and almost fell. She heard Sliv laugh, and her heart grew cold.

If your enemy has a better weapon than you, take it away from him. That was another thing Olav had said. Moving as swiftly and fluidly as ever she had, Nahala strode forward, stabbed her staff between the wizard and his amulet, and flung it into the air. It flew to her hand. She slung it over her own neck.

With the amulet, Nahala could protect not only herself but her master and weapons instructor as well. Nothing could harm them. They could leave Kheshem behind. If need be, they could cross the desert in perfect safety, with nothing more than Olav's sword to protect them. Clutching the stone, she cried in triumph, "Take me back to this morning!"

Nothing happened.

Ushted smiled urbanely. "The amulet will take you back no further than when you first put it on. Nor do you know how to use it." Extending his hand, he added, "I am aware that Sliv told you I am not a great wizard. But if you honestly doubt I can protect myself, then by all means attempt to throw those knives I see your hand yearning toward."

The butt of a spear struck Ushted hard in the side of the jaw, sending two teeth and a gout of blood into the air. He fell and a sandaled foot trod upon his neck to hold him captive. In a small, puzzled voice, he gasped, "But that's not what happened—"

Sure hands spun the spear about and drove the business end through his rib cage, piercing his heart.

Ushted the Protector, also called the Uncanny, was dead.

The woman who had appeared out of nowhere had precious stones everywhere: on her many rings, on her even more necklaces, on her bangles and bracelets, and set into her cheeks and earlobes. A curved sword hung at her side. The long black spear that she drew back up from the wizard's chest, lethal though it was, looked not half so deadly as did she herself.

This apparition was the most wonderful thing Nahala had ever seen in her life. A heavily embroidered skirt hung down past her knees and was slit on either side almost to her waist, revealing multicolored leggings beneath. A leather vest or breastplate, marvelously crafted with the image of the desert sun, was fretted with amber beads and yellow citrines so that it dazzled the eye. A small leather cap held her braided hair in place. She was strong and stocky and everything that Nahala had ever dreamed of someday becoming.

Her heart went out to this radiant creature. "Who . . . who are you?"

The warrior-woman smiled a stony smile and pulled out from beneath her vest the exact same amulet that Nahala now wore. "Why, don't you know, dear? I'm *you*."

Talking, they walked back up the mountain.
After he recovered from his stunned paralysis, Sliv had, of course, bolted like a marsh rabbit. In a flash, Nahala's knives were in her hands. His back was wide and inviting—and then gone. She hadn't thrown.

"That was wisely done," her older self had said. "Kill no more than you absolutely have to."

"Olav said that to me!"

"Yes, he did."

Now, however, Nahala peered anxiously up the trail. "Shouldn't we be hurrying?"

"Hush." Nahala's future self smiled reassuringly. "We have all the time in the world."

*The fight did not last long. When they came in sight of her, the dragon-*witch was crouched anxiously over Olav's body, watching his pulse quicken. Without challenge or battle cry, the warrior Nahala ran straight at her. When, hearing the rush of footsteps, the witch straightened, Nahala cut through both amulet thongs and her throat with a single slash of her scimitar, so that the hag could neither escape nor call down a curse upon them. With a gesture, however, the witch-woman summoned her dark, fluid substance back to herself.

She was midway through changing back into her lizard form when Nahala's spear thrust into her heart.

The dragon fell like a great black wave, smashing foulness everywhere. At her demise, the cavern collapsed in on itself, burying both her and her two remaining amulets under enough stone to build a new city with.

The warrior Nahala threw back her head and ululated in triumph.

Nahala, watching it all and shivering with joy, knew: *That's me. That's who I'll grow up to be!*

When it was over, both Nahalas turned toward Olav, lying motionless on the ground. His skin was pale but his breathing steady. It was obvious he would recover.

"Look at him!" said the warrior Nahala, and there was a fondness to her expression. "Oh, he is lovely in his youth, with his beard so black and his limbs so strong. Do you not agree?"

Young Nahala turned toward Olav and, to her amazement, heard herself say, "Yes, he is. Oh, he is indeed."

"Just be sure, when he wakes up, to let him think he did the deed himself. You know what a child he can be." At which words, the older woman touched her amulet and faded back into the neverwhere of times to come.

This is the tale of Olav the Merchant, known also as the Dragon Slayer. For many years, he and his wife guided caravans across the desert. On occasion they encountered brigands, whom they slew without mercy. They had many children. In time, he became rich, retired to a villa near the sea, grew fat, and died old. May such great good fortune come to us all!

CAMOUFLAGE

Patricia A. McKillip

Patricia A. McKillip (patriciamckillip.com) has written many fantasy novels over many years, among them *The Forgotten Beasts of Eld*, the Riddle-Master trilogy, and, most recently, *Kingfisher*. She has won World Fantasy and Mythopoeic awards for her work. Her short story collections include *Wonders of the Invisible World*, *Harrowing the Dragon,* and *Dreams of Distant Shores*. She lives in a small town on the Oregon coast with her husband, the poet David Lunde.

Old Professor Seeley was droning again as he darted bee-like among his students, dropping exams on their desks: papers on some, oddments or more recognizable objects on others. It was his last year before retirement, Will remembered, stifling a yawn as he watched the ancient wizard turn and stop, stop and start again as if in some forgotten dance around the students and the aisles. Occasionally his mustachios, long and white as sea-lion tusks, puffed with his breathy humming. He had made his way two or three times to the desks before and behind Will, pulling items out of his pockets, dragging others out of his sleeves. But so far, he had danced away from Will, after dropping a paper, a pair of sunglasses, a flower, a palm-sized harp, a party hat under the bemused gazes of others.

"There," he announced finally, and Will's head came up abruptly, the urge to nap forgotten.

What about me? he thought, appalled at the idea that he might have to take the History of Ancient Sorcery class all over again. *What did I do wrong? What did I not do?* he wondered frantically. It was mostly just history, very little actual experience with hoary spells; like most history, it was neither memorable nor particularly useful, especially not to the Magical Arts degree.

"Professor Seeley?"

"Look again, Mr. Fletcher," he heard clearly within the language of bees the professor had returned to, buzzing behind his nose again as he wandered back to his desk.

Will glanced down at his own empty desktop. And there it was, coming clear against the pale wood: a small spiraling hillock of dark stone, looking very much like a lump of petrified dung except for the odd, colorful glitter across its surface.

He stared at it, reluctant to touch it. Finally, he prodded it gingerly with one finger. He heard half-stifled snorts of laughter around him.

"Might there be a problem, Mr. Fletcher?"

"No," he said, and sighed. It was his own final year as well, the seventh of seven, and midway through what was called "the Winnowing" by the masters and "the Hell-Harrow" by the students. Already, three of his closest friends had vanished in that final year, culled by the mercilessly constant testing.

Even Laurel. There one night and gone the next. He contemplated her glumly in memory: she of the wild gold-green hair, and the long, long bones, her fingers like new, tender twigs that seemed to break into blossom when she touched him. Even she.

Well, he thought, gazing at the bleak little pile on his desk with something like a stirring of interest. *I can go and find her if I get kicked out of here.*

A blue, wrinkled, bloodshot eye opened in the stone. "Really, Mr. Fletcher," he heard in his head as his bones melted and tried to pour him under his desk. "Don't give up so easily. Anyway, nobody likes being a consolation prize."

He straightened himself, his mouth tight, holding back a protest. It was fair, he conceded, that voice invading his head. Professor Seeley would be aware of the entire class throughout the test period, in case they got lost, or into trouble, or ran off in despair.

The eye in the stone closed; the professor's public voice returned. "By now you are all familiar with the seventh year tests. Some of you will find yourselves in unexpected places; others will remain here. There is no advantage to those with tests on paper. Much of the past exists in written form these days; it is no less difficult. Just remember that you are facing the burgeoning early elements of magic and sorcery, some of which you may not recognize. Do your best to see and define what you have been given. Think about the words you would use to define what I've given you. Remember: always, always the language is the magic. And take comfort in this: in the long history of this school, no one has ever died taking a test."

"Cold comfort," Will muttered.

And then he was out, who knew where, standing among trees and light and a long hillside of meadow grass, the wind roaring like a dragon around him.

"My stone—" he said on a hiccup of panic, turning circles around himself, searching the grass. It was nowhere, his test; he had forgotten it, left it behind; he had already failed.

A slit in the air opened above his feet; the stone spilled out of it, thumped on his shoe. He gazed down at it, both relieved and sorry to see it. No eye opened to glower at him. The wildly waving grass blades blowing back and forth across the stone loosed jewels of light, then doused them in shadow, flowing and vanishing in a seemingly endless cycle. Mesmerized, he bent over it. The glittering melted completely away under his shadow, left only very ancient dung.

Reluctantly, he bent and picked it up. A memory of the dry, humorless voice of one of his early teachers surfaced in his head: *To have power over a thing, name it. To name a thing, know it. To know a thing: become it.*

"Shit," said Will, which pretty much summed things up.

All color left the sky. Snow began to fall.

Sydney heard Gauda sing the camo-dragons out of the sky before the storm broke and they turned themselves into snowflakes.

Her voice meant food. It meant sleep. It meant morning, wake, move. It meant attack. Begin. End. They had heard it since they were tiny. Gauda had grown up with them; they had been children together. The camo-dragons would have followed her voice anywhere.

So would Sydney, the first time she heard Gauda sing. Almost anywhere, anyway. Exactly where Gauda kept that voice, Sydney could not fathom, the girl being otherwise small-boned, slender, with a habitually absent look about her young, round face from listening for dragons. She had begun to sing before she learned to speak. For her, the dragons showed themselves, recognizing, even before she knew, what she was born to be, even before she could say the words: dragon-singer.

Her voice, sometimes deep and lovely, at other moments soaring outrageously only to slow suddenly, soothingly into a tranquil lullaby, held the camos in thrall, told them what to do. *Come to me,* she said now. *Come out of the winds, the clouds. Come and be trees.*

Sydney watched them settle among the branches. The trees had great, strong, feathery, deep green boughs that swayed in the harsh winds as easily, as gracefully as kelp in the flow of the tide. As the camos swooped down and clung to the trees, they shed their misty, cloudy lines to mirror the massive, fringed limbs, the colors of trunk and needle, until they themselves became the windblown, soughing giants. Gauda could recognize the dragons instantly. Sydney, looking carefully, constantly lost the boundaries where tree stopped and camouflage began. They had grown very quickly, she knew: from a sweet handful of dragon into a small aircraft of camo. It seemed impossible that a winged plane parking itself up a tree should be so difficult to spot.

"All home?" she asked Gauda. They had put together a mixed jumble of language: something Latinate mixed with various local expressions, along with a few well-traveled gestures and slang phrases of merchants and traders.

Gauda nodded no, still singing. In her culture, a nod was a no. She held up one finger, indicating the missing one. Then the finger rose high, pointing at the sky, whose vague blur of color was fading rapidly beneath a cloud. She caught the brief glimpse of a great, frosty eye before it dropped among the branches and became a pinecone. Gauda shook her head then: *All home.*

Under the fading daylight, enormous fires had turned the stark peaks, snowy ledges, and distant slopes into a field of fallen stars. Shadows rapidly melting into dusk moved endlessly through the flickering light: a city on foot, the numbers incalculable on two feet or four. Soldiers and beasts of various kinds hewed and hauled what seemed entire forests; others shoved the wood onto the fires. Huge milling crowds circled the fires like the rings of exploded moons and planets. Beyond the forest, within which entire herds were spitted and roasted, a chasm of black cut through the mountains, marking the human boundary. On the far side of the chasm, the storm flowing across it had dropped snow endlessly onto empty crags and slopes.

Within the grove of camo and tree, there was no fire. Gauda and Sydney were both covered head to foot in thick, furry cloaks gleaming with animals' claws. Sydney was a mage; Gauda was magical in unpredictable ways. Between them they knew a dozen different ways to produce fire. But fire was a complex language to the dragons, and Gauda was singing them to sleep now. Before midnight, she would rouse them again, send them to feed among the leftovers fallen, along with smoldering spits, into the embers of the massive fires.

She held up her finger again, this time to her lips, which were smiling. "All asleep," she said softly.

And then they weren't, head after head untucking from wing, wings uncoiling, claws causing the huge trees to shudder as they stretched, searched, eyes appearing and disappearing, colored like cloud, then tree bark, then gold. A sudden flame from one of the camos, like a brief question, flared in its mouth, reflected in its eye, and directed human attention to something in the dusk beyond them.

A man stood in the distance down the sloping meadow, riveted and staring at what he should not have been able to see. The camo-dragons, all awake now, stared motionlessly back at him. He seemed to have drawn the storm over their heads. Snow began to fall, most likely caused, Sydney thought, by the way he was dressed. At that altitude, in that harsh, blanched season, he wore khakis and a short-sleeved shirt.

Startled, Gauda reverted to her own language.

"Whathu?" she said, or maybe, "Farlu?" The words were muffled behind her hands. The dragons shifted, rousing at her uncertainty, her tension. The young man, his wide eyes flicking incredulously from Gauda to the camos to Gauda again, took a step backward and sat down abruptly in a snowdrift.

Sydney, reading his mind without compunction, gave a sudden laugh.

"Tell them there's nothing for us to fear," she said to Gauda, adding a gesture: opening her hand, tossing fear away, making light of it. Tension, a palpable danger, melted out of the girl and, as quickly, out of the dragons. She hummed gently, soothingly, and they settled their claws, refolded their wings, melting again into tree.

Sydney walked down the slope to the stranger, held out a hand, and hauled him out of the drift. He was trembling badly, and his eyes, still wide, were full of dragons.

"Are you ever a long way from home," Sydney marveled. His eyes came back to her, seeing her a little more clearly, and with sudden hope.

"Are you taking the final for one of Dr. Seeley's classes, too?"

"No," she said briskly. "I'm studying the camo-dragons. I work for the War Department."

He almost sat down again; she gripped him, held him upright. "Where are we?" he pleaded.

"Oh, about twenty-two centuries ago. What on earth kind of class is Dr. Seeley teaching these days?"

"History of Ancient Sorcery." His voice had all but disappeared. "Please. Where are we?"

"Crossing the Alps. Along with give or take fifty thousand men who speak a dozen different languages, thirty-seven elephants—no, twenty-nine now; they don't like the cold either—five camos, two mages or four, depending on who's talking, and one of the greatest generals in history. Make that three mages. You see them better than I do."

"See what?" he said faintly.

"The dragons."

He was silent, staring at the trees again. "They flicker in and out . . . I think I'll just flunk the test and go home. I never much liked history anyway."

"Don't be afraid. As Dr. Seeley says, no one ever died taking one of his tests." She felt his surprise and smiled. "I've looked into his methods. The War Department keeps track of everything that could possibly be useful. And it's very interested in camo." She tugged at him; he still seemed frozen in place. "Come on. Gauda has ways of kindling a fire that won't disturb the dragons. You don't have to fear them. They're part poda, and very intelligent."

He took a step finally, and spoke. "Poda?"

"Cephalopoda." His silence exuded a blank, a question mark; she answered it, preparing now for a startled flock of question marks. "Octopus."

The war-mage had left Will speechless again: he kept looking for huge eyes and bulbous bodies, long, long legs—or were they arms?—dangling down between the trees boughs. Nothing but dragons and trees, his eyes told him. The dragons looked big enough to carry him aloft on their backs. He studied their shifting shapes, picked out their silhouettes against the true trees, whose boughs rode the wind, gesturing, flowing, conducting invisible orchestras. The camo-dragons were the calm within the storm. They only rippled now and then, mostly at the edges, as though stirred by a gentle flow of water. Tide, he thought incredulously, and made a noise the woman interpreted as a question.

"It's not a concept," she said, "intuitively grasped." Her hand on his elbow was a concept he did understand and was grateful for: somehow she was sharing the warmth of the bulky, furry coat with him, as though she had opened it up and invited him in. Even his nose was beginning to thaw. "The octos seem to see with their skin; they camouflage themselves in the ocean as easily as we breathe. That's what we're studying here in the camo-dragons as well."

"The War Department."

"Of course. Methods of camouflage. It's a no-brainer, really. Instant invisibility for human combatants. Except, of course, for the weapons they carry. Others are working on that."

He glanced at her amazed, his eyes squinting against the merciless wind. She looked a few scant years older than he, and at the same time centuries older, unconflicted by the thought of inventing new and different ways to kill. Her lean face was nicely boned, her dark hair whitened only by snow, her smile easy, fearless, and somehow expecting the ridiculous. He wondered, uneasily, exactly how powerful she might be.

"You don't want to know," she said, breaking every rule he had been painstakingly taught about trespassing into someone else's thoughts. She smiled, again with that faint quirk of mockery. "As far as manners go, consider who I work for."

Somewhere ahead in the swirling snowflakes, an elephant trumpeted.

"War elephants," the mage said, and left him floundering again in the idea that even after twenty-two centuries, generals still looked to nature to inspire the nature of war.

"Do you have a name?" he asked. They had nearly reached the grove; a low, gentle fire that had come out of nowhere brushed the massive trunks with warmth.

The mage flashed her amused smile. "Take it."

486

"It's aggressive and patronizing to go into someone's mind without asking. That's what we're taught. Not to mention dangerous."

"Sydney."

"What?"

"That's my name. Sydney Culver. Graduate of the Hannibal Military Academy's Magical Arts of War division. And you? Since we're asking?"

"Will Fletcher. On my final year at Hallowgrove University, majoring in magical arts."

"Ah. What's that year called? Winnowing?"

"Hell-Harrow." He sighed. "I might actually pass if I survive this."

The other mage, ringed by dragons, was still humming sweetly to the sleeping beasts. Will's own eyes grew heavy as he gazed at her fire-lit profile. He would have bet that everything within range of that lullaby, including generals, war-elephants, and earthworms, would be sleeping by now.

"This is Gauda," the mage Sydney said, and went on to say a few incomprehensible things with her voice and her hands. Gauda smiled at him briefly, and with interest, before her attention went back to the dragons. Barely a teenager, Will thought, amazed, with all that calm and that power. She glanced again at him curiously; he smiled and she said something in her unfathomable language to Sydney.

"She thinks your taste in clothes is really weird."

"She did not say *weird*. *Weird* wasn't even invented back then. Now. Whenever we are." He paused, blinking up at a pinecone among the needles with a fiery eyeball wavering in and out of it, churning with color and fixed upon him. "All right," he conceded. "But khakis in a snowstorm don't come anywhere close to the weirdness that must have gone on to make a baby camo-dragon."

She tilted her head, considering the matter. "It helps to know something about the anatomy of octos and dragons."

He started to do some considering himself, and then decided not to. "I don't think—"

"Sea-dragons used to be common in most of the oceans. We have evidence that they could mate with fire-dragons, most successfully, according to lore, during thunderstorms. Then the oceanic temperatures began to change, and the sea-dragons died out, except in the warmest waters. Octos, however, thrive in any temperature and can grow over thirty feet long. If a sea-dragon with fire-kindling abilities and a large enough octo meet at the perfect time, there's nothing to stop the octo from passing its sperm to anything it wants, including sea-dragons, fire-dragons, and even, if some local artwork and tales are any more than prurient—"

"No. Really? Humans?"

She shrugged. "It's being looked into. Can the octo's camouflage ability be passed to humans? What's impossible, these days?"

"Cell phone service in the past?"

Her mouth slid upward into a wry slant. "That's being looked into, too."

Gauda said something, gesturing at the trees. The last open eye had vanished; the camos were dreaming, their outlines flowing and rippling peacefully, melting in and out of the branches. The wind shifted; Will got a face full of smoke and the smell of hot, charred meat. He made a sound. Gauda, adept at interpreting odd noises and gestures, murmured something at the trees, then vanished.

"Where did she go?"

"To fetch us some supper." Sydney took off her cloak then, and draped it over Will's shoulders. He smelled the musty fur, felt the little claws on his bare arms, cool and prickly. He hoped the small, faceless beasts would remember that this was not his fault. His fingers, warming finally, felt the stone locked in his grip; he dropped it into a furry pocket inside the cloak. "Don't worry," Sydney added, "I won't be gone long."

"You're leaving me alone with the dragons?" he said, appalled.

"What are you worried about? You're almost a mage. Do some almost magic if they scare you."

"But—where are you going?"

"To find us a drink. I know where the commanders keep their wine."

She vanished. Will, surrounded by dreaming dragons, wondered if he would ever see the future again.

The attacking army came out of the gorge just as Sydney passed the elephants.

She heard the clamor and roar in the snow-streaked dusk beyond one of the distant, enormous fires. The attackers must have made paths up the steep gorge, she guessed, the one thought to be too deep and dangerous for thousands on foot, along with horses, elephants, and supply wagons. A strange army invading that part of the mountains without permission, treaties, or gifts, and leaving ravaged forests and charred bones behind, must have annoyed the locals, who, it sounded like, were out for blood.

The war-elephants woke to the familiar sound and blared back at it. Their keepers, who ate and slept in the elephant pavilion, came running to free the beasts and arm themselves. Various musical instruments sounded alarms, sang orders, beat the rhythms of battle. Suddenly there were armed men everywhere, drawing swords, fitting arrows to bows, mounting horses and shouting commands, shields and armor flaring, vanishing constantly as the warriors moved in and out of the strange twilight of fire and snowfall and fading light.

Sydney, remembering the young man innocently taking his final exam, wondered what exactly his professor was using for a brain.

When the trumpeting elephants charged out of the pavilion and into the huge, twin waves of armed men, one wave marginally paler and hairier than the other, that crashed together where Sydney had been standing, she was already back in the grove of camo-trees.

She nearly bumped into Gauda, who was staring, wide-eyed, up into their branches. Sydney glanced around for Will, then closed her eyes, ruthlessly searching for his rather glum and unappealing mind.

She opened her eyes after a moment, wondering if Professor Seeley had actually come to his senses and rescued his student. There seemed no sign of him. Gauda said something, then repeated it with a gathering tension in her voice, before she reached out, caught Sydney's arm, and said the same incomprehensible thing.

"I can't understand you," Sydney reminded her in the language they more or less shared.

Gauda pointed upward at the camos, then held out her spread fingers. Four, they said to Sydney, who gazed at them incomprehensively a moment, before her own eyes widened in horror.

"Four," she said faintly.

"Four," Gauda echoed, shaking her head, then added her thumb to the spread. "Five camo-dragons. I have five dragons. There are four."

Sydney tried to imagine the morose young man actually climbing a tree and pulling himself onto a dragon's back. "No," she said flatly. Not even a clash of armies on top of an alp in the twilight could have terrified him more than a camo-dragon rousing at the sound.

Gauda spread both hands wide in an ancient gesture probably older than language: *Then what? Then where?*

A dragon spoke, a streak of gold fire, just as the battle spilled across the crest of the meadow, harsh shouts, clashing metal, elephants and humans trumpeting together under the smoky blur of huge, hand-carried torches. Dark wings spilled open; Gauda sang suddenly, fierce, searing phrases that Sydney had never heard before. A battle cry. They were war-dragons after all, and Gauda had been trained to battle. The camos took to the air, then landed in the snow, becoming white shadows glowing faintly with inner fire. Gauda said something incomprehensible again to Sydney, who understood it just fine.

"I'm coming, too," she said promptly, and clambered onto the huge, warm, leathery back behind Gauda. Camos in battle: that was, after all, why she was there. "The War Department will love this."

Gauda sang again. Wings of snow and dusk caught wind and rose, as the battling armies flowed down toward them, trampling a bloody swath into the snow. The camos took on hues of fire and shadow as

490

Gauda guided them uphill. Her fighting voice, strong, fearless, and lovely, broke through the cacophony of battle, startling the attackers, who saw at most a stream of gold fire, nothing of dragons or the invisible mages. Someone sent a stray arrow in their direction, causing a furious answering billow of flame from the camos, which melted snow into a flow of gold down the slope, tossing warriors off their feet, carrying them off in an avalanche of dragon-fire and snow.

"They don't discriminate," Sydney breathed, "between armies. Neither do the elephants," she added, watching one wading into battle that suddenly reared at a misaimed lick of camo-fire, throwing its rider and trumpeting furiously before its massive forefeet came down on the rider, as well as a couple of warriors heaving their swords at one another. Their screams were lost in the tumult. Gauda shook her head absently, agreeing with whatever Sydney was saying; her voice, true as beaten metal, did not lose a note in the mayhem. "But," Sydney answered herself, remembering where and when she came from, "it's not dragons we'll be using as camo."

She was silent again, hearing a change of tone in Gauda's voice. Fire did not discriminate between armies; neither did dark. But the camos, instead of spilling their gold at anything that moved, seemed suddenly better at hitting the right army. They heard something more precise in Gauda's singing, Sydney guessed. The camos stopped drifting, flew more closely together, and waited, maybe, for a certain phrase from Gauda. They had all been raised together, and Gauda must have learned their language along with her own as they grew.

She mulled over the complexity of it all, wondering how to translate the ancient camos, the dragon-singer Gauda, and opposing armies to the advantage of a War Department in the very far future.

The answer appeared with stunning ease and startling clarity in a splash of dragon-fire: the student-mage, Will Fletcher, on the back of the missing camo, flying toward the sound of Gauda's voice.

It was the last thing he intended to do. It wasn't even on the list of things he least intended, nowhere even near the things he would never ever do, like jumping off a mountain or offering himself to a hungry shark. It was the camo's idea. He was stirring up the fire, glanced up, and saw a single eye the color of the fire, luminous, intelligent, staring down at him. His throat went dry; he froze. Then, under that small, baleful flame of dragon's eye among the branches, he felt an odd sense of curiosity.

What magic, he wondered, was behind that eye?

The question, he realized, was mutual.

He stood motionlessly, one end of the stick with which he had been prodding the fire now being eaten by it. Wings seemed to flutter through his thoughts; he felt himself camouflaged, mirroring his surroundings; he became a tree trunk, a branch, a snowbank, a flame, even, feeling an instant of bulk and power, a dragon. But always himself, the man standing in the dark stirring the fire, and realizing suddenly that the flame charring the stick was about to eat his fingers.

He dropped it, and glimpsed the octo's eye, deep in the dragon-mind, and then its hidden eyes, everywhere within the dragon's skin.

I want to see everything, he thought, entranced, *through your eyes*.

Then see, the dragon said.

He didn't remember moving; he was just there on the camo's back, watching as the attacking army began to spill out of the gorge.

He heard Gauda sing.

At first it was her voice, and he between the dragon's wings, listening.

And then it flooded into him, song rolling over him, through him, until it became his breath, his skin, his heartbeat. *Be wild*, it said. *Be fearsome. Be fire and night, let your blood sing, let me hear you. Let your heart sing to me as I sing to you. Let your heart be flame, send it singing, flying into the face of death.*

The dragon roared. So did Will, riding the fire, yelling his head off until he remembered, with sudden surprise: *But I'm only human.*

He felt his own body again, looked out of his own eyes at the battle lines below, lit by the dragons, by the huge fires, and by the torches pulled out of them, warriors slashing at the twilight with fire in one hand, swords streaking the air with liquid silver light and then with blood.

He thought: *I don't have fire.*

But he felt an odd warmth against one knee, as though something in him had kindled and lit. The camo-dragon, all dark shadow and flame, let loose a volley into a tangle of fighting men; they parted, shrieking, and Will saw the wild hair and beards and furs on one side, the helmets and armor on the other. Gauda's voice swept into him again: *Recognize the difference. Remember it. Protect the army we travel with. You know them, my wonderful, my astonishing beasts. See them with my eyes.*

I am wonderful, Will thought, amazed. *I am astonishing.*

His heart swarmed, seethed with fire, kindled by that fierce and lovely voice. But he had no way to make the fire real, let it flow, stark and terrible, toward the raucous enemy.

I have no way to kill.

Below, in the glow of fire, he watched a man with a spear stalk another man on horseback, whose armor, polished bronze and silver, as well as the jewel set in bronze on his helmet, seemed to mark his high rank. He fought warriors on both sides of his horse, methodically and skillfully, as the spear-stalker, dodging one soldier, fighting another, cleared a path for himself toward the man on the horse.

Protect, Gauda insisted.

I have no weapons, Will thought in frustration, wanting to obey her, wanting to defend, protect. He tried to direct the camo's attention to the stalker, but nothing would distract it from Gauda's voice.

Then he remembered the oldest weapon in the world.

He recognized the warmth at his knee, and pulled it out of the inner pocket of fur. It glittered in the dragon-fire with its own dark, inner fires. The warrior below lifted his spear, drew his arm back to throw it at the rider, and Will dropped the dragon-dung on his head.

He saw, in one final, brief moment, the warrior staggering, the spear slipping from his hand; he rubbed his head, then stared furiously, bewilderedly upward, searching the dark and the snow for flying soldiers and invisible dragons.

Then he was gone. Night was gone. The noise, the shouts and terrible cries, the flourishes of trumpet and drum and elephant trunk, the sear of dragon-flame unrolling like silk shaken across the dark, stopped. The cold stopped. Will's breath stopped.

He was back in the classroom, sitting at a desk. The room was empty but for Professor Seeley, seated behind his own desk and tossing the petrified dung lightly in his hand, waiting, apparently, for Will to return to the future.

"Very good, Mr. Fletcher."

Will glanced down; the cloak of little animals had vanished along with everything else. He gazed at the professor wordlessly, blinking, trying to see what it was he had done.

"Was it?" he asked finally. He shifted a little; his bones still worked, if not his brains. "What did I do? I didn't do much."

"You brought something very, very valuable back from the past."

"I don't know what. Last I saw of that stone, I dropped it on some stranger's head."

"You brought back a question."

Will stared at him. "You mean like, why did you send me there in the first place? I haven't a clue. I don't feel that I've flunked the test as much as I feel I haven't even started it yet."

The smile that swept across the old professor's face startled him. "Yes! Yes. Exactly, Mr. Fletcher. You have brought the magic of the past into the present. Now what will you do with it?"

"Is this part of the test?" Will asked fuzzily.

"No." He tossed the stone suddenly to Will, who flailed wildly but managed the catch. "It's life."

Will, mesmerized once again by the dark, lovely colors glittering constantly over the lump, remembered the camo-dragon in his head, and then the powers guiding the dragons. His eyes widened. He breathed. "Shit."

"Indeed, Mr. Fletcher. Sydney Culver will be looking for you. Twenty-two centuries into the past, you caught the eye of the future. And a charming eye she has, too."

"What should I do?"

The professor scratched thoughtfully at his chin. "Well. You rode the camo-dragon. You must have learned something."

Will stared at him. "Did you really send me back there?" he demanded. "How did you—how could you—Or did you just re-create the world you wanted me to see? In my head?"

"With Ms. Culver in it?"

"But how—all that snow, those mountains—"

"Stones have very long memories, Mr. Fletcher . . . You simply saw what was there, beneath the surface. You possess some very unusual talents. You camouflage them very well. You hardly recognize them."

"What should I do?" Will asked confusedly.

"Finish your tests, get your degree. Who knows, after that? Maybe go and work for the War Department. Be a saboteur for peace."

"But—" He stopped, possibilities fanning through his head. "She'd know," he said abruptly. "She'd recognize the camouflage. And I'm not that heroic."

"You rode the dragon, Mr. Fletcher."

"So did she."

"But you looked out of its eyes. Into its heart."

"How do you—" He stopped again, gazing at the aged professor, wondering suddenly about his very long life, what those ancient eyes had seen and out of what dragon's vision. "There's so much I don't know . . ."

The old wizard smiled again, inordinately pleased about something Will couldn't see. "The perfect place for you, Mr. Fletcher. The perfect place to begin."

WE DON'T TALK ABOUT THE DRAGON

Sarah Gailey

Hugo Award winner **Sarah Gailey** (sarahgailey.com) is an internationally published writer of fiction and nonfiction. Their nonfiction has been recently published by *Mashable*, the *Boston Globe*, and Tor.com. Their most recent short fiction credits include *Fireside Fiction*, Tor.com, and the *Atlantic*. Their debut novella, *River of Teeth*, was a Hugo and Nebula award finalist. Their recent books include their debut novel, *Magic for Liars*, and a young adult novel, *When We Were Magic*.

Cecily is six years old, and there is a dragon in the barn.

Cecily knows what you are thinking. You are thinking that something will have to be done about the dragon. You are thinking that a dragon should not live inside a barn, and that this story will be a story about what is to be done about the dragon.

But you're wrong. Nothing needs to be done about the dragon, because there's no problem with having a dragon in the barn. Cecily knows that this is true, just as she knows that she must never discuss the dragon with anyone in town. She knows it's true because it has always been true. It will always be true.

The dragon is not to be discussed. If Cecily brings up the dragon over the dinner table, her mother will reach over and shake her by the back of her collar, and then after the plates are cleared, her father will give her A Talking-To about her attitude. He will make her feel very aware of the fact that he is big and she is small and he is strong and she is not. She will go to bed with a knot in her belly, and she will toss and turn all night, and she will wake up afraid.

Cecily does not want to wake up afraid, so she doesn't bring up the dragon except in sideways looks she shares with her brothers and her sister. Once, she tried to share a sideways look with her mother. That did not go well. Cecily has learned to be careful with her, too.

There is a dragon in the barn, and it is just the way things are.

Cecily is eight years old, and there is a dragon in the barn.

Going near the barn is hard. The dragon radiates anger, a kind of hot oppressive anger that looms tall and thumps heavy. Cecily knows this because every time she goes near the barn she feels hot and sudden fear. The red paint on the outside of the barn is peeling like an all-over scab, and the big barn doors loom too tall for no reason Cecily can see, and the whole thing sits on Cecily's father's land like a stain on a new dress. The grass around the outside of the barn is green, which doesn't make any sense, because the barn is so hateful and cruel that everything near it should be blighted.

It is Cecily's turn to feed the dragon. She chews on a sourgrass stem and stares at the barn from a distance, holding a bucket of iron shavings that her father brought home from the foundry where he works. He says that he works there because it's the best way to get iron shavings for the dragon, and whenever he says this, Cecily's brothers slide each other those forbidden sideways looks, because they know that when they are old enough they will have to work at the foundry, too. They will be the ones coming home at dusk, sweating and scarred, their pockets full of iron scraps to drop into the bucket by the kitchen door.

The bucket is thick plastic with a metal handle. The handle has a kitchen rag wrapped around and around it to keep it from digging into Cecily's hand too hard. It's enormously heavy—a month's worth of pocket-iron is in there, so the bucket is all the way full, and that means it needs to be emptied. Cecily spits out the chewed-up sourgrass stem.

She knows what you are thinking: if she doesn't feed the dragon, then maybe it will go away. After all, it isn't trapped in the barn. It just likes to stay there, because there's iron and darkness and owls and other things that dragons like. Maybe, you are thinking, if Cecily stops feeding the dragon, it will go away.

But you're wrong. Cecily has to feed the dragon, because it's her turn, and because the bucket is all the way full. If she doesn't feed the dragon, then the bucket will overflow. There will be scraps of metal on the floor. Her mother will look at her with grave disappointment, will tell her that she should go to her bedroom until her father gets home, and it won't matter if Cecily tries to clean up the spilled iron, because her mother will have decided that she needs fixing. She will go to her bedroom and clean it and tidy it, hoping that her cleanliness there will make up for her other failures, and then her father will come home and her mother will tell him what she has done, and she will be afraid, and then all her fears will come to pass.

Cecily has to feed the dragon. It's her turn. That's just the way things are: sometimes there's a dragon in the barn, and it's your turn to feed the dragon. Cecily is eight years old, and even she understands that this is how the world works. She would explain all this to you if she had time, but she has to do her chores.

Cecily is ten years old, and there is a dragon in the barn.

The ladder to the hayloft has not gotten less scary over the years. It's so high up, and it's not fixed to anything—it just leans up against the outside of the barn, even though Cecily's father keeps saying that he really ought to strap it down with plumber's tape or a cross brace or something. The metal gets wet in the winter and hot in the summer, and no matter what time of year it is, the whole thing wobbles and shakes and creaks in ways that make Cecily feel like there's something yanking at her bellybutton from the inside. The bucket is still heavy, too, and she's starting to wonder if maybe it's getting heavier as she gets older, because surely it should feel easier to carry by now.

The dragon is still angry, and his anger still radiates through the wood grain of the barn like heat rising off asphalt. Cecily has almost gotten used to it, although when she's finished feeding the dragon, she always runs away from the barn as fast as her legs will carry her.

Climbing the ladder one-handed has gotten easier, so at least there's that. Cecily braces the forearm of her bucket-carrying hand against the frame of the ladder to keep her balance every time she has to take her free hand off the ladder to grab at a higher rung. That forearm—her left—is scarred from all the times the ladder's been sun-baked to scalding, from all the times she's slipped and caught herself hard on the frame. She has an angry scab on her chin, too, from the time last month when she didn't catch herself. She fell hard that day, bouncing her chin off the rung of the ladder that her foot had been on just a moment before.

Her mother scolded her when she came back to the house spitting blood. Her mother told her to take her time, be more careful, not to rush. Then her mother sent her back outside with an ice cube in her cheek to suck on, because there was iron scattered all over the ground at the base of the ladder and the dragon still needed to be fed. Cecily remembers the way the ice crunched between her back teeth as she picked through the weeds to find all the iron she could. She managed to fill the bucket back up all the way, and then she climbed the ladder again, because the dragon needed to be fed.

Of course, you are thinking that Cecily could just open the barn doors up and get to the dragon that way. After all, the barn doors are on ground level, and they're well oiled and easy to open. Her father opens them once every six months, when he goes in to try to talk to the dragon, to ask it to leave. Every time he does this, he swears that he's going to make it stick this time, that he's going to look that dragon in the face and tell it to get out of the barn for the good of his family. Every time, he tells them that things are really going to change.

You are wondering why Cecily doesn't just open the barn doors, why she carries a heavy bucket of scrap iron up a dangerous ladder, why her brothers do that when it's their turn to feed the dragon, why the dragon is there at all. You are wondering why they feed the dragon from the hayloft instead of from the ground.

Cecily has asked this question herself, which was tricky, because asking questions about the dragon isn't allowed. It's not that she's ever been told it's not allowed, but she knows it's not allowed the way so many things are not allowed—like telling her mother that there's too much pepper on the pork chops or making a joke about how much her oldest brother hates working at the foundry. No one says not to do these things, but if she does these things, a weight will descend on the room like a fog, and her father's eyes will go dark and cruel, and everyone will find quiet excuses to leave the room before the weight in the room congeals into a consequence.

But the day Cecily fell off the ladder, her tooth fell out at dinner, and her father asked what happened to her with real concern in his voice, and she gathered her courage and she told him.

"I fell off the ladder," she said.

"What were you doing on the ladder?" her father asked, which struck Cecily as strange, because there's only one reason why she would be on the ladder. But then she realized that she was being tested somehow, that there was a right answer and a wrong answer, and she thought hard before giving her reply.

"The bucket was full," she said. Her oldest brother exhaled softly beside her. Her mother took a long sip of water. Cecily read these movements as signs that she'd answered her father correctly, because no one was looking at her with warning, and no one was moving toward the door.

"You'll be more careful next time," her father said, cutting a piece of chicken but looking at Cecily's chin. "That's going to scar, I bet. Shame. Right on your face."

This is the part where Cecily needed an awful lot of courage, because she knew that it was supposed to be the end of the conversation. Her father had told her how not to make the mistake again, and he'd said something very slightly cruel about the consequence of her mistake, something that could pass for an observation but that would stick with her for a long time (*shame*, she would think that night as she tried to fall asleep, *shame*). This was the part where one of her brothers was supposed to change the subject, to ask their father for advice about a problem at school or at work.

But Cecily swallowed around the nothing that was suddenly taking up her entire throat. She reached under the table and grabbed her middle brother's hand, and he squeezed her fingers and he gave her the courage she didn't have enough of.

"Maybe I could go through the door next time, instead of using the ladder?" She said it in as reasonable a voice as she could.

Cecily's mother put her knife and fork down on her plate and glanced toward the kitchen door. "I should check on the kettle," she said, which was silly because the kettle wasn't on, but no one would say anything about that because they were trying to figure out their own excuses to leave the room, and if one person's excuse was silly then everyone else's excuse might be silly, too.

"You don't need to check the kettle," Cecily's father said. "Stay. Let's talk about this idea Cecily has."

Oh. That was new. The raw patch on Cecily's chin throbbed. Cecily and her brothers exchanged glances, wondering if this was a trap.

"Well, I just wondered—"

"You didn't wonder," Cecily's father said, pointing at her with the tip of his knife. "You decided that you know best."

Cecily's oldest brother stared at his lap. Yes, it was a trap, and it was already too late for any of them to escape. Cecily would have liked to say that she didn't decide anything, that she didn't think she knew best, but that would have been arguing, and arguing is even worse than deciding. A small, quiet part of her whispered that maybe she *did* know best, and after all, why couldn't her ideas be good? She cupped that small, quiet part of her in her hands and crushed it, fast and merciless.

"I'm sorry," she said, looking at her father's hands because she was supposed to look at him when she was talking to him but she wasn't supposed to look willful.

"Why are you sorry?" he asked.

Oh. That was new, too. She looked up at her brothers for help, but they looked as confused as she felt.

Another trap.

"I'm sorry for saying something stupid," she said. "I didn't think—"

"No," her father interrupted, "you *didn't* think."

When he said that, Cecily's eyes burned with tears, because this, at last, was familiar territory. She knew what to expect. As her father talked about her attitude and her thoughtlessness and everything else that was wrong with her, she swallowed those relieved tears back, because they'd only make things worse. She also swallowed back laughter, because this, at last, was the easy part.

So, you may wonder why Cecily climbs the ladder instead of simply opening up the barn door. Cecily would tell you why, herself, if she knew how to say it. But she is only ten years old, brave and bony and trying not to fall off a wet ladder, and it's too hard to explain to a stranger who has never sat at her dinner table.

Cecily is thirteen years old, and there is a dragon in the barn.

She takes the bucket up the ladder every week now. Both of her brothers work at the foundry, and bringing home iron is their contribution to the dragon. She's strong, and the bucket doesn't seem as heavy as it used to, although it's still heavy enough to dig grooves into her hands even with the kitchen rag wound around the handle. One of her brothers did put some cross bracing between the ladder and the barn, so it's fixed in place now and she can climb it almost as fast with the bucket in her hand as without it.

Every summer, Cecily goes swimming in the deep part of the creek. Some of the boys from town like to dare each other to jump off a high rock, and they holler on the way down and try to make the biggest splashes they can. Cecily joins them sometimes. She used to get water up her nose, but this summer her middle brother taught her how to hold her breath and push a little bit of air out through her nostrils so that she doesn't come up spluttering.

That's how the dragon's anger feels now. Cecily has learned how to be okay, how to breathe and climb and let the anger pass over her in waves, and she's not afraid of it. She's started to wonder if it's really anger, or if it's something else, something that only dragons feel, something that she's always thought of as anger because she never knew how to look out for anything different.

And because, you know. It's a dragon. You would assume it was angry, too.

Usually, Cecily takes the bucket up the ladder and pulls it into the hayloft behind her. Usually, she scrambles into the hayloft on all fours, dragging the bucket across the wood with one hand and feeling her way to the edge of the loft with the other. Usually, she tosses the contents of the bucket over that edge, and she listens to the sound of the dragon huffing and the scrape of its claws in the dirt and the dark. Usually she leaves as fast as she can.

But that's not what she's going to do today. She's decided. She's been deciding for months now, and she's been chickening out for months, and today's the day. She's going to do it. Really, she is.

She climbs up the ladder. She scrambles into the hayloft. She feels for the edge of the loft.

She swings her legs over the edge.

She sits.

"Hello?" she calls down into the darkness. There is no answer.

Cecily picks up a piece of scrap iron out of the bucket, a big sharp curly piece, all black at the ends, that must have hurt whichever of her brothers had to carry it home in his pocket. She drops it between her knees and hears it hit the dirt a ways below her. Then comes the sound of the dragon moving, a sound like scrap iron shifting in a bucket, a sound like the frame of a ladder rattling, the sound of a house settling in the night when it's dark and you're six and you're scared of monsters and you only hope that a blanket will hide you from whatever's in the walls.

"I got my period today," Cecily says. Her eyes are starting to adjust, and she can see that one part of the darkness below her is denser than the rest. "Seems like it should be a bigger deal than it is, but Mom just gave me a menstrual cup. I wish she'd let me use tampons," she adds, although she isn't sure if that's true or if maybe she's just saying it because it's something different that doesn't hurt too much to long for. "Anyway, there's nobody I can tell about it other than her, and she doesn't think it matters that much. So I thought I'd tell you."

She throws another piece of scrap iron down, a flat piece the size of her palm. She can't hear the dragon eating, but she can kind of see it moving, unless that's just her eyes playing tricks on her.

"I thought you'd be scary," she says. "I thought my period would be scary, too. I always think everything will be scarier than it is, but it all just kind of feels flat and weird and sometimes I wish I could die because it would be like running away forever and no one could ever be mad at me again—" She claps her hands over her mouth. She's never said that out loud before. Where did all of that come from?

You are thinking that the dragon played a trick on her. You are thinking that maybe this is a dragon that feeds on emotions, that maybe it is pulling them out of her and hurting her in a way she doesn't understand. You are thinking that her father was right to keep her from opening the barn door.

Cecily is thinking those things, too. But then she takes her hands away from her mouth, and she drops half the bucket of scrap iron off the edge of the loft, and she starts talking again, slower. She tells the dragon so many things—secrets and feelings and fears and wishes. The dragon listens, or maybe it doesn't, maybe it just eats what she's given it. Maybe it completely ignores her.

She doesn't care. She's never been able to talk to anyone about these things, and now she can, and they rise up in her like a shiver racing up a spine. Here is someone who will not get angry at her for feeling afraid or alone, someone who has time to listen to her, someone who might not be on her side but who definitely isn't the enemy.

Finally, Cecily has found someone who she can talk to about the fact that there is a dragon in the barn.

Cecily is sixteen years old, and there is a dragon in the barn.

She has been coming to the hayloft once a week for the last three years. She tells the dragon everything. She doesn't know if it's listening to her or not. She doesn't need to know. She told it about her first kiss (two summers ago, at the creek, when Nolan dared her to kiss him instead of daring her to jump off the rock). She told it about her mother falling down the stairs (it happened right in front of her, and she felt a bigger jump of terror than she would have predicted, but the next day everything went back to normal and her mother was just as distant as always, only with a big bruise on her leg). She told it about running away from home, back when she was making plans to run away from home, and she told it about deciding that the risk of getting caught wasn't worth the reward of making it to the city and disappearing forever.

"Besides," she added, chucking a handful of iron between her feet, "if I disappeared, who would feed you?"

Today, she's in the barn, and she starts talking before she even finishes climbing the ladder.

"Nolan kissed me again," she says. A cobweb catches at her hair, and she swipes it away as she crawls toward the edge of the loft, shuddering—she hates that feeling, the cling and drag and the phantom itch of tiny legs on her neck. "He kissed me! I went to town to get eggs and he was there, and he walked me home, and he kissed me right at the edge of the field, can you believe it?"

Cecily knows that she should be suspicious of this boy. You don't need to tell her that. She knows that boys are trouble, and she knows that she's not allowed to date, and she knows what her mother and father would call her if they found out about Nolan. She knows because they found out about it the last time Nolan kissed her, at a big picnic for the foundry workers and their families. Nolan's father works at the foundry, and he found Nolan and Cecily kissing inside the big inflatable bouncy castle. It was there for little kids to play in but no little kids were playing in it, so Nolan and Cecily decided to go inside and see if it was as fun as it used to be, and it turned out that it was, and then they fell down and they fell together and it didn't feel like they were in there a long time but it was long enough that Nolan's father came looking for them.

She knows the risks, is the point. But it's Nolan, and he holds her hand in his and he strokes her thumb with his thumb and he cups her chin in the crook of his index finger, and she thinks, maybe, possibly—

"I think I love him," she tells the dragon.

The dragon makes a sound that Cecily has decided is a sigh. A fresh wave of that feeling drifts through the barn like cold water mixing into warm—that feeling that she used to think was anger, but now she's pretty sure is just hunger. She drops more iron.

"I think I'm in love with him," she says, "and I think I want to bring him home to meet Mom and Dad."

You're right—that does sound risky. It is risky. It will not go well. Cecily's mother and father will not be happy to hear that she wants to bring this boy home. But Cecily will be sitting between her brothers when she tells them, and her brothers will hold her hands under the table and give her courage she doesn't have, and she'll stay calm and reasonable and she'll be brave, and eventually, her father will throw his hands up and say that he'll just have to meet the boy and see for himself.

When Nolan comes over for dinner, he will bring flowers for Cecily's mother and whiskey for her father. He will be nervous, and he will be achingly polite. Cecily's father will interrogate him in a way that is supposed to seem playful but is still menacing. Cecily's mother will not say whether or not she approves. Cecily's middle brother will pronounce him acceptable, and when everyone else has gone to bed, her oldest brother will knock on her bedroom door. He will fold her into a tight hug and tell her that she found a good one, and when he pulls away from her, there will be tears in his eyes because he knows that she's found someone who makes her shine.

The next week, Nolan will come back for another dinner, with more flowers and more whiskey, and he will establish himself as the one who holds Cecily's hand under the dinner table.

Cecily is seventeen and a half years old, and there is a dragon in the barn.

There is a ring on her finger.

She climbs the ladder and she's carrying the bucket in her left hand like always, and the handle of the bucket makes the ring dig hard into the soft place where her finger meets her hand. It hurts so much, and she makes a mental note to put the ring on a chain around her neck the next week, the next time she has to climb the ladder.

If it wasn't for that pain, she would feel those waves of hunger. She's sure now that it's hunger she feels, and not anger—she's gotten used to the way it intensifies as she climbs the ladder, to the way it comes in waves if she takes too long throwing more iron down to the hulking shadow in the barn. She doesn't usually pay attention to it, but as she climbs the ladder this time, it's enormous, enveloping, overwhelming.

Or at least, it would be, if it wasn't for the pain in her finger. All her attention is on that pain, and it's just the same as when she digs her nails into her palms to get through one of her father's tirades or one of her mother's long, cold silences. She notices the sharpest hurt, and she ignores the rest.

When she gets to the loft, and she sets the bucket down on the wood, the pain in her finger vanishes, and then she notices the hunger. It's blistering, white-hot, and absolute. It crushes the breath from her lungs, and she tries to make a sound, some kind of oh-no sound, but she can't, because the second she opens her mouth it's choking her, more hunger than she's ever felt before, more hunger than she's ever imagined, and it's in her brain, and it's in her belly, and she can't stand it.

She throws the entire contents of the bucket of iron off the edge of the loft, and the hunger dies away a little, enough for her to cope. She gasps, heaves, drags the back of one wrist across her brow to keep sudden sweat from dripping into her eyes.

"What was that for?" she asks, breathless and indignant. There is no answer from below—only the sound of the dragon moving. She can still feel that hunger, but it's drifting around her like the heat of a summer day now, instead of pointing at her like a flamethrower. "Shit's sake," she whispers. She turns the ring around on her finger nervously. "Anyway," she says, "I'm getting married."

Nolan asked her the night before. They were on a blanket in the field behind the barn, far enough away that the dragon's hunger didn't reach them, and they were looking up at the stars. Nolan was due to start working at the foundry the next week, and he wanted to ask her before he started working there. She knew he was going to, knew because her middle brother had told her that Nolan had showed up to ask her father's permission.

"He wanted to make sure that I really wanted it," she tells the dragon. "He said he was sorry to spoil the surprise, but he wanted to make sure that I wasn't getting stuck in anything on account of not knowing how to say no." She shakes her head at the shifting mass in the darkness, listens to the dragon's slow, deep breathing. "I told him that I want it more than anything."

She keeps telling the dragon about Nolan asking her to marry him—about how he got down on one knee, and he gave her the gold ring that his grandmother left him, the one with a little diamond chip in it. When she says the word *gold*, another blast of hunger hits her, fresh and brutal, and she curls into a ball and waits for it to die away.

"I don't have any more iron, I'm sorry," she cries. When she apologizes, the force of the hunger ebbs, and she straightens. "I'll ask if we have any extra somewhere," she says. "I promise. Anyway—I suppose

I'll have to tell Nolan about you, won't I? So he can bring iron home, and then maybe we can feed you together."

If that second blast of hunger hadn't been so cruel—if it hadn't been so desperate and urgent and overpowering—maybe Cecily would have heard the sound of her father climbing the ladder. Maybe she would have heard him coming into the loft. But I don't think she would have. After all, the dragon was below her, and even when it wasn't doing anything, it was a big living animal, breathing and shifting its weight and creaking like an old ship. Its scales rasped on the floor, and its claws dug into the earth, and it was made of noise even if it wasn't always easy to figure out what it was doing based on the sounds it made.

"Tell Nolan about who?" Cecily's father was right behind her when he said it, and she jumped about a mile. She would have fallen right off the edge of the hayloft except that her father caught her by the collar. He hung on to it longer than he needed to, gave it a little shake, and she remembered being six years old, mouthing off at the dinner table, that feeling of being small and weak and afraid and not knowing why.

But it's just a little shake of the collar, and Cecily will not make a big deal about it, even if it does put a familiar knot in her belly.

"I just meant that Nolan would need to know about my chores," she says. She doesn't know why she feels afraid to say the word *dragon*.

"And why on earth," her father says, "would he need to know that? You just need to go to the barn for five minutes once a week. Why do you need to explain that to anybody?"

Cecily has fallen into a trap. She knows it, and you know it, and I know it. Because the thing is, she isn't supposed to talk to the dragon. She isn't supposed to talk to anyone. She's not stupid; it's occurred to her to wonder what her father is doing in the loft, why he followed her here, what kind of trouble she's in. He must have found out about the hours she spends up here each week.

The easy thing to do would be to agree with him, and to go back to spending just a few minutes up here each time the dragon needs feeding. But then Cecily would lose this place, this dark, musty barn where she can talk about being afraid, where she can talk about wanting things. She has already crushed so many small pieces of herself in the name of being safe and keeping her father happy with her, and in this moment, she can't remember *why*.

"I need to tell Nolan because he'll be my husband," she says. "And I don't want to have secrets from my husband."

This is the wrong answer.

Cecily's father grabs her wrist in his hand that has always been bigger and stronger than hers, and his grip is tight, tighter than it needs to be, but he's making a point about how *much* bigger and stronger he is. "You think you're going to marry that boy?" he says. "You think you're going to run off and abandon your responsibilities here? You think that's a smart idea?"

Cecily wants to say that she knows her father knew about Nolan proposing to her, but that would get her brother in trouble and it would make things worse, there's no point, *mustn't argue*. Her father pulls her toward the door to the hayloft, toward the ladder, and for a moment she's terrified that he's going to throw her out of it. She yanks her wrist away from him, breaks his grip, stumbles backward.

He shouts, and she doesn't know for sure what kind of mistake she's made until she tries to get her balance. She sets her foot down on the floor of the loft, but there's no floor there. There's only darkness.

She falls.

It's a shorter fall than she always feared it would be. She drops like a piece of scrap iron, and she lands hard on her back, and the phrase "the wind was knocked out of her" isn't adequate to describe the dying-feeling of all the air leaving her at once. She knows that this hurts, she knows that falling that distance hurts, but she can't feel the pain yet because of the simple shock of landing.

And then there's the realization of where she is, and there is no time for fear, because the dragon is on her.

Cecily does not hear her father scrambling down from the hayloft, because all she can hear is the scraping of scales, a sound that was like rustling from a distance but that is like a fork on a dinner plate close up. She does not hear her father unlatching the barn door from the outside, because all she can hear is the bellows *whoosh* of the dragon breathing. Breathing right next to her, iron-stink breath in her hair. She does not hear the barn door scraping open, wood on metal, rust protesting, because all she can hear is her own heartbeat.

Sunlight streams into the barn, and Cecily sees the dragon.

It is smaller than she imagined, all this time. That does not mean that it is not big. Its eye is close to hers, a dinner plate, and its mouth—

(Oh, Cecily is afraid, she is more afraid than she has ever been.)

—its mouth is on her left hand.

Teeth, on her wrist. Wet on her fingers, she can't distinguish feelings like "tongue" because her hand is inside a dragon's *mouth* and that's about the limit of what she can process right now. Scales, black as oxidized iron—she's aware of those but they are in the periphery because the dragon's teeth are around her wrist.

She wonders why the dragon has not bitten her hand off yet. And then she hears her father's voice, shouting something that will not resolve into language. She remembers his grip on her wrist, too.

She pulls her hand away from the dragon's mouth, slowly, gingerly.

It lets her go.

Cecily pushes herself to her feet. She watches the dragon's eye, the strange pupil contracting in the sunlight. She lifts her hand to see if it is bleeding, and when she does, the sunlight catches on the ring Nolan gave her.

The dragon watches, and hunger pulses in the air around it like a heartbeat.

Cecily has spent years telling the dragon everything about herself. She has told it every wish and want that she has experienced since she was thirteen years old. She has told it about dreams, and about longing, and about lust. She has told it about her hopes. She has told it about her needs.

She thought it wasn't listening, but she understands now: the dragon has told her the same things. It's told her about its hunger, every time she's seen it. It's asked her for the only thing she ever had to give it, and what she had to give it never quite felt like enough, and she understands, now, why it never quite felt like enough.

Cecily slips the gold ring from her finger. Behind her, her father shouts for her to stop. He steps toward her, and he is radiating the old familiar anger, big and strong, scary on purpose.

The dragon looks at him, and he stops. He has faced it again and again, failed to make it bend to him every time. Today will not be different. The dragon knows this and Cecily's father knows this, too.

Cecily places the ring in her palm. She is already planning how she will apologize to Nolan, but she thinks that he will understand.

The dragon lowers its head like a horse to a sugar cube. Cecily doesn't feel lips or a tongue, but she does feel the click of the dragon's teeth against metal.

And then the ring is gone, and for the first time she can remember, the dragon's hunger is gone, too. Not just bearable, not just ignorable—completely, entirely gone. Cecily can breathe, although her ribs ache from the fall she took. The air tastes like dust and sunlight and clean sweat and timothy hay, and the dragon isn't hungry anymore, and Cecily's father is silent behind her.

"You're not supposed to eat iron," Cecily whispers. "You're supposed to eat gold."

The dragon does not answer. It looks toward the open door and shifts its wings, so much like a bird that Cecily can't help but laugh a little. Her laugh dies in her throat when she sees threads of bright gold spreading through the membrane of the wings, slowly at first and then faster.

"No," her father says. "No, it's—you can't give these things what they want, Cecily, you don't understand, you have to let them know who's in charge or else—"

"Or else what?" Cecily murmurs, and her father doesn't answer her the way he usually would because he's distracted by the dragon walking toward him. He steps backward, out of the barn, and the dragon steps forward, slow and sinuous. The gold is still spreading through its dark wings like fire eating at the edge of kindling; when it steps into the sunlight, it spreads those wings wide, stretching them until they block out the whole of the barn door. Cecily follows it.

For the first time either of them can remember, the dragon is not hungry, and Cecily is not afraid.

Cecily is eighteen years old, and there is no dragon in the barn. The barn is empty, and there is a dragon in the sky above her house, and she will talk about it with whomever she chooses.

MAYBE JUST GO UP
THERE AND TALK TO IT

Scott Lynch

Scott Lynch (scottlynch.us) was born in St. Paul, Minnesota, in 1978. He is the author of the World Fantasy Award–nominated *The Lies of Locke Lamora* and its sequels, and his short fiction has appeared in a number of anthologies. In 2016, Scott traded the plains of Wisconsin for the hills and valleys of Massachusetts, and married his longtime partner, fellow SF/F writer Elizabeth Bear.

After Saipan in the summer of '44, Emery Blackburn had a lot of adjusting to do. First, to the sudden acquisition of a pair of Japanese bullets, one in each leg, and then to the painful tedium of evacuation to a hospital ship. Next came hepatitis, which got him kicked all the way back to Hawaii. Not the postcard Hawaii of legend, either, the one with hot-and-cold-running nurses and more gentle white beaches and ice cream than a sober convalescent could take. In Emery's case, all the nurses came from the cold side of the tap, and the only intimate acquaintances he made were the mechanical slings that dangled his slowly healing legs in place. He spent two months in bed thinking of himself as half man, half catapult.

Once upright, he learned to adjust to shambling with a crutch, then to stumbling without one, then to walking almost normally, just in time for the doctors to finally tame the wracking of his liver. His eyes, which he examined in a mirror not more than thirty times a day, gradually lost the bright tinge of a ripe mango. However, Emery was never fated to rejoin the 4th Marine Division. His next major adjustments were to (in precise order) the existence of atomic bombs, the surrender of Japan, the end of the war, and an honorable if expedited separation from the Corps.

They cut Emery loose in late '45, thirty pounds lighter and walking with a hoppy little cartoon hitch because of it (and the never-quite-fading ghost of those holes in his thigh muscles). His bank account was reasonably insulated with an E-3's back pay, and he supposed he was lucky to have a medal with George Washington's head on it to remind him thereafter of the crucial difference between cover and concealment. He could have got one of those by not surviving, too.

The journey back to Carbon County, Wyoming, wasn't comfortable. Emery was an advance drop in a wave of a million similarly unemployed men then washing ashore, and he was four years out of sync with the civilian world, so everything was harder than it needed to be and slower than shit rolling uphill. Still, he was good at adjusting by that point, and in due course he adjusted himself home to Reunion Creek, population 315 plus one. There he adjusted to the hollow feeling of being in a town that no longer held any living relations and to the sudden realization that he'd come back by dumb reflex. Emery stared down the barrel of full-on manhood, twenty-four and feeling about two hundred, and wondered just what the hell he'd thought this old familiar nowhere had to offer him for the long decades that needed filling.

That took care of the spring of '46, a good lengthy sulk, a proper mope to which still-waters-run-deep sorts like Emery Blackburn occasionally feel entitled and don't hold against themselves. He looked for clues at the bottoms of beer cans and found only tin. Eventually, he adjusted again, picked himself up, let the sun burn him and the mountain winds push him around a bit. Clear-eyed and copacetic, he felt ready to make a move, and started hunting for the one to make.

That was when the storms blew through, the dry thunderstorms, rainless crackling things under licorice-black clouds, the storms that blotted out the sun for days and ate radio waves like candy, and when they had passed, pouring up into the night sky like dark exhalations, why, goddamn if there weren't dragons in the world.

The fuss was considerable and it came in every flavor you might expect. Preachers took to their street corners, columnists burned holes in their typewriter ribbons, and the airwaves were lively with cranks proclaiming their apocalypse of preference. Martial law was declared, undeclared, then reinstated in an ever-shifting patchwork. Civil defense administrators who'd missed the chance to test their fancy training against Axis bombers seized their clipboards and ran toward the sound of planning committees. Air-raid sirens came out of garages, not to mention gas-attack rattles, air horns, drums, and flares. Everyone signaled everyone else as often as they could, for reasons that were largely unclear, for about a week. Congress declared a general emergency and the states called out the National Guard, whose first task was usually to smash the barricades some enterprising locals had thrown across their nearest crossroads. Things got more orderly in a hurry.

After all, Emery reflected, the nation was only barely demobilized to begin with, the sinews of coast-to-coast military discipline had slackened only a touch, and maybe it was a fortuitous moment for absorbing the uncanny. Real, live dragons were a lot to take in, but then again, what about a six-year war that had killed fifty million people? What about jet planes, rockets, the fall of a few empires, Fat Man and Little Boy? Also, the creatures appearing in the wake of the black storms promptly set about eating people and livestock, and that had a way of focusing attention on matters of immediate practicality.

Hollister J. Beech had been the sheriff of Carbon County since just before or just after the invention of the wheel. Accounts differed. Beech had no close friends, but a few middle-distance ones, including Emery's late father. That was how the younger Blackburn knew him well enough to nod hello as the lawman stumped into Buckhorn Jack's Famous Oyster Bar (famous since 1934 for having no oysters), where Emery had more or less holed up since actual monsters started appearing in the hills around Reunion Creek.

"Did you ask for the Marine Corps when you signed up, Emery, or did Uncle Sam play spin the bottle?" was not what Emery had expected by way of a return greeting.

"I wanted the Marines, Sheriff."

"About what I thought." Beech was a wind-chiseled sort, all creases and squints under enough hat for any three men, and he leaned against a post while he fixed Emery with a measuring look. "Means you're a certain sort of brave and a certain sort of foolish, and I'm in the market for both qualities. Heard you got shot, too. Bad?"

"My legs." Emery half consciously ran a thumb along one seam of his trousers, feeling for the hole that was no longer there under the fabric. "Bad enough at the time, sir, but I guess I'm spry these days."

"Catchin' lead tends to make a man cautious, in my experience. The right sort of cautious. Those shotgun pellets I took in '28 did more to smarten me up than most of the books I ever read. Look, Emery, what I'm gettin' at, why I came down from Rawlins is—do you think you'd object to having a gun in your hands again? You got, y'know, any issues?"

"Uh, just magazines, sir." Emery coughed and sat up straight. "Sorry, Sheriff. That was a dumb-ass joke. What I mean is, I think I'm okay, and what are we even talking about here?"

"Lots of trouble comin', Emery. Big mess to clean up. Federals are gonna be in on it, army, state police, everybody. But I ain't goin' anywhere. Got a remit for another special deputy or two." Beech jerked a finger at the window, and Emery saw that he'd come to town with something like a convoy, a couple of sedans and a Jeep. Five men milled around, smoking, rifles slung at their shoulders. "Monsters in the woods, by God. We'll handle it same as coyotes or horse thieves. Take the calls. Do the business. Fill out the paperwork and bill the county."

"You want . . . you're offering me a job as a deputy?"

"That's right. On behalf of the good people of Carbon County, I'm lookin' for another buddin' Saint George. You're young, you're trained to take orders and handle firearms, and I know you ain't married. No offense. But what we gotta do will be hard and weird and dangerous." Beech grinned and tipped his hat. "If it's any consolation, the pay will also be terrible and your boss will be a duplicitous sweet-talker who delights in passin' the aforementioned paperwork off on everyone else. Now, you got a 'Semper Fi' left in you, son?"

Emery didn't know what to say. He wasn't exactly thirsting for adventure. If he'd ever had anything to prove, he felt he'd already proved it on landing beaches and in hospital beds, beyond anyone's right to question, until the end of his days. In later years, after much thought, he would finally conclude that it was just nice to be wanted, to be invited, to have someone come along and say "You're the man for the job," even if one of his qualifications was that he wouldn't leave a widow if something bit his head off. He nodded.

"Good show. Hop up outta that chair and ride with us. We'll get you sworn in." Beech gave his suspenders a tug that had the air of old ceremony and started for the door. "Then we'll get some coffee and sandwiches, and go dragon hunting."

Two days later, Emery shot his first dragon. He wasn't the only one.

The missing persons report came in overnight, so they left Rawlins at the red crack of dawn, tires grinding up veils of alkaline dust on US 30. They passed a checkpoint, olive-drab Deuce and a Half trucks

521

parked in a row, National Guardsmen filling sandbags and manning heavy weapons. Emery spotted a quad-mount machine gun and a pair of 37mm anti-tank guns, their crews staring out into the lightening haze. Unless Emery missed his guess, they were equal parts bored and confused and terrified. Nothing had attacked any of the actual towns in Carbon County yet, not that he'd heard, and that was both a blessing and a complication. Until one of the creatures from the hills and forests actually showed itself, the mere idea of a dragon would steadily enlarge itself in the idle imaginations of those men. It would be thirty feet tall, then forty, then eighty, and then they'd all flip their brains like omelets and soak their pants the first time a sage-grouse squawked at them from a bush. LCpl Blackburn had been there, brother.

Emery saw straightaway that Sheriff Beech's plan to roam with a posse of special deputies was forward thinking. The National Guard and the ad hoc local militias were camping, setting up perimeters, guarding towns and mines and railroads, and that was a dandy public service, but there was no clear command authority yet, no center of communications, and in a place as big and barren as Carbon County, there were too few resources for too many chores. The National Guard wasn't going to send tanks out to investigate every phone call from an old-timer who heard a noise down by some creek, nor were they going to handle routine incidents like drunks or auto collisions. Beech intended to go about his usual business, and just by coincidence bring along enough firepower to tackle anything with claws and scales that poked its nose out along the way.

Elk Mountain loomed on the southern horizon as they drove out. Two hours later, they were on its northeastern side, on foot, a few hundred yards up from the old Steadman ranch, which had contained people until sometime the previous day. Two upper-story windows were smashed, plus a doghouse and a ramshackle livestock pen had been busted up, leaving smears of blood along with the splintered wood.

There were no useful tracks, just a report of something big moving upslope, and so they set to walking.

They were seven men spread out in a line, gingerly pacing their way up a tree-bounded draw, smoking and joking and pretending they all felt just fine. The sun stroked Emery's shoulders with increasing heat, like a painter dabbing on layer after warm layer, but the wind blowing down from the mountain's white-dusted peaks was cold, too cold. He didn't like it. The strange but familiar bulk of an M1 Garand rifle was tucked against his right ribs in an underarm hang, and three spare clips clinked gently in a pouch at his left hip. Puffs of gray dust swirled up waist-high in time with the winds, then blew down past them, like ghosts fleeing the scene. There were no bighorns, no deer, no birds, nor even any bird noises, and as they ascended, the jokes thinned out into silence.

Sheriff Beech had the middle of the line and a fine pair of binoculars, but it was Kinnock Iron Cloud who first pointed at the tree line and drew their eyes to the thing watching them from it. He used a concise and traditional call to tactical alertness: "Jesus H. Coal-Mining Christ, look at that shit!"

It moved immediately into full daylight, gleaming, sinuous, pebble-gray, with mottled black stripes like a tiger's. Horned and crested, it had a serpentine wedge of a head and limbs like something out of a magazine article on dinosaurs Emery had read years before. Its wings were folded tight; its body was lean, probably twenty-five feet from nostrils to tail, and the golden eyes that fixed on them had an eerie power even at a distance of ninety yards.

"Oh, hell," said Beech. "Don't even bother with the head, boys! Damn thing's the size of an elephant. Break it down, legs and joints."

Heart pounding, Emery knelt, brought up the Garand he'd zeroed just the day before, and laid his sights on a myth. Then the myth started to move, and showed the nest of knives it had for teeth. The rifle was a cold hard habit that kept Emery's mind from wandering, and so as volley after volley of smoke and noise rose around him, he squeezed off his first eight, slow and on the mark, then moved to reload while the spent clip was still in the air. Eight, steady. Reload. Eight again.

The dragon made it forty yards. Once they had all recovered themselves and stopped dancing around like adrenalized, temporarily deafened chickens, they counted a total of ninety-seven rounds expended from their collection of Garands and hunting rifles.

"God Almighty," yelled the sheriff as he surveyed the corpse. The blood was steaming where it touched the ground, fuming up like something in a laboratory, and the air smelled like metal. "I gotta get a photographer out here. Look at this mess. Look at how lucky we were! We're gonna need big-game pieces. Elephant guns."

"You're gonna need stretchers and blankets," said Iron Cloud, returning from a brief examination of the trees from which the dragon had emerged.

Emery got just close enough to see what he'd found. Sheep, mostly, still as stuffed animals. Behind that, a pair of booted feet could be seen. A woman's feet, sticking out from under a torn plaid skirt. The rest of her was in assorted places nearby.

That was Emery's first. After that, his hands would never be empty long enough for a rifle to start feeling unfamiliar.

So it was war again, basically, across Wyoming and the world. The first black storms scattered dragons from Iceland to New Guinea, from Germany to Poughkeepsie, and after a few weeks of fighting, there came a fresh wave of storms to deliver more of the hungry things. Like Emery, people adjusted, refined their solutions, studied their opponents, and mostly pointed bigger guns at them.

There was no explanation, not that scientists could ever pry out of the creatures. No mysterious comet, no wave of flying saucers, no gateway to the center of the earth that had suddenly been flung open. Museums of natural history filled up with fresh dragon bones, and all the comparative anatomists swore by their microscopes that the dragons were carbon-based, warm-blooded, oxygen-breathing reptilians with no connection to any known fossil record from our planet.

"Reckon I know where they came from," said Darius Barlow, oldest of Beech's special deputies. They were all gathered at the county offices one quiet night in late '47, enjoying one of the occasional closed-door cribbage games they all agreed never happened at the county offices. "Reckon it was your goddamn people."

Sitting directly across from him, Kinnock Iron Cloud, half Arapaho, let the corners of his mouth pull apart in that plausible approximation of a smile reserved for the placation of big-talk jackasses.

"You know what I mean," continued Barlow. "Could be doing anything up there on the reservation. Could be calling this shit, dancing it up, making a deal with all those things."

"Hey now, Dare, that's bonkers," said Otho Sullivan.

"You know what's bonkers? *Dragons* are shittin' bonkers!" Barlow slapped the table. "They're real, so what *else* might be real, huh? Why not magic? You got cousins putting these things out there in the world, Iron Cloud? You all laughing at us behind our backs, pulling down county money while the dragons get your revenge for you?"

"It's got nothing to do with us," said Iron Cloud, more calmly than Emery would have thought possible. "I can prove it. Plain and simple logic."

"Can you, now?" said Barlow.

"If *my* people, by which I will generously assume you mean the Arapaho and not the fuckin' Anglo-Dutch, had the power to call up a bunch of dragons and make a deal to bring the white man's business to a screeching halt, why the hell wait? We would've done it eighty years ago, dumbass."

Tense silence held for a few seconds, and then Barlow barked a laugh.

"Ah, shit," he said. "You may have me there."

"All you suckers would work for me now, assuming you could speak a civilized language. If you couldn't, I'd stick your asses on a tiny reservation. In Maine." Iron Cloud casually set down one of his cards. "That makes the count fifteen, two points for me. Moving that peg on the board is as far as my revenge goes, gentlemen. When it comes to dragons, we're all in it together."

That was a fine sentiment, not entirely supported by the facts of the case.

Existing human wars ground to a halt, but new ones started up, all thanks to the black storms, which became a near-monthly recurrence, with their fresh cargoes of monsters. News from around the world was bewildering.

On the radio, Emery heard some Soviet minister or another proclaiming that "the Union of Soviet Socialist Republics has no dragon problem," which struck him as the clearest possible indication they were up to their collarbones in claws and scales, same as everyone else.

In places like Chicago and New York City and Washington, D.C., the war against the dragons was absolute, and absolutely surgical. Neighborhoods were quartered and re-quartered every week, parklands scoured, thick walls manned day and night. In less populated areas, the war was waged with a more flexible vigor. In New Mexico, atomic weapons tests were conducted against nesting concentrations of dragons. In Wyoming and Montana, Army Air Force planes used napalm and rockets to support people like Emery, whose involvement was more cost-effective for their own side and more sporting for the other.

Dragons couldn't actually fly, thank God, but the ones with wings could do an impressive sort of hop and glide, which was how that first one had ravaged the Steadman place without leaving a mess of tracks. Nor could they breathe fire, but there were reports that some of them were venomous, which Emery judged a darkly comical cherry on top of the carnivorous sundae. The smallest dragon he encountered in his first three years as a special deputy was sixteen feet long, and even it had jaws like a hydraulic press. If a critter like that chomped you in half like a county fair hot dog, the hell did it need to poison you for, too?

Emery and his colleagues responded with whatever they could

cadge from sympathetic National Guard noncoms, federal grants, and even the occasional unguarded supply truck or Quonset hut. The Carbon County special deputies hit the field with BARs, light machine guns, and sport rifles chambered up for the .458 Winchester Lancelot, purpose-designed for dragon control. For a while they even had a bazooka, which notched up a steady stream of kills and was stored in an unlocked shack, on the honor system. That worked surprisingly well, until the spring of '51, when Darius Barlow got it into his head that the postmaster of Medicine Bow was fooling around with his wife during Barlow's extended absences on department business. That postmaster's 1940 Buick Super, fortunately uninhabited, took a high-explosive rocket through the trunk. Barlow was all but horsewhipped out of his job by old Beech, but this didn't prevent a stony-faced National Guard colonel from taking their bazooka away like a disappointed father shit-canning a BB gun.

Procedures evolved, manuals were written, and even if what they all achieved (the army, the guard, the Wyoming Highway Patrol, the local sheriffs and their increasingly permanent "special deputies") was more of a weird, bloody equilibrium than anything resembling the old normalcy, well, at least they were keeping busy. The official radio parlance for a dragon became "CZ," Charlie Zebra, which stood for "crypto-zoological." Internally, the sheriff's department took to calling them "Fox Delta incidents," with the "Delta" meaning dragon and the "Fox" standing for exactly what you'd imagine it to stand for.

Emery didn't mean to lose count of the Fox Deltas he handled, but the work was absorbing and the damn cases just blurred together. Some dragons favored hills and gullies; some of them loved forests. Some of them stole a sheep or two at odd intervals, and some of them tore the walls off family dwellings to get at everyone inside. They all went down if you pulled the right triggers often enough, though, and they all had to be hauled away for special disposal afterward. There was nothing biochemically awry, not that any scientist could ever tell, but dragon flesh and dragon blood simply wouldn't nourish terrestrial soil. It was almost like a magic curse. Anyhow, there were plenty of old mines and quarries perfect for filling up with rotting Fox Delta detritus, and while the smell was god-awful ghastly discombobulating, it wasn't like there were many people living near such places to file complaints. In the summer of '52, as he was hosing down the steamy, stinking bed of the truck they used for Fox Delta corpses, Emery suddenly realized that it had been weeks since he'd even remembered to keep a tally of dragons killed. So it went.

In '53, Dane Burkholder got stepped on by the largest Fox Delta anyone had yet seen in Carbon County, a forty-five footer. Two months later, Otho Sullivan got too close to the foam in a freshly dead specimen's mouth, and it turned out that what the venom did looked much like a sudden heart attack, from an observer's perspective. In '54, Kinnock Iron Cloud moved his last cribbage peg. He didn't get his in the field, where his wariness was legend, but in a ravine off US 30, doing twenty miles per hour too fast in the rain. He'd always had a lead foot. In '55, Sheriff Beech, hard up for funds and volunteers, brought Miss Delia Sanchez of Dixon on board as the first special deputy in the state to hail from the distaff side of human affairs. She was a flyweight brunette, but the things she did with a bespoke Weatherby dangerous-game rifle put her in the heavyweight class all the way. A week with her on overwatch, drilling neat holes in the foreheads of some very scary scalies, was all it took to shut down foolish teasing indefinitely.

In September '56, Hollister J. Beech, gray as campfire ashes, announced that he was unclipping his badge for the last time. He'd wrestled with monsters as well as anyone could, but Emery knew he was tired of late nights and bad dreams and the drinking that never fixed either problem, tired of begging for support from state and federal agencies that seemed ever more inclined to let places like Carbon County fend for themselves like border marches in some medieval adventure story. Emery Blackburn, a certain sort of brave and a certain sort of foolish, had been taking correspondence courses at Beech's behest for two years. When Beech put out the word that Emery would stand for election as his handpicked successor, that was that, and Emery came first in a field of himself. Sheriff Blackburn it was, just in time for the next phase of the whole mess.

"I don't understand," said Emery, his knuckles white on the black Bakelite handset of the phone. It seemed to be his new catchphrase. He was trying it out on all sorts of people, from state legislators to governor's aides to the smiling federal types who floated through every now and then, dispensing handshakes and good wishes and very little else. Those boys always came in by helicopter, the roads being what they were. "I really don't understand, sir, how I'm supposed to tell people to stay in their homes when it's obvious a dragon . . . Yes, sir, yes, I do know that. Ahem. What I mean to say is, when it's obvious a Charlie Zebra can invite itself in through the wall or the roof anytime it pleases . . . Well, of course they have guns, everybody does these days, but that's just farting into a high wind unless . . . No, sir, I am *not* fixing to be disrespectful. I just think that somebody ought to put in a good word for reality every now and . . . hello? Hello? Damn it all to hell!"

"Productive exchange of ideas?" said Delia Sanchez, who was using the spare table in the corner of the sheriff's office to strip and clean a mesquite-stock bolt-action rifle nearly as big as she was.

"Miracle of modern government." Emery ran his hands through his bristly hair, which seemed to be perched a touch higher up the front slope these days. "Government invites me to arrange the miracle. I can't have any more money, because we're not Laramie or the railroad or the big mines, and I can't have more heavy ordnance, also because no money, and I can't have more proper deputies, because no money and no ordnance, so here we are. I get to tell people to try locking their windows and pulling the blinds at night in case a dragon comes by, but when it's time to fill out the casualty report, I have to be sure to type *Charlie Zebra* so some sweaty-palmed pin-dick a hundred miles from danger doesn't get scared reading about it! Aw, I'm sorry, there I go."

"That's a dime for the harsh language fund," said Delia mildly. "Asshole."

"I'll put us down for two." Emery penciled a pair of hash marks on a yellow pad already thick with them. Ready cash being something of an issue, the harsh language fund was conceptual.

Three years now, Emery had been doing a sheriff's job, and well, but it was no longer just a sheriff's job. It was two sheriffs' jobs, maybe three, and all his deputies felt the stretch. The black storms rolled on, and the dragons came with them, and the old way of trying to beat back the strangeness was out of fashion. Road crews were jumpy and needed to work under guard, so the state and county highways deteriorated, people traveled less, and there was sand piling up in the gears of the economy. Local militias helped, sometimes, but the fact was that little towns were going dark. People struck out for the well-defended bigger cities, if they could, and if they were, shall we say, desirable types in the eyes of neighborhood associations. Some people fled to their kinfolk; some left the state. Some hunkered down in place and cut off all contact, until time or dragons did for them.

Emery's team, and the teams like them all over the sparser parts of the country, could no longer afford to root out every dragon that got reported. Just the really noisy ones, the aggressive types, the confirmed man-eaters. War had become mitigation.

"Sheriff, I got a nasty customer for you." Claire O'Dell, full-time part-time clerk for basically every department still functioning in the county, came in without a knock and handed Emery a slip of paper. "Up by the Ferris Mountains. Muddy Creek militia tried to roust it."

"Four dead." Emery crumpled the report. "Well, that adds a certain sparkle to the morning, doesn't it?"

"And it's a talker," said Claire as she swept back out, toward another phone ringing somewhere. "Yelled all kinds of strange things at the folk that got away."

"Sweet Lord," Emery muttered. Sheriff Norbert Tuck up in Laramie County had supposedly dealt with some talking dragons, but Emery had only ever faced the mute and militant kind.

"Ready when you are, Sheriff," said Delia.

"For what? I don't want to just sit here and invest more money in the harsh language fund, but the boys won't be back for another five or six hours." His other four deputies were out that day dealing with, of all things, a busload of prisoners facing out-of-state extradition. "God dammit, ten cents. This situation sucks, ten cents."

"Well," said Delia, and then, after a pause: "If it's a talker, why not maybe just go up there and talk to it?"

"Talk to it." Emery rubbed his eyeballs. "*Talk* to it. That's a stupid plan, Delia. Stupid, stupid plan."

"If it wasn't for stupid plans, Sheriff, doesn't seem to me we'd have any plans at all around here."

Emery laughed in a putting-a-party-hat-on-a-sob sort of way, then sighed, then jabbed a finger at his deputy. "You and your things, in the Jeep in five minutes. If I'm going up there to speak softly, you're coming as a big stick."

"Wouldn't have let you leave me behind."

"Uh-huh. You got your running feet on today, Delia? Just in case I fuck this up?"

"I never back myself into corners, Sheriff." She slid her reassembled rifle into its leather case and zipped it tight. "And that's another ten cents from you."

Everything was wrong with the air and the light on the way up the hillside. It was inside light somehow escaped outside; golden amber beams of sun that hung in the air, languid, a light so rich you all but smelled it, and tasted the dryness of dust flecks that floated in it like microscopic sea creatures, flickering in and out of visibility. It was warmer than September ought to be, at least here, where Emery walked alone up a sagebrush slope well clear of a line of birch and aspen on his left. The west Ferris

Mountains reared high overhead, white cliff faces rippling softly as ever-changing cloud shadows passed over them. It wasn't unpleasant, but it was definitely wrong. Dragon weather. Things just happened around them. Winds blew harder or colder, temperatures got whimsical, snows melted in January or reappeared without shame in the middle of July.

That gitchy feeling, and the four smashed bodies he'd found about fifty yards back down the trail, told him he was close. Still, he kept his rifle slung, his stance easy, trying not to look as though he were up to something.

He found his perpetrator easily enough. The dragon was equally uninterested in subterfuge, and had some heft to back up its arrogance. Thirty-five feet, maybe, chest and front haunches slabs of bullish power, scales a shade of dusty honey slashed with networks of old scars. The creature was perched above a half-eaten cow, Hereford by the looks of it. *More like Goneford*, Emery couldn't help thinking to himself.

"Ahem," said Emery, halting at a distance of about thirty yards. Then, louder: "Excuse me!"

The beast peered at him, tapped its claws on the ground, pushed itself back slightly. Shreds of meat clung to the whorls and wrinkles of its lower jaw.

"Why do you seek my pardon, little one?" The dragon's voice had the timbre of a bulldozer engine.

"Um," Emery said, shivering at the straight-up weirdness of what he was doing. "I don't. It's a, you know, attention-getter. Means I'm sorry to have to bother you."

"Are you, though?"

"Partly. Duty's a hell of a thing. Look, I'm Emery Blackburn, sheriff of Carbon County, and that's where you're presently, well, stealing cattle, among other things."

"The strong take," growled the dragon, "or they prevent others from taking. I was not prevented. That is all. The meat is mine, this place is mine. You carry your fire-tube in abeyance, or you would already be slain. You may be yet. Why have you come?"

"Conversation." Emery slid his hands into his pockets to control their desperate urge to clutch his rifle sling. "Heard you were the talking sort, figured we could maybe work something out. You, uh, killed four of my people."

"Your kin?"

"No, uh, my constituents. It's a thing we have. I suppose I'm responsible, for situations like this, after . . . there's trouble."

"The trouble was brief. Your constituents attacked me. I slew them. I did not want the strange trash they carried. I wanted the good blood of a heifer, and found it. All is well."

"Look, is there any way I could politely ask you to just . . . leave?"

"No."

"I do not wish to threaten you."

"Then do not." The dragon turned back toward its unfinished meal. "And you may continue breathing."

"Okay. Asking politely's out, that's fine. Threats are a bad idea. I do enjoy breathing. Look, shit, do you know what a coin toss is? You play poker? Tic-tac-toe? Anything like that?"

The dragon's head whipped back toward him, eyes bright, and Emery fell back a step despite himself.

"You would try conclusions with me?" the dragon said. "Assail me in wisdom? A challenge of the minds?"

"I . . . yes. Yes, I would." Emery had a vision of a cheering crowd, the president of the United States draping a heavy gold medal around his neck, and on the face of that medal the words HISTORY'S GREATEST DUMBASS. "What the hell. I would challenge you, if it would make you leave."

"Such could be your binding."

"If I challenge you and win, then, I, uh, bind you . . . to leave this mountainside, in fact, to cease and desist all activities in Carbon County, Wyoming, henceforth and forever. Deal?"

"Should you lose," said the dragon, "I shall break your every limb, snap the bones inside your thin flesh, and hang you from a tree by the roadside, where you will scream my praises to all your kind who happen by, warning them away from my territory, until the mercy of death claims you."

"That is a vivid and straightforward promise, I suppose."

"As I am challenged, I call the contest. Let riddles be our trial. Who wins five, wins all. Begin."

"Riddles. Shit. Okay." Emery felt trickles of sweat sliding down his back like little spiders. "Okay. Two, um, Americans are walking on a street, you see. Two Americans on a street. One American is the father of the other American's son, so what's the relation of the two Americans?"

"Wife and husband," said the dragon. "Do I look like an idiot?"

"I decline to answer that. Wait, is that your riddle?"

"Of course not. First point is mine. Now this: What is thin as night and soft as sand, will break the teeth but not the hand?"

"I have"—Emery stared at the dragon for nearly half a minute—"Absolutely no idea."

"Then the second point is mine. Ask your next riddle."

"Wait, what was the answer to yours?"

"Winners get answers." The dragon grinned, the first time Emery had ever seen such an expression of raw, undeniably intelligent smugness on a fanged snout the size of a writing desk. "Losers get broken and hung from trees. Ask your next riddle."

"If that's how it is." Emery paced theatrically for a moment. "Who was the American League home-run leader during the regular 1953 season?"

"That's no riddle," growled the dragon. "That is historical trivia from your scuttling little world. A ploy without dignity. The third point is mine."

"Hey, I didn't agree to any such rule—"

"If you can't tell what a riddle is," said the dragon, "you are less than a child, and I shall simply kill you now."

"Al Rosen, that's the answer I was looking for, but sure, a death threat is equally compelling. Third point's yours."

"Listen well. The sun can never find me, the moon can never hide me, all men give half their lives to me."

"Ugh," said Emery. "Sorry. Drawing a blank."

"You are going into a tree, little Sheriff Emery Blackburn." The dragon chuckled. "Choose your next question wisely."

"I already have." Emery cleared his throat. "My final riddle. The fuck is your problem?"

"What?"

"You heard me: The. Fuck. Is. Your. Problem?"

"Trifling, half-witted little piss-jester! Your life is forfeit. That's no riddle!"

"I'd say it's actually the defining conundrum of your existence," said Emery as he gave a mocking two-fingered salute, which was a pre-arranged signal for Delia, who was supposed to have been using all the time he could buy her to quietly slip into a good firing position a few hundred yards back.

The trick to head-shotting a draconic target, as when shooting an elephant, was to picture an imaginary line on the forehead directly between the creature's eye sockets and to place your shot in the middle of that line. Delia favored 450-grain copper-jacketed tungsten carbide armor-piercers, which meant the creature was angry with Emery only for another half second or so before its cares were made irrelevant. A flat *crack* echoed over the rocks and trees, and Emery had to dash clear as the dragon's body flopped forward and rolled twenty or thirty yards down the slope, just missing him. Delia came up a few minutes later and joined him beside the steaming corpse.

"You two have a good visit?"

"Well, I found out it wasn't a baseball fan," said Emery. "Nice shot."

"Thanks. Dandy skull on this one. Looking at it now, I think if I'd been a couple inches off to either side, it would've just glanced—"

"Think I like you better when you let me pretend you're infallible, Delia." Emery's hands were trembling. He shoved them in his pockets again, told himself it was just a cold wind, but the air around the dragon remained a golden false summer, and it stirred not at all.

They went back the next day, every deputy in tow, to get the bodies of the poor bastards from Muddy Creek, and to haul down the carcass of the riddling dragon, which became a complex matter when they spotted not one but three other Fox Deltas moving about in plain sight at various points in the surrounding valley. Avoiding a tangle with one or more of them would require some interesting driving, as they had been known to take severe offense at the sight of humans handling dragon remains.

"What happened to the tanks?" said Special Deputy Howard Jones. "What happened to the planes, the artillery, the radio network? Why are they just letting this go on?"

"I've been asking the same questions," said Emery. "The phone calls keep getting shorter and shorter."

'61 was the year they laid out the first Exclusion Zones, and the fellow from the Department of the Interior who helicoptered in to explain things was as chipper as a whiskey priest with new bottles to hide.

"We're not sealing these areas off. We're not putting up fences or any nonsense like that. Waste of taxpayer money. All we're saying is, if you wander into those areas, or choose to stay there in some sort of unincorporated community, we won't be providing services, we won't send anyone after you. You're on your own."

Emery stared at the maps spread before him, his deputies, and a dozen other Wyoming sheriffs in the briefing bunker on the outskirts of the fortress-city of Cheyenne. Red lines crosshatched out all the areas within the continental United States in which the state and federal governments were essentially giving up and letting the Charlie Zebra anomalies roam free. Emery saw very little that surprised him. The blue symbols of special security zones enclosed the big cities, the major coal and uranium areas, the suburbs around Minneapolis, the farmlands of Wisconsin and

Iowa, plus long straight rail and highway corridors. Everything from Boston to Atlanta was locked up tight. The red zones were all over the west, the empty far north, most of the deserts. Mississippi, northern Louisiana, Georgia, and Alabama looked like they'd had an outbreak of map measles. Emery didn't need to be told who mostly lived in those places. Reservations were all EZs, too. Wind River Reservation, a few counties to the northwest, was completely blotted out with pay-no-mind lines. Emery wondered if the inhabitants would even be able to tell the difference.

"You haven't exactly been providing services," said Emery, with deliberate mildness. "Nor sending anyone out as is."

"I was speaking in the plural. All civil authorities, from Washington on down. This only makes your job easier, Sheriff! You're Carbon County, right? The jurisdiction you need to worry about just got forty percent smaller."

"My budget's already eighty percent smaller, relative to ten years ago. Any chance it might bounce back into proportion?"

"Aw, Sheriff, come now. Pragmatic decisions must be made. We've got a lot of resources, but they're not infinite."

"Not out here, they're not," said Mac Nimmo, sheriff of Sweetwater County, with a scowl. "You're amputating, is what you're doing."

"Oh, be reasonable," said the man from DOI, whose dark suit was starting to get even darker under the armpits. "It's nobody's fault, but we have to face the facts. The Charlie Zebra situation, it's an act of God, a sort of parallel ecology, and we can save everyone a lot of time and money and risk by simply not poking at it."

"Didn't need to get this bad," continued Nimmo. "We've had years to fight, years to keep their numbers down, but we never had the right tools or support."

"The situation wasn't amenable. We couldn't keep the whole country on a war footing forever!"

"Nope." Nimmo paused to light a fresh cigarette. "Just the right parts of it."

"I can't believe what I'm hearing. I thought you men would be

delighted! Where's that famous spirit of the west, that, uh, rugged in-
dividualism?"

"If you're leaving us such a peach of a situation," said Emery, "why
don't you stay on out here for a while, get yourself some sort of liaison
position? See how we get on with our spirit of the west and our thriving
dragon population."

"Charlie Zebra," said the federal man.

"Charlie Zebra should be hanging out with Huckleberry Hound,
my friend. Those things are dragons! You want to set the nomenclature,
get us some goddamn money, some new guns and machine tools, some
vehicles that aren't falling apart!"

"They're messin' up the weather," said Nimmo. "They're out there
howling and moaning to one another, night after night, and it's doing
something. It's warmer every year, where it oughtn't be. Growing season lasts longer."

"Now that's just a local anomaly, Sheriff. Don't talk nonsense." The
federal man suddenly seemed very nervous. "We all hate the black storms,
of course, but there's no systemic proof of any lasting meteorological effects
since the Charlie . . . dragon incidents began. Just no proof at all. Don't
frighten yourselves or your constituents with that kind of loose talk."

That kicked off another few minutes of generally fruitless shouting, followed by profuse apologies from the Department of the Interior man, who claimed his schedule was tight and he was already
overdue to fly to his next meeting. That came as a surprise to his pilot
and flight engineer, who had to be retrieved from lunch, but they had
their chopper spun up and vanishing over the hills with commendable
speed.

"Amputating," repeated Nimmo. "This ain't a state now, it's a phantom limb. What chance you reckon those Exclusion Zones don't get any
bigger in a few years, Blackburn?"

"No bet," said Emery. "I think we're all gonna find out what it's
like to live on the rez."

"Not the sort of thing a lawman should admit," said Nimmo, "but I confess I never much cared for the concept of poetic justice. Was kinda hoping I could die peacefully of old age before I ever had to face any."

"Maybe the dragons can accommodate you."

"Well, we're accommodating them, ain't we?"

Howard Jones was the first department casualty of '63. The evacuation of the smaller towns and hamlets was in full swing, and Howard was so busy helping an old lady get every last one of her caged chickens onto a truck, he didn't notice the little dragon, just eighteen feet long, that padded up behind him, equal parts curious and hungry. Jones fought well with his sidearm, but a Police Positive was just a noisemaker for a funeral against a target like that.

E. B. Daglish, distraught at the loss of his closest friend, handed in his badge the next day and lit out for parts unknown. Half the remaining county population followed his example that year, one way or another.

Emery's department killed thirty dragons in '64, then half as many in '65. The old need was gone. There just weren't enough places left to terrorize or enough slack-brained militia types running around and getting stepped on.

In the long summer of '66, the dragons did discover the joys of uprooting and playing with telephone poles, so at least Emery had a reason to get out of bed until that blew over.

By '68, the Exclusion Zones had metastasized as foreseen. Most of Carbon County was an amusement park for dragons. About a thousand people remained holed up together in Rawlins, guarded by lovingly folk-crafted mud walls and ditches and scrapped-car barriers. They had good wells and secure fields, and the growing season was half a month longer no matter what anybody from Washington said, so with that and supplies from the one secure route to Cheyenne, nobody had to tighten their belt much.

Emery remained sheriff, and his department consisted entirely of Delia Sanchez. The caseload was mild. The people that remained were neighborly, a curious combination of hurt and invincible, proud of the rugged outpost they were keeping, bitter that they had been left to keep it. In Rawlins, the postal service came in once a month. In the suburbs of Maryland, the city walls were forty feet high. The baseball games were packed, the stadiums guarded by Oerlikon cannon emplacements, the ice-cream vendors equipped with backup generators in case anything made the power flicker.

Dragons stalked the Wyoming landscape at leisure, congregating in packs as large as seven or eight, and all around them a curious rewilding was taking place. Deer, moose, longhorns, wolves, and coyotes surged in numbers, and were even seen following dragons around. It was as if the creatures were practicing some sort of stewardship, satisfying themselves with a more leisurely predation.

More strange weather. Chinooks blew cold without reason, but even in winter the days were mild and the sunlight was honey-rich. The telephone lines hissed and crackled even when there wasn't a cloud visible for miles. The world seemed heavy with invisible possibilities, as if the sky itself were vibrating.

Not many dragons bothered with human livestock any longer, but a few, just a few, were inexplicable assholes. Delia Sanchez died in '71 handling a thirty-foot talker as it spouted nonsense and smashed sections of defensive wall. She couldn't find a vantage point for a distance shot, so she got point-blank, using six rounds to do the job. She was close enough as she squeezed off the last one that the dragon's dying tail-lash took her off her rooftop perch, breaking her neck.

The town doctor told Emery she hadn't felt a thing, that her troubles were over now, and Emery graciously held back from punching him in the face.

A request to Cheyenne for a pine coffin was denied, as was a request for a funeral announcement, an honor guard, or literally anything, any damn thing they could be bothered to cough up. The voice on the radio told him that local deaths were strictly local problems, over and out.

The townsfolk stepped in, pushed Emery respectfully aside, cobbled together a fine box in no time. They hung dragon claws around her neck and buried her with her gun, in the back of her garden.

After the funeral, Emery walked back to his office, locked the windows tight, pulled the shades. He contemplated one of his remaining rifles, before settling on the long-barreled Smith & Wesson Model 29 that had sat long and little used in a desk drawer. He strapped it on, slid it in and out of its holster a few times, then nodded and loaded the shells. He left the office with just those six, wanting no reloads, incapable of using them in any case. After locking his office door, he set the key on the indefatigable Claire O'Dell's desk, in a spot where she couldn't miss it.

"Maybe just go up there and talk to it," he whispered, as he gassed up the department's last remaining Jeep from five-gallon cans.

It was mid-evening as he drove out, under a cloudy carnation-colored sky, and nobody at the gate asked his business.

There were always dragons lurking about near Rawlins Point, up a slope just northwest of town. Emery drove up, flashing his lights and honking his horn as he approached, and he was gratified to see five pairs of golden plate-sized eyes staring at him from within the lengthening shadows of the rock. He screeched and rattled to a halt about thirty yards in front of the creatures.

"Hey!" Emery yelled. "Hey up there! Any of you know how to talk? I need directions!"

His request had eventually amused them. He was pretty sure that was the only reason they'd given him answers. They claimed the dragon he sought was farther north, up beneath the purpling heights of the Ferris Mountains, and they spoke of a green vale between two running waters. It was there, all right, a valley like an emerald cyst between Birch Creek and Cottonwood Creek, surrounded by smooth round rises of scrub and rock. Twilight was coming down, the sky a star-specked cobalt shot through with ripples of orange fire. In the trees, lights that were obviously not fireflies drifted in gentle clouds, and the air smelled like heated copper. Emery went in on foot, judging it more respectful than rolling up in the Jeep.

The dragon, the only dragon there (and very sufficient it was) lay curled and coiled in the midst of scattered white bones. Its chest was broader than a Sherman tank, and in length, it had to be pushing sixty feet. Its scales were metallic scarlet, its eyes deep pits of molten light, and it moved its wings as it regarded him, stirring the air of the glade, casting the drifting lights onto new courses.

"Killer," the dragon said without preamble.

"Likewise, I'm sure," said Emery.

"The whelps informed me of your approach."

"I told them I wanted the biggest, oldest, wisest whatever-you-are they knew how to reach. Seems they steered me right."

"That remains to be seen."

Emery stepped forward, slowly and deliberately, arms akimbo, until he faced the dragon directly. The beast responded by lowering its head nearly down to his, peering at him over nostrils bigger than Jeep head-lights, exhaling soft rumbling breaths that smelled of blood and felt like jungle steam.

"You're doing something to this place," said Emery.

"We breathe our world into yours," said the dragon. "We sing our world into yours. It's only yours for another few turnings."

"We could have stopped you."

"Yes." The dragon clicked its teeth together, making a noise like a hundred swords rattling in scabbards. "With care. And pain."

"I'm old," whispered Emery. "I've been broken and I've been tired and I've been sore and confused, but tonight I feel old for the first time, and I don't understand how any of this got so bad."

"Little killer. You and your . . . pack stood your ground too long, for people who gave you nothing in return."

"They act like they don't need the same air. Like they can lock themselves away and command us not to believe what we see with our own eyes. The indifference, the arrogance, and the world is just . . . folding up around them!"

"Your people could have fought us for everything, and presented it to your children with proud and bloody hands. What *did* you fight for, in the end? Another few turnings to sleep." The dragon raised a single claw, slowly, almost tenderly, and tapped Emery's shoulder. "I have breathed the memories of this place, the violence you have done, and I return to you the riddle you didn't realize you were asking. Humans . . . *the fuck is your problem?"*

"I sorely wish I knew," whispered Emery.

"And now?" said the dragon.

"Would it make any difference?" Emery rested a hand on the butt of his gun. "If I tried, if I won?"

"No," said the dragon with a sigh. "No, little killer, the time is past, and it would change nothing. I'm old, too, on a different scale, but I'm no more crucial to the change than you are."

Emery stood there, hand on weapon, and the dragon never broke his stare. It rose, though, with alarming smoothness, and backed off roughly ten man-sized paces.

"I believe this is traditional. It will alleviate something of your disadvantage, at least. The weapon you carry might be powerful enough to make this fair. Are you resolved that we should do this?"

"I thought I would be," said Emery. "I really thought it was all I could do. Come up here and let someone or something else just decide it all, for Christ's sake."

"And what have you learned?"

"You're not at all like the piece of work I had that riddling contest with."

"A rather grandiose description of the affair."

"Sonofabitch never answered my last question, did he?"

"*What have you learned,* Sheriff Emery Blackburn?"

"I'm old. Sure, I'm old. But suddenly I feel like I've still got an adjustment or two left in me. Maybe you do, too. Fuck shooting. Come back to town with me."

"What?"

"As my guest. Accept my hospitality and protection. Meet everybody. Have some beer and chat awhile."

"To what end?"

"I lost count of how many of you I've killed over the years, and it hasn't done a damn thing. You're apparently inheriting the planet, and my whole country's dissolved and left us to fend for ourselves, so what's stopping us? Come to town. Tell us about yourself. Tell us how to get along with your friends. We could build you houses. You could run for mayor. Who cares? Adjust. Like we maybe should have done years ago."

For the second time, a dragon smiled at Emery Blackburn.

For the first time, he smiled back.

A NICE CUPPA

Jane Yolen

". . . dragons eat their foes for breakfast with a nice
cup of Lapsang souchong . . ."
—ERIN MORGENSTERN, *The Night Circus*

She set the cup down
with a paw scaled in red.
So like her mother's, he thought,
the red of knight's blood
newly spilt. It made him
love her the more.

She'd been this particular
since her egg days, preferring
the yak dung taste
of Lapsang souchong
to the nestly niceness
of chamomile, his own tea.

But then females were always
the tougher ones, wriggling

out of the elastic embryo
and through the hard shell
with scarcely a dent
in their egg tooth.

He shuddered and took
another small sip
of the raw, hot brew.
He had much to say to her,
a plea, a proposition, a proposal,
a world to throw at her feet.

He hoped he would not be eaten
for his impertinence.

So comes snow after fire,

and even dragons have their endings.

—J. R. R. Tolkien,
The Hobbit, or There and Back Again

ABOUT OUR POETS

Nebula Award–nominated **Beth Cato** (bethcato.com) is the author of *The Clockwork Dagger, The Clockwork Crown*, and the Blood of Earth trilogy. Her short fiction is collected in *Red Dust and Dancing Horses and Other Stories*. She's a Hanford, California, native transplanted to the Arizona desert, where she lives with her husband, son, and requisite cats.

C.S.E. Cooney (csecooney.com) lives and writes in Queens, whose borders are water. She is an audiobook narrator, the singer/songwriter Brimstone Rhine, and author of the World Fantasy Award–winning short story collection *Bone Swans*. Her novella *Desdemona and the Deep* was published in 2019. Her poetry collection, *How to Flirt in Faerieland and Other Wild Rhymes*, features her Rhysling Award–winning poem "The Sea King's Second Bride," and her short fiction has been collected in *Mad Hatters and March Hares, Sword and Sonnet, Clockwork Phoenix 3* and *5, The Year's Best Science Fiction & Fantasy*, and published in *Lightspeed, Strange Horizons, Apex, Uncanny*, and elsewhere.

Amal El-Mohtar (amalelmohtar.com) is an award-winning writer of fiction, poetry, and criticism. Her stories and poems have appeared on Tor.com and in magazines including *Fireside Quarterly, Lightspeed, Uncanny*, and *Strange Horizons*; in anthologies including *The Djinn Falls* in *Love and Other Stories, The Starlit Wood: New Fairy Tales,* and *Kaleidoscope: Diverse YA Science Fiction and Fantasy Stories*; and have been collected in *The Honey Month*. Her short fiction has won the Nebula, Locus, and Hugo awards, and her poetry has won the Rhysling Award in 2009, 2011, and 2014, and in 2012 she received the Richard Jefferies Poetry Prize. Her nonfiction has appeared in the *New York Times* and NPR Books and on Tor.com. She became the Otherworldly columnist at the *New York Times Book Review* in February 2018. In her (few) hours of rest, she drinks tea, lifts weights, plays harp, and writes letters to her friends by hand.

Theodora Goss (theodoragoss.com) was born in Hungary and spent her childhood in various European countries before her family moved to the United States. Although she grew up on the classics of English literature, her writing has been influenced by an Eastern European literary tradition in which the boundaries between realism and the fantastic are often ambiguous. Her publications include *In the Forest of Forgetting*, a short story collection; *Interfictions*, a short story anthology co-edited with Delia Sherman; and *Voices from Fairyland*, a poetry anthology with critical essays and a selection of her own poems. She has been a finalist for the Nebula, Crawford, and Mythopoeic awards, as well as on the Tiptree Award honor list, and has won the World Fantasy and Rhysling awards. Her debut novel, *The Strange Case of the Alchemist's Daughter*, was nominated for the Nebula and World Fantasy awards, and was followed by *European Travel for the Monstrous Gentlewoman* and *The Sinister Mystery of the Mesmerizing Girl.*

Jo Walton (jowaltonbooks.com) has published fifteen novels, most recently *Lent*. She has also published three poetry collections, two essay collections, and a short story collection. She won the John W. Campbell Award for Best New Writer in 2002, the World Fantasy Award for *Tooth and Claw* in 2004, the Hugo and Nebula awards for *Among Others* in 2012, and in 2014 both the Tiptree Award for *My Real Children* and the Locus Award for Non-Fiction for *What Makes This Book So Great*. She comes from Wales but lives in Montreal, where the food and books are much better. She gets bored easily, so she tends to write books that are different from one another. She also reads a lot and enjoys travel, talking about books, and eating great food. She plans to live to be ninety-nine and write a book every year.

Jane Yolen's (janeyolen.com) eyes are on 400 books, though her count at the moment stands at 383. She has more than enough under contract to make that number, but another number troubles her. She's recently turned eighty-one. Will she get to see number 400? If so, there will be a big party. In 2019, she won five awards! The Jeremiah Ludington Award for her body of work and two Anne Izard Storytellers' Choice Awards for *How to Fracture a Fairy Tale* and *Once There Was a Story*. Plus two awards for her Holocaust novel, *Mapping the Bones*, which took home the Golden Kite Award from the Society of Children's Book Writers and Illustrators as well as the Massachusetts Book Award for best YA novel. She will have several books out in 2020, including *Midnight Circus*, a collection of her dark stories and tales. Also, she is in a band. At eighty-one!

ABOUT JONATHAN STRAHAN

JONATHAN STRAHAN is a World Fantasy Award–winning editor, anthologist, and podcaster. He has edited more than ninety books, is reviews editor for *Locus*, a consulting editor for Tor.com, and co-host and producer of the Hugo-nominated *Coode Street Podcast*.

CREDITS